BLOOD GOLD IN THE CONGO

PETER RALPH

The crocodile and the scorpion:
a Congolese parable

One afternoon in Kinshasa, a scorpion asked his friend the crocodile to help him cross the majestic Congo river. 'I have to cross over to Brazzaville but don't know how to swim. As you swim with such ease and elegance, let me climb on your back so we can leave without further ado.'

The crocodile replied: 'Dear scorpion, I know you and the reputation of your kind. Once we get to the middle of the river, you'll sting me and we'll both drown.'

'Why would I ever do such a thing? asked the scorpion. 'If I sting you and you die, I'll drown with you.'

The crocodile thought for a moment and agreed to help the scorpion. 'Climb on; let's get moving before nightfall.'

They left the shore and headed for Brazzaville. As the lights of Kinshasa started to fade and their destination appeared on the horizon, the scorpion had a sudden urge and stung the valiant swimmer in the neck.

'Why did you do that?' asked the crocodile, who was nearing the end of his tether. 'I'm exhausted; we're never going to make it!'

Just before they disappeared under the murky water, the scorpion whispered: 'That's the way it is. This is Congo. Don't try to understand.'

(Congo Masquerade, Theodore Trefon, Zed Books, London in association with International African Institute Royal African Society Social Science Research Council).

Prologue

It was ninety-five degrees, and there wasn't even the whiff of a breeze. Beijing's Bird's Nest stadium was packed. Joseph Muamba looked up from the track, searching for his adoptive parents.

Eight events of the Olympic decathlon had been completed, and while only in ninth place, he was within range of the leaders. He had conserved his energy for the final two events. Greg Foreman, his Californian coach, signaled with his hands as Joseph balanced the javelin in his right hand. Memories flooded back to his childhood in a small village in Katanga Province in the Democratic Republic of the Congo. He had learned to throw a spear from the time he'd taken his first steps and killed his first impala when only eight. He'd been equally adept at spearing fish in the local river.

Joseph's ebony skin shone with perspiration as he charged toward the throwing line. His right bicep bulged as he drew his arm back and hurled the aluminum missile into the stratosphere. There was a gasp and then spontaneous applause.

"Joseph Muamba, or as Americans know him, Joseph Rafter, has just thrown a personal best of seventy-nine meters. That's six meters farther than his nearest rival and puts him in the bronze medal position," Ted Cosell, the NBC anchor, said.

"His story is remarkable," Angie Madigan responded. "He could've tried out for the U.S. team, but instead opted to compete for his birthplace, the Democratic Republic of the Congo. I bet there are seventy million Congolese rooting for him and hoping he'll win their first-ever medal."

"He may not have made the U.S. team," Cosell said, "but he would've been the first athlete chosen for the Congo. They've been competing for more than fifty years without ever gracing the podium. If this young man can win a medal, he'll be a national hero."

"I've got my fingers crossed for him, Ted, but his fastest time in the fifteen hundred won't do it. If he's going to win bronze, he'll have to beat his PB by twenty seconds. It's been a great effort to get where he is, but I can't see it happening."

"Angie, he hasn't been seen at any of his regular training venues in LA for the past three months. Rumors have it that Greg Foreman has had him in Mexico City training at altitude."

"Well, we'll soon find out if it worked. He'll have to run at least four minutes, forty seconds to get a medal, and guys of his physique just don't do it. Have a look at him. He could be a running back for the Giants. Nope, it isn't going to happen."

Joseph let his body go loose as he waited for the starter. He had run a PB in Mexico City two weeks before returning to LA to taper for the Games. He had wanted to run a trial at sea level, but Greg had insisted he conserve his energy for the big day. Greg had pushed him to the maximum in Mexico, and he'd regularly vomited in the thin air, his lungs starved of oxygen. Now he was going to find out whether the agony had been worth it.

Maya Tansi, a twenty-four-year-old nurse at Kinshasa Mercy Hospital, couldn't sit still. A small group of medical staff sat around an old television, waiting for the fifteen hundred to start. Maya paced the small room willing Joseph to win. She would run every step with him. It had been fourteen years since she'd seen him.

The starter fired his pistol, and Joseph went straight to the lead. The stadium was like a cauldron, and heat shimmered off the track, but Joseph was oblivious. He didn't hear the roaring of the crowd or the grunting and gasping of the runners behind him. He was twelve again and running to escape a raging white rhino that had set its sights on him. If he could just make it to the jacaranda tree, he would be safe.

"Fifty-six seconds for the first lap," Angie screamed, "he's lost his marbles. There's no way he can keep that pace up."

Still, Joseph accelerated, waiting for the pain to sear his lungs, but he felt nothing. He was floating and looking down at the mean old rhino from the top of the jacaranda. As the bell rang for the last lap, Greg stood near the fence waving a red towel, signaling to Joseph that if he could hold his form for the last three hundred meters, he would win gold.

"Joseph Muamba's opened up a huge lead," Ted Cosell shouted, "but I think he'll stop and the pack will overtake him."

Joseph was now hurting. Sweat ran down his forehead and into his eyes, his throat was parched, and his lungs felt like they would explode. He was in a daze but could sense the crowd. They were on their feet cheering. Cheering for him. He glanced over his shoulder at the two-hundred-meter mark to see where his nearest rival was and nearly stumbled. *Focus, concentrate, and hold your form,* his brain screamed. With eighty meters to go, the noise was deafening, and he felt something lift him from outside his body. Now he was surging with renewed vigor and as he crossed the line, the stadium erupted in applause.

"Four minutes, fifteen seconds," Angie said, "he's beaten his PB by forty seconds. If it's legal, it's one of the all-time great Olympic performances. He's definitely got silver, and only Germany's Wolfgang Boesch can deny him gold."

"'If it's legal'? What are you suggesting, Angie?"

"I'm in shock. Have you ever seen a better performance? He clocked eleven seconds for the last hundred. That's impossible! For his sake and the Olympics', I hope he's clean. We don't want another Ben Johnson."

"Boesch's failed by a mere three seconds. Joseph Muamba is the gold medalist in one of the greatest upsets in sporting history. Congratulations to the young man. This victory puts Greg Foreman on the world stage as a coach."

"Joseph Muamba could be a male model. He's good-looking, articulate, has a great family, and to date, his drug tests have been squeaky-clean. Providing nothing shows up in his urine, blood, and saliva, advertisers are going to be beating a path to his door," Angie said.

Joseph half jogged, half danced along the track with his hands held over his head, sucking up the applause and atmosphere, before he saw Greg waving his red towel and holding the Democratic Republic of the Congo's distinctive blue, red, and yellow flag. He ran over to the fence, embraced his coach, and draped himself with the flag. His mother and father worked their way down the aisle toward him. Tears were streaming down his father's face as he reached out and put his hands on Joseph's shoulders. "I'm so proud of you, Joseph. I'm still pinching myself. I love you."

"I love you too, Dad."

"You were wonderful," his mother chimed in. "You deserved to win after all your hard work."

Maya Tansi saw more than Joseph's victory. She saw the love he had for his adoptive parents and their love for him. Tears streamed down her cheeks. She didn't know whether she was happy for him or sorry for herself.

In Kinshasa, the capital of the Democratic Republic of the Congo, ten million Congolese celebrated like there was no tomorrow.

Chapter 1

Frank and Michelle Rafter were in their late forties when they got the news every parent dreads. Their son, Brent, and daughter, Dianne, had gone out to do some Christmas shopping. On their way home, a speeding Ford F-100 driven by a drunken driver, ran a red light and T-boned Brent's Honda. The small car was no match for the truck, and Dianne died instantly. Brent lingered on for two more weeks before his parents consented to turn his life support off and donate his organs.

Frank and Michelle's grief was unendurable. They contemplated suicide rather than living with the unbearable pain. Frank took extended leave from Capel & Lambert, the firm of Los Angeles stock brokers he had founded. Michelle cut all her social ties, and they moped around their palatial Beverly Hills mansion compounding each other's heartache. More than twelve months elapsed before Frank returned to work, and by then he'd aged twenty years. Life had lost all purpose and meaning for Frank and Michelle when a well-meaning friend asked them whether they'd consider adopting. They were appalled by the suggestion, but the seed had been sown. As time wore on, they warmed to the idea.

They were model adoption applicants, pillars of the community who were successful and affluent, but they failed one critical condition. They were too old. If they adopted a baby, they would be in their early seventies when the child turned twenty-one. The authorities were kind and gentle but advised them not to apply, as their application would not be considered. Being rejected helped them turn their focus back on life. They complained bitterly to politicians and influential contacts about the unfairness of the regulations. Their contacts were sympathetic, but rules were rules, and after four years of trying, they were no closer to adopting.

They had all but given up hope when one of Frank's closest friends

— George Faraday, an entrepreneur and director of more than a dozen mining exploration companies in Africa — asked, "Frank, would you be interested in adopting in the Congo or Senegal? If so, I can help."

"I don't know."

"I understand." Faraday smiled. "You don't want a black kid."

The blood raced to Frank's face. "I couldn't care what color the baby is," he said, "but I wouldn't want him or her to feel any pressure later in life as a result of having white parents."

"You're not going to get a baby, not even in Africa. You're going to get an orphan or a kid whose family can no longer afford to look after him. The child could be as young as five or as old as fourteen."

"I'll have to talk to Michelle and then my lawyers. I'll get back to you."

"By all means, talk to Michelle but forget the lawyers. They'll say you can't do it, and that you'll be breaking hundreds of laws. There's no point calling me if you're going to talk to your lawyers."

The following day, Frank called Faraday and asked him to find out what could be arranged.

In less than two weeks, George Faraday located a boy who had just turned twelve, in a small village in Katanga. "Frank, if you like him and grease the right palms, he's available for adoption. Better still, the Catholic missionaries have taught him a smattering of English. That's a bonus. We'll fly to Kinshasa and clear it with General Bodho, who's a friend of mine. Then we'll hop a flight to Lubumbashi. After Kinshasa, it's the next-largest city. The village is eight hours north of Lubumbashi by gravel road."

"What does the army have to do with child adoption?"

"Nothing happens in the Congo without the general's imprimatur. If he says it's okay, the adoption papers and passport are just a formality. And more importantly for you, it's all legal."

"How much is it going to cost?"

"Thirty thousand cash. They like greenbacks. Fifteen thousand for the general, twelve thousand split between the chief of police and the colonel in Katanga, and three thousand for the boy's family."

"The family only gets three thousand?"

"For them, it'll be a small fortune. The boy's the oldest of eight kids.

Three thousand's enough to ensure they won't have to sell another one."

"It's disgraceful, George. I want to pay the family another twenty thousand."

Faraday sighed. "You'll ruin everything. If the powers that be find out you've paid more, they'll take it off the family and run you out of the country, or perhaps even kill you. A boy is worth three thousand and a girl fifteen hundred. You start paying more and other families will find out, and they'll want more. You'll ruin their economy. You don't know how these people work. Just do as I tell you, and everything will be all right."

Frank shook his head but said, "I'll call Michelle and tell her to start packing."

"Michelle can't come. Jesus, we're going into one of the most dangerous places on the planet. The Congo's on the brink of civil war, and the rebels are about to overthrow President Mobutu. We'll be in an area of Katanga known as the 'Triangle of Death.' Here's the deal, Frank, we get in and get out as fast as we can. Tell Michelle it's eighty-five degrees in the shade, the humidity's unbearable, we'll be on dirt roads, there's no running water, there are huge mosquitoes, we'll be sleeping in tents, the snakes are enormous, and we'll be lucky to get home without dengue fever or malaria. I don't think she'll want to come after hearing that. We'll fly out on Friday."

After Frank described the hardships and danger, Michelle reluctantly agreed not to make the trip but was worried about her husband. "Don't fuss," he said. "I'll be in and out like lightning. George said we'll be back home in five days."

"God, I hope he's right. I'll pray for you, Frank. Call me as soon as you have our son. I want to buy shoes and clothes for him."

"How am I going to get his shoe size?" Frank laughed. "He'll probably be barefoot or wearing sandals."

"You can guess, and I'll do the rest. Call me."

Air France 117 departed LA at 7:00 a.m. on Friday; twenty-nine hours later, after refueling in Paris, it landed at N'djili Airport, in Kinshasa at 9:00 p.m. The taxi stand was crowded with light blue and yellow old Volkswagen and Mazda sedans. Frank and Faraday climbed into a battered Mazda for the ten-mile trip to the Hotel Memling. The taxi stunk, and the air conditioning blew hot air. Faraday crunched his body up so his head wouldn't hit the roof and closed his eyes, but Frank was fascinated by the pandemonium taking place on the road. The taxi driver turned up the radio's volume and clicked his fingers to the beat of the reggae, seemingly oblivious to the cars and vans beeping and swerving in and out of unmarked lanes. When they reached the city, the streets were bumper to bumper, and the sidewalks were swarming. Frank had never seen so many beggars before. There were the blind, the shockingly disfigured, and those missing limbs.

Kinshasa was a mixture of old French architecture and contemporary buildings. When the taxi pulled up at the modern, Belgian-managed Hotel Memling, Faraday opened his eyes and said, "Let's check in and get cleaned up, Frank. General Bodho will be here in an hour."

Chapter 2

Three children, whose ribs protruded from the rags they were wearing, sat in the shade, next to a hut constructed of sticks and mud with a grass roof, in a remote village in Katanga. The heat was oppressive, and dust covered the children. Twelve-year-old Joseph Muamba was two years older than Maya Tansi and Yannick Kyenge. They looked up to Joseph and called him "Boss."

"I have something important to tell you," he said. "Let's go to the forest."

"It's too hot and too far," Maya moaned. "Tell us now."

"It's only a fifteen-minute walk, and we'll be cooler in our hideout," Joseph replied.

"I'm with Joseph," Yannick said. "If you don't want to come, you can stay here, Maya."

"Shut up, Yannick," Maya said, getting to her feet.

The dust was soon replaced with grass as they trudged toward the dark forest. "I love the jungle," Yannick said.

Joseph was strangely quiet, and as they entered the forest, there was an eerie silence broken only by the sounds of animals and the dripping of water from the branches and leaves. The canopy of trees blocked out the light and the rays of the sun, but it was still hot and humid. Four hundred yards into the forest they stopped in front of a huge, dying baobab tree before making their way behind it. Joseph pushed away the dense foliage surrounding it to reveal a cavity as large as a door. They had bored small holes in the trunk so that they could see if anyone was coming. Tiny slivers of dull light came through the holes as they waited for their eyes to adjust to the darkness. They squatted down on the cool moss growing over the roots and Yannick said, "What is this important news, Boss?"

"I'm leaving the village. My father has sold me to a wealthy American."

Maya was horrified. "My parents would never sell me," she declared. "Why don't you run away and hide here in the jungle? We could bring you food. I can't stand the thought of you not being with us."

"Maya loves Joseph. Maya loves Joseph." Yannick laughed, fending off the young girl's blows.

"Shut up, you two. The maize crop has failed, and my father is down to his last scrawny goat. Your family is no better off, Maya. Where are you going to get food?"

"You could live off pythons and manioc roots. What are we going to do without you, Boss? Please don't go," Yannick pleaded.

"Even without me, my father has nine mouths to feed. Everyone will perish unless he can feed them. Once I'm in America, I'll find a way to escape and return home. I'll be back before you know it. They are paying $3,000 for me. My father will be able to buy grain, vegetables, goats, and pigs."

"How much is $3,000?" Maya asked.

"I heard my father say it's nearly three million francs."

"Three million francs?" Maya gasped, her big brown eyes lighting up in astonishment. "I didn't know there was that much money in the world. Your father's going to be rich."

"Soon everyone will be better off," Joseph said. "It's rumored the Americans are planning to build a gold mine. If they do, there will be jobs for everyone. The village will no longer be reliant on the seasons or the river for its food."

"I heard the same," Yannick said. "My mother and father are getting jobs at the mine. I am too."

"It's only a rumor," Maya scoffed, "and my parents think it will be years before anything happens. The mining company wants a guarantee it will be safe from the rebels. How can anyone guarantee that? Besides, you're too young, Yannick. Look at you. You're too skinny to swing a pick and not strong enough to carry gold."

"You have such a big mouth, Maya. You think you know everything."

"Stop it," Joseph said. "I heard my father say if it goes ahead, anyone over ten will be able to get a job. You might be a miner, Sis."

"I'll never go down a mine," Maya responded. "I'm going to be a doctor."

"How?" Yannick taunted, but before the young girl could respond, he said, "When are you going, Boss?"

"The Americans are coming tomorrow."

"No, it's too soon!" Maya said. "It's so unfair, Joseph. You should run away."

"If I did, Sis, I would bring hurt and shame on my family. When you're older, you'll understand," Joseph said with false bravado.

On his last night in the village, Joseph lay on a grass mat listening to the breathing of his siblings and parents. The howls of the village dogs were punctuated by the snarling of lions in the jungle. He killed an ant crawling across his chest and popped it into his mouth. His hunger was greater than his fear, and warriors didn't cry, but try as he might, he couldn't fight back the tears. The hut was tiny, so Joseph, fearing he might be heard, clamped a hand over his mouth.

Finally, splinters of sunlight penetrated the hut, ending a sleepless night. His father looked at his feet, unable to make eye contact with his eldest child, while his mother wept profusely. The bluster of yesterday had vanished, and Joseph was scared — scared in a way he'd never been before.

An hour after sunrise, two Jeeps and a truck sped into the village, throwing up dust and stones. Soldiers carrying AK-47s jumped from the back of the truck and took up positions around the village. The fear on the faces of the villagers was clear as day. A man fighting a losing battle to keep his stomach contained in a jungle green army shirt, climbed out of the first Jeep and, in a booming voice, shouted, "I am Colonel Zamenka. Where is Joseph Muamba?"

Two white men were perspiring heavily in the back of the first Jeep.

One of the four men dressed in navy blue in the second Jeep got out and said, "And I am Major Ibaka."

Ibaka's girth was only slightly less than Zamenka's. The two obese men stood like peacocks, preening themselves in front of the frightened villagers. Joseph's father, head hung low, pushed his son toward the peacocks.

"Put him in the back of the truck," Colonel Zamenka said, nodding to one of the soldiers.

"No," one of the white men said, "he will travel with me."

"There is no room in the Jeep. Can't you see that?" Zamenka said scornfully.

"Two of the police officers will travel in the back of the truck, and Joseph and I will take their places."

"No," Ibaka said, "I need my men near me."

"For Chrissakes, Frank, drop it," the taller man hissed. "They'll kill us as soon as look at us."

The other man pulled out his wallet and emptied it. "I'll pay $600 for those two seats, Major Ibaka. What do you say?"

"He says yes," Zamenka said, greedily eyeing the cash. "Give it to me."

Ibaka was going to protest when Zamenka spoke rapidly to him in a mixture of French and Lingala. The police officer cringed under the barrage and then signaled two of his men to get into the truck.

Maya stood at the front of the villagers, tears streaming down her cheeks. Yannick was next her, his jaw set and his lips compressed as he willed himself not to cry. Joseph bit his lip and looked at the white men with smoldering, hate-filled eyes.

Frank shepherded the boy into the back of the Jeep and put his arm around him in an attempt to comfort him, but Joseph pulled away like he'd been struck by a cobra.

Ten months after Joseph was taken, Maya's parents, desperate for food and with six younger children to feed, did the unimaginable and sold her to an elderly South African couple.

Chapter 3

It was 8:00 p.m., and Michelle Rafter waited nervously at LAX to greet her new son. She saw the tall figure of George Faraday first and then, a few minutes later, her husband trying to rest his hand on a young boy's shoulder. Even from a distance, she could tell the boy was not happy.

Michelle kissed Frank and then bent down to embrace Joseph, who recoiled without warning. He scowled, and his eyes were defiant. She hadn't expected his reaction, surprise and hurt filled her face. She looked at Frank, who was slowly shaking his head and mouthing, "Give him time."

Despite their best efforts to engage him, Joseph didn't speak on the forty-minute drive from LAX to Beverly Hills. Frank glanced in the rearview mirror and noted that despite Joseph's attempts to remain impassive, he was open-mouthed as he stared out the windows. Frank couldn't imagine what it would be like being dragged from a dusty village in Africa to the snarling roads and high-rise buildings of Los Angeles. His biggest fear was that twelve-year-old Joseph might to be too old — and not smart enough — to assimilate.

Dianne's and Brent's rooms were shrines in the eight-bedroom mansion, and hadn't been touched since the day of the accident. Michelle had spent ages preparing Joseph's bedroom, and pictures of famous football players, baseball players, and rock bands adorned the walls. There was a desk at the end of the bed with a television, desktop computer, and laptop sitting on it. The wardrobe was full of trendy clothes, and a three-drawer dresser crammed with under-clothes, socks, and T-shirts was next to the double bed. Slippers, sandals, shoes, and two pairs of Nikes were on the floor of the ward-robe. When Michelle showed Joseph to his bedroom, the young boy's demeanor didn't change.

Later, when Michelle and Frank were having coffee in the

living room, she said, "He's not what I expected. He's so sullen and unfriendly."

"He'll be all right," Frank replied, but without conviction. "He's scared. You should have seen him at the Lubumbashi airport. If it hadn't been for the flight attendants, we never would've got him on the plane. He was like a wild animal. We have to give him time."

"God, I hope we haven't made a mistake. We're too old for this. He didn't even smile when I showed him his bedroom."

Frank laughed. "When I peeked in, he was asleep on the floor. No blankets, sheets, or pillow. Ron Patterson's coming here in the morning. He's fluent in French and a good communicator. I'm hoping Joseph might relate to someone of his own color."

At 2:00 a.m., the lights around the Rafters' house lit up the gardens, the sprinklers came on, and security sirens broke the peace. Michelle Rafter opened the bedroom window and saw Joseph, fully naked, squatting on the lawn. "Oh God, what have we done?"

"I'll get him," Frank replied.

A few minutes later, Michelle heard the toilet continually flushing and realized Frank was teaching the boy about indoor plumbing. When he got back to the bedroom, Michelle said, "He must have used the toilets on the plane. What's wrong with him?"

Frank paused before responding. "He didn't eat or drink anything on the plane, and when the flight attendants asked him if he wanted to use the toilet, he shook his head. On reflection, I don't think he understood."

"Does he know what to do now?"

"I think so," Frank replied. "I showed him and saw a flicker of understanding in his eyes."

"God, after you told me about the missionaries I thought he'd at least be partially civilized."

"It could've been worse." Frank laughed. "He could've crapped in the pool."

Ron Patterson was a gentle, intellectual young man who worked as a trainee at Capel & Lambert between semesters. He didn't fully understand Joseph's dialect, but his knowledge of French enabled him to glean a smattering of what Joseph was saying. It was apparent he was scared, missed his homeland, and blamed the Rafters for what had happened to him. For the next three months Ron spent every spare minute he had with Joseph, and while the young Katangese's English improved, his attitude did not.

"Mr. Rafter, he has a chip on his shoulder," Ron said, "and I don't like saying this, but he hates you. He told me you stole him from his family, and he'll never forgive you."

Frank sighed. He was starting to think he was fighting a losing battle. "Does he have anything good to say about anyone or anything?"

"No, but here's something interesting. I asked him to watch television as a way of improving his English and his communication skills. The only thing he watches is football, and he already has a good understanding of the game. He knows all the 49ers' players."

"Really?"

That night, Michelle asked, "How long can we go on like this?" as she turned her bedroom lamp off. "He never smiles, never says please or thank you, and Ron says he hates us. Face it, Frank, he's a savage, and he's too old to change."

"We have to give him more time. Ron says the Catholic missionaries in Katanga imbued him with a sense of religion and he believes in God. His English has come along in leaps and bounds. Perhaps after he goes to school and makes some friends, he'll change."

"You can't be serious. If he gets into trouble at school, he'll kill someone. If he's not happy here, shouldn't we send him back to the Congo?"

"He's our son, darling, and there's a civil war festering there. We're not sending him back. He'll come around."

Frank rarely left the office early, but Ron Patterson had given him an idea that he wanted to try. It was late afternoon when he pulled into his driveway and drove up to the garage. He strode up the stairs with his hands behind his back before knocking on Joseph's door and opening it. He was barefoot and sitting cross-legged on the floor watching a replay of the 49ers and the Lions. "Who's your favorite player?" Frank asked.

"Steve Young," Joseph replied through pursed lips.

"I thought so," Frank said, pulling his arm from behind his back to reveal a football. "Want to throw some?"

Joseph's face lit up in a huge grin, and he jumped to his feet and took off down the stairs. His throwing, while erratic, was incredibly powerful for someone so thin. When Frank dropped a catch, the young boy burst out laughing. They threw until dusk, and even then, Joseph didn't want to go into the house. Over dinner, he talked incessantly about the 49ers, Steve Young, and the catches Frank had fumbled. Frank winked at Michelle. The breakthrough they'd been praying for was upon them.

In January 1995, the Rafter family took a flight to Florida to watch the 49ers thrash the San Diego Chargers at Joe Robbie Stadium in Super Bowl XXIX. As Steve Young threw his sixth touchdown, Joseph nudged Frank and said, "Dad, one day I'm going to be the 49ers' quarterback on a winning Super Bowl team."

Frank smiled. It was the first time Joseph had called him *Dad*.

Michelle ruffled his curly hair and said, "It's good to have dreams."

"In two months, it's your birthday. Would you like to have a party with your school friends?" Frank asked.

"Is it my choice?"

Frank laughed. "Within reason."

"Can we go to a Dodgers game instead? The three of us?"

"Consider it done."

Frank winked at Michelle. The Rafter family was at last a happy unit.

Chapter 4

Joseph became an above-average student and brilliant at any sport. He was a lightning-fast sprinter, a good distance runner, had a strong arm, and loved baseball and football. Worried that Joseph might not be able to defend himself against the bigger kids, Frank took him for self-defense lessons. Within two weeks, his trainer — a former world-ranked boxer — said, "Mr. Rafter, I'm taking your money under false pretenses. Your boy's good enough to be a Golden Gloves champion. He's a natural."

The self-defense lessons were cancelled, and soon Frank and Michelle's weekends revolved around driving Joseph to sporting events and watching him participate. His adoptive parents' love had eroded his resentment, and he spontaneously returned their affection.

While waiting for their events, the other kids played with their Gameboys, and it didn't take Joseph long to pick up another obsession — computer games.

Almost every month, Frank hosted a poker night for his buddies where they drank beer, ate pizzas, and told lies. They played five-card-draw poker, in which bluffing played a big tactical part. Joseph watched the men play before going to bed and soon picked up the game. By the time he was fifteen, he was playing regularly. His father loved quoting old sayings, and one of his favorites was, "You can tell a lot about a man by the way he plays poker." Joseph had watched these men play for years, knew all their "tells," and rarely lost. He had grown into the all-American boy. However, his idyllic world was soon to suffer a terrible setback.

He had just completed his last year at high school when news of the brutal slaying of his birth father and two brothers crushed him. It came as an awful shock. The village had been attacked by rebels desperately seeking food. Joseph's father and family had fought bravely to protect their livestock. Forty men, women, and children were macheted to death, and their bodies were burned beyond recognition. Nothing had been heard from his mother and other siblings, but Joseph hoped they had fled into the jungle.

His first reaction was to beg to return to the Congo to help his family, but Frank spent hours convincing him of the futility — and danger — of that. The president had been assassinated, and the Congo was in the grip of a bloody civil war. Lubumbashi International Airport was in the hands of the rebels, and the only way to Katanga from Kinshasa was overland. It would take weeks of travel over dirt and potholed roads, half controlled by the government and half controlled by the rebels. Joseph came to realize there was nothing he could do and in the end, acceded to his father's logic.

That night, as they lay in bed, Michelle said to Frank, "I'm glad you talked him out of going back. I think I'd die if we lost him. God, his father was only forty-four, and here we are in our early sixties."

"Life expectancy in the Congo is only forty-five."

"That's shocking. Why do they die so young?"

"Malnutrition, disease, childbirth, and civil war, in no particular order," Frank said.

"What a horrible place."

"Yes, but it shouldn't be. It's sitting on $32 trillion worth of mineral wealth, and should be one of the most prosperous and healthy nations in the world. It's a beautiful country."

"Why isn't it?"

"Corruption at all levels of government and exploitation by foreign mining companies. Let's say I have a gold mine there, and I should be paying $100 million in taxes plus an honest wage to my workers. I find a friendly government minister or high-ranking army officer, transfer $5 million to a bank account in the Caymans for him, and voila, my tax and labor problems are gone. That's why the roads and infrastructure are almost non-existent. The government would be lucky to receive 10 percent of the tax revenue it should be collecting."

"That's outrageous. Don't they have trade unions?"

"They do, but how would you feel if you were a trade union leader staring at half a dozen AK-47-toting soldiers under the command of an eye-rolling, frothing-at-the-mouth captain or major?"

"I can understand why the rebels are trying to overthrow the government. Will the people be better off if they win?"

"It's sad," Frank said, turning off his bedside lamp. "Their leaders are Marxists, and their followers are bloodthirsty thugs. The type who killed Joseph's father. The Marxists will do what Mugabe did in Zimbabwe with the same terrible results. They'll kill or kick the foreigners out and nationalize the mines and farms. They'll go to wrack and ruin, and the country will be even worse off."

"Why can't the blacks run the farms and mines?"

"They can. It's got nothing to do with color and everything to do with education. When Mugabe gave the farms to the blacks in Zimbabwe, they burned the farmhouses and crops. The pristine fields of wheat, maize, and corn of only twenty years ago are now barren fields of weeds, and Zimbabwe is a basket case. Of course, Mugabe lives in a palace and is as corrupt as the Congolese leaders. Had he given the farms to educated blacks, like Joseph, those farms would be no less efficient and productive than if they'd been managed by the whites."

"Give me a hug. I'm glad Joseph will never set foot in that horrible place again. He's ours, isn't he, Frank?"

"He's ours, darling."

Two years later, the Rafters received notification of the death of Joseph's mother. She had died three months earlier after tuberculosis had ripped through the village, killing more than fifty villagers. Unable to afford vaccination, and her immune system weak from malnutrition, she had been unable to fight it off. According to the government's notification, she weighed just sixty-eight pounds at the time of her passing.

Joseph wept, and asked to return again, this time to look after his remaining siblings.

"I don't know how to say this, Son, but there have been hundreds of thousands killed in the war, and even more have starved to death or died from diseases. The probability of your brothers and sisters being found alive is remote. I'm sorry," Frank said.

"I won't know if they're alive unless I go home."

Frank sighed. "This is your home, Joseph. You know you'll never make it back to Katanga alive. Bravery and self-sacrifice are noble but only if they achieve something. Your death won't accomplish anything. The war will eventually end, and then you can return home. Your siblings, if they've survived, will still be there."

"If you hadn't bought me, I'd be dead."

Frank paused and rested his hand on Joseph's shoulder. "I don't own you. You are free to do what you want. I adopted you, and no father could love a son or be prouder of him than me."

"I love you too, Dad," Joseph said, squeezing Frank's hand. "You're right, but one day I will return."

Later, Joseph lay on his bed reflecting. He was surrounded by material items he had come to take for granted: the television, desk, computers, library, pictures of his sporting heroes, the wardrobe laden with clothes and shoes, the baseball mitt, football, and helmet. He was living the American dream, but the deaths of his parents and siblings tore at his conscience. Why had God chosen to take him from the poverty-stricken Congo and deliver him to the land of milk and honey? Had he stayed in Katanga, could he have saved his parents and brothers'? How many of his siblings were still alive? Where were they? He knew God had saved him for a greater calling but didn't know what it was.

Joseph tried to block the troubling thoughts from his mind, pondered his fate, and fell into a fitful sleep.

Chapter 5

When Joseph turned eighteen, Frank and Michelle surprised him with the gift of a Ford Taurus. They didn't say anything, but it was equipped with every conceivable safety device.

By the time he commenced college, he was over six feet tall and weighed nearly 190 pounds. The skinny little African boy had morphed into Superman. He was popular but had only one close friend. Floyd Coffey was a sports-mad African-American who, unfortunately, didn't have the skills to make it to the top in any sport. Instead, determined to stay involved, he studied sports journalism. Because of their love for sport, Joseph and Floyd became inseparable. Joseph's relationships with girls were plentiful, but he was careful not to let them become serious. He knew he had a greater calling in life — though what that calling was, he didn't know yet.

As he learned more about America, he became curious to find out how the world's financial levers worked and grew obsessed with economics and politics. He knew Frank and Michelle were Republicans, and while he never said anything, the policies of the Democrats appealed to him more. Ron Patterson had undertaken his undergraduate degree in economics at UCLA before completing his master's. Joseph decided to follow in his footsteps. At UCLA, one of his professors said, "You're a fantastic athlete, Joseph, but if you want to be the best, you need to specialize in one sport."

"But I like all sports," Joseph responded.

"Perhaps you should take up the decathlon." The professor laughed.

The decathlon was an event Joseph had never thought of, but when he looked at the ten disciplines, nine held no fear for him. Only the pole vault caused concern, but when he cleared four meters at his first trial, it was just a matter of how high in the future.

During semester breaks, Joseph worked at Capel & Lambert doing everything from photocopying to preparing research reports. Capel & Lambert occupied floors thirty and thirty-one of the Stanford Building on Wilshire Boulevard. The boutique firm known as Capel's boasted some of California's wealthiest citizens as clients. It was one of the few firms in the U.S. that got its clients in and out of the tech boom early. When the NASDAQ crashed in March 2001, most of Capel's clients were in cash.

When Joseph finished college, joining Capel's as an analyst was a no-brainer. Where else was he going to get an office, a PA, and a parking space in the underground garage for the Mercedes convertible his parents had given him for his twenty-first birthday? Not to say anything of a starting salary of three hundred thousand. He was a fixture at parties and always had a gorgeous girl on his arm, but eschewed drugs or alcohol. Obsessed with winning Olympic gold, he knew clean living and eating were essential to attaining that goal.

Also critical to that goal was how Capel let him have unlimited time off for training, and paid his travel expenses. Being a senior partner's son sure had its benefits. However, he knew how lucky he was and, when he was at the office, worked long hours to produce detailed, highly rated research reports. The firm's brokers welcomed and seized on Joseph's research to add to their clients' wealth. If there was any angst or jealousy, it came when his co-workers discovered he had opted not to try out for the U.S. Olympics team.

In June 2007, Joseph traveled to Indianapolis with his coach, Greg Foreman, for the U.S. Outdoor Track and Field Championships, where the best he could manage in the decathlon was sixth. He performed dismally in his pet event, the javelin, failing to throw sixty meters. The fifteen hundred meters, always his Achilles' heel, was a disaster, and the five minutes and thirty seconds he clocked was his worst result in two years. Greg went ballistic, saying, "Forget gold. You're not even going to make the team."

Joseph laughed, seeming unperturbed. "I'll be first chosen."

"Oh yeah? Tell me how."

"I'll be competing for the Congo. That's where I was born."

"You don't think you're good enough to make the U.S. team?"

"Of course I am. Forget the last two days. I'll peak in August next year and win gold. I've been racking my brain over who I should represent. I owe this country everything, but even if I win gold, it won't have much effect. If I win gold for the Congo, I'll never be forgotten. Does it make any difference to you?"

"I'd prefer it if you were in the colors of the U.S., but I understand your reasoning. I'm happy to keep coaching you for as long as I can. Were you tanking today?"

Joseph laughed. "Dad says the best cards are the ones in your hand you haven't played. Everyone will write me off after they see my Indianapolis results."

In late 2007, Frank Rafter called his old friend and client, George Faraday, and told him to pull some strings so his son could be selected by the DRC to compete in the Beijing Olympics.

"He easily exceeds the U.S. qualifying standards," Frank said.

Faraday chuckled. "It wouldn't make any difference if he didn't. He could have two left feet, and I could still get him selected. It just comes down to how much you're prepared to pay."

"Hang on. He at least has to meet the Olympic qualifying standards."

"You still don't understand how the Congo works. For enough money, they'd rig a history of past events where he smashed the qualifying standards. There's nothing you can't buy in the Congo. It's subject only to price."

"You won't have to rig anything with Joseph. He's got the score on the board."

"That helps," Faraday said. "We won't have to pay as much, but you'll still be looking at twenty thousand."

"It's worth it. He'll win gold."

"Don't get your hopes up, Frank. I know he's an exceptional athlete, but he's not ranked in the world's top ten. Don't forget, the German decathlete Wolfgang Boesch hasn't been beaten for six years. He's a freak."

"You'll see, George. You'll see. Talk to your contacts in the Congo and pay whatever you have to. And George, don't breathe a word to Joseph. He's a proud young man and would hate it if he knew we were bribing corrupt officials."

Greg Foreman was reluctant to leave the athletes he was training in LA, but if money shouted in the Congo, it talked discreetly in the U.S. After an hour-long meeting with Frank Rafter — and the receipt of a large check — Greg saw the light and agreed to coach Joseph exclusively.

In early May 2008, they traveled to La Loma Altitude Training Center in San Luis Potosi, Mexico. They both knew Joseph's weakness was the fifteen hundred meters, and he'd have to take forty seconds off his PB if he were to win gold. Many American and international athletes were training at La Loma. Greg and Joseph, anxious to keep their training secret, took off early in the morning to run in the woods. It averaged eighty-four degrees during the day, and Greg pushed Joseph to exhaustion, knowing it was the only way he could pump endurance into the young man's legs and lungs. Once a week, late at night when there were no lights and no one was around, they would go to the track, and Joseph would run a time trial.

Every third day, they trained at the track for the other events in the decathlon, focusing on the javelin because it was Joseph's strongest event. They concentrated on technique rather than distance, and subsequently the length of Joseph's practice throws was of no concern to his rivals.

On their last night in La Loma, Greg took Joseph to the track just before midnight and told him not to hold back. Four minutes and twenty seconds later, Joseph flashed past the finish line. He'd beaten his PB by thirty-five seconds, and Greg knew he'd run at least ten seconds faster at sea level. When they climbed aboard the plane for LA, Greg knew he had the favorite for gold in Beijing.

Chapter 6

Team U.S.A. led the medal tally at Beijing with 110 medals, but surprisingly the U.S. public and media were captivated by Joseph Muamba's achievements. By the time he left Beijing, he had done more than fifty interviews and was sick of the press. Two of those interviews were with his old high school friend, the gangly Floyd Coffey. Over dinner, he said, "I don't understand, Floyd. There are plenty of athletes on the U.S. team who won gold. The media's not hounding them for interviews. My cellphone hasn't stopped ringing."

His friend smiled and whistled through the gap in his front teeth. "You're a novelty. You live and train in the U.S. and yet competed for the Congo. Add winning their first gold and running a sensational fifteen hundred, and you have your answer."

"Well, I hope it's over soon."

"It's going to be even worse when you get back to the U.S. You're the flavor of the month. Perhaps we can help each other."

"How?"

"Give me an exclusive interview when you return," Floyd replied.

In the Congo, pictures of Joseph and stories of his feats dominated the media and he was lauded as a national hero, despite not having set foot in the country for fourteen years.

Frank and Michelle Rafter were beside themselves with pride. It wasn't every day your son won Olympic gold in the toughest event in the world. Michelle bought him the strangest present: a gold chain and what looked like a gold ingot pendant that, when pulled apart, was a USB flash drive.

"You're always losing or looking for USBs. Wear this one around your neck, and you'll never have to stress again."

"You think of everything, Mom. Where would I be without you?" Joseph said, warmly hugging his mother. "I love you."

"I love you too, Joseph."

When Joseph's flight from Beijing landed at LAX, he groaned when he saw the waiting media pack. "I'm sorry," he said, "I've signed a contract with Mr. Floyd Coffey for an exclusive interview."

The media took no notice and plied him with questions as he pushed his way through them, saying, "No comment. No comment."

The following Sunday night, Floyd interviewed Joseph for ninety minutes in prime time on CBS. Millions across the nation were glued to their screens, enraptured by the story of the little boy from the Congo who grew up in the U.S., and won Olympic gold. The media continued to call, but Joseph refused to take their calls and didn't respond to their messages. The interview propelled Floyd to interviewer stardom, just as he had hoped.

On his first day back in the office, Joseph was swarmed by staff and clients. Delighted by his success, they wanted to congratulate him and bask in his glory. Family friend and client, George Faraday, was particularly anxious to see him, and had arranged a meeting with his father.

"Good morning, George. What's so urgent?" Frank Rafter asked, taking a chair at the head of a twenty-seat boardroom table, with Joseph on his right and Faraday on his left.

"President Bodho wants Joseph to return to the Congo for a ticker-tape parade. He'll send the presidential 707 for him. He'll get a red-carpet welcome and stay at the palace. It's a great opportunity."

Frank rested his hand on Joseph's forearm. "Bodho was one of the army officers we paid to get you out of the Congo."

"Will he remember me?"

"Not likely," Frank said. "He probably sold lots of kids, but he wasn't the only one. Other generals and politicians were doing it too, and he never saw you. Do you remember Colonel Zamenka?"

"Yes. He was fat. He was at the village the morning you took me."

"It's General Zamenka now, and he's the army's strongman. He keeps Bodho in power," Faraday said.

"What's this great opportunity, George?" Frank asked. "As if we don't already know."

"The Congo's sitting on trillions of dollars of untapped mineral wealth. I haven't spoken to Bodho or Zamenka for years. They're too big-time for me now. I'm still doing smaller deals, but there's no door Joseph couldn't open. We could provide the means by which the world's biggest miners access the Congo."

"What type of deals? And how are you doing them?" Joseph asked.

"Smaller entrepreneurial ventures. I help folks with capital find profitable projects. I assist with permits, tax, and labor. And there's still only one way to do business in the Congo. The guys who have been helping me have a limit on the size of the projects they can approve."

Joseph studied the tall man with rapidly receding gray hair, a craggy face, and a hawkish nose. From the minute he had set eyes on him in the village all those years ago, he'd felt an instant dislike. Still, Faraday was his father's friend, and he had to show him respect.

"I think you're overrating my value, George."

"No, I'm not. Bodho would do or pay anything to see you in Kinshasa," Faraday said. "Frank, we have the opportunity to make hundreds of millions, perhaps even billions. Let's not blow it."

Joseph was about to protest when Frank raised his hand. "George, my son's not some pawn who's going to make you rich."

"You're missing the point," Faraday said. "It would be good for the Congo, good for American companies, and good for us. What's wrong with that?"

"What do you think, Joseph?"

"I'm eventually going to go back, Dad. It might as well be now."

"Will you visit your village?"

Before Joseph could reply, Faraday said, "No, it's far too danger-ous. The rebels have been running amok in Katanga. Besides, you wouldn't recognize it. The gold mine they built a few years after you left has had a huge impact. Houses have replaced many of the huts."

"You know you're not going to be able to change anything," Frank said. "I don't want you to go back if you think you're going to be the country's savior. The rebels are still active, but the country would be no better off if they won. It's still a dangerous place."

"Dad, I know how dangerous and corrupt it is. I've read the terrible stories on the Internet. I'm not going there to be the messiah. I'm going to visit for a few weeks and then return home. Don't worry."

"Joseph will be safer there than he is here," Faraday chipped in. "He'll be surrounded by soldiers night and day. Bodho wouldn't survive if anything were to happen to the nation's new hero. You have no idea how popular you are among the people."

"George is probably right, but your mother's going to be distraught. Don't say anything. I'll talk to her. I don't want you flying on a 707. It must be fifty years old. We'll charter a plane for the duration of your trip."

"I can fly commercial," Joseph said.

"I know you can, but then Bodho won't be able to give you the red-carpet treatment. Besides, I want you to be able to call the crew at any time, so the plane's ready to go. I don't want you staying at the palace either. If something goes wrong, I want you to be able to get out in a hurry. George, there's a new five-star hotel in the diplomatic quarter. That's where you and Joseph will stay."

"Yeah, the Kempinski Hotel," Faraday replied, "but you can't insult Bodho. He's invited Joseph to stay at the palace. He's going to treat it as a slap in the face if Joseph says no. You can't do it."

"You can smooth it over. Tell them the Department of Commerce officials are traveling with Joseph, and they want to stay at the same place as him."

"What if they say we can all stay at the palace?"

"For fuck's sake. Say there are CIA agents traveling with him. It'll ensure there's no invite."

Joseph frowned. He knew his father was worried because he rarely swore.

"Dad, don't worry, nothing's going to happen to me."

"We're all going to get rich." Faraday grinned as he stood up and shook Joseph's and Frank's hands. "I'll charter a Gulfstream. Let's aim to fly out at midday tomorrow."

Later in the afternoon, Joseph entered his father's office and said, "Dad, I don't need George with me."

"You don't like him, do you?"

"No."

"Why?"

"I don't trust him. Call it a sixth sense."

"George has been good for this firm and is well-connected in the Congo. You'll need him if there's any trouble. You don't know anyone there."

"No, but I still speak the language. I've never forgotten it."

"If I could get away, I'd come with you, but I wouldn't be as valuable as George. You're wrong about him. He's a good man."

"Yes, Dad."

"I can't be with you, but I do have something for you," Frank said, handing Joseph a cellphone. "It's the most advanced in the world. It can pick up satellites from anywhere, and if need be, the sun will charge it."

"God, it sounds like something CIA agents use."

"You're not wrong."

"How did you get it so quickly?"

"George isn't the only one who has contacts." Frank smiled.

"I'm sure my iPhone would've been fine."

"Perhaps. Make sure you download your contacts before you leave."

"Sure, Dad, but I think you're worrying too much. The chartered jet and phone are overkill."

"I'd rather overkill than leave you high and dry."

Chapter 7

Eight years after Joseph and Maya were taken, the New Dawn Gold Mining Company — wholly owned by Liberty Investments, incorporated in Mauritania — finally commenced operations just four miles from the village. Cyclone and razor wire fenced off 300 acres. Private security guards with rifles slung over their shoulders and holstered pistols, patrolled the internal perimeter. On the outside, sixty of the army's finest sauntered around waving AK-47s and Kalashnikovs. Before investing in the mine, the owners of Liberty Investments had wanted a guarantee it would be safe from attack. There was no way the rebels could match the firepower on display.

There were two distinct mines within the enclosure. One was an open-cut mine where low-grade ore was blasted and dug up by enormous excavators and trucks. The operators and drivers of this equipment were highly skilled, and white. They were Afrikaners, Americans, Australians, Canadians, and British, and all were paid a fortune to put up with the heat, mosquitoes, and the jungle. It was not all hardship, though. At night they lived in a camp within the enclosure where the accommodations were air-conditioned modular huts containing well-stocked refrigerators. However, not even the hum of diesel generators could drown out the sounds of the jungle.

The second mine was underground, where the ore was of a far higher grade. A large tunnel was sunk, and shafts leading to the ore deposits were shored up with timber beams. Explosives and machines were used to drill and blow out the shafts. Then the debris was loaded into trucks and hauled to the surface. After the shafts had been cleared, workers armed with little more than hand picks extracted the quartz. The work was back-breaking and dangerous, and the workers, except for the supervisors, were Congolese. The mine's management made a token contribution to safety by issuing hard hats and flimsy work boots, and then deducted the cost from the workers' wages. If management had been able to fasten light globes directly to workers' heads rather than putting them in hard hats, they would have done so. Their real interest was making sure the miners could see to work, not to remain safe. However, it was pointless having cheap workers who couldn't see. The mine operated two twelve-hour shifts, seven days a week, and the workers earned between three and four dollars per shift. There was no sick pay, and if a worker was injured at the mine, it was his or her bad luck.

The company excavated a massive open tailings dam approximately a mile from the mine and two miles from the river. The mine pumped waste, including cyanide solution and heavy metals, into the tailings dam.

The mine was adjacent to a gravel road connecting Northern Katanga to Lubumbashi — the same route Joseph had taken on his way to America. The road had cut travel times massively, and what had once been a three-day trip from the village, was cut to only eight hours. The villagers could access emergency medical services anytime, the only exception being the wet season when all roads flooded.

Once New Dawn became established, it became the primary route for tons of cyanide tablets the mine purchased for spraying the ore and extracting the gold. This posed a huge threat to the fauna and flora. If it rained and a truck loaded with cyanide tablets crashed and they liquefied, the ecological catastrophe would be enormous. These circumstances, in a Western country, would make a government most unlikely to grant a mining permit. If it did, it would insist on cast-iron assurances that the cyanide was secure and that nothing could go wrong.

The Congo was different, and the size of the bribe determined the government's actions. Most of the locals were not surprised when the road was closed to them and its use became exclusive to the New Dawn gold mine, the army, and the police. Without other traffic on the road, the risk of an accident — and thus a cyanide spill — was minimized.

Marc Boucher, a hard-nosed Canadian from Quebec with a ferocious temper, was New Dawn's manager. The workers who built the mine's infrastructure talked about Boucher in fear and awe. He was small but pushed them to exhaustion and sometimes death. His oil-slicked black hair and mustache resembled Hitler's. With a baton under his arm, he marched around the mine, not hesitating to beat those he saw as malingering. Usually accompanying him was his superintendent: the Afrikaner Gert Botha, who sported pearl-handled revolvers on his hips and whose shirt could barely contain his massive chest. The workers cringed in trepidation at the mere sight of him.

Suffering from drought and floods, the local villagers welcomed the opening of the mine. Dressed in rags, starving, and with the flesh hanging off their frames, hundreds lined up for jobs on the first day. Most were barefooted, and for them, three dollars a day was a fortune. In contrast, the whites, the security guards, and the soldiers looked healthy and well-fed.

As the villagers jostled in line, Botha shouted into a megaphone. "*My naam is Gert Botha. Ek is die myn superintendent. Jy sal my bel mnr Botha of Sir, en sal net praat wanneer gepraat. Nou stop stoot, sal daar werk vir almal van julle.*"

Eighteen-year-old Yannick Kyenge stood in the middle of the long line. He understood enough Afrikaans to know the Afrikaner was the mine superintendent and had to be addressed as "Mr. Botha" or "Sir." Workers were not permitted to speak to him unless spoken to. Most importantly, Botha had said there would be jobs for everyone, at which Yannick breathed a massive sigh of relief. He was over six feet tall but weighed only 120 pounds. His face was gaunt, and his ribs protruded, but finally there was hope. Four years earlier, the rebels had attacked his village, killing the males and raping the women and children before slaughtering them. Yannick had cowered in the jungle, frozen with fear as he watched his mother and father die. He had resolved never to cower again, but later when faced with another atrocity, he had failed miserably.

After soldiers had been out on a mission, their commanders often allowed them to pillage and plunder villages as a reward for their efforts. This time was no different: They had come in the middle of the night, drunk and looking for sex, and killed anyone who got in their way. Again, Yannick ran and hid in the jungle along with seventy or so other villagers. He had watched the officer in charge, Colonel Zamenka, waving a whiskey bottle in one hand while inciting his soldiers to commit even worse atrocities. When Zamenka ripped the dress off sixteen-year-old Safi Muamba, her mother had charged him with a knife. Zamenka withdrew his pistol and put a bullet through her forehead. Twenty minutes later, when he had finished with Safi, he had taken a knife and slit her throat from ear to ear. Her screams still haunted Yannick. As dawn was breaking, the soldiers had dug a mass grave and heaped the bodies into it before soaking them in petrol. The stench of burning flesh hung over the jungle.

Five days later, there was an article in *The Congo Daily Times*. Soldiers had entered a small village in northern Katanga and found it deserted. Further inspection revealed the horror of fifty tick- and rat-infested bodies in huts. There was no indication of violence, and the soldiers — scared a contagious virus might have killed the villagers — bravely donned masks and incinerated the bodies.

Chapter 8

More than five hundred men, women, and children per shift worked in the underground mine and toiled through unbearable heat, driven relentlessly by merciless Afrikaner supervisors. Shaky cages, with a carrying capacity of one hundred workers, bumped their way deep into the bowels of the earth in the endless pursuit of gold.

When blasting occurred in the poorly ventilated mine, debris and dust filled the shafts. In most underground mines, there is a designated safety area — but there wasn't in the New Dawn gold mine. The supervisors wore face masks and respirators, but the workers were given nothing and breathed dust all day. A club across the shoulders or behind the knees was the punishment for slacking. Workers regularly suffered broken arms and legs as a result of the brutality of their supervisors. Two weeks after the mine opened, the first worker died of malnutrition and exhaustion. His body was hauled out as if nothing had happened, and the supervisor in charge drove his remaining workers harder to make up for the loss. Deaths from blasting, mine collapses, accidents, and exhaustion soon became regular occurrences.

The supervisors spoke a mixture of Afrikaner, English, and Dutch, but it didn't take long for the workers to understand them.

"*Werk jy lazy Kaffir,*" the supervisors would scream as they laid into some hapless soul with truncheons.

"*Kem saam met my*" were the words the workers most feared. They meant "come with me." When the supervisors took someone away, it was a rarity to see them again.

Yannick worked hard and kept his head down but resented the cruel Afrikaner supervisors. When he tried to organize labor to confront the bosses for better wages and conditions, he got absolutely no support. The other workers were simply too scared.

Two years after the mine became operational, Katanga experienced torrential rains and floods. The underground mine flooded, and it was impossible to operate heavy equipment in the open-cut mine. A mile away, the tailings dam overflowed, and after a few more days of teeming rain, the dam wall collapsed. Thousands of gallons of red, toxic muck, spread across the land below the dam, relentlessly making its way toward the river. Within ten days, everything surrounding the dam was dead or dying — grass, weeds, trees, and animals. Worse, the river the villagers relied on for drinking water and fish was polluted for more than a hundred miles. Dead fish floated on the surface, while the carcasses of birds and animals littered the banks.

Half an ounce of gold was tiny and, at market price, worth a year's wages. The temptation to steal was overwhelming, and guards carried out random strip searches at the close of every shift. Rags barely covering workers' bodies were searched by one guard, while two others performed full-body searches: first the hair, then behind and in the ears, the mouth, the nostrils, under the armpits, the anus, the vagina, below the testes, between the toes, and the hands. When they found a small nugget, they severely beat the guilty worker. Many were maimed, some were killed.

In the early days, Yannick swallowed small nuggets and recovered them after they passed through him. But he soon found it was impossible to get more than half the market price, and when he rejected dealers' offers, they threatened to report him to the mine. When he got the cash, it was hard to spend it without drawing attention to himself. Buying livestock was out of the question. In the end, Yannick decided stealing wasn't worth the risk. Many others did not.

It was midday when Yannick's shift finished, and he was about twentieth in line as workers filed out of the mine. The guards had dragged an attractive young girl out of the line, and she stood naked, hands above her head, while they searched her. A few minutes later one of the guards let out a yell of exultation and held up a small rag she had concealed in her vagina. The other guard was on his two-way, and Yannick could hear Gert Botha's booming voice. The line started to move again, but workers were ordered to assemble in front of the mine, where Mr. Botha would address them.

It was a stinking hot day, and the guards held the naked girl in front of the assembled workers as Botha stormed toward them.

"Wat is your naam?" Botha shouted.

"De-Deshna," the trembling girl said.

"Hoekom jy het steel?"

The bewildered girl did not reply, and the back of Botha's hand crashed into her right eye.

"She doesn't understand. Don't speak fucking Afrikaans shit. Speak French or English."

Botha spun around to see his boss standing a few meters away. *"Ja,* Mr. Boucher."

Yannick, watching the exchange, could see that Botha disliked Boucher's intrusion but was scared of the smaller man.

Botha turned his attention back to the girl, whose eye was swollen and nearly closed. Tears streamed down her cheeks, and she hung her head.

"Why did you steal the gold? Who helped you? Tell me their names and I'll go easy on you."

The girl shook her head and muttered something indecipherable.

The sun was oppressive, and Boucher knew what was going to happen. He put his baton under his arm and walked back to the comfort of his air-conditioned office.

Two supervisors leered at the girl. Botha looked at them and said, *"Fok haar en dan* kill *haar."*

One of the men started to undo his fly, and Deshna screamed. For the next thirty minutes, the two men raped and sodomized her. Only her screams and cries broke the silence.

Yannick thought he would vomit and wanted to yell *charge.* Leaders were possessed of great courage and knew others would follow them. But Yannick didn't know whether anyone would follow him and was too scared to take the risk. Fear gripped him again, and he closed his eyes, unable to watch the atrocity. He'd heard the screams before, and they brought back terrible memories.

Deshna was lying in the dirt, bleeding heavily, when one of the guards put his pistol behind her head and pulled the trigger. Blood, brain, and bone splattered everywhere.

Botha hadn't looked at what the two men had done to Deshna. Instead, he stood — arms folded, pearl-handled pistols on his hips — and stared at the workers' terrified faces. Once he heard the shot, he shouted, "You have seen what happens when you steal. We have been too soft on you. Remember, if you thieve, you will die. Now get back to work."

As Yannick shuffled out the gates, he felt a surge of anger and implored those around him to band together. "We outnumber them fifty to one. We must never let it happen again. Next time we will attack them."

A few glanced at him, but no one responded. Fear had paralyzed them.

Chapter 9

In the months following Deshna's murder, Yannick continued to agitate the other mine workers to take action against the supervisors and management. His words went unheeded even as the brutality meted out by the Afrikaner supervisors intensified. Men, women, and children were routinely bashed, often for no other reason than to set an example. Fear reigned. If a worker reached the surface without having been beaten, it was considered a good day.

The whites responsible for operating the heavy equipment and setting and detonating charges at the open-cut mine were treated vastly differently. Generously paid and living in relative comfort, they were untouchable. The clearing away of clay and rock at the open-cut mine by use of explosives was a regular occurrence. While the underground mine was less than a mile away, the workers were never brought to the surface when blasting took place at the open-cut mine. Safety procedures did not exist at New Dawn.

Three weeks before Joseph's jet landed at N'djili, powder monkeys extensively primed the open-cut mine with explosives. When detonated, the explosions were intense and had the same impact as a midlevel earthquake. Four miles away, the ground at the village trembled. Shaken animals in the jungle roared and snarled. Terrified, screeching birds took flight.

The underground mine shook, and huge clouds of dust concealed the entrance. Eight hundred yards below the surface, a poorly constructed mine shaft collapsed under the weight of hundreds of tons of rubble. Yannick was working in a shaft a level above and raced to help. The dust was suffocating. When he reached the shaft, he faced a wall of rock and rubble. Miraculously the cables to the cages remained intact, and many panic-stricken workers rushed to board them. Others joined Yannick and started to pull rocks away from the collapsed shaft in a futile attempt to save the screamers trapped under tons of rock. But within an hour, the screaming stopped, there was only the silence of death. After three days of drilling and looking for air pockets where the workers might have survived, the rescue was called off. Forty-seven men, women, and children were unaccounted for and presumed dead. Wives, husbands, mothers, fathers, and friends mourned their lost ones. An undercurrent of anger swept through the surviving workers.

The deaths made Yannick physically and emotionally ill, but he finally had some dissent and outrage he could exploit. The workers and their families were still scared, but anger outweighed their fear. Yannick was determined to ensure that the mine was safe, wages were increased, and conditions were improved before the workers went underground again. He had heard Marc Boucher threaten Gert Botha with the loss of his job if the mine wasn't restored and operational within four weeks. Yannick knew this was his window of opportunity.

Chapter 10

Joseph asked his mom if they could say their farewells at home, but she was determined to go to the airport. As the limousine stop-started through the LA traffic, she sat next to him, holding his hand. Frank sat opposite, casually chewing gum, but his stomach was churning.

"Tell me you're not going back to your village," Michelle said, tightly gripping his hand.

"I don't know, Mom. I don't think I am."

"The Congo's a horrible, dangerous place," Michelle persisted, "and life is cheap. Please be careful."

"According to George, soldiers are going to guard us around the clock. I'll be safer there than I am here."

A tear ran down Michelle's cheek, and there was a tremor in her voice. "I'll die if something happens to you."

"He'll be all right. He can look after himself," Frank said without conviction.

As the limo pulled into the departures area, Michelle said, "We won't come any further. If we do, I'll break down, and I don't want you to remember me in a mess of tears. Please come home to us."

Frank shook Joseph's hand and said, "Safe trip, Son. Follow George's lead. He knows what he's doing. We'll see you in two weeks."

"Sure," Joseph said, giving his mom one more hug before climbing out.

As the limo drove away, Frank and Michelle waved. To Joseph, they looked like they'd just been to a funeral.

Faraday was already on the Gulfstream when Joseph boarded. A flight attendant who was part of the hired crew offered him an orange juice. Joseph gazed around the cabin in astonishment. There were only eight large seats in two pods of four facing each other.

"Hello, Joseph. Isn't it great?" Faraday said. "You want to see the boardroom? There are two separate bedrooms at the rear, too. Oh, I nearly forgot, there's a fully stocked bar. It sure is the way to travel."

"Yes," Joseph said, doubt written all over his face.

"You're worried about the cost? Don't be! We're gonna make so much money, by the time we get back, you'll be able to buy one of these."

Joseph was about to respond when two men boarded. They nodded to Faraday and made their way to the second pod of seats.

"Who are they?" Joseph asked.

"State Department officials. I told them Frank didn't want you to stay in the palace. They're happy if we use them as an excuse."

"State Department? Why? Dad said if anyone came with us, it would be Department of Commerce officials. Aren't our meetings going to be about trade, investment, and development?"

"I'll let them explain the details, but they want to ensure the Chinese don't get their hands on a massive uranium resource. Don't fight it. These guys have way more power than the hacks from the Department of Commerce. When they learned of the potential size of the deals, particularly the uranium deal, they insisted on coming. We won't have to bullshit Bodho, even though I'm sure he'll invite them to stay at the palace too. Don't worry, they're going to say they can't accept because it breaches the department's rules. It worked out perfectly. I'll introduce you to them once we take off."

"There's no hurry. We're going to be in the air for nearly thirty hours."

"No, that's what it would've taken if we'd stopped in Paris to refuel. The State Department has arranged for us to refuel at Nouakchott in Mauritania. I tell you, having those two guys with us is going to be a big plus. We'll be landing in N'djili in twenty-one hours," Faraday said, looking at his watch. "President Bodho will have the red carpet rolled out for you."

"I hope not," Joseph said.

The two guys from the State Department were somber, and while they politely asked a few questions about the decathlon, their focus was on U.S. business and investment in the Congo.

"I don't understand why you guys are involved," Joseph said. "I thought the Department of Commerce handled trade matters."

The more senior of the two, Jack Costigan, clenched and unclenched his meaty hands before responding. "The fucking Chinese got into the Congo, and they've been ripping the guts out of it. That gold medal you won is our chance to get back in again."

"How did the Chinese manage that? What did they do that we didn't?"

"Nothing. They're as cunning as shithouse rats. The size of the bribes they paid was outrageous, and then they built hospitals, schools, roads, and infrastructure. They obviously didn't do it out of the goodness of their hearts, though. They screwed the workers and paid way below market prices for the commodities they bought. However, they made it appear as if they cared for the people and their communities. When the veil's pulled away, they're far worse than us. Slimy bastards."

Joseph's face clouded over. "So our companies are screwing the Congolese, and the Chinese companies are screwing the Congolese. The only difference is they're doing it in a nicer way."

A vein in Costigan's bull neck started to throb, and Faraday cut in. "No, you've misconstrued what Jack said, Joseph. The Chinese, because of their dirty deals, have kept the West out of the Congo on significant developments for years. We want to help the Congolese people."

"Sure," Joseph said, but only to smooth things over — he was already having his doubts about his new companions.

With the help of Costigan, Faraday had arranged for senior executives of BHP, Barrick, Freeport, Alcoa, Newmont, Anglo American, and a few smaller mining companies to be in Kinshasa at the same time as Joseph. Faraday was licking his lips. He had never been able to get any business from the big miners. Now they were falling over themselves to use his services. He was going to be rich beyond his wildest dreams.

The Gulfstream touched down in N'djili at 4:30 p.m. When the door opened, Joseph looked down from the top of the mobile stairway at an army band, before staring in amazement at tens of thousands of cheering faces. A red carpet stretched across the tarmac, and a group of officials were waiting at the foot of the stairway. One of the officials signaled, and the military band struck up the "Debout Congolais," the country's national anthem.

"How cool is this?" Faraday beamed.

"It's terrible," Joseph replied. "I never expected anything like this."

"Don't keep them waiting."

Joseph recognized President Bodho from his photos. He wasn't tall, but he was massively obese, and his navy blue suit wrapped around him like a tent. General Zamenka, who was of similar build, was standing next to the president in full military regalia, including medals and ribbons. A third man, also in uniform sporting the insignia of a colonel, stood with them. He was taller, and also had a generous girth, but nothing like the size of his boss's. Half a dozen steps farther back was a group of politicians and public servants.

As Joseph neared the bottom of the stairway, President Bodho grabbed his hand and embraced him. Camera flashes erupted, and television crews pushed closer, capturing every moment. When Bodho released him, General Zamenka repeated the performance. Then they stood on either side of Joseph while photographers pressed in, taking more photos. The third man, Colonel Gizenga, was more subdued. When Joseph looked into his eyes, they were dark and foreboding.

One of President Bodho's aides took Joseph by the elbow and directed him to the motorcade waiting at the end of the red carpet. Joseph got into the back of a black Mercedes. Bodho took the seat on the other side, pressed a button, and the rear half of the car's roof slid away. He stood on the back seat and beckoned Joseph to join him. The crowd started applauding, and flashing camera bulbs momentarily blinded Joseph. He felt Bodho's arm around his shoulders and involuntarily tensed. General Zamenka climbed into the front seat, and the Mercedes rolled slowly across the tarmac, followed by twenty other black sedans. Motorcycle police took up their positions on either side of the motorcade. Joseph turned to look back at the motorcade but couldn't see Faraday or the State Department officials.

Thousands of Congolese lined the road, cheering and waving distinct DRC flags. Large pictures of Joseph and the president hung from the light poles. Joseph fought to hold his balance when the Mercedes hit ruts in the road and swerved to avoid deeper potholes. *How can the road between the capital and the airport be in such a state of disrepair?* Joseph wondered.

As the motorcade neared Kinshasa, the crowds pushed closer, and it slowed to a crawl. Cheering Congolese threw streamers, and Joseph felt paper dropped from buildings falling on his head. Someone in the crowd started chanting, "Muamba, Muamba, Muamba," and within a few minutes, it became a crescendo. Bodho smiled and threw an arm around Joseph while waving with his other hand.

Two guards saluted as the motorcade turned into the presidential palace. Joseph gasped. All he'd seen on the drive from the airport was poverty: children dressed in rags, crumbling roads, and old, faded buildings. The palace, rolling green lawns, and gardens that he was now staring at would not have been out of place in Versailles or London. When the motorcade stopped at the front of the palace, a valet opened the president's door, and another ran around and held Joseph's open.

"My valets will show you to your room, where you may refresh yourself, and if you're tired, perhaps take a nap. Dinner will be in the Great Hall at eight o'clock."

"Thank you, Mr. President."

As Joseph followed the valet down the corridor, he was struck by the grandeur. Marble and gold leaf tiles glistened, and some of the sculptures were breathtaking. The first valet unlocked the door to his room, which was the size of a small house, and said, "I'll return just before eight. There is a platter of fresh fruit on the table, mineral water in the refrigerator, and a well-stocked bar. If there is something not to your satisfaction, or you need help, there is a red button next to the bed. Press it and I'll come running."

The valet carrying his suitcases followed Joseph into the room and asked, "Would you like me to help you unpack?"

"No thank you. I won't be unpacking."

After the valets had left, Joseph laid out a clean set of clothes before going to the toilet. The taps, showerheads, and grates in the bathroom were gold. When he returned to the living room, he took a seat in a large period chair and kicked his shoes off. He felt his feet sink into the lush, beige carpet, put his hands behind his head, and pondered what the night might hold.

Chapter 11

Joseph entered the Great Hall through enormous, gold double doors just before eight o'clock. A young girl dressed in a white sleeveless blouse showing just a trace of midriff and a colorful, full-length skirt took him by the hand and showed him to a chair next to the head of the table. The high-backed, red-cushioned chairs were regal. Sitting opposite him were General Zamenka and Colonel Gizenga. He glanced down the long table. Military personnel sat in the first ten chairs, and politicians and administrators, including George Faraday and the two State Department officials, occupied the next thirty. Embroidered red and gold drapes ran the full length of the walls, huge chandeliers sparkled, and the table was set with gold candelabras, matching cutlery and gold-leafed crockery. Three paces behind each chair, young girls stood at attention, waiting to serve their respective guests. Joseph was still taking in the decadence of the room when a fanfare of trumpets erupted, and everyone at the table stood up. The president swept in, a security guard on either side of him, and took the chair at the head of the table. Looking up, he held his hands out in front of him and moved them downward, and his guests sat back down.

President Bodho rested his hand on Joseph's arm. "You will enjoy the food. I employ the world's finest French chefs. The quail was flown in from Paris this morning, and the wagyu from Tokyo. The truffles are from Italy."

"I'm sure I will, Mr. President."

While they were talking, waiters carried bowls of exotic foods to the table, and the servers attended to their guests' needs.

Malt whiskey was the president's drink of choice, and bottles lined the table. Joseph knew there would be little change out of $2,000 a bottle. When his waiter came to fill his glass, he put his hand over it and said, "No, thanks."

"What is wrong?" Bodho asked, his booming voice carrying the length of the table.

"Nothing, Mr. President. I just don't drink alcohol."

"Why? You have won the gold. You don't need to worry anymore."

"Mr. President, I'm going to defend my title in London."

"For the U.S. or the Democratic Republic?"

"The Democratic Republic."

Bodho's scowl disappeared and was replaced by toothy, raucous laughter. "Then I forbid you to drink alcohol. You must bring more honor to our country by again winning gold."

Colonel Gizenga, chimed in, "I understand you used to live in Katanga."

"Yes, in a village in the northeast."

"Are you going to visit?"

"I don't know. I understand the rebels control much of the north."

"Ah, so the famous decathlete is too scared to go back to his old home," Gizenga sneered.

Joseph fought back a surge of anger. "I'm not scared. I'm just following the advice of the State Department."

"I control Katanga," Gizenga said. "I'm flying back tomorrow. If you want to visit your village, six of my men will provide you with more than enough protection so long as they have Kel with them."

"Kel?" Joseph asked, looking puzzled.

"Kalashnikov," Gizenga said, thumping his leg while the military men and president roared with laughter. "Six Kalashnikovs is enough to wipe out all the rebels if the cowards would only fight. Let me know if you want to go back. You will not be at any risk."

"Why did you refuse my invitation to stay at the palace?" the president asked, slurring slightly. The whiskey bottle in front of him had only a few inches left in it.

"The State Department wanted me to stay with their officials. I think they want to ensure the mining executives will have access to me. The last thing our government wants to do is insult you, Mr. President."

"Our government?" Zamenka said. "We are your government. What do you mean? Those mining executives will go home with nothing without our support."

"I have dual citizenship. I have responsibilities to the country in which I live."

"Yes, and you used that dual citizenship to gain a place on our Olympics team because the U.S. wouldn't have picked you," Gizenga chipped in.

"Rubbish," Joseph said. "I would've been the first selected. I wanted to give something back to the people of my country of birth."

"Then why did your friend pay a bri—"

"Enough," Zamenka said, glaring at Gizenga.

"What?" Joseph said. "What did you say?"

"He didn't say anything," Zamenka said. "Would you like some company tonight?"

"I don't understand."

"Do you fancy any of the young girls?" Zamenka asked, swiveling his bulky neck to look around the room.

"No," Joseph said, suppressing a look of disgust. "I'm tired from the flight. I need sleep. If you don't mind, Mr. President, I'd like to go to my hotel."

"But you will miss my head chef's pièce de résistance — lemon soufflé," the president slurred, downing the last of the whiskey bottle in front of him and shouting for more.

"Thank you, Mr. President, but I don't eat sweets."

"You don't drink alcohol, don't like girls, and don't eat sweets," Zamenka said. "What do you like?"

"Sorry, General."

Gizenga beckoned one of the soldiers standing at the doors.

"Your friend seems to be enjoying himself," Zamenka said, nodding toward George Faraday, who was talking animatedly and drinking champagne. "I don't think he'll be going back to the hotel with you."

"That's all right. He can come when he's ready."

"Your luggage is being taken to the car. Follow me," Gizenga said.

"Thank you for your hospitality, Mr. President. Thank you, General. Goodnight."

Gizenga showed Joseph to a black Range Rover. There were Jeeps in front of and behind it, each carrying four soldiers. Half a dozen motorbikes flanked either side of the convoy.

"Is all this necessary?"

"Kinshasa is not Los Angeles," Gizenga said, closing the door behind Joseph. "If anything were to happen to you, we would be the laughing stock of the world."

Joseph cringed as the motorcade roared through the city. People on the streets smiled and waved to him.

It was just before midnight when they reached the Kempinski Hotel. Screaming young women surrounded the entrance, and the bellboys had to fight their way through to the Range Rover. Joseph got out, and the soldiers formed up on either side of him, and pushed their way through the crowd.

"You're like a rock star. What's it feel like?" One of the soldiers grinned.

"Terrible."

The foyer was even worse. The hotel had cordoned the women off, but they continued to push forward, screaming, "Joseph, Joseph, Joseph!"

The hotel manager directed the soldiers to the elevators and handed Joseph a key, saying, "We upgraded you to a suite, Mr. Muamba."

As the doors started to close, Joseph heard a woman cry out in Swahili-French, the dialect of his village, and a nickname he hadn't heard in fourteen years.

"Boss, Boss, don't you remember me?"

Joseph turned around, putting his hands out to stop the doors from closing, and saw a stunning young woman with tints of blonde in her long, dark, cascading hair. She was wearing a sleeveless, multi-colored knee-length floral dress cinched at the waist and jeweled sandals.

"Maya!" he said. "Maya, is it really you?"

"Yes, Boss," she said, flashing gleaming white teeth while her big brown eyes sparkled.

"Let her through," Joseph said.

Maya pushed her way through the noisy crowd with the help of the soldiers.

"You look stunning," he said.

"I can't hear you."

"Let's go up to my room," Joseph said, holding the elevator doors open.

The soldiers smiled, and one winked before saying, "Goodnight."

Chapter 12

One of the bellboys held the door open to the suite on the twenty-second level, and Joseph thought he heard Maya gasp. There was a sofa, television, dining table, a coffee table and two recliners in the living area. Maya walked over to the desk positioned next to the window and said, "You can still see lights on the Congo River. It will be a beautiful view in the daytime."

"Would you like me to unpack, sir?" a bellboy asked.

"Thank you, no," Joseph replied, pulling out his wallet and tipping him generously.

After both bellboys left, Maya said, "I've never been in such a luxurious room."

"Would you like a drink?"

"Thank you. Mineral water, please. What does it feel like to return as the country's all-conquering hero?"

"Surreal. Do you speak English?"

Maya laughed. "Have you forgotten Swahili? It sounds funny spoken with an American accent. Half of Kinshasa speaks English. Of course I do, but you wouldn't have noticed me had I not spoke in Swahili."

"Sis is all grown up. How come you're in Kinshasa? When did you leave the village?"

"Please don't call me that. I'm not your sister."

"And I'm not your boss. Now tell me about yourself."

For the next ten minutes, Maya related what had happened to her and how she had been adopted.

"My God, I can still remember you saying your parents would never sell you. We met the same fate."

"No, we didn't," Maya said. "My adoptive parents were looking for a slave. I cleaned their house, washed and ironed their clothes, did the shopping and cooking, and looked after the garden. There was no love. The only good thing they did was to ensure I got a good education. However, when I wanted to study medicine, they told me poor black girls didn't become doctors. They were nothing like your adoptive parents."

Joseph looked puzzled. "I don't understand. You don't know my parents."

"No, but I saw them on television after you won in Beijing. They love you, and I could see how much you loved them. You got lucky."

"I would have been dead by now had I stayed in the village, and yes, I got lucky with my adoptive parents. They are kind, generous, and loving. I've only been here a day, and I already miss them. When did you return?"

"As soon as I turned eighteen, I left my adoptive parents in South Africa, and I'll never go back. I studied nursing for two years in Johannesburg before returning. I've been back for nearly five years and have a good job at Kinshasa Mercy Hospital."

"Are you married? Do you have a boyfriend?"

"Do you typically ask such personal questions?" Maya said, her eyes dancing. "No, I'm like you. I'm single."

"And how do you know I'm single?" Joseph replied, drawing his chair closer.

"I know everything there is to know about you. I've read all of the articles on the Internet. The all-American boy, successful at college, successful on the track, successful in business. Your voice sounds so strange. You talk like all the other Americans. Why isn't such a famous man married? Why doesn't he have a girlfriend?"

"I just haven't met Miss Right," Joseph said, and then paused. "Do you believe God put us here for a greater calling?"

"Oh, you've become religious. So many American sports stars are. No, I deal with death every day. Not just from disease, from child-birth, bashings, assaults, and murder. I don't have the luxury of thinking about greater callings in life. When you live here, you focus on survival."

"Then why did you come back?"

"The Congo is my home. You're an American boy. Why didn't you compete for the U.S. in Beijing?"

"I don't know. I told myself it was because I'd get greater recognition and be helping the country where I was born. That's untrue. I've been asking myself the same question. Maya, if you knew so much, why didn't you call or email me?"

Maya smiled. Her moist lips were full, and her perfect teeth glistened. "I did. I presume my emails went to junk, and you never returned my calls. I might just as well have called President Obama."

"I'm sorry. I never got your messages."

"Of course you didn't. You probably receive thousands of calls that your secretary thinks are of no account. Like mine."

"Have you been back to the village?"

"Yes, every year since I returned. It's hard to get time off from the hospital, and it takes four days to get to the village."

"It only took a day fourteen years ago. How can it take four days?"

"The road from Lubumbashi is closed. Only the New Dawn mine, police, and military are allowed to use it. The mine's management has enormous influence. If our people get sick, they usually die before making it to Lubumbashi."

"The country's gone backward. Do you still have family here?"

"My parents are dead, but I have a brother and sister in the village." Maya smiled sadly.

"Are any of my family still there?"

"No, Anatole fled with the last of your family to Tanzania."

"What do you mean? Anatole was only six when I left."

"He was fifteen when soldiers attacked the village and killed your mother and Safi. He was the eldest living member of your family."

"No! No!" Joseph exclaimed, hanging his head before looking up. "My mother wasn't killed. She died of TB."

"Is that what they told you?" Maya frowned. "I'm sorry."

Joseph stood and paced around the room, clenching and unclenching his fists. "No! That's not true. How do you know? You weren't there."

"No, but Yannick was, and he told me. He saw it all."

"Yannick is still in the village?"

"Yes."

"What did he tell you?"

"Not that much detail. He hid in the bush and watched. He's still ashamed of himself. I comforted him and said he shouldn't be. If he had tried to intervene, they would've shot him. They killed more than fifty of our people."

"Are you certain?"

"I believe Yannick. I pressed him for details, but he blames himself. He told me he was a coward and then clammed up."

"I feel sick."

Maya rested her hand on Joseph's forearm. "I'm sorry you had to hear it from me. I didn't know the government had told you lies."

"I was with some senior military people tonight. I'll find out what happened."

"You're going to ask them?"

"I am. I have to find out."

"For someone's who's supposed to be smart, you're naïve. They know I'm with you, Joseph. When you ask them, they'll know I told you. They'll torture and perhaps even kill me. You can't breathe a word. You're not in Los Angeles now."

"It's that bad?"

"It is."

"How is Yannick?"

"He's the same height as you but half the weight. It's easy to detect those who are corrupt here — they look well-fed. Yannick walks with a hunch, probably caused from working in the mine. He looks twenty years older than you."

"I don't understand. The mine was meant to bring prosperity."

"It's brought nothing but misery. Workers are paid three dollars for a twelve-hour shift without breaks. If they get sick or injured, they don't get paid. And then there are the deaths. Around one a week, and the company pays the widow or parents $100. That's what life is worth. $100!"

"Why does Yannick continue to work there?"

"What else can he do? The country is barren, and there are no fish in the river to catch."

"How can that be?"

"The mining company built a holding pond and – "

"Yes, all gold-mining companies do. It's used to store waste cyanide and residual metals."

"I know," Maya said. "Yannick told me. Please let me finish."

"Sorry."

"When the torrential rains came, they breached the holding pond's walls, and the waste covered thousands of acres of land before seeping into the river. It killed every fish for fifty miles and all of the foliage abutting the river. Animals and birds died in the thousands."

"There was nothing reported. Nothing on the Internet."

"The mine is in the middle of nowhere, and it's the Congo. What did you expect? An exposé in *Time* magazine? It's not California, you know. A tailings dam burst at another mine a hundred miles north of the village. Somehow Greenpeace found out and sent two of their people to snoop around. They disappeared off the face of the earth."

"It's worse than when Mobutu ruled."

"Yes. Yannick said the people are sick of it, but they're scared. He's been agitating for change, but he's fearful the others won't follow him. He says he's not a leader, and the Afrikaner supervisors and guards are brutal."

"I'm shocked," Joseph said.

"Are you going to visit the village?"

"I was, but now I know my family's not there, I'm not sure. Probably not."

Maya curled her bottom lip in disgust, and her eyes narrowed. "You don't want to see Yannick after all these years. You don't want to ask him what happened to your mother and sister. I guess I'm privileged to be in Kinshasa, or you wouldn't have seen me. I lived in South Africa but never left the Congo. You're a shallow, soft American boy. I shouldn't have expected more."

"Hang on," Joseph said.

"No, *you* hang on," Maya said, jotting something on a piece of paper before standing up. "It's nearly two o'clock. I have to go. Here's my phone number. If you like, you can call me, but I won't hold my breath."

As they reached the door, Maya turned around and kissed him on the cheek. "I always dreamed of kissing you," she said. "I know I may not see you again."

Joseph had been exhausted before, but now he was wide awake. Talking to Maya had been like talking to a stranger. She was a beautiful young woman, but the past fourteen years of their lives had been vastly different. It was only natural they would not connect. Was the information about his mother and sister factual? Why was life at the New Dawn mine so cheap?

The hotel had Wi-Fi, but Joseph didn't know how fast or secure it was. He connected his laptop to his cellphone and Googled the New Dawn Mining Gold Company. There were a few pictures taken from outside the fence on the website, plus the usual public relations rubbish. The mine produced three hundred thousand ounces per annum for the benefit of Katanga and the Democratic Republic of the Congo. According to the website, hundreds of Congolese were prospering as a result of being employed by the mine. The name of the mine's manager was Marc Boucher, but there was virtually no information about him.

Joseph then Googled "New Dawn Gold Mining Company + ownership" and discovered that Liberty Investments, incorporated in Mauritania, was the holding company. Liberty's directors and shareholders were lawyers resident in Mauritania. It was evident the lawyers were holding the shares in trust for the beneficial owners, whoever they might be — most likely foreign investors or corporations.

Googling Marc Boucher also proved fruitless. The only times he was mentioned were all related to New Dawn. The beneficial owners had gone to a lot of trouble to ensure they were well-hidden. It would be nearly impossible to find out who they were. Despite this, Joseph emailed Ron Patterson and asked him to find out all he could about New Dawn, Liberty Investments, and Marc Boucher. Capel & Lambert's tentacles were long, and perhaps Ron would come up with something.

Chapter 13

Joseph had gotten less than four hours of sleep, but the adrenaline kicked in, and he felt refreshed and alert. When he entered the hotel's Riviera restaurant at 7:30 a.m., he saw George Faraday and the two State Department officials at a table near the window. They looked seedy, there was no food in front of them, only cups of coffee. Faraday finished talking to the group at an adjoining table as Joseph sat down.

"You were smart leaving when you did," he said. "We were still drinking malt whiskey at two o'clock. I can't remember how we got back to the hotel."

"They wanted us to stay at the palace," Jack Costigan said, "but we declined. They brought us back by motorcade. I'm surprised you didn't hear us."

"You know who's at the table behind me?" Faraday said. "A delegation from BHP — you know, the world's biggest miner. They want to use my services."

"George, I know who BHP is. Who doesn't? I'm going to get something to eat from the buffet. Is anyone else eating?"

"We'll stick to coffee," Costigan said.

When Joseph got back to the table, the two officials had gone.

"They aren't seasoned drinkers and couldn't stand the sight of food," Faraday said.

"It's good," Joseph said, putting a forkful of egg, tomato, and steak into his mouth. "You should have some. What have we got planned today?"

"The guys from Greenmount Mining, a private consortium, are presenting to General Zamenka at ten o'clock. It's a copper project in northern Katanga with a capital investment of $800 million to get it off the ground. It's not huge, but could be a nice little earner," Faraday said, rubbing his hands together. "We'll be there for moral support and to tidy up any loose ends after the Greenmount people leave."

"To work out the size of the bribes," Joseph said bitterly.

"Jesus! Don't mention bribes, especially not in front of those guys from the State Department. They'll have a fit. Anyhow, they're not bribes, they're government charges."

"Paid into numbered accounts in Hong Kong, the Virgin Islands, or Liechtenstein?"

"Don't get all moral. These deals are good for the Congo and the people. They create jobs, prosperity, and a better country."

"And they're good for you, George."

"Good for us," Faraday said. "After all, you're the principal man."

Joseph's face clouded over. He didn't want to be responsible for putting dirty deals together and robbing the Congolese people. He took a sip of coffee and then, looking directly into Faraday's eyes, said, "When I was a little boy, I remember you helping to peg out a gold mine near the village. What happened to it?"

Faraday dropped his eyes. "I don't know. I can't remember. It was a long time ago."

"You spent a lot of time at the site. Surely you didn't do it for nothing. Who paid you?"

"I recall it was a four-million-ounce resource with a fifteen-year life, but I couldn't get anyone interested because of the rebels. Everyone I pitched to wanted the government to guarantee the rebels wouldn't disrupt operations. It was impossible to get."

"That's not such a bad memory, George." Joseph frowned. "At today's prices, the resource is worth $7 billion. You must have been angry when you didn't get anything for your work."

"Oh, don't worry, I got paid. I had some valuable government approvals. I sold them to a group of investors who were prepared to gamble on the army eventually clearing the rebels out."

"Do you remember who the investors were?"

"No. Jesus! What is this? Why are you so interested in something I did so long ago? I can barely remember it."

"Does the name Liberty Investments ring a bell?"

Again Faraday dropped his eyes. "No."

Joseph knew he was lying but didn't understand why. "Have you heard of a dude named Marc Boucher?"

"No. Look, what's this about?"

"It's nothing," Joseph said. "How are we getting to the palace?"

"We're getting picked up at 9:45. I'll meet you in the foyer."

Later that morning, when their three-vehicle motorcade complete with motorcycles sped through the streets of Kinshasa, Joseph noticed some sharp contrasts with the prior day's spectators.

Around fifty human rights protestors holding placards marched in a circle at the front of the palace gates. They made no attempt to block the motorcade, and the demonstration was peaceful. One man who was slightly taller than the others caught Joseph's attention. He had a jutting jaw, pronounced cheekbones, and a goatee. He stared at Joseph through bloodshot eyes and slowly shook his head. The sign he was carrying said, "Stop the army murdering innocents."

"Who are they? How come they're protesting? Who's the guy with the goatee?" Joseph asked.

"They're troublemakers," Faraday replied. "That's all. His name is Paul Blundo. He's a Communist sympathizer."

"What does he mean about the army murdering innocents?"

"I don't know. Probably rebels killed by the soldiers. Don't be concerned. It's all lies."

The motorcade pulled up at the front of the palace. The soldiers led Faraday, Joseph, and the Greenmount people through double doors into a large meeting room. General Zamenka sat at a long, elevated table with three advisers on either side of him. In front of the table were two rows of chairs. The heavily armed soldiers took up positions on either side of the doors.

"How is your hotel? Did you sleep well?" Zamenka asked.

"Quite comfortable, and yes, I had a good night's sleep," Joseph replied.

"Really?" Zamenka smirked. "Really?"

"Yes," Joseph replied, puzzled by the general's smirk. "It's the first time I have seen the river. It is magnificent. Can you swim in it?"

"I can't." Zamenka laughed. "But that's because I can't swim. If I could, I wouldn't, though. It's dirty, and there's always the chance of a crocodile lurking."

"So close to the port?"

"I am told children and dogs regularly disappear. If you want to swim, use the hotel's pools."

"Thank you. I will."

"I know now why you didn't want a girl last night. You already had one back at your hotel. I hear she is beautiful — I can understand why you were anxious to get back," General Zamenka said, looking down at Joseph.

"She's an old friend," Joseph said.

"An old friend." Zamenka laughed, slapping his thigh, and his advisers joined in the laughter.

"What's he on about?" Faraday whispered.

"Nothing. Forget it."

The Greenmount people were well-prepared, and for the next three hours, they pitched their proposal by PowerPoint, by video, and by rolling out maps and detailed plans. George Faraday added explanatory comments when Zamenka's advisers raised queries. Zamenka looked bored and occasionally dozed off, only to wake up with a start and demand to know what was going on. No one dared laugh.

After the Greenmount people had finished their presentation and left, Faraday said, "It's a good project, General. It will result in thousands of jobs, receipt of foreign currency, and significant tax revenue."

"Yes, yes, I know," Zamenka said, and then, looking at Joseph, he began speaking in Lingala.

Much to Joseph's surprise, Faraday responded in the same dialect, and the two men engaged in animated conversation. Joseph could only understand the occasional word, but it was apparent Zamenka was dominating the conversation, and while Faraday was shaking his head, the look on his face said he was acceding.

A few minutes later, Zamenka stood up, shook hands with Faraday, and embraced Joseph. "I'll see you tomorrow," he said, then ordered his soldiers to take them back to the hotel.

As soon as they were in the car, Joseph said, "I never knew you spoke Lingala. Hardly anyone in the village spoke or understood it. I picked up a few of your words. What were you discussing?"

"I've been coming here for forty years. They say there are twenty languages and more than two hundred dialects spoken in the Congo. There would only be a handful I don't understand. General Zamenka didn't think a national hero should hear our conversation. He was protecting you."

"Rubbish! He doesn't trust me. How much did he screw out of you?"

"Greenmount's investment just increased to $900 million."

"$100 million," Joseph said, "payable in the Virgin Islands or Zurich, I suppose."

"It's nothing," Faraday replied. "They're getting one of the best copper resources in the world. It's worth north of $3 billion."

"I understand how private consortiums like Greenmount can pay bribes, but how do the big public companies do it? They've got responsibilities to shareholders. Surely their boards don't condone criminal acts?"

"There are always ways." Faraday laughed. "Are we having dinner tonight?"

"I think I'll eat in my room," Joseph replied. "The travel's starting to take its toll."

Chapter 14

Out of respect, Joseph had had his cellphone on silent for the meeting with Zamenka, but had seen an email from Ron Patterson pop up and was dying to read it. Disappointingly, Ron hadn't come up with anything on Liberty Investments. He said there were a maze of different lawyers' and accountants' nominee companies behind Liberty, so finding who controlled and owned the shares was impossible. The real owners had gone to a lot of trouble to conceal themselves, but this wasn't unusual — the keystone to international money laundering and tax avoidance was secrecy.

Marc Boucher was another story. He was a mining gun for sale to the highest bidder. Better known as Jacques Le Roux, he had managed gold mines all over Africa and had a reputation for extreme brutality. In early 2001, he had authorized blasting at an underground mine in South Africa without evacuating the workers, and twenty miners had died. The South African authorities had charged him, and there was a newspaper photograph of him standing in front of the court surrounded by well-dressed white men, presumably lawyers. He had applied for bail and, once it had been granted, had absconded to the Congo, where he changed his name to Marc Boucher. The South African government's numerous extradition applications had fallen on deaf Congolese ears.

Joseph quickly Googled Le Roux and got more than two hundred hits, mainly newspapers. He was a ruthless operator who always took a percentage of the gold mined, rather than working for a salary. The owners, whoever they were, surely must have known Boucher's background before they hired him. Joseph pondered for a few minutes before emailing Ron, asking him to dig around the archives on George Faraday and to look at his deals in Katanga around 1992 to 1995. He also asked him to find out who owned the mine where the workers had been killed in South Africa.

Joseph lay on the bed, staring at the ceiling, and reflecting on how everything in life had a reason. Why had his life been spared by a white man who he had hated but now loved? Why had he won gold in Beijing? Had soldiers killed his mother and sister, and if so, who ordered their deaths? Why was he back in the country of his birth?

The answer to one of those questions lay in his village. Perhaps once he had an explanation, the fog hanging over his destiny would lift. He Googled airports in Katanga and then brought up a map of the province. Satisfied with his calculations, he punched Maya's number into his cell. She answered, "Maya Tansi speaking."

"Maya, it's me."

"Ah, Mr. America. I didn't think you'd call. Are you calling because you want to or feel you have to? Is your conscience troubling you?"

"That's silly. Of course, I want to meet up with you again. That's why I'm calling. I'm going to the village on Saturday morning. I want to see Yannick. Can you come with me?"

There was a long pause. "It's such short notice. I'd like to, but I can't. The hospital's short-staffed, and there's no way I'm going to be able to get eight days off."

"Eight days? You'll be back in Kinshasa on Sunday night."

"That's impossible. Even if we're on the first flight and could use the road from Lubumbashi, which we can't, it would still take nearly twelve hours. We'd arrive at nightfall and have to return at first light in the morning. Oh, and I realize you're a national treasure, and they might let you use the road, but it will only be with a full army guard. I don't fancy traveling with thugs and rapists. The only other route takes three days. It's not Los Angeles, you know."

"So I keep getting told," Joseph said. "Are you quite finished? I have a private plane we can use. We can fly out of Kinshasa at 6:00 a.m. and land in Lubumbashi just after eight. From there we'll take a helicopter, and even with one stop to refuel at Kilwa, we'll be at the village just before midday. How does that sound?"

"You own a plane? Oh my God! I don't believe it."

"It's not mine. My father chartered it for the trip. He worries about my safety."

"And the helicopter?"

"I haven't arranged it yet, but there's nothing the State Department guys can't seem to do. I'm going to ask them in the morning. Don't worry, there won't be a problem. Are you coming with me?"

"Yes, yes, of course I am."

"Where will I pick you up?"

There was another pause. "I-I'll meet you at the airport."

"Maya, I don't care where you live. There's no reason to be ashamed."

"I'm not. I said I'd meet you at the airport."

"As you wish. Don't be late."

"I won't be — and, Joseph, thank you for thinking of me. Goodnight."

He went to bed early, pulling the sheet up around his neck. He wondered whether he'd find his calling when he returned to his village.

The following morning, George Faraday and Jack Costigan were having breakfast when Joseph entered the restaurant and told them what he had planned for the weekend.

"I don't like it," Faraday said. "Some of the world's most influential mining executives are here. They're going to want to be looked after and entertained over the weekend."

"I'm sure you can take good care of them."

"What? I thought you said we were going to Katanga."

"Not we. Just me and a friend."

"That's not happening. I told your father I'd look after you. I'm not letting you out of my sight."

"Look after me?" Joseph laughed. "I don't want to be rude, but these are my people, and you are old and weak. I can protect myself, but I don't want to be worrying about you."

"No, I'm coming, and that's final."

"George, this is a private matter. I'm going back to my village to hopefully see my siblings. They fled the village, but I'm hoping they've returned. I don't want you there. I'll be back on Sunday night for next week's round of meetings. If that's not satisfactory, I'll be on a commercial flight to LA this afternoon, and you can handle Bodho, Zamenka, and the mining companies yourself."

"Jesus!" Costigan said. "You wouldn't. We're just starting to make ground."

"Yes, I would."

"I'm going to talk to your father. I'm responsible for you."

"Do whatever you like, George, but nothing is going to stop me. You seem to think I'm still the twelve-year-old boy you bought all those years ago. I'm not!"

"It's only two days," Costigan said. "He'll be okay. If the negotiations fall apart, we'll be a laughing-stock. Worse, the Chinese will be here the minute we leave."

"All right, Joseph, have it your way," Faraday said, "but you have a funny way of showing gratitude."

"Gratitude? You virtually strong-armed me into coming, and you weren't doing it for me. I was your meal ticket into the palace. Don't talk to me about gratitude, George."

"Funny that. I didn't hear you objecting when I told you how much money we might make, and how you might own your own Gulfstream."

"No, I didn't, because of the respect my father has for you, but understand this — I don't like the way you make money. It's dirty," Joseph said, standing up. "I've lost my appetite. I'll meet you in the lobby in half an hour. Jack, will there be any problems arranging the helicopter?"

"Consider it done."

Chapter 15

The first glimmer of sunlight peeped over the horizon as Joseph's motorcade pulled into the airport. President Bodho and General Zamenka had insisted he take a security detail, but he had tactfully declined, saying he wanted to spend some time with Maya alone. After much debate they had agreed but wouldn't hear of him getting a taxi.

Maya was waiting in the terminal. When she saw him, she gasped. "God, you're huge," she said, trying to get a hand around his bicep. "Why are you carrying your cellphone in an armband? You're not going on a training run, are you?"

"You saw me the other night. I haven't changed since then," Joseph said, laughing. "And it's safer on my arm than in my pocket."

"You weren't wearing a T-shirt then. Of course, I knew you were big, but you're far more muscly in real life than you appear on television. I watched every event in the decathlon, and you looked small next to that German."

"Compared to Wolfgang, I am. He's six foot eight inches tall and weighs 260 pounds. Give me your bag."

"I'm fine, thanks. It's light. I'm so excited."

"Okay, let's get moving."

As they climbed the stairs, they were greeted by the flight attendant, who said, "Good morning, Mr. Muamba. What a beautiful green your blouse is, Ms. Tansi."

"Thank you," Maya said, gazing around the plane. "Joseph, I can't believe this is just for us. I've never seen anything as luxurious. It's so extravagant. How many crew members are there?"

"Captain, co-pilot, and flight attendant. That's it. Kick your Nikes off and put your feet up," Joseph said, sitting down.

Maya took the seat opposite him. "It feels almost wrong to be wearing jeans in this opulence. I should've worn my best clothes."

"You chose well," Joseph said, as the plane taxied into position for takeoff. "If the village is anything like what it was, we're going to come back caked in dirt."

Twenty minutes later, the flight attendant took their breakfast orders, and after he'd gone, Maya said, "It's embarrassing. We have one person dedicated to looking after us. You live an amazing life."

"It's unusual for me too. I've been on small charter planes, but nothing like this."

"How was your week?" Maya asked. "Did you do a lot of big deals?"

Joseph pushed his chair into the upright position, clenched his hands, and looked out the window. "We're flying over the richest and most concentrated mineral resources in the world, and the people are getting nothing for them. It's terrible. No deal gets done without Bodho, Zamenka, and who knows how many others getting paid off. The Western companies and the Chinese are raping the country. The people get paid a pittance, and the copper, gold, and cobalt is transferred out of the country at way less than market value, so the government collects no taxes. It's shockingly corrupt."

"You must have known of the corruption before you came back. You'd only have needed to spend an hour on the Internet."

"Of course, but I never realized the extent. I didn't think public companies listed on the world's largest stock exchanges paid bribes."

"And they do?"

"Yesterday an Australian mining company agreed to pay nearly $500 million to rehabilitate the environment, compensate landholders, build roads, and provide housing rather than huts. George Faraday told me Bodho and Zamenka will provide invoices and documentation to support the payment, but the country will be lucky to see $100 million. God, the Australians were found guilty of paying $300 million in bribes to Saddam Hussein. Apparently, they didn't learn anything."

"Are they the worst?"

"No, they're all the same."

"What about the Chinese?"

"They give the appearance of being fair and caring. They build roads, medical centers, and hospitals, but for every dollar they spend, they get four back. They're the same as the Westerners, but rather than brutal rape, they do it gently. The leaders of the American companies hate their slyness."

"Poor Boss," Maya smiled, reaching over and taking his hand. "It's the Congo, and it's not going to change just because you won a gold medal. I worked late last night and only got a few hours' sleep. I'm going to have a short snooze. Would you like to read the *Times?*"

"Sure."

Maya pushed her seat back and closed her eyes. The sound of Joseph rustling the newspaper soothed her into a light doze, but she jerked upright upon his exclamation, "Jesus!"

"What's wrong?"

"Sorry," he said, holding up the newspaper and pointing to a photo on the bottom of the front page. "I saw him. He was in front of the palace protesting two days ago. He hanged himself in prison."

"Paul Blundo," Maya said. "He was a thorn in the government's side, exposing politicians, administrators, and the army for what they are. He didn't hang himself. How could he? What would have he used? The first things they take are shoelaces and belts. The number of prisoners who 'hang themselves' is staggering."

"Are you saying they murdered him?"

"He and many others," Maya said, closing her eyes again.

About thirty minutes from Lubumbashi, the plane hit light turbulence, and Maya woke up with a start.

"It's okay," Joseph said. "You were out like a light. I was watching you. Who would've thought a skinny, scruffy kid would grow up to be so beautiful?"

"And I was thinking about you. You were so serious when we were kids, and nothing has changed. You're only two years older than Yannick and me. Yet, when we were little, it seemed like so much more. That's why we called you Boss." Maya laughed. "Is it so hard to smile? Don't you have a sense of humor?"

"Perhaps if you'd seen and heard what I have in the last few days, you too might find it hard to laugh."

"Oh, Joseph, I've lived it for the past five years. Everyone in the Congo has. It's a way of life. You've been enjoying the land of milk and honey. That's why you're shocked. Welcome to my world."

Joseph bit his bottom lip and said, "You'd better tighten your seatbelt."

"Will the Blackhawk be waiting for us when we land?"

"I doubt it's going to be a Blackhawk." Joseph smiled. "The pilot's going to be waiting for us."

"Ah, a smile. Now that wasn't so difficult, was it?" Maya teased.

Joseph looked down on Lubumbashi and observed, "It's a sprawling city."

"Nearly 2 million people, and it's developing at a breakneck speed."

The plane taxied to a standstill. Joseph thanked the crew and asked the captain to be ready to go at 7:00 p.m. on Sunday. Waiting at the bottom of the stairs was a man with cropped blond hair, a jutting jaw, and a physique similar to Joseph's. He held out his hand and said, "I'm Chuck Bennett, your pilot. It's an honor to shake the hand of the greatest athlete on the planet. Would you mind writing a short note to my son, Andy, on the trip? He's only seven, but he'd kill to have something written by you."

This guy's in the services. Where did Costigan dig him up? I wonder if he's a SEAL. "It'd be a pleasure, Chuck," Joseph said, before introducing Maya.

"This way, folks. The big bird's humming and ready to go."

The helicopter was a Sikorsky and far larger than Joseph had expected. Sitting in the front seat was another man who had shaved black hair and was a little smaller than Chuck. "Who's that?" Joseph shouted over the whine of the rotors.

"Brett Kronk, my co-pilot. I'll introduce you once we're onboard. Come on, let's go."

Joseph smirked. *These guys are Marines or SEALS and the copter's big enough to carry an arsenal. How did Jack Costigan arrange to fly them in, or are they based in Katanga?*

A few minutes later when they were at cruising altitude, Joseph asked, "Where are you guys based?"

The two Americans looked at each other before Bennett said, "Lubumbashi?"

"Who are you with?"

"We freelance," Bennett said.

"Where'd you learn to fly?"

"Hey," Bennett said, handing Joseph a pen and pad. "I nearly forgot. Can you write that note?"

"Sure."

Kronk spoke for the first time to ask, "What was it like knowing you had to take nearly a minute off your personal best in the fifteen hundred to win gold?"

"Yeah," Bennett chimed in, "but wasn't it that enormous javelin throw that won you gold?"

Every time Joseph asked them what they were doing in Lubumbashi, they changed the subject back to his sporting exploits. Bennett was friendly and gregarious, while Kronk was curt and to the point. *Good cop, bad cop,* Joseph thought.

Maya looked down at the green canopy and said, "Isn't it beautiful? Nature's umbrella."

"Some of those trees are two hundred feet tall and have trunks nearly forty feet in diameter," Bennett said.

"I know," Maya said. "I usually travel through the forest on the way to the village."

An hour later Joseph looked down on a small town with dirt roads, clay and thatched huts, some corrugated iron and brick houses, and a few concrete buildings. "I thought Kilwa would be larger," he said.

"It is." Bennett grinned. "This is Pweto. We arranged to refuel here before leaving Lubumbashi. We'll be at your village in half an hour and won't need to stop on the way back."

The airstrip was around a mile long, and the copter touched down next to a corrugated iron building with a flat roof. A small tanker appeared from nowhere, and Kronk said, "Why don't you stretch your legs?"

The heat was oppressive, and tsetse flies buzzed around them. "I can't believe we'll be home in half an hour," Maya said.

"Home," Joseph repeated wistfully. "It's strange to think of the village as home after all the years I've spent in California, What do you think of the pilots?"

"They seem to know what they're doing. Why do you ask?"

"No reason. I think they've finished refueling. Let's go."

Twenty-five minutes later, Joseph said, "There's a gold mine three miles to the east of the village. Please fly over it."

"New Dawn," Bennett said. "Sure, no problem."

The helicopter swept over the mine and circled. "Go lower," Joseph said. "Go as low as you can."

"Hold on," Bennett said.

"Jesus!" Joseph exclaimed.

"What's wrong?" Maya asked.

"Look at the excavators and trucks. They're not moving. No one's working. It looks deserted."

"It's Saturday," Maya said.

"Mines never stop, not even on Christmas Day," Joseph replied. "There's something wrong. Chuck, fly over those huts. I want to see if there's any sign of life."

Maya pointed. "There's a small group of men."

Chapter 16

Ten men were standing in a circle surrounding a man who was speaking and gesticulating. They seemed to be enjoying what he was saying, and smiles filled their drawn faces. Without exception, they were skinny and dressed in rags and sandals. Three of them were carrying spears, and the others were armed with rifles.

"Go lower," Joseph said.

"I don't know what's going on," Bennett said, "but I don't want to get too close to those rifles. One lucky shot to our fuel tanks, and we're history."

"They're not worried about us," Joseph said. "They're not even looking up. They're too busy listening to that guy in the middle. Go lower."

Bennett took the copter down to a hundred feet. The men looked up, worry written across their faces, but they didn't raise their rifles. Joseph noticed Kronk caressing an M16 that appeared to have materialized from nowhere. Suddenly Maya screamed, "It's Yannick! It's Yannick!"

"Which one?" Joseph asked.

"In the middle. The one doing the talking."

The hunched-over man was nothing but a bag of bones and looked about forty. "Are you sure?"

"Of course," Maya said, opening a window and shouting down to Yannick.

"He can't hear you, Miss," Bennett said.

"Put it down," Joseph said.

Bennett looked worried and glanced over at Kronk, who shook his head.

"Jesus," Joseph yelled, pointing to a yard that housed approximately fifty vehicles — four-wheel drives, trucks, trailers, excavators, and graders. "Put it down over there. We'll walk back."

Bennett landed about four hundred yards from the men. Maya leaped out through the dust and started to run. Joseph easily caught up to her and grasped her elbow. "It's too hot to run. Yannick's not going anywhere."

"I'm so excited. I haven't seen him for nearly a year. He's going to be so surprised and when he sees you ..." Maya stopped. "I'm lost for words. I don't know what he'll do when he sees you."

Joseph glanced back at the helicopter. The two Americans were following close behind. Both were carrying M16s.

When they were eighty yards from the men, Maya shouted, "Yannick, Yannick," and he broke from the group and jogged toward her.

They embraced, and Yannick asked, "What are you doing here?"

"Can't you see who I have with me?" she replied.

Joseph looked at the tall, gaunt man with the pockmarked face carrying three spears and couldn't see a trace of the Yannick he'd once known.

"Boss," he said, "you came back. I would've never recognized you if I hadn't seen your picture in the newspapers. I wondered whether you would visit."

"Hello, Yannick," Joseph said, extending his hand. "It's good to see you again."

"God, you are massive. It's easy to see you don't live in Katanga."

"Yannick, why isn't the mine working? Where is everyone?" Joseph asked.

"Last week the company installed X-ray machines to detect workers stealing gold. Everyone has to pass through them at the end of their shifts. Yesterday a young boy was found with a small nugget inside his stomach. They were all set to remove it with a knife when the workers revolted. They would've killed him. We took their guns," Yannick said, nodding at the men holding rifles behind him. "We told them they had nothing to fear, but we were officially on strike. Despite this, they still ran. We want more money, better safety, improved conditions, and the X-ray machines removed."

Joseph frowned. "But where are the workers?"

"They went back to their villages," Yannick said, wiping his bloodshot eyes. "They'll return when they're needed."

"Are you the only workers still at the mine?" Maya asked, glancing at the small group.

"No, another eighty are spread around the mine. Some are underground, others are guarding equipment, but most are enjoying themselves in air-conditioned huts."

"Did you hurt the guards or wreck any equipment?" Joseph asked. "Was there any violence?"

"No," Yannick replied, "all we did was take their rifles. We had to, or they would've turned them on us. Life is cheap here. It's a peaceful strike."

Joseph looked back at the helicopter. There was no sign of the Americans. "Is there a toilet I can use?" he asked.

"In the big boss's office." Yannick nodded toward the largest hut. "There won't be anyone in there. Everyone's scared he'll find out and take revenge when he returns."

Boucher's office, Joseph thought as he walked over and let himself in. A metal desk sat in the center of it with a fabric high-backed chair behind it and half a dozen plastic chairs in front of it. There were a few papers and a computer on the desk. Joseph opened a door behind the fabric chair, and there was a tiled bathroom adjoining another room that housed a double bed.

When he returned to the office, he noticed that the thermostat on the wall read seventy degrees. Marc Boucher certainly worked and lived in comparative comfort. Joseph scanned a few invoices on the desk for equipment parts and was about to leave when his hand brushed the keyboard and the screen sprang to life. *He obviously didn't think to turn it off before fleeing*, Joseph noted. He took the USB from around his neck and plugged it into the tower. A few minutes later he joined the others. "We're going to the village now, Yannick. I need to talk to you. Will you come with us?"

Yannick looked dubiously at the helicopter. "I don't know. I'm needed here."

"Oh, come on," Maya wheedled, grabbing his hand.

They were halfway back when the rotors started spinning, blowing up a cloud of yellow dust. Yannick looked uncomfortable, and Maya said, "Don't be concerned. I'd never been in one before today. You'll be amazed by the views."

Five minutes later, the helicopter landed on the outskirts of the village. "Will you want to go back to the mine?" Bennett asked.

"I don't know," Joseph replied. "Probably not."

"We'll put the chopper in the shade of the forest then."

"What are you going to do while you're waiting?" Joseph asked.

"Don't concern yourself," Kronk said. "We'll be here when you need us."

"I can't wait to see my brother and sister," Maya said. "What are you two going to do?"

"Is our old meeting place still standing?" Joseph asked.

"It hasn't changed since you left. It's been dying for twenty years but refuses to succumb," Yannick said. "I can only give you a few hours. I have to get back to the mine. When Mr. Boucher and the others come back, I need to be there to handle the negotiations."

Chapter 17

Joseph and Yannick trekked across the grass toward the jungle in silence. There was none of the old banter. They were like strangers, and Joseph sensed he might never again truly know the frail man walking beside him. Maya was different. She had been educated and had seen the world. Yannick had never known anything except the village and the gold mine.

Time had stood still for the baobab tree. Joseph patted its trunk and said, "It looks like it'll be dead in six months, just like it did when we were boys."

"After you left, Maya and I never set foot in it. Then Maya was taken, and it just became a sad memory," Yannick said.

"I'm going to check the entrance," Joseph said, walking around the trunk. "Ah, the foliage is much heavier, but it's still the same."

Yannick was squatting in front of the baobab and asked, "What do you want to know?"

"Maya told me you witnessed the soldiers murder my mother and little Safi. Tell me what you saw."

Yannick's legs started shaking, and he got to his feet. "It was horrible. That pig Zamenka killed them both, and I watched like the coward I am."

"You're not a coward, Yannick. What could you have done? Sacrifice your life to achieve nothing? That would've been stupid."

"You would've attacked them."

"Zamenka was about to murder my mother and sister. Of course I would've attacked him, and you know what would've happened? They would've killed me. Would I have saved them? No! Don't beat yourself up. Tell me what happened, and don't spare me. Maya said it was soldiers. Were there more than Zamenka? I want to hear everything."

For the next hour, Yannick related everything he had seen. Joseph listened, distant and impassive. "Zamenka raped Safi. It was brutal. I can still hear her screams. She was still fighting when he slashed her throat. I said 'soldiers' to Maya because I couldn't talk. They raped every young girl and boy in the village. What are you going to do, Joseph?"

"I don't know," Joseph lied. "Tell me what happened to your parents."

"The soldiers attacked the village six months earlier, but your family got away that time. I hid, and my parents got butchered. You said you'd have attacked because it was your mother and your sister. I froze. I couldn't move." Yannick looked haunted and hung his head in shame.

Joseph reached out and rested his hand on Yannick's shoulder. "I know what I said I'd do, but it doesn't mean I would have. I wasn't here. I didn't experience the terror. You did. You can't fight guns with spears. Maya told me that Anatole fled with my brothers and sisters to Tanzania. Have you heard anything about them?"

"They never made it across Lake Tanganyika. I was told that Anatole made a raft, but the lake is over forty miles wide. They never stood a chance."

"All gone," Joseph muttered. "All gone."

A tear trickled down Yannick's cheek. "I'm sorry, but I have to get back to the mine."

"Do you know who owns it? Have there ever been any visitors who looked like they might be owners?"

"No. It's run by a Canadian, Marc Boucher, and an Afrikaner, Gert Botha. Most of the supervisors are Afrikaners. Other than the army, and police, there are never any visitors."

"Yes, I know about Boucher and Botha."

"There's a death every week. Sometimes more. There are no safety procedures underground. Workers die in cave-ins, from blasting, from exhaustion and malnutrition. Then there are those murdered for malingering or stealing gold. It's hell on earth."

"Why do you still work there?"

Yannick shrugged fatalistically. "The rivers and streams are polluted with cyanide and heavy metals. Nothing survived. There are no fish, birds, or animals. The foliage on the banks is dead, and when the tailings dam overflowed, it destroyed thousands of acres of fertile land. The little we make from the mine is all that keeps us alive."

Joseph clenched his fists, anger rising with every new revelation. "The gold mine was meant to bring prosperity, but it has brought nothing but hardship and death."

"I'm sorry, Joseph. I have to get back. I'll come to the village tonight. We can talk some more then."

Deep in their own thoughts they got up and walked in silence to the edge of the forest, when the peace was broken by a sharp clattering in the distance. "What's that?" Joseph asked, as his cellphone rang.

"Machine guns," Yannick said, his face stricken with fear. "Oh God, it's coming from the mine."

"Yes," Joseph shouted, putting his cellphone in speaker mode.

"It's Chuck Bennett. We're above the mine. Four choppers carrying about thirty troops just landed. They're randomly killing workers. We've been getting reports that rebels have taken over the mine. Where are you?"

"On the edge of the forest."

"Take refuge there. These bastards are killing everything that moves. Some of them are starting to get into the trucks. They'll be at the village in less than ten minutes. Get in the forest and hide. We'll get to you when we can."

Joseph could hear the sound of machine gun fire in the background and then Kronk screaming, "Christ, they've got two SAMs, and they're aiming one at us. Take it down, Chuck, take it down behind those trees." The words stopped, and sounds of chaos took their place.

"Hello? Hello?" Joseph shouted, before losing the the connection. He put his cellphone on vibrate before turning to Yannick. "Go back to our hideout, and make sure we can still access it. I'm going to get Maya."

"I'm coming with you," Yannick replied.

"No, you'll never keep up with me. You'll be more valuable in the forest. Now go!" Joseph shouted, arms pumping as he sprinted toward the village.

The first villagers were already racing to the safety of the forest, but there was no sign of Maya. Sweat dripped into Joseph's eyes, and he ran with an urgency he'd never experienced before. The sound of shells exploding and machine guns filled the air. He pulled his cellphone out of his pocket and blindly took photos of the chaos, carnage, and destruction without focusing. The village was in mayhem, and panic-stricken villagers tried to gather their families before making for the forest. Some were foolishly taking their belongings, while others were helping their elderly parents. Joseph ran around the huts searching desperately for Maya, and then he saw her distinctive green blouse.

"Maya! Maya! Come quickly, we must go."

She was disoriented and in shock. "I-I can't find Grace and Roland. I can't leave without them."

A hut fifty yards away was hit by a shell and disintegrated. Joseph grasped Maya's hand and shouted, "If they're not here, they've already gone. Come on. There is no time to waste."

Knowing white would stand out, Joseph took his T-shirt off and crammed it into the pocket of his jeans. Then they were running, charging toward the forest with hundreds of others. Bullets zinged around their heads, and some unlucky villagers were killed or wounded before their very eyes. Joseph heard the helicopter and looked up expecting to see the Sikorsky. Instead, he saw soldiers hanging out the sides of a chopper shooting at the villagers. He half dragged, half carried Maya to the edge of the forest. When they entered, he slowed to a fast jog. "Are you all right?"

Tears ran down Maya's face, and she choked on her words. "Where-where are Grace and Roland?"

"I'm sure they'll be all right. How did you become separated?"

"I went to visit an old friend for a few minutes, and then the shooting started. When I got back to their hut, they were gone."

As they got closer to the baobab tree, they could hear voices. Joseph pushed the foliage away. There were at least thirty men, women, children, and babies hiding inside the trunk. "I heard you from fifty yards away," he said. "We'll all be dead if the soldiers hear us. You have to be quiet. So quiet you can hear a fly breathe."

A few of the children laughed nervously before their wooden cavern became silent.

Yannick whispered, "The soldiers are too scared to go into the depths of the forest. Perhaps we should have kept on going."

"Providing we don't make any noise, they'll never find us here," Joseph replied, pushing his way to the front of the trunk so he could look out of one of the tiny boreholes.

Chapter 18

Joseph saw a young boy around six or seven hiding under a large fern about eighty yards away. He was tempted to go get him but knew the soldiers were nearby. If the boy didn't move or make a sound, they'd never find him. As he stared at the boy, he felt his cellphone vibrate. "Are you safe? Are you hiding?" Bennett asked.

"Yes," Joseph whispered.

"Turn your cell off. They may be able to trace it from the chopper they've got flying over the jungle. Turn it on when you're sure they've gone. Good luck."

"Okay."

There was no response. "Hello," Joseph whispered before turning his cellphone off.

Two huge soldiers carrying machine guns came into sight about twenty yards from the young boy. They were laughing, and one had a cigarette hanging out the side of his mouth. Then the laughing stopped, and one put his finger to his lips. Joseph watched, knowing they had heard something. They skirted around the area, prodding the barrels of their guns into the surrounding palm fronds and ferns. Then one reached down and lifted the struggling, screaming boy up by the neck. The other backhanded him and shouted, "Shut up!"

"Don't knock him out," the other said. "It's more fun when they're moving and struggling."

The boy's screaming was replaced with whimpering as the two soldiers laughed and joked about their prize. One of them walked forty yards away to stand guard before turning and shouting, "Don't be long. Then it's my turn."

The boy, who knew what was going to happen, struggled frantically as the soldier spat his cigarette out and started to undo his belt.

Yannick was watching from an adjacent borehole when Joseph whispered, "Spear."

"What?"

"Give me a spear. I need a knife too. Does anyone have a knife?"

"Wha-what are you going to do?" Maya asked.

"Shoosh. No noise. I'm going out there," Joseph whispered, grasping the knife. The handle was attached with a piece of duct tape, but the blade was sharp.

Maya and Yannick had their eyes glued to boreholes as they watched Joseph creep slowly toward the soldier and the boy. Moving from tree trunk to tree trunk, he was like a ninja, but they knew the sound of a twig cracking would see him dead. An animal roared in the distance, and the soldier looked directly at a dense clump of vines where Joseph was hiding. Maya gasped and said a prayer. Then the soldier, whose pants were down around his ankles, turned his attention back to the boy and tore his shorts off in one brutal movement. As he seized the boy's hips, Joseph stepped out from behind a tree and hurled the spear. It drove through the soldier's chest with ferocious velocity. He crumbled onto the foliage without a sound. In an instant, Joseph was next to the boy with his finger up to his lips. "What's your name?"

"Moise," the boy sniffled.

"Listen to me, Moise," Joseph whispered, as he dragged the soldier's body into the bush. "When I get behind that tree, I want you to start screaming. When the other soldier asks where his friend is, say he's having a shit. Don't worry. I'll protect you."

A few minutes later, the other soldier made his way over to the boy, as Joseph watched from behind a nearby tree. Finding his companion gone, he yelled, "Henri, Henri, where are you?"

When the boy replied, the soldier laughed. "You little fool. You should've run when you had the chance. Now it's my turn."

As the soldier started to undo his belt, Joseph moved, slicing deep into his jugular vein. Blood gushed from the soldier's neck, and he gave a last gurgle as he died. Joseph dragged him deep into the bush before picking up both men's Kalashnikovs and spare magazines. "Let's go, Moise," he said.

The shooting had died down, but Joseph could still hear the helicopter as he held the foliage back so Moise could enter the hideaway.

There was stark silence but not the silence of fear — the silence of awe. Some of the villagers reached out to touch and congratulate Joseph while others were speechless. "Boss," Maya choked, fighting back the tears, "you were so brave."

"I should have done it," Yannick said, hanging his head.

"My friend," Joseph said, resting his hand on Yannick's. "You are brave, but you are not strong. It's not your fault. You've been malnourished for years. Those soldiers are far too big and powerful for you. The next time they come into the forest, you will have machine guns. It will even up the fight."

Maya was still in shock. "How long are we going to have to stay here?" she sniffled.

"It'll be nightfall soon," Yannick said. "The soldiers would never dare come in here at night. We'll be safe then."

It was dusk when they left the safety of their hideaway, and congregated with hundreds of other villagers on the edge of the forest to check on the village they loved. It was in flames, they could hear soldiers shouting, and the villagers who hadn't been lucky enough to get away, screaming. Joseph turned on his cellphone and started taking photos. A few minutes later, it vibrated. "Yes," he said.

"Are you all right?"

"Is it safe to talk?"

"You're on a secure frequency. Don't worry."

"Okay, I'm okay."

"Good. We want you to head north through the jungle. It's going to be at least two days before we can pick you up. Someone goofed up in Katanga. It seems no one knew you were going to be in the village when they attacked. The Congolese have rushed out a media release claiming you've been kidnapped by the rebels. It's all face-saving because the U.S. government is going ballistic. It's a major international incident."

"And so it should be. The army's slaughtered the villagers and burned down their huts for no reason."

There was a long pause before Bennett said, "You don't understand, Joseph. No one cares what happened to them. Your disappearance is the international incident. The mine and village haven't rated a mention. If it were up to us, we'd pick you up now. It's not, though, and until the respective governments come up with a diplomatic solution, there's nothing we can do."

"How did you get my cellphone number before? Who are you working for? Who are you?"

"Sorry, I can't answer those questions. Turn your cellphone on at noon and six o'clock in the evening each day for five minutes. Don't worry, we're gonna get you out. Head north. The army's not going to give up on finding you. We just want to make sure you don't get killed when they do. You need to put as much distance between you and the village as you can."

"How many workers were killed at the mine?"

"More than fifty. Two white guys returned with the troops. We think they're the bosses."

"Fifty! And how many at the village?"

"We don't know."

"Someone's going to pay for this."

"You can worry about that after. Are you going to be all right in the jungle for the next few days?"

"Of course."

"Good. We'll talk at midday tomorrow."

Across the Congo, drums beat frenetically through the night, sending a message of hope: *A great leader has returned to deliver us from poverty and oppression.*

Chapter 19

Maya had been certain that Grace and Roland had been killed. She was overjoyed when she saw them standing on the edge of the forest. Once the shooting started, they had been sure she and her friend would run for the forest and headed that way. When they found out she had been looking for them, they were overcome with emotion. Maya was overjoyed and immediately smothered them in kisses and hugs. After the hugging and kissing was over, Joseph outlined his plans, saying they should travel as a group. Grace and Roland thanked him for his offer but said there was nothing for them in Kinshasa; they would prefer instead to stay and help rebuild the village.

"I'm the same," Yannick said. "It was my idea to go out on strike. Many of my friends are dead because of me. I cannot leave. What will the people think?"

"But you can't go back to the mine. How are you going to live?" Joseph asked.

"There is always something to eat in the forest."

Joseph reached for his wallet and took out all the notes. There was more than $1,000 in U.S. currency. "I'm not going to be able to buy anything in the forest, am I?" he said, pressing the money into Yannick's hands.

"Tha-that's what I earn in a year," Yannick said, unable to adequately express his gratitude.

"Give me details of your bank account," Joseph said. "I'll see you never go hungry again."

"Thank you, Boss." Yannick grinned.

"It looks like it's you and me, Maya. Are you going to be able to rough it in the jungle for two days?"

"Far better than you. I'm not a soft American boy." She giggled.

"What about Moise?" Yannick asked. "Who will look after him?"

"His family, of course," Joseph responded.

"His family is dead. Mother, father, and siblings. He was the only one who got away."

"My God," Joseph said, squatting down. "Moise, come over here."

The sad little boy threw his arms around Joseph's neck, and he felt Moise's warm tears running down his back. Joseph patted him on the head and whispered soothingly, "Would you like to come to America and live with me?"

"Yes, yes," the little boy whimpered.

"Then it's resolved," Joseph said, standing up with Moise still clinging to his neck. "Moise will come with Maya and me tomorrow."

At daylight the following morning, thanks to Yannick, Joseph, Maya, and Moise ate a small meal of dry fufu bread.

"Do you want to take a machine gun?" Yannick asked.

"Too noisy," Joseph said. "If I had to use it, it would mean we were about to die. Two spears, a knife, and a machete would be far more useful."

"That's easy," Yannick said. "I also have two canteens of water, two cigarettes, and a box of matches. I've put the matches in a plastic bag so they won't get wet."

"Thank you, but I don't understand. I don't smoke," Joseph said, looking puzzled.

"You've forgotten. Your feet, legs, and body are going to be covered in leeches. The safest way to get them off is by using a cigarette."

"Of course. Where did you get them from?"

"See, Boss, you're not the only one who can perform miracles. I crept back into the village last night."

"What is left of it?"

"They looted nearly everything before destroying half the huts and burning four houses."

"Bastards," Joseph said. "They will pay."

"You don't understand the ways of the Congo," Yannick said. "You've been away for too long. The scorpion now only kills when it's sure it won't be killed."

Joseph shook Yannick's hand, hoping destiny would one day

unite their vastly different worlds. "Let's go," he called and headed off deeper into the jungle with Maya and Moise close behind.

Even though the sun couldn't penetrate the canopy, the forest was as hot as a sauna. The foliage was dense, and the ground, while springy under their feet, was laced with massive tree roots. Thick vines hung from the trees, and drops of water fell from the leaves. The brilliant greens of huge ferns and palms blended with the stark browns of tree trunks. Joseph set a punishing pace, and within two hours, Maya said, "Slow down, we can't keep up with you, and little Moise's feet are bleeding."

Joseph knelt down, looked at Moise's feet and wiped the blood away. They were covered in tiny cuts, but he hadn't said a word. "You're a brave little boy. From now on, you'll ride on my shoulders."

"I need to sit down for a few minutes," Maya said, sipping from her canteen. "We're miles away now. I don't know why we're still rushing."

"They're still looking, and we don't know what they'll do if they find us. Come on," he said, throwing Moise up onto his shoulders.

Moise was light, but Maya was glad Joseph had to slow down for overhanging branches and vines. Even so, she still found it hard to keep up. Joseph paused and said, "We're making good time. You take the lead, Maya. We'll go at your pace."

She was saturated with perspiration and moisture from the drops falling off the leaves. "I feel yucky," she said. "I'd kill for a cold shower."

Her clothes clung to her like polyethylene and left little to the imagination. For so long, Joseph had only known her as a little girl, and her transformation confused him. Fourteen years ago, he had never seen her as his girlfriend, and his feelings for her had been the same as his feelings for Yannick. Now as he watched her shapely butt bouncing from side to side with every stride, he smiled to himself. His memory was of a gawky ten-year-old, but now she was a woman — all woman.

An hour later, he turned his cellphone on and said, "We have to stop. It's nearly midday, and I have to take a call. Let's take fifteen minutes."

"I'd love something to eat," Maya said.

"Later," Joseph said. "I'll find something for dinner."

Right on cue, his cellphone vibrated, and Chuck Bennett said,

"You're making spectacular time. You've done nearly sixteen miles today. You can take your foot off the accelerator. The army has no idea where you are. They've left a dozen men and a chopper here. The rest have gone back to Lubumbashi. The government's official line with the media is that they suspect the rebels have captured you. Oh, and they carted two of their men away in body bags. You wouldn't know how they were killed, would you?"

Joseph ignored the question. "What's the unofficial line?"

"Do you know Colonel Gizenga?"

"Yes, he's a pig and a bully."

"Well, he led the troops yesterday. He thinks you panicked, ran into the jungle, and got lost. Lucky he doesn't know the capabilities of your cellphone."

"He thinks I'm a coward?"

"Yes."

"Chuck, before you go on, who do you work for?"

"We're freelancers for the government. We help out in tight situations. If we get into trouble, we're on our own. In this case, Jack Costigan told the Congolese we're assisting the State Department, and know roughly where you are. It's blown our cover in the Congo, but it also means they won't try to blow us out of the sky."

"When are you going to get us out?"

"I don't know. Hopefully in the morning. It's still being arranged. The Congolese government can't be seen with egg on its face. The diplomats are working it out. With luck, I'll have something when I call you this evening."

Before Joseph turned his cellphone off, he called his father on his direct line. "Dad, it's me. I can't talk for long. No matter what you hear, I'm okay. I'm not in any danger. Tell Mom not to worry."

"We were told you were in the middle of a shootout between rebels and the army, and no one knows what happened to you."

"That's not true. I'm unharmed and safe."

"Why didn't you take George with you?"

"I have to go, Dad. Love you."

The call had been as clear as if his father was standing next to him.

Chapter 20

Joseph knew they were in no danger, so he slowed the pace to a walk in the afternoon. Moise told them his four siblings were teenagers, and he had come along as an accident. He had been out playing when one of the first shells hit his family's hut. The old woman next door saw it explode and told Moise it had killed everyone, and he should run for it. "What's going to happen to me?" he sobbed.

"I'm going to take care of you," Joseph said.

Maya turned and frowned. "How are you going to look after him?"

"I don't know, but if he wants, he can come back to the U.S. with me."

"How?"

"I'm sure I can arrange it."

"He must have uncles, cousins, and other relations. Don't you think they will want to care for him?"

"I don't have anyone else," Moise whimpered. "Only the woman who lives in the next hut."

Joseph was about to respond when a clap of thunder shook the forest. The canopy became transparent as bolts of lightning lit up the sky. He had noticed it getting darker but wasn't surprised when he felt Moise flinch on his shoulders. Maya also looked shaken. "A little rainstorm," he said, "let's find some big palm fronds to shelter under."

A few minutes later they couldn't hear themselves talk as torrential rain pounded the canopy. Huge drops fell onto the palm fronds, which wilted, and bucket loads cascaded over the sheltering trio.

"That was a bright idea, Boss," Maya shouted over the sound of the rain, a huge grin on her face.

Thirty minutes later the forest became lighter, and the rain abruptly stopped. They were drenched, and hungry. Huge drops continued to fall from the trees while the fierce sun added ten degrees to what was already a sauna. Maya felt something on her neck and screamed as she tried to pull it off.

"No, Maya!" Joseph shouted. "It's a leech. Don't pull it off."

"I know," she said, "but it's revolting."

Joseph tried to remove the water from his hands as best he could before pulling out the plastic bag. One of the cigarettes had broken, so he lit half and burned the leech off.

"Oh, thank God," Maya said.

"Now take your top off."

Maya's top clung to her, and she couldn't get it over her head.

"Let me help," Joseph said, slowly rolling her blouse off. Her stomach was taut, her skin glistened, and the matching green bra she wore left little to the imagination. Joseph let out an involuntary gasp as he raised the cigarette to her back and for the second time thought, *she's all woman.*

"What are you doing, Boss?"

"There are three on your back. Don't move while I get rid of them. Check the inside of your bra."

She pushed the cups of her bra away, looked down, and said, "That's a relief – there's none there."

"I'm sorry, you're going to have to take your jeans and shoes off too."

Blood-filled, fat, black leeches covered her legs. They were also between her toes and under her feet. When Joseph had burned the last one off, he said, "Look down the front of your panties."

"There's none," she said. "God, I'm glad that's over."

"It's not. Turn around."

Joseph pulled her panties down and opened her cheeks before burning the last leech off. "Now it's over," he said. "Moise, it's your turn. Then you can do me, Maya."

The sun beat down on the huge umbrella of leaves, but there were puddles on the muddy, slippery ground, and still the droplets fell. "The farther we walk, the more leeches we're going to get on us," Joseph said. "Let's try to find a clearing where we can camp for the night."

"I'm hungry," Moise said.

"So am I," Maya chipped in.

"I'll find some berries and some manioc roots once we have a place to camp," Joseph said.

"Manioc roots? I'm not eating manioc roots. If you don't cook them properly they can kill you," Maya said. "Anyhow, how are you going to get dry wood to light a fire?"

"Have you forgotten the jungle? There'll be dry twigs and wood inside hollow logs and trees. A fire won't be a problem. There's a little patch roughly a hundred yards in front of us where the sun's shining through. We'll camp there."

"I'm tired. I'm wet. I'm hungry," Moise said.

"Shoosh." Joseph pointed. "We just got lucky. There's our dinner."

Sunning itself in the clearing was a wet, curled-up black python. Joseph carefully put the spears and the knife on the ground and ran his finger over the machete. "This won't take long," he said, edging toward the snake.

As he raised the machete, the snake reared. Joseph shouted as rows of teeth penetrated his forearm. The creature curled around him, pinning both his arms. Desperate, he fought with every ounce of strength, all to no avail as the snake tightened its vicelike grip. He could feel it constricting with every breath and knew it would eventually crush him to death.

Maya screamed in horror and then, as quick as a flash, picked up the knife and drove it between the eyes of the snake, again and again. When Joseph felt the coils releasing, he reached down, picked up the machete, and severed the monster's head. The body writhed for a few seconds before it was still.

"You saved my life," Joseph said. "You're so brave."

Maya was trembling uncontrollably, and as he went to put his arm around her, she shied away. "Your arm is bleeding."

"Don't worry. It's not poisonous."

"I know. I wish I had some antibacterial cream to kill any infection. Here, let me wash it," she said, picking up her canteen.

"Bad snake," Moise said, giving the snake's body a healthy kick.

Joseph and Maya burst out laughing.

"I'm going to gut it," Joseph said, picking up the knife. "Then I'll scavenge some dry branches and build a raging fire."

At six o'clock, Joseph's cellphone rang, and Chuck Bennett asked, "How are you holding up?"

"We're okay. When are we getting picked up?"

"Tomorrow morning. There's a clearing below a break in the canopy three miles to the north. Make your way there as soon as the sun rises."

"Will you be there?"

"Yes, but as I told you, it's a face-saving exercise for the Congolese. The rest of the world sees them as having lost you. Now they're going to be seen as rescuing you. Do you understand?"

"What will I tell Gizenga?"

"What he wants to hear. You shit yourself when you heard the shooting and ran. He'll tell you what to say to the media."

"What a load of bullshit."

"Don't spoil it, Joseph. An awful lot of diplomatic work went into this deal. If the Congo wasn't the most-resource-rich country in the world, we would've pulled you out last night."

"I won't. Is the jet still at Lubumbashi?"

"Yes."

"Good, I need you to do me a favor. I've got a young boy with me. His name's Moise. I'm going to leave him with my cellphone so you can find him after Maya and I have been picked up. Take him to the plane."

"Shit! I can't do that. Do you know what you're asking?"

"I've told you what I want. Call Jack Costigan and get it cleared. Let him know I could get used to living in the jungle. If his answer's no, tell him not to send the Congolese rescue team in. Do you understand, Chuck?"

"He's not gonna like it."

"If the answer's 'yes,' call me at six in the morning. If it's not, don't bother."

An hour later, they sat around a blazing fire using the metal tips of the spears to barbecue twelve-inch snake steaks. Joseph had cut thirteen and was cooking them all just in case tomorrow didn't pan out.

"I'm glad the mosquitoes have gone," Maya said. "They were eating me alive."

"They don't like the fire," Joseph replied.

"This is the best snake I've ever tasted. Isn't it nice to be dry again?" Maya said.

"Watch the ribs, Moise," Joseph cautioned, "clean them with your teeth."

A steamy haze engulfed the forest, and Maya asked, "Will the fire last through the night, Boss?"

"I'll make sure it does because it'll keep us safe. You saved my life today, Maya. Without you, that snake might have eaten me."

"He might've eaten a soft American boy, but a Katangese warrior would've been far too tough." Maya giggled.

As they were talking, Moise tipped over, sound asleep. Joseph took his T-shirt off and draped it over him. "Poor little Moise."

"I know you mean well, Joseph, but how are you going to take care of him?"

"I told you. I'm taking him back to the U.S. with me."

"You can't just take someone home with you. There are passport, visa, and citizenship considerations. Besides, when are you going to get the time to look after him?"

"The paperwork won't be a problem, and no matter what happens, he'll be better off in the U.S. than here."

"You're so serious. You always have been." Maya yawned.

"Come over here. You can use my shoulder as a pillow." Joseph smiled.

"And you have such a lovely smile," Maya said, snuggling up to him.

Joseph kissed her, and when they pulled apart, she said, "I always dreamed of kissing you."

"You said that at the hotel."

"Yes, but tonight was a real kiss. I'm sorry, I'm so tired I have to sleep. Goodnight."

Chapter 21

It was six o'clock, and the birds were singing when Joseph felt his cellphone vibrate. The embers of the fire were still glowing, and Maya and Moise were starting to stir.

"Yes," Joseph answered.

"Jack Costigan's not happy, but he agreed to your demands. You need to be at the clearing within two hours. Make sure the boy stays hidden. We won't land until you're on your way back to Lubumbashi. Good luck with Colonel Gizenga."

"Thanks, Chuck, but there's been a change of plan. I can't leave Moise in the jungle by himself. It's too dangerous. We'll be at the clearing in ninety minutes. Be waiting for us. You can tell Gizenga where we are after Moise is safe."

"Jesus, Joseph, why do you have to make things so hard?"

"Can you do it?"

"Yeah, we'll be there."

"Is everything all right?" Maya asked.

"We have to move," Joseph said, chewing on a piece of the snake while dowsing the fire. "Come on, Moise, snap out of it. Are you two having anything to eat?"

"Not snake," they both responded.

Joseph wrapped the remaining pieces in his T-shirt and knotted it.

"Why did you do that?" Maya asked.

"Just in case things don't go according to plan."

When they reached the clearing, the chopper was waiting. Joseph lifted the little boy off his shoulders and knelt down. "Moise, meet Chuck and Brett. They're going to look after you. If I don't see you tonight, I'll make sure I do in the morning. You'll be safe with them."

Maya gave Moise a quick hug, and then Brett took his hand and led him to the copter.

"Jack Costigan's gonna tear strips off you," Bennett said. "He's an angry man."

"You already told me he's pissed off," Joseph replied. "He won't be tearing strips off anyone. He needs me far more than I need him. Have you told Colonel Gizenga where we are?"

"Not exactly, but he's not far away. We'll make contact once we're in the air."

"How did you know where we were after I had turned the cellphone off?"

"I thought you would've guessed. The phone's CIA-issue."

"What else does it do that I don't know about?"

Bennett laughed. "I can't answer that."

"Can't or won't?"

"Both. I have to get going. I'll see you in Lubumbashi."

"Sure. Take good care of Moise and don't feed him too much. His stomach's shrunk, and it'll only make him sick."

As they watched the helicopter ascend, Maya said, "I couldn't keep my eyes open last night, but I wanted to ask you about those two soldiers you killed."

"Not soldiers, vile thugs. What would you like to know?"

"Have you thought about them?"

"You mean, do I have a troubled conscience?"

"Yes."

Joseph smiled, but his lips were compressed. "Do you have a troubled conscience about killing the snake?"

"Of course not."

"It's the same with me. Like the snake, they were reptiles."

"I know what Yannick told you about your mother and Safi. Are you going to kill General Zamenka?"

Joseph's eyes narrowed. "If I get the opportunity. I want to see his face after I tell him why he's going to die."

Maya shook her head. "You're a good man. I was wrong when I called you soft. You're tough. I'm glad. You're going to need to be."

Joseph was about to respond when they heard the thumping of a chopper. It was larger than the Sikorsky, and when Gizenga got out, he had five of his men with him. He shook Joseph's hand, held his nose, and said, "Fuck, you stink."

Joseph unwrapped his T-shirt and said, "Would you like a piece of snake, Colonel?"

Gizenga looked at one of his men. "Get him a clean shirt and get rid of that shit."

One of the other soldiers was leering at Maya, so Joseph stepped in front of her. "What are you staring at?" he demanded.

"He didn't mean anything," Gizenga said. "She's an attractive girl. He's allowed to look. I wouldn't upset him if I were you. Unlike you, he didn't run from the village with his tail between his legs. I know how you won your gold medal now. You're a terrific runner. You ran so far you got yourself lost. You didn't need to worry. We killed most of the rebels."

Gizenga's men smirked and nudged each other.

Joseph was fuming but forced himself to maintain his composure. "I only saw terrified, unarmed villagers whom your soldiers chased into the forest. I saw their village go up in flames. I didn't see any rebels. Are you sure you and your men weren't jumping at shadows?"

"You'd be wise to be more careful with your mouth. Two of them were murdered. Like me, these soldiers would like nothing better than to avenge their brothers."

Gizenga's using the two thugs I killed to prove rebels were attacking the mine. Shit! "I'm just saying I didn't see any rebels."

"Of course you didn't. You were too busy running. You would've needed eyes in the back of your head. You've embarrassed our government. I would've left you in the jungle, but the president insisted we find you."

This time, the soldiers broke into laughter, slapping their thighs and each other on the back.

"How did you find us?" Joseph smiled through compressed lips.

"Never mind," Gizenga snapped. "Let's go."

The silence on the flight back to Lubumbashi was palpable. No one offered Joseph and Maya anything to eat or drink. Gizenga ignored them by sitting in the seat next to the pilot. Sullen soldiers stared defiantly at them. Joseph put his arm around Maya, smiled, and told her not to be intimidated.

As the helicopter landed, Gizenga turned around and looked at Joseph. "The media's waiting. Follow my lead and watch your smart mouth. Remember, it's a long way to Kinshasa, and I can stop your jet from ever taking off."

Flash bulbs popped, and television cameras pressed closer as Gizenga led Joseph and Maya from the chopper. Gizenga put his arm around Joseph's shoulders, smiled, and said, "Our Olympic hero got lost in the jungle after fleeing from the rebels. I'm pleased to say, thanks to the tireless efforts of my men, we have managed to rescue him just in the nick of time. Who knows whether he would've survived another night in the jungle?"

"What did you eat and drink, Joseph?" a reporter asked.

"Nothing," Gizenga responded. "He was on his last legs when we found him."

"Did the rebels try to kill you?" another reporter asked.

"I don't know. Once I heard gunfire, I made for the safety of the jungle."

"He made a wise decision," Gizenga said. "If he had waited, he mightn't be with us today. The rebels killed two of my best soldiers in the jungle."

"How did you cope, Ms. Tansi? Were you scared?"

"No, not at all," Maya said. "I knew Joseph would protect me."

"The naivety of youth," Gizenga said, shaking his head.

"You must be grateful to Colonel Gizenga and the Congolese army for saving you," a planted stooge said.

Joseph looked down at his feet and mumbled, "Yes, if it were not for Colonel Gizenga and his men, we would still be in the jungle. We appreciate the trouble and time they took to find us."

Gizenga patted Joseph on the back and said, "No more questions. They need food and rest."

The reporters, photographers, and camera crews applauded and broke up.

Gizenga removed his arm from around Joseph's shoulders. "You did well," he said. "Don't stir up any trouble in Kinshasa. I'd hate to hear your girlfriend had had an accident."

Chapter 22

As Joseph and Maya made their way up the stairs of the jet, an excited Moise — wearing a light blue T-shirt, jeans, and Puma sneakers — greeted them. The two Americans and the flight attendant were sitting in the front seat, drinking beers. "He's a real live wire," Chuck Bennett said. "We took him shopping while we were waiting for you. He likes the clothes but won't keep the sneakers on."

"That's kind of you, Chuck. Thanks for looking after him. Hey, Moise, let me get some photos of you in your new clothes."

"We probably won't see you again, so we wanted to say goodbye," Bennett said.

"Yeah," the dour Brett Kronk cut in, "and we wanted to warn ya. We don't know if they bought your story about running and getting lost. They know you're a friend of Yannick's and think he's the rebel leader."

"That's rubbish. You know there were no rebels."

"Yeah, but we overheard a conversation. They blamed him for stirring up the trouble at the mine. They think ya might have helped him. Be careful. Your gold medal is not gonna help ya with these pricks."

"Thanks for your help and advice," Joseph said, shaking their hands as they stood up.

"See ya, Moise," Kronk said, patting the little boy on the head.

Joseph looked at the flight attendant and said, "Tell the captain to take off as soon as he can get clearance."

"Yes, Mr. Muamba."

"Would you like to take a shower, Maya?"

"After you." She giggled. "Gizenga was right about one thing. You stink."

Thirty minutes later they were wearing white fluffy nightgowns and matching slippers while sipping hot chocolate and eating chicken salad sandwiches. Moise was stretched out in his seat, sound asleep.

"What are you going to do when you get back to Kinshasa?" Maya asked.

Joseph involuntarily felt the USB around his neck. "I don't know. The army murdered seventy-four innocent people. Someone has to pay."

"Are you going to tell the president?"

"I don't think so," Joseph replied, thinking of Gizenga's warning. "He might have condoned it."

"I was thinking the same. Nothing will happen. No one's going to be charged. They never are. It is the way of the Congo."

"There's more than one way to skin a cat."

"You have a plan?"

"The bones of one," Joseph said. "I intend to see Gizenga and his murderous thugs brought to account."

"How are you going to look after Moise when we get back?" Maya asked.

"I've been wondering the same thing. I'll find a way."

"I can look after him. There's always one of us at the apartment. I'm sure my girlfriends will be willing to help. Are you really going to take him back to the U.S. with you?"

"That would be a big help. And yes, I want you to come with us too. Is your passport current?"

The flight attendant returned to tell them the captain was preparing to land and to fasten their seatbelts.

"Everything's easy for you," Maya said. "I have a good job at the hospital. If I did go, there's no certainty I'd get it back when I return. I'm probably already in trouble for not going in yesterday."

"They will re-employ you, and you won't be in any trouble." Joseph yawned. "That's something I can guarantee."

"God, you're full of yourself." Maya smiled. "And yes, I have a current passport."

"I don't mean to be. I just know it's something the president's advisers will be able to fix if I ask them."

"I'm sorry, Joseph. Try to lighten up. Sometimes it's like you're carrying the weight of the world on your shoulders."

The plane made a soft landing, and Joseph turned on his cellphone.

There were more than a hundred emails, and he quickly scanned the senders, smiling when he saw Ron Patterson's name. He glanced out the window and saw a stressed George Faraday standing at the front of a three-vehicle motorcade. He would wait until he was at the hotel before reading Ron's email.

Joseph and Maya, still wearing nightgowns, left the plane with Moise, rubbing his eyes, close behind them. George Faraday was at the bottom of the stairway. "I need to talk to you," he said.

"Not now," Joseph replied.

They traveled in silence until the limo pulled up in front of an old, three-level cream-colored apartment building. Joseph patted Moise on the head and gave Maya a peck on the cheek. "I'll see you both soon," he said.

As the door closed, Faraday said, "Jesus, what happened? I knew I should have gone with you. Did the rebels try to capture you?"

"There were no rebels. The miners went on strike, and the army came in and murdered them. Seventy-four! Seventy-four murdered, and their village burned to the ground! The soldiers drove trucks from the mine, and I guess New Dawn paid for the helicopters they flew in on."

"Bu-but the newspapers reported rebels killing two soldiers. General Zamenka confirmed it."

"Come closer, George," Joseph said, then dropped his voice to a whisper. "I killed them. They were going to rape the little boy I brought back."

Faraday's face collapsed. "You did what? Christ, if they find out, you'll never get out of the country alive."

"They won't find out. It's convenient for Gizenga. It gives credibility to his bullshit story about rebels. George, who did you sell the mine to?"

"I told you, I can't remember."

"Yeah, you did." Joseph smiled grimly.

"Why did you bring the boy back with you?"

"The soldiers murdered his family. I'm taking him back to the U.S. with me."

"What? What? You can't!"

"I can and will. Set up a meeting with Jack Costigan tonight. Tell him we'd like to have dinner," Joseph said, as the motorcade stopped in front of the hotel. "I'm going to take a nap for a few hours. Message me with a time."

As Joseph walked into the foyer, staff and guests burst into spontaneous applause. He smiled and waved but didn't stop. He was dying to get to his room and turn on his laptop.

Ron's email covered all of the negotiations Faraday had entered into, to sell the gold mine in Katanga fourteen years earlier. Unfortunately, it appeared Faraday had failed to make a sale and had elected to go it alone. Ron did point out there was a draft agreement on file, but the name of the proposed buyer was blacked out. The only letters Ron could make out were "PLC," which suggested the proposed buyer had been a British company. *Did George cut the firm out of negotiations to avoid paying commission and then do the deal privately?* Joseph wondered.

Disappointed, he plugged in the USB, copied it to his laptop and started reading emails. After a few minutes, it became apparent that Boucher's immediate boss was a man named Thibault, who kept in contact via a Gmail address. From his name, Joseph guessed he was French or Belgian. An email from Boucher to Thibault included a summary of New Dawn's budget for the current year. Targeted gold production was three hundred thousand ounces with a value of $540 million. Boucher was getting 5 percent of the gross paid quarterly. No wonder he was ruthless and pushed the workers so hard. New Dawn transferred Boucher's profit share to a company controlled by him in the tax haven of Mauritius and claimed it as fully tax-deductible management fees.

Loans to the New Dawn mine aggregated $50 million, but it paid more than $100 million a year in fully tax-deductible interest to a company incorporated in the Virgin Islands. Thibault authorized payments to many recipients with bank accounts in tax havens, for professional fees, consulting fees, engineering fees, and technical advice. There were even payments to companies who supposedly provided mine safety and environmental information. Two $20 million payments transferred to a bank account in the Caymans for professional services rendered by someone or something simply referred to as "Z" intrigued Joseph. It seemed Thibault authorized all payments more than $5 million. Other than those, Boucher was in full control.

An email from an international firm of tax accountants set out New Dawn's prior year's tax liability of $375,000 on gold sales of $497 million. The Congolese government had granted an exploitation permit for the mine in Katanga. Around $500 million of gold per annum was being extracted, but New Dawn was paying a meager $375,000 in tax. *No wonder they call it an exploitation permit,* Joseph thought. It also accounted for why there were virtually no paved roads in the Congo. New Dawn paid virtually no tax, didn't provide any safety or health benefits, grossly underpaid its workers, and — when they went on strike for better wages and benefits — killed them with impunity.

Joseph was determined to go through the thousands of emails in the deleted folder, but for the time being he had had enough. His cellphone beeped, and the text message from Faraday said, "7:00 p.m. dining room." He had two hours to fill in. It was 9:00 a.m. in Los Angeles when he called Ron Patterson.

Joseph's relationship with Ron had changed over the years. When he was a young boy, he had been accountable to Ron as his teacher, but their roles had reversed. Perhaps it was because he was the boss's son. Perhaps it was because he was a champion athlete and had won an Olympic gold medal. The most likely reason was that Ron was quiet, passive, and reactive rather than proactive.

"Ron, this is Joseph. Thanks for the information."

Chapter 23

"Joseph. Jesus! You've been on every news channel and the front page of all the newspapers. They're saying you were lucky to get away with your life. Did the rebels try and kidnap you?"

"No, the army and the government lied. I'm fine. There were no rebels. The workers from the New Dawn mine went on strike. Seventy-four of them, men, women, and children, were slaughtered by the soldiers. They're using the rebels as an excuse."

"That's tragic. What does it have to do with finding out who owns New Dawn?"

"Nothing. It was just a coincidence. The army's covering up mass murder. I want your help in exposing the bastards."

"How-how can I help?"

"You're a computer expert. I'm going to send you photos of the massacre. I want you to anonymously send them to the media, Greenpeace, and the United Nations. I know Greenpeace will act quickly and travel to the remains of the village within the week. Oh, send copies to the International Monetary Fund. If the IMF turns off the funds, those in power in the Congo will have no choice but to act."

"Does your dad know what you're doing?"

"I'm going to forget you said that, Ron. I hadn't finished. I want those photos on Facebook, Twitter, and Instagram. Flood the Net. I want the world to know what happened."

"Joseph, don't take this the wrong way, but did anyone else have a cellphone? If they didn't, it's going to be obvious who took the pics."

The two Americans had cellphones. "Don't worry. Some of the soldiers are sure to have had cells. And, Ron, drop whatever else you're doing and get those photos out in cyberspace. I have to go."

Joseph entered the hotel's brasserie just after seven o'clock. The décor was typical of five-star hotel restaurants, but only three tables were occupied. Jack Costigan and George Faraday had their heads together at a corner table. Costigan stood up, extended his hand, and said, "You can't imagine how much trouble you caused. You created a major international incident. We've had to pull strings at the highest level to smooth things over. The Congolese want to know why you went back to your village without an army escort. They say they offered. Did they?"

As Joseph sat down, Faraday was shaking his head. "Yes, they did offer, Jack, but I don't like traveling with murderers. I'm sure your men have told you there were no rebels. I don't know why you're upset. I didn't do anything to cause the trouble."

"You still don't get it, do you? It's not our country. We're visitors. We don't know what goes on here, but we sure as hell don't want to upset the government. We've finally got our foot back in the door at the expense of the Chinese. We don't want to alienate President Bodho or General Zamenka."

Joseph fought back a surge of anger at the mere mention of Zamenka's name. "You're right. It's not your country, but it is mine. You know what happened, but you're more worried about trade and diplomacy than the lives of poor villagers. You need to take a good look at yourself."

"Joseph, you can't talk to Jack like – "

"Shut up, George. Jack's big enough and ugly enough to stand up for himself."

"You're out of your depth, way out of your depth," Costigan said. "Leave government relations to the experts."

"Happy to, but what do you intend to do about the seventy-four workers murdered by the Congolese military?"

Costigan rolled his eyes, turned his palms up, and looked at Faraday. "If we hadn't arranged those two pilots, you'd still be in the jungle, probably dead."

Joseph laughed. "It's you who have no idea, Jack. I could've lived in the forest for months. Long enough to cross into Tanzania and safety. I didn't need your help or protection."

The table descended into an uncomfortable silence. Faraday looked around for a waiter. Costigan looked down at the polished timber floor. Joseph rested his arms on the table, a grim smile pasted on his face.

Faraday finally broke the silence. "Can we talk about the next two days? Prescott Uranium is presenting, and the total investment over ten years is $20 billion. If they're successful, the mine will be constructed by Fachtel America. It's a great resource and will be a monumental deal for us."

"It's more than that," Costigan said. "It's the largest unmined uranium resource in the world. The Chinese have had their greedy eyes on it for years. We can't let them get their hands on it. We have to win this deal."

"I've looked at Prescott's proposition, and there's no way the Chinese can match their technology and expertise. If we knew the Congolese were going to base their decision on merit, Prescott would be in the driver's seat," Faraday said.

"Jesus, George, you've been coming here for forty years. When was the last time the Congolese made a decision based on merit? Just make sure Prescott does what it has to do to get the green light."

The waiter served their drinks: Jim Beam for Costigan, beer for Faraday, and mineral water for Joseph. After they'd ordered their meals, Faraday muttered, "I guess it won't be less than $500 million."

"Just make sure you get it done. I don't want to know figures. Do what you have to do, but don't tell me," Costigan said.

"You know Prescott's going to pay an enormous bribe, Jack, but you don't want to know. Is that what you call diplomacy?" Joseph frowned.

Before Costigan could reply Faraday said, "Don't worry, I won't let the Chinese beat us."

"Will I be needed tomorrow?" Joseph asked.

"Of course you are. When you were reported missing, I thought President Bodho was going to have a shit fit," Faraday replied.

"From what Jack said, you haven't missed me too much. You've still managed to close deals."

"They were small," Faraday said. "Prescott is the big one. I'm going to need you."

"Yeah," Costigan said, "if the Chinese get hold of that uranium, there's going to be hell to pay back home. The secretary himself has said this deal is a must-win. I'd hate to face him if the Chinese wrangle their way into a winning position. It can't happen. It can't!"

Joseph, tired of business talk, changed the subject. "Jack, I brought a seven-year-old boy back with me. The army killed his family when they attacked the village. I want to take him home with me. I've taken some photos. Can you arrange a passport, visa, and whatever other papers are needed? Do them in the name of Moise Muamba. No, on second thought, make it Moise Rafter."

Costigan nearly choked on his whiskey. "Are you stupid? Why did you bring him back? I can't and won't arrange the papers. There are orphanages in Kinshasa. They'll take him."

"Jesus, Joseph, your parents are too old to look after a young kid," Faraday said.

"You say you know my father. If he were in the same position, he wouldn't dream of leaving Moise behind. I'm not going to, either. Pass on my apologies to President Bodho, but I won't be able to attend any further negotiations. If Moise is going to fly out with me on Saturday, I'll need every minute I have to arrange a passport for him."

"You won't get any documents without his parents' or guardian's consent, and with his parents dead, it isn't going to happen," Costigan scoffed.

Joseph ignored the State Department man and said, "George, I'm going to get my father to transfer $50,000 to me tomorrow. When you apologize to the president, can you ask him if he has time to see me tomorrow night? Call me as soon as you know."

"You-you have to be there tomorrow. If you're not, they won't even start the negotiations. You have to be there!" Faraday said.

"Sorry, I won't have time."

Costigan looked flustered and signaled the waiter, telling him to bring the bottle of Jim Beam and leave it. "Send the boy's photos to my cellphone. I'll get the documentation sorted out. You're a real smartass, aren't you? I should've left you in the jungle."

Joseph stood and smiled through compressed lips. "Thanks, Jack. I'll have to call it a night. I have to prepare for the Prescott meeting. I'll see you for breakfast in the morning."

A few steps from the table, Joseph heard Costigan hiss "bastard!"

Chapter 24

Joseph woke early, reached over for his cellphone, and clicked on the news services. The first headline he read on *Reuters* was "Massacre in Katanga." There were photos of the village being shelled and burned. *AAP* had gone with "Soldiers Slaughter Civilians" and reported that United Nations peacekeepers were on the way to the village to interview the survivors. *Bloomberg's* headline was "Tragedy in the Congo." Thousands of comments from outraged readers sat below the articles, but Joseph didn't have time to read them. Ron had done a great job.

The mood over breakfast and in the limo on the way to the palace was icy. Costigan and Faraday made no mention of the headlines flashing around the world. However, Costigan's demeanor suggested he knew and had most likely been woken by a call from the U.S. in the early hours of the morning. Four senior executives from Prescott Uranium were traveling in the limo immediately behind.

Surprisingly, President Bodho, General Zamenka, and their advisers were already sitting behind the long table when Joseph and the Prescott team entered the room. The president stood up, came around to the front of the table, and hugged Joseph. "We were worried about you. Were you harmed in any way?"

"Thank you for your concern, Mr. President. I am fine."

"Thanks to our army," General Zamenka cut in.

"Did the rebels fire at you?" Bodho asked.

"I didn't see any rebels. Only villagers, and no, they did not shoot at me. They only had spears and old rifles. I doubt they'd even fire."

The president frowned and looked at Zamenka, who said, "Why did you run then? What were you scared of?"

"I ran because the soldiers were firing at random. They didn't seem to care who they hit. That's why the villagers ran too."

"How would you know what a rebel looks like?" Zamenka asked. "Especially when you were running like a rabbit. Do you have eyes in the back of your head?"

The advisers smirked.

"I'm telling you what I saw. I didn't see anyone firing at the soldiers."

"And yet two were killed," Zamenka said.

"Were they shot?" Joseph asked.

"No. One was killed with a spear, and the other had his throat cut."

"Perhaps it was the villagers," Joseph said. "I don't know. Maybe they were defending themselves."

"Defending themselves by slashing a soldier's throat from behind? I don't think so." Zamenka sneered. "I think the villagers were befriending and hiding the rebels. Sure, a few innocents may have been killed, but if you couldn't tell the villagers from the rebels, I'm sure my soldiers couldn't either. There's collateral damage in all battles."

Zamenka's far smarter than I gave him credit for. He's turned my words back on me. "There were seventy-four deaths, General. Many were women and children. They're far more than collateral damage."

"The important thing is you're back with us, safe, and well," Bodho said, growing tired of the conversation.

"Did you take any photos?" Zamenka asked.

"No, I was running."

"Ah, yes, of course, you were running." Zamenka laughed. "And then you were hiding with your girlfriend. Did she keep you warm at night?"

The advisers joined the general in raucous laughter.

I'm going to enjoy killing you. "I built a fire to keep us warm."

"Enough," Bodho said, looking at Faraday. "What do you have for us?"

For the next six hours, the Prescott Uranium team — with the help of Faraday and Costigan — pitched their proposal for the massive yellowcake resource in Katanga. As the meeting was wrapping up, Joseph said, "May I speak to you regarding another matter, Mr. President?"

"Go ahead."

"There was a young boy in the village. A shell or grenade hit his family's hut and killed everyone. He has no living relations. I looked after him in the jungle, and we bonded. With your permission, I would like to take him back to the U.S. with me. Mr. Costigan is handling the paperwork with your diplomatic officials, but I would greatly appreciate it if you could use your influence to smooth the way."

Bodho shifted uneasily and glanced at Zamenka, who shook his head. "Do you intend to adopt him?"

"Yes."

"I don't know."

"I'm sure the world will admire your generosity and compassion, Mr. President."

"Yes," the president said, brightening up.

Joseph smiled. "And who's to say he won't win an Olympic gold medal for the Congo in sixteen years' time?"

"Yes, yes," the president beamed, "give the boy's name and details to my aide, and I will sweep the red tape away."

Joseph could feel Costigan staring at him in the limo. "You didn't need to involve the president. The paperwork's already in transit, and there would've been no holdups. I hope you haven't messed things up."

"I haven't," Joseph replied. "I would've been uncomfortable had I not informed him."

"Bullshit! You don't trust me, and you think by getting the president involved, you won't get done over. Did you see Zamenka's face? He was fuming. I'm betting he's doing his level best to talk the president out of letting Moise go with you. You're a real smartass. You might've outsmarted yourself this time."

"I don't think so. If I'm right, by tomorrow morning, the president will need all the media help he can get. Not to say anything of a convenient distraction."

"You're such a smartass. Where do you think those photos on the news services came from?"

"I have no idea. Jesus, Jack, I don't want to fight with you. I told the president about Moise because I didn't want him finding out from someone else. Let's start over again."

"That's a good idea," Faraday said. "We still have to close the Prescott deal tomorrow. Let's present a unified front. We can discuss it over dinner."

"It'll have to be breakfast," Joseph said. "I'm eating with Maya and Moise tonight."

The following morning, the front page of *The Congo Daily Times* carried the story of New Dawn workers being shot and killed by the army because they had gone on strike. The journalist said workers who had survived claimed the soldiers were flown in on helicopters hired by New Dawn. On arrival, the soldiers used New Dawn's trucks to mount their attack on the village. At the end of the long article, the journalist posed a question: "Is the army on New Dawn's payroll?"

International news services continued their barrage, and some suggested the Congo should be subject to sanctions. Joseph knew that was unlikely to occur as the Congo was too rich in resources for any of the Western plunderers to run the risk of losing access.

Television news showed a Greenpeace team landing at N'djili Airport and immediately boarding another flight for Lubumbashi. The rest of the world was turning up the heat on the Congo's rulers.

Jack Costigan wasn't happy. He knew the news could only harm Prescott's bid and, more importantly, his future.

When Joseph entered the meeting room, President Bodho looked morose, and General Zamenka was scowling. The government advisers had their heads down staring at the table. Bodho looked up and said, "I've arranged to do a prerecorded television interview at midday about the attack on the mine and the village. I want you with me. All you have to say is you were lucky to escape from the rebels with your life."

"But, Mr. President, I told you I didn't see any rebels. I only saw workers, villagers, and soldiers. I can't lie."

"You won't be lying," General Zamenka said. "I have personally spoken to Colonel Gizenga. He has given me his word that he saw rebels attack the mine. Surely you don't doubt his word?"

"I saw villagers killed by soldiers. I saw huts blown up. I saw villagers fired on as they ran."

"Collateral damage," Zamenka said. "Sad, unfortunate, but accidents happen."

"Here's the problem," President Bodho said. "I thought it would be easy to arrange a passport and documents for the young boy. It is not. My aide tells me the public servants who handle these matters are upset that I'm bypassing protocols. I want to help you, but it is awkward. Do you want to help me?"

I can't see you taking any notice of your public servants. Joseph glanced at Jack Costigan, who had a grim smile on his face and was imperceptibly shaking his head. "I don't know. I don't want to lie."

"Mr. Faraday," Zamenka said, looking directly at the Prescott executives, "we were approached by the Chinese last night about the uranium project. Their proposition was attractive, but we said we were dealing exclusively with you. Would you like to continue the negotiations on that basis?"

Before Faraday could reply, Costigan said, "Yes, yes, General, we would like to conclude a memorandum of understanding before we leave."

Bastards! I don't care about Prescott Uranium, but I can't leave poor little Moise behind. "The newspapers say the United Nations and Greenpeace are on the way to the mine and village. The villagers will tell them there were no rebels. If I do what you're asking, I'll look like a liar."

"No," Zamenka said, "you are a national hero. The people will believe you, and the liars will be exposed."

"All right, I'll do the interview, but only if I can mention that the soldiers killed some of the villagers."

"Accidentally killed," Zamenka said, nodding to the president. "Mr. Faraday, you may continue with your presentation."

On the way back to the hotel, Costigan said, "Welcome back to the Congo, Joseph. Now you know what it's like to sell your soul. I've been doing it for years."

"The only reason I did the interview was to protect Moise. Perhaps you were right, Jack. I shouldn't have mentioned him to the president."

"Don't beat yourself up. They would've found out. Zamenka has an honors degree in extortion."

"At least the public will get to hear there were villagers killed by the soldiers."

"Yeah," Costigan said unconvincingly.

Joseph sat on the end of his bed, watching the interview with the president on the early evening news. He watched it in its entirety and then quickly flicked to another channel's news. It was the same. They'd cut the part about the villagers being collateral damage. Joseph felt ill and put his head in his hands. *Costigan's right. I'm out of my depth.*

The drums beat furiously deep into the night. The man they had thought of as their savior was a traitor.

Chapter 25

Maya was sympathetic when Joseph called and told her how Bodho and Zamenka had coerced him into doing the interview and then tricked him. "You have been away for a long time," she said. "It is the way of the Congo. You did the right thing. Moise would have been destined for a life of fear and poverty had he stayed here. With you, he can make something of himself."

"I feel terrible. I have let Yannick and the villagers down. They will use what I said to make sure Gizenga and the soldiers never face court."

Maya gave a sarcastic laugh. "They were never going to face court. There is no justice here — only torture and beatings for those who seek it. Paul Blundo was a man seeking equity and justice. Look what happened to him. Murdered in prison by guards who made it look like he committed suicide."

"I'm not sure you're right. The United Nations investigators and Greenpeace are going to find out the truth. When they do, they'll bring pressure to bear on Bodho. The International Monetary Fund and the World Bank might threaten to cut off funds if the culprits aren't brought to trial."

"If the IMF cuts off funds, Bodho will turn to the Chinese. The West will never let it happen. The thought of the Chinese getting their hands on more of the Congo's resources drives them crazy. You know that."

"Perhaps," Joseph said. "I know Bodho has the army in his pocket, but he's also conscious of public opinion. Otherwise, he wouldn't have been so anxious to be driven around the streets with me."

"Poor Joseph. Nothing here is what it seems."

"Can you get word to Yannick and tell him they blackmailed me? I did not betray him. I had to save Moise."

"Yes, the drums will beat out the truth tonight."

"Maya, are you coming back to the U.S. with me?"

"Why do you want me to?"

"To meet my parents."

"Why do you want me to come?" Maya persisted.

"I'm fond of you. I like being with you."

"Do you love me?" she giggled.

"I don't know. My heart beats faster when I see you. You are so different from the scruffy little kid I once knew."

"And you're still the same. So serious. So bossy. But you no longer understand the Congo. Are you coming back?"

"Yes."

"Then I shall come to the U.S. with you because when you return to the Congo, you'll need me to look after you."

Joseph smiled. "We leave on Saturday morning. I have one last banquet to attend on the president's cabin cruiser on Friday night. Faraday said it's decked out like the Queen Mary."

"Yes, it's opulent. The despot knows how to spoil himself. Do you know what he named it?"

"No."

"Numero Uno." Maya replied, her disgust apparent.

The sun was sinking below the horizon when Joseph walked across the gangplank and boarded the yacht. There was a solid breeze, and the water was choppy. "It's nearly three hundred feet long," Faraday said, "and has more than a dozen staterooms, a helipad, a movie theater, a billiards room, and elevators. Have you ever seen anything like it before?"

"It's stunning."

"Yeah, and at forty knots we could do the five miles to Brazzaville, on the other side of the river, in less than ten minutes. There are regular flights from Kinshasa. They take four minutes. It has to be the shortest airline route in the world. Let's find the dining room."

There was a long table in the dining room without any chairs. It was laden with food. Lovely young girls carried plates around so the guests could eat at their leisure. Sofas and recliners surrounded the perimeter of the room. President Bodho and General Zamenka were engaged in an animated conversation with their advisers. Zamenka had a glass of whiskey in his hand, and when he saw Joseph, he beckoned him over. "Are you glad to be going back to the U.S.?" he slurred as a hostess asked Joseph what he would like to drink.

Before he could respond, Zamenka laughed. "He only drinks lemonade and mineral water."

Oh, how I'd love to smash your face in, Joseph thought, and then an idea dawned on him. "I'll have the same as what the general's drinking. It's my last night, and I'll be able to sleep it off on the plane tomorrow."

"That's better," Zamenka said, pounding Joseph on the back with a meaty hand. "Let's sit down."

"Are you happy with the negotiations? Did you find the two weeks fruitful?" Bodho asked.

"I did, Mr. President, and the Prescott uranium mine is going to add enormously to the country's revenue."

Joseph saw Zamenka smirk and wink at the president. Joseph had not attended the final negotiations with George Faraday, Prescott's CEO, and the Congolese, but the wink told him as much as a thousand words.

"Yes, yes," Bodho said, picking up a turkey leg and devouring it.

Faraday had told him not to bring the television interview up, but Joseph had to know what happened. "Mr. President, I was disappointed to see the part of the interview about the villagers being collateral damage cut."

The corners of Bodho's mouth turned up, and he said, "I didn't watch it. I suppose the channels had time constraints and edited it. I'm sorry."

Zamenka had a huge grin on his face. "Let's not talk about unpleasantness on your last night. There are some attractive girls and plenty of staterooms you can use if you're inclined."

"It's been years since I've had a drink," Joseph replied. "I'm enjoying this whiskey. If it's all the same to you, I'm going to have another."

"Good man," Zamenka roared. "Let's get doubles."

A few minutes later, Joseph stood up, glass in hand and went to the bathroom where he tipped nearly all the whiskey down the toilet.

When he got back to the sofa, he drank the rest and said, "You're slowing down, General. I'll get myself a refill."

"You think you can outdrink me?" Zamenka said, badly slurring his words. "They'll carry you off this boat before that happens."

Joseph glanced out the window. It was a moonless night, and the wind had sprung up. "I have to go to the bathroom," he said.

"You're spending a lot of time there."

"I'm sorry, General, I feel a little sick."

"Ah, now I understand. And you thought you could outdrink me. If there was an Olympic gold medal for drinking, I would win it." He laughed.

When Joseph returned, he was holding his head. "I have to go up on deck and get some fresh air," he moaned.

"I'll come with ya," Zamenka slurred while signaling one of the hostesses to fill his glass.

They left the buzz of the banquet behind and struggled up the stairs with their arms around each other. There was no one else on the deck. It was warm, but the wind was howling as Joseph staggered to the bow, and put his head over the rail. "Put your fingers down your throat and throw up." Zamenka said. "You'll feel better."

Joseph turned around. "I'm already feeling better. Maybe it's the fresh air. General, Colonel Gizenga told me you were heroic and personally led the attack on the rebels who'd encroached on my village. I was amazed. I didn't think you'd get involved in the fighting."

Zamenka's face clouded over. "I-I don't remember."

"According to Colonel Gizenga, one of the rebels tried to knife you, and you shot her in the head. He told me if you hadn't responded instantly, she would've killed you."

"Yes, yes. I remember." Zamenka smirked. "The bitch had a skinny daughter. I had my way with her. I nearly split her open. You should have heard her scream. When I finished, I cut her throat from ear to ear. I made sure she wasn't gonna spawn any more rebels."

Joseph stood up straight, showing no sign of intoxication. In one swift movement, he turned the general around, so his back was against the rail. "The woman was my mother, and the little girl was my sister," he said, spitting the words out.

Zamenka was drunk, but fear overcame him. He started to tremble as Joseph gripped his lapels. He looked over his shoulder and then in one move hurled the two-hundred-eighty-pound Zamenka into the river.

"Hey!" a voice shouted.

Joseph turned to see one of Zamenka's bodyguards and shouted back, "Man overboard," and dived over the rail.

The current was running fast in the same direction the boat was traveling, and Zamenka was floundering only thirty yards from Joseph. In fifteen strokes, Joseph was next to the panic-stricken brute. "Prepare to die," he hissed taking a deep breath before putting his hands on Zamenka's shoulders and pushing him under. The general struggled and fought desperately as Joseph pushed him ever deeper into the murky, black water. After ninety seconds, Joseph felt him go limp and swam to the surface. He could see the yacht turning around, and then a Zodiac craft was charging toward him. He held his arm up out of the water and shouted. A few minutes later, he was hauled into the inflatable. "Where is the general?" one of the soldiers asked.

"I couldn't find him," Joseph said, gasping heavily for effect. "I tried. God, I tried."

After fruitlessly looking for the general for another ten minutes, they turned back to the yacht. The Zodiac powered up the lowered ramp at the stern, and Joseph got out.

George Faraday was waiting in the shadows. "Jesus, what did you do? The president wants to see you."

"I'll shower and put something dry on first."

"Now," one of the soldiers growled. "The president wants to see you now."

The soldiers led Joseph to a room, which contained a desk and a dozen chairs. Bodho sat behind the desk with soldiers on either side of him. Jack Costigan was standing in the corner, his face drawn and his lips compressed. "What happened?" Bodho asked.

"General Zamenka fell overboard. I dived in and tried to save him. I did everything I could," Joseph said, water still dripping from his clothes.

"That's not what this man says," Bodho said, nodding at a soldier standing on the left of him. "He says you threw the general over-board. Did you?"

"It's ridiculous," Joseph replied. "The general was sitting on the rail and overbalanced. I lunged and tried to grab him. I had no reason to hurt him. If I had, would have I dived in and tried to save him?"

The president beckoned the soldier to bend down, and they spoke in whispered tones. After they'd finished, Bodho looked up and said, "He says he made a mistake, and what you say is true. He saw you lunge and thought you'd thrown the general overboard. He didn't realize he'd fallen off the rail, and you had tried to pull him back. He is sorry and apologizes to you."

Joseph lifted his hand and nodded to the soldier. "I can under-stand how he misinterpreted what he saw. Apology accepted."

"You better take a shower, and we'll head back to Kinshasa. Find him some dry clothes," Bodho said to one of his aides.

"Aren't you going to try to find him? He might still be alive," Joseph said.

"He couldn't swim," Bodho replied. "He is dead. He might already be crocodile food. You were courageous."

"Thank you, Mr. President, I only wish I could have saved him."

"I was going to see you off tomorrow," Bodho replied. "In the circumstances, it would not be appropriate. Thank you for your valiant efforts. I'll say goodbye now."

"Goodbye, Mr. President."

Joseph could feel George Faraday staring at him as they got off the yacht. "George, contact the captain. I want to be on the plane and out of here by five o'clock in the morning."

"That's in four hours."

"Yes. Arrange it. I'll meet you in the foyer at four-fifteen."

"What about Maya and Moise?"

"I called Maya earlier. She'll be ready."

"All right," Faraday said, shaking his head.

Chapter 26

Joseph packed and then paced around his room, regretting he hadn't said three o'clock. Adrenaline was pumping through him. He hadn't had time to think when he killed the two soldiers, but Zamenka's death was premeditated. He had no regrets but knew that had he been a second later, the soldier would've seen exactly what he had done. Fate had saved his life by taking him to America. Fate had saved him from the python, and now it had saved him again. The sense of being spared for a greater calling was stronger than ever, but he still didn't know what it was.

This time, there were no cheering crowds on the way to the airport or a red-carpet departure — just dark, quiet streets and anxiety among those leaving. On the plane, Joseph smiled grimly when he told Maya about the terrible accident on the yacht. She looked at him in the same way Faraday had. Only Moise was bubbling with excitement, racing up and down the plane's aisle, oblivious to the adults' tension. Two hours later, he — along with everyone else except Joseph and Maya — was asleep.

"He's a beautiful little boy," Maya said, as she looked at him curled up on the two seats in front of them. "How are you going to care for him?"

"Mom and Dad will help. He'll be okay. I'll be with him at night and on the weekends."

"When are you going to find time to train?"

"Moise's more important than defending my gold medal. After the last two weeks, the Olympics are no longer as significant as they once were."

"Joseph," Maya said, holding his hand, "do you feel better?"

"Avenged. I'm glad the butcher is dead, but I know they'll replace him with someone equally as evil."

"Will you still go back to the Congo?"

"I don't know. At the start, I thought I could change things. Now I'm not as sure. Life is cheap. It could be a turning point if the government brings Gizenga and his thugs to trial. My interview with Bodho probably killed the chance of legal action, though. I feel so guilty."

"You had no choice," Maya said, squeezing his hand. "Who's to say what the United Nations and Greenpeace will find? Don't give up hope."

"I won't," Joseph replied without conviction.

"I'm tired," Maya said, resting her head on his shoulder. "I'm going to sleep."

Joseph put his arm around her. He was still hyped up and knew there was no point in closing his eyes.

It was just after midday when they touched down at LAX. Customs officials came out to the plane, and thirty minutes later they were in the arrivals terminal. Michelle Rafter pushed her way through the crowd, threw her arms around Joseph's neck, and kissed him. "I was worried sick. I'm glad you're back. Don't ever do that to me again," she said, still clinging to him.

"I wasn't in any danger, Mom. I promise."

Frank Rafter was bending down talking to Moise. "My son told me all about you. He said you might win an Olympic gold medal one day too."

Maya stood with Faraday and the State Department officials watching the Rafters. She again had mixed feelings. The love she had seen on television at the Beijing Olympics was overwhelming, and Joseph's adoptive parents were nothing like hers. His father was hugging him, and his mother hadn't left his side. She was pleased but also envious.

"Maya, Maya," he shouted, "come and meet my parents."

Michelle kissed her, and Frank shook her hand. "Joseph tells me you're a childhood friend. It's a pleasure to meet you."

On the drive to the house, memories flooded back for Joseph as he watched Moise, his face glued to the window, staring in astonishment at the hundreds of cars flashing around him and the high-rise

122

buildings. More memories were to follow when Michelle showed Moise to his room. Clothes were on his bed; shoes, sandals, and Nikes were next to it; and a three-drawer dresser was overflowing with socks, underwear, and T-shirts. Michelle had gone a step further, and pictures of the 49ers' quarterback covered the walls. Maya gasped when she saw her room and the four-poster double bed with drapes. She had never been in a house as large or luxurious. After they had settled, Joseph grabbed a football. "Come on, Dad," he said, "and you too, Maya and Moise. I'll introduce you to American football."

Moise was a good catch, but his hands were too small to get a grip on the ball, and he couldn't throw with any power. "I'll buy you a smaller ball tomorrow," Frank said, ruffling the little boy's hair before picking up the ball and unleashing a fast throw.

Maya was another story. She could not only catch but was soon throwing with surprising speed and power. "I'm going to sign you up for the 49ers," Joseph laughed.

"See, it's not hard to smile," Maya responded. "I like it when you lighten up."

After dinner, when Michelle, Maya, and Moise had gone to bed, Joseph sat across from his father in the study. "Who's going to look after the boy?" Frank asked.

"I am," Joseph said.

"How? Are you going to retire? I thought you brought Maya back to help you."

"It never entered my mind. Maya used to be like my sister when she was a little girl. Now I'm romantically attracted to her. It's strange. I want to see if we can set our cultural differences aside. She calls me a soft American boy."

Frank smiled. "She's a stunning young woman. It's not hard to understand your attraction. How long is she going to stay?"

"I don't know. She's a nurse in Kinshasa but wants to be a doctor. Do you think you can get her into UCLA?"

"Possibly. No, make that probably. Let's go back to the boy. How are you going to look after him when you're at work or training?"

"I thought you and Mom might be able to help."

"I'm sixty-eight, and your mother's sixty-six. We're not going to be around forever."

"You're in terrific condition, Dad. That rocket you threw nearly knocked me over."

Frank frowned. "You've taken on a big responsibility, Son. You might have to hire someone to help you out."

"Dad, I told you the army killed all of his family. If you were in my shoes, you would've done the same."

Frank reached over the desk and squeezed Joseph's forearm. "I'm not critical of you. You're right, I would've done what you did. I'm just trying to work out what's best for Moise. Lighten up."

"Thanks, Dad." Joseph grimaced. "The adoption papers are in the name of Moise Rafter. Mom's always said she'd like a grandson."

"Yes, but I don't think an instant seven-year-old is what she had in mind." Frank laughed. "Do you think you'll go back to the Congo?"

"I don't know. It might depend on Maya, but if she's studying medicine here, I can't see myself going back for a long time. It's corrupt, and I felt sick listening to some of the deals George Faraday put together."

"Your mother will be delighted if you never set foot in the Congo again. She missed you terribly. So did I. We were distraught when you were in the jungle and no one knew if you were dead or alive. We thought we'd lost you. Then you called. It was such a relief."

I wish I hadn't told George about those two thugs and the snake. I hope he keeps his mouth shut. "It was nothing, Dad. I was with Maya and little Moise. Staying in the jungle for two nights was no hardship for us. We were in no danger."

"I'm glad. I want you to take a week off to help Maya and Moise get acclimated. The firm can afford it. Those deals you didn't like George doing were lucrative. Make the most of your break. There's a lot for you to do at the office when you return."

BOOK 2
JUSTICE IN THE CONGO

Chapter 27

Joseph had intended to continue his investigations into the New Dawn Gold Mining Company on his return from the Congo. There were thousands of emails to read, and he was still determined to find out who the real owners were. However, he had little spare time. Michelle enrolled Moise in a local school, and Joseph played with him and helped out with homework every night. He hadn't realized being a father would be so time-consuming. When he returned to work, there was a backlog to catch up on, and with his newfound fame, there was always a client wanting to see him. His relationship with Maya also took time. He was attracted to her but still had visions of her as his little sister, and it troubled him. She had wanted to return to the Congo after a month in Beverly Hills, but Joseph had dangled the carrot of studying medicine, and she had taken it.

"As soon as I'm qualified, I'm returning," she said. "I can make a real difference in Kinshasa."

"I'm happy to go back with you during semester breaks," Joseph replied. "You don't have to wait until you're qualified."

"What do you see happening with us?"

"With us? I don't understand."

"You were so anxious to bring me back to America with you. Surely it wasn't just because you wanted to see me become a doctor." She smiled.

"That was part of it."

"Joseph, can I ask you a personal question? You might find it offensive. I hope not, but I need to clear the air."

"Go ahead."

"Are you gay?"

"Jesus, why would you ask me something like that?"

"It's been six weeks since we reconnected in Kinshasa. We've been together nearly every day. We've gone on long walks holding hands, you've taken me to nice restaurants, and we've been to the movies. Last weekend watching the sunset over Santa Monica was romantic, but there was no romance. In all that time, you haven't made a move."

Joseph put his hand to his mouth to conceal a frown and then, unable to hold a straight face, roared with laughter. "No, I'm not gay, and if you remember, Moise was with us in Santa Monica. What did you expect me to do?"

"Well, if you're not gay, is it me?"

"Maya, I used to think of you as my little sister. Now you are a beautiful young woman. I'm confused. We're going to be living under the same roof for the next three years. What if we started something and it didn't work out? It might mess with your studies, and you might leave. If that happened, it would break Moise's heart. He loves you."

"Oh my God. I don't believe you. I've never heard you laugh so loudly. It was so great to hear, and now you're back to the old, serious Joseph. All relationships are risky, and many fail, but don't you wonder about us?"

"Of course I do, but you're going back to the Congo, and I'll probably stay here. You're right. I'm an American boy. I love Michelle and Frank."

"You mightn't know it yet, but you're not staying here. Do you think the calling you keep talking about is coming from California? It's coming from the Congo. I can see how attached you are to your parents, but your calling isn't here."

"When I see that petulant face, it brings back memories," Joseph said. "It's the same face you used to pull when I called you 'Sis.' Your expression hasn't changed a bit."

"Really?" Maya giggled. "We'll have to see about that."

That night, just after midnight, Maya crept into Joseph's room, took her nightgown off and put it at the end of the bed. His back was to her, and she put a hand over his mouth and snuggled into him. Three hours later she whispered, "I better get back to my room."

"Not now," he murmured.

"Yes, I have to. I don't want your mom or dad catching me leaving your room in the morning."

"Okay," he said, kissing her.

"I have a question."

"Go on."

"Do you still think of me as your little sister?" she giggled, jumping out of the bed before he could respond.

Six months after they had returned from the Congo, Joseph and Maya were planning their marriage. He was happy and content. Moise had assimilated far better than he had fourteen years earlier and had put on a needed eight pounds. Joseph had read thousands of emails between Marc Boucher and the man called Thibault without finding anything more. He hadn't lost interest but had lost the drive, and he'd gone from reading emails every night to reading them when he had some free time. Even Maya had lost some of her earlier doggedness. They didn't know it, but the drums of the Congo were on the verge of erupting.

Their first indication was a long, detailed letter from Congolese law firm, Banze & Yaz. They were representing Colonel Gizenga and twenty soldiers, who had been charged with war crimes including: arbitrary detention, torture, rape, and murder by the Congolese military prosecutor. The most serious charges related to the execution of twenty-five men, six women — one of whom was pregnant — and three children. Banze & Yaz were also representing Marc Boucher and Gert Botha, who were facing charges of incitement and aiding and abetting the soldiers by hiring the helicopters that had taken them from Lubumbashi to the New Dawn mine, and providing them with company vehicles.

Joseph was amazed. Jack Costigan had told him there was no possibility of Gizenga and his thugs ever being charged. He was also shocked. Paul Banze had watched the Bodho interview and wanted him to return to the Congo to appear as a defense witness. Failing this, Banze had arranged with the court for Joseph to appear by video. He hung his head. There was no way out, not that he was looking for one. He wanted to return to the Congo, not as a witness for the defense, but as a witness for the prosecution. He could only do this by exposing the Bodho interview as a lie.

Still staggered, Joseph called Costigan, who told him the United Nations report into the massacre had been damning and had come down hard on the army. The World Bank and International Monetary Fund had threatened to turn the cash tap off, and President Bodho blinked.

"I don't get it," Joseph said. "Didn't you tell me if the West turned his cash off, Bodho would go to the Chinese for funds?"

Costigan laughed. "Do you remember those deals you and George Faraday put together?"

"Of course. Get to the point."

"When they were getting done, Bodho and Zamenka were holding deposits from the Chinese on the same projects. The Chinese never got their deposits back. Bodho burned his bridges with them. He's got no one to turn to. The only way he could ensure the continuing flow of funds was by agreeing to put Gizenga and the others on trial. He knows the world is watching. Are you going back?"

"I don't know. I'll discuss it with my family over dinner tonight. Thanks, Jack."

Chapter 28

The Rafter family's dinner table was in an uproar. "I don't want you going back," Michelle said. "If you must, you can testify by video. They've given you that option."

"Mom, my testimony won't have any impact if I do it from here. I'll have no credibility. I'm going to repudiate what I said in that interview with the president, and I'm going to say why."

"You're a fool," Maya said. "When they find out what you're up to, they'll kill you before they let you near the courtroom."

"If you go, I'm coming with you," Frank said.

"So am I," Maya said.

"Neither of you are," Joseph responded. "They blackmailed me last time because they knew I was desperate to take Moise home. I don't want anyone with me who they can use in the same way."

"I don't want you to go," Moise sniffled, ketchup dribbling down his chin. "What will happen to me if you don't come back?"

"I'll be back, don't worry about me, Moise," Joseph said, reaching out and putting his arm around the young boy. "Grandma and Grandad will look after you while I'm gone, and Maya will still be here."

"Why is it crucial for you to go?" Michelle asked. "The United Nations built its case without you. How do you know your testimony will be important?"

"Mom, this could be a turning point. Everyone told me Bodho would never permit a trial. Perhaps this is the start of change."

"Oh, you really are a fool," Maya said. "Bodho called the trial because of what you said in that television interview. You're not just a defense witness. You're their star witness. When they find out you're appearing for the prosecution, they'll have you killed. The police will pick you up, and you'll disappear off the face of the earth."

"Jack Costigan said the world is going to be watching. I don't think they'll try anything."

"No, no, no!" Maya shouted. "You haven't lived there. You don't know. Bodho doesn't care what the rest of the world thinks."

"Joseph, Maya's right. You don't have to go. The UN must have enough evidence. Why do you have to go?" Frank asked, the food on his plate hardly touched.

"It's hard to explain. I thought the calling had gone, but when I read the law firm's letter, it was like a message from God."

"Oh, shit! You just want to hear yourself," Maya said, standing up. "Sorry for swearing, everyone. I've lost my appetite. I'm going to have an early night."

Michelle started to clear the table, and Moise went to do his homework. "When are you going?" Frank asked.

"Wednesday, if I can get a flight. It'll give me a few days to talk to the prosecutor."

"I'll charter a jet."

"Don't be ridiculous. It'll cost a small fortune. Besides, I'd rather not draw attention to myself."

"Don't worry about the money. I'm sure plenty of private jets land at N'djili. No one will know you're on the plane, but if you have to get out in a hurry, I don't want you having to line up for a commercial flight. George will make sure your entry's low-key."

"Dad, I know George is your friend, but I don't like or trust him. He's not coming with me."

Frank paused, knotted his hands together, and whispered, "I know what you did. George told me. Did you kill Zamenka too?"

"I slipped up when I told George about those two thugs. They intended to rape Moise. And yes, I killed Zamenka. He murdered my mother and raped and murdered my sister. George had no right to tell you. You can see why I don't trust him."

"No, Joseph, I can't. He's a good friend of mine, and if he hadn't told me, he wouldn't be much of a friend. He says they suspect you killed Zamenka. They'll be watching you like hawks. Your mother and I will feel far better if George is with you. He knows them."

"I'm sorry, Dad. The answer's no. I wonder who else he told."

"No one. He swore he hasn't told anyone other than me."

"If only I could believe that. Don't worry about a private jet. I'll get a commercial flight. I can look after myself."

"You won't compromise on George. I'm not going to compromise on the jet," Frank said, jutting out his jaw. "And make sure you take at least ten thousand in cash. You never know whose palm you might have to grease."

On Wednesday, Maya didn't go to college, Moise didn't go to school, and Frank didn't go to work. Along with Michelle, who had tears streaming down her cheeks, they were all at the airport to bid farewell to Joseph. Maya's anger had been replaced with fear, and as they kissed, she whispered, "Please come back to me."

"There's nothing to worry about."

Moise clung to his leg saying, "Don't go, don't go."

Frank was outwardly stoic, but his gut was churning as he shook Joseph's hand. "I've arranged some security for you," he said. "Good luck."

"What? What have you done?" Joseph asked.

"Don't be angry."

"I have to go. I'll see you in three weeks," Joseph said, abruptly turning, fearing he too might start crying.

He took the stairs to the jet two at a time, thinking it was a waste of money. A smiling flight attendant said, "Good morning, Mr. Muamba, the others have already boarded."

Jesus, if George Faraday's on the plane, I'm throwing him off. "Thank you," he growled, as he entered the main cabin.

"Why so grumpy? I thought you'd be glad to see us."

"Chuck, Brett, what are you doing here?"

"Once our cover was blown, our value fell through the floor, didn't it, Brett?" Bennett laughed. "Your dad's got a lot of influence. Someone from the Department of Justice strong-armed our boss, and here we are. We're your unofficial bodyguards."

"Jesus," Joseph cursed. "You can't be with me."

"Settle down," Kronk said. "You'll never see us, and yeah, we won't be able to go everywhere ya do. We know we're not gonna get in the palace, but if they try to kill ya, it's not gonna happen there. We'll be in the places where they are likely to try. We won't cramp your style."

"You know everything there is to know about me. Tell me what qualifies you as bodyguards."

Bennett winked at Kronk, grinned, and said, "We're former SEALs. Does that meet your specifications?"

"I thought so," Joseph said. "I don't need you. I can look after myself, but it's obvious what I want doesn't count. I'm going to appear as a witness. I'll be safe in court. I don't want you turning it into the last shootout at the O.K. Corral."

"That'd make me Wyatt Earp and him Doc Holliday." Bennett laughed. "In case you've forgotten, you'd still be in that jungle in Katanga if it weren't for us. Lighten up."

If I'm told to lighten up one more time, I'll explode. "I wouldn't, you know. I'd have crossed into Tanzania. But yes, you saved me a lot of time and trouble."

"On a lighter note, the message you wrote to my son was fantastic. He took it to school and showed the other kids. He was the envy of his class," Bennett said.

"You've got a wife and young son. Why aren't you home with them? Why do you do such a dangerous job?"

"Someone's gotta stop the baddies. Isn't that why you're going back to the Congo? And don't you have a fiancée and son?"

"Fiancée? No, not yet, but I guess I know what you mean. It's a calling."

Bennett laughed. "I wouldn't go that far. It's a job someone has to do, and we happen to be good at it. When you depart the terminal, you'll be approached by a limo driver and asked whether Maya is well. You'll reply, 'She's in excellent health.' He's one of ours and will be stationed at the hotel for your use."

"Jesus, how many of you are there?"

"Just three."

Twenty-nine hours later, it was 3:00 p.m. Kinshasa time, and the captain informed them they'd be landing in an hour. Joseph switched his cellphone on and called the prosecutor's office. Within a few minutes, he was speaking to Yuma Lidy, the prosecutor, who said he'd be pleased to see him at nine o'clock in the morning.

Chapter 29

There were no cheering crowds or red carpet when the Gulfstream landed. Joseph was relieved. The two Americans remained on the plane, saying they would catch up with him later. They had booked rooms on either side of him at the Memling.

The Congolese driver standing next to the limo was gargantuan. "Is Maya well, sir?" he asked.

"She's in excellent health."

"Did you have a good flight, Mr. Muamba?" the driver said, holding the rear door open.

"Jesus, you've got the deepest voice I've ever heard. Compared to you, George Clooney is a soprano," Joseph said. "Call me Joseph. What's your name, and how is it you're working with Americans?"

"Leon, and I've heard all the voice jokes a hundred times before. It's better if I call you 'sir' or 'Mr. Muamba,' sir. I will be on twenty-four-hour call for the duration of your stay. It is not unusual, and I often drive exclusively for foreign diplomats. My parents took me to the States when I was ten. I have a degree in economics and politics and a post-graduate degree in computer science, and I'm fluent in six languages. I was with the CIA for ten years. I returned to Kinshasa a few years ago and own a limousine hire business. It's the largest in the city."

"What a great cover for a spook," Joseph said. "What made you come back?"

"I'm surprised you would ask. The same reason you're here. I love this country and feel sorry for the people. I thought I could make a difference, and I have, but it's nothing compared to what you can do."

"Perhaps," Joseph said. "Perhaps."

Yuma Lidy's wood-paneled office was small and dusty. Crammed bookshelves as high as the ceiling concealed three walls. Stick-on notes, press clippings, and phone messages covered the fourth. Neatly arranged folders bound with pink ribbon covered the floor to the right of Lidy's cluttered desk. A small window overlooked the street. Joseph sat down on a badly worn leather chair and studied the little gray-haired man sitting opposite him. "This is most irregular, Mr. Muamba," he said. "You are listed as a witness for the defense. Does Mr. Banze know you are here?"

"Let me explain, Mr. Lidy," Joseph said, and then related what had occurred at the mine, the village, and in the jungle.

"You're going to go to court and tell the world the president lied and blackmailed you. You're a brave man," the prosecutor said, shaking his head. "If you appear as a defense witness and repeat what you've just told me, defense counsel will ask the court to treat you as a hostile witness."

"Hostile?"

Lidy smiled. "Not in the way you are thinking, Mr. Muamba. If you don't say anything to defense counsel before the trial, he will rightly expect your testimony to help his clients. When it doesn't, he will treat you as hostile and do everything in his power to discredit you. He will tell the court you said you'd support the defendants, and your testimony is the antithesis of what you told him. You will be called a liar. He will use the interview with President Bodho to support his assertion and say your claim about the president blackmailing you is rubbish. He will keep you in the witness box for as long as he can and try to break you down."

"What are the options?"

"I will notify Mr. Banze you are appearing as a witness for the prosecution. It will throw the cat among the pigeons. He will, of course, realize you are going to repudiate the comments you made in the television interview with the president. The only reason the president didn't block the trial was that your testimony made it almost certain Colonel Gizenga and his soldiers would be acquitted. I'm going to enjoy this trial."

"I'm pleased. Who else do you have as witnesses?"

"Some mine workers and villagers. We also have a friend of yours, Yannick Kyenge. He was my star witness before you appeared."

"Yannick. Can I see him?"

"I'm afraid not. He's appearing at significant risk. We have him at a hidden location, and he will remain out of sight until called. He'll testify, and then we have to get him out of court before they arrest him. Colonel Donatien and his men have been hunting Yannick. They're ruthless. Have you heard of Donatien?"

"No, should I have?"

"The plan is that after Colonel Gizenga is acquitted, he'll be promoted to general, and take over the role performed by the late General Zamenka. Donatien will take Gizenga's place in the hierarchy. He's a dangerous man. The people are terrified of him. Don't be surprised if he tries to dissuade you from testifying."

"I'm not worried. I'm not easily bullied. Can you call me as your first witness?"

"Yes, but why?"

"I want to sit through the whole trial. If you call me as, say, the fourth witness, I'll miss the testimony of the first three. I want to hear everything."

"I understand, but I'll ask you again. Why?"

Joseph stared directly into Lidy's eyes and said, "I don't know, but it's important. There is much I don't know. I think this trial will provide some of the answers I'm looking for."

Lidy stood up. "I have a lot to do," he said. "Can you come back tomorrow morning and I'll take you through my examination? After we're finished, we'll go over what you can expect on cross-examination. You're going to have to steel yourself. It will be a harrowing experience. On the positive side, you have made my day, Mr. Muamba. Thank you."

"Call me Joseph. One question before I go. Why are Boucher and Botha appearing before a military court? They're not soldiers."

"Military courts here have the power to try civilians. It's not unusual."

"Interesting."

"Watch your back," the little man said. "When word gets out, some people are going to be livid. Ruthless people! What do you have planned for the rest of the day?"

"Nothing much. I'll go back to my hotel room and send some emails. Don't worry about me. I can look after myself."

"Don't underestimate what I said, Joseph. Please be careful. I'll see you in the morning."

Back in his hotel room, Joseph turned on his laptop. At last, he had some time to peruse the emails and the few documents Marc Boucher had saved. He hadn't permanently deleted his emails, and there were more than one hundred thousand in the deleted items folder. Joseph knew the names of the real owners of the New Dawn Gold Mining Company were somewhere amongst those emails. Most of the exchanges were with the mysterious Thibault, but some of the emails were to and from suppliers, accountants, and lawyers. Joseph read them slowly, looking for a location, a bank, or a third party he could link to Thibault.

He was crouched over his laptop, deep in concentration, when there was a pounding on his door. "Joseph Muamba, please open the door."

"Who is it?"

"Colonel Donatien. I need to talk to you. Let me in."

God, that didn't take long. I'd like to tell him to get lost, but that might not be wise, Joseph thought. He opened the door to see soldiers carrying machine guns on either side of a heavyset, smiling officer. "Welcome back to Kinshasa," he said, extending his hand. "I am Colonel Donatien."

Joseph felt Donatien attempt to crush his hand but remained impassive. When Donatien realized his grip had had no effect, he eased the pressure. As he did, Joseph applied full force for a split second and watched the officer's face contort in pain. "How can I help you, Colonel?"

"There is a silly rumor going around that you're testifying for the prosecution. President Bodho is quite disturbed. He is concerned about you. As you know, perjury is a serious crime. I told him the rumor was unfounded. I'm right, aren't I?"

One soldier had worked his way behind Joseph, the other was on his right, and Donatien was in front of him. "Colonel, you can tell the president I will be telling the truth. He doesn't have to worry about me perjuring myself."

Donatien looked perplexed. "So your testimony will be no different than what you said in the television interview with the president?"

"I will be telling the truth," Joseph repeated.

Donatien's confusion quickly turned to anger. "Are you going to see Mr. Banze before the trial?"

"I have no reason to."

"You are stupid!" Donatien shouted, his face only inches from Joseph's. "You will not get bail after we charge you with perjury. You'll languish in prison waiting for your case to come to trial — that's if you're lucky. Unavoidable accidents occur in prison, terrible accidents. You mightn't even get to see the inside of the courtroom."

"You omitted to say I might hang myself," Joseph said. "It's a regular occurrence, isn't it?"

The soldiers pressed closer, eyes narrowed, and lips turned up in sneers. "You have a smart mouth. What are you even doing here? This is not your country. You're an American. Go home, while you still can."

"I'm sorry, I can't, and you'd be wise to remember the United Nations, Greenpeace, and the rest of the world are going to be watching this trial. You might let the president know. It will look bad if one of the witnesses gets thrown in prison."

"You dare threaten the president. You are stupider than I thought."

Joseph pushed past the soldiers and opened the balcony door. "It's starting to smell in here. I'm busy, Colonel. You can leave now. Close the door after you."

"We will meet again," Donatien said. "I won't forget today."

Less than a minute later, there was a light knocking on Joseph's door. He flung it open, expecting to see Donatien.

Instead, it was Chuck Bennett. "From now on, when you go out, one of us is going to be with you. Those pricks mean business."

"They won't try anything while the trial's going on."

"And here I was hoping Donatien was wrong when he called you stupid." Bennett frowned. "If they get the chance, they'll kill you, trial or no trial. Your problem is that you've been away far too long."

"You bugged my room?"

"It's for your own good," Bennett said, brushing past Joseph to close the balcony door. "Don't go out on the balcony, and keep the drapes drawn."

Joseph shut down the laptop just before midnight and was pulling back the covers on his bed when his cellphone rang. He scowled after glancing at the display and answered, "Hello, George. What I can do for you?"

"Christ, what are you doing? Why didn't you tell me you were going back for the trial? The Congolese are going crazy and threatening to cancel those deals. If the Chinese wrangle their way back into Prescott's uranium project because of you, there'll be hell to pay with the government. Why couldn't you have stayed away? You think you can call their president a liar and get away with it? You're mad! Your testimony's gonna be worth diddly squat after they finish with you. They might even throw you in a cell, or worse."

"They're bluffing. They've already done the Chinese over. They've got nowhere to go."

"Jesus! You're wet behind the ears. The Chinese will soon forget what's owed to them if they can get their mitts on that uranium. Alternatively, Bodho will leave it in the ground if he has to, or hawk it to the Japanese or French. You know nothing. Don't forget, if things go awry, your father's going to lose out big-time too."

"Here's the thing. I can't lie in court. I'll say I was dazed when I did the interview with the president, and it was only later I recalled the events in their entirety. Oh, and George, have you remembered who bought New Dawn off you?"

"No, I haven't. You need to be careful about what you say because once the genie's out the bottle, you can't put it back in."

"I know what I'm doing."

"If only it were true. You're a fool. You've upset a lot of powerful people, here and there," Faraday said ominously and hung up.

Chapter 30

Surly-looking soldiers dressed in short-sleeved camouflage green shirts milled around the steps of the military court. Ugly stares followed Joseph from the time he got out of the limo until he entered the court building. Brett Kronk was by his side, telling him to move quickly. One of the prosecutor's assistants led Joseph to a small room where Mr. Lidy was sitting at a table. "Good morning, Joseph. How are you?"

"I'm fine, thank you, Mr. Lidy."

"You know the procedure. The opening addresses will be completed by lunchtime. I'll call you as my first witness immediately after. In the meantime, don't leave this room. There's nothing the soldiers can do, but they will try to intimidate you."

"I'm not easily intimidated," Joseph said.

At 1:00 p.m., Joseph entered the courtroom to a gallery packed with a haze of camouflage green. The judges, three officers dressed in military tunics, sat behind a bench draped in the Democratic Republic of the Congo's flag. Mr. Lidy and his team were sitting at a small table. The defense lawyers were at an identically sized table on the other side of the aisle. The defendants were seated on the left of the bench. Joseph was sworn in, and for the next two hours, Mr. Lidy skillfully took him through his testimony. Colonel Gizenga glared at Joseph, shaking his head when he did not agree with something. Boucher and Botha were next to the colonel, defiance written all over their faces. "Your witness," Mr. Lidy said, well satisfied with his work.

Paul Banze stood up, stretched, and smiled at Joseph before saying, "Are you a liar, Mr. Muamba?"

Lidy was immediately on his feet, shouting, "Objection."

"I'll allow it," the senior judge said.

"I'll ask you again, are you a liar?"

"No."

"But you admitted to telling lies less than an hour ago. Didn't you admit to lying on national television?"

"Yes, but – "

"Just yes or no will suffice, Mr. Muamba. You testified there were no rebels at the mine or village. How did you come to that conclusion?"

"They were miners and villagers. Not rebels."

"How could you tell? Wasn't it your first visit since being taken to America fifteen years ago? How could you distinguish a villager from a rebel?"

"I did not see anyone attack the soldiers. All I saw was workers fleeing from soldiers who were throwing hand grenades and firing at random."

"Are you asking this court to believe it was simple villagers who killed those two soldiers?"

"I don't know. Perhaps the villagers were defending themselves."

"Really?" Banze smirked. "One of those poor soldiers had his throat slashed from behind. Are you suggesting his death was in self-defense?"

"He could've been raping or killing someone's wife, daughter, or son," Joseph replied.

An audible gasp came from the gallery, and an already tense courtroom teetered on exploding.

"Could've?" Banze shouted. "You didn't see anything. It could've been the rebels who killed him. How do you know it wasn't?"

"There were no rebels," Joseph calmly replied.

The cross-examination continued in the same vein for the rest of the day, and most of the next. Lidy was passionate and was up and down objecting, but the judges rejected most of his objections. Paul Banze finished by saying, "Mr. Muamba, you have no credibility as a witness. You have proved yourself to be an unmitigated liar. You – "

"Objection," Lidy shouted. "Where's the question?"

"I'm leading up to it, Your Honors," Banze responded.

"I'll allow it," the senior judge said.

"I'll ask you again, are you a liar, Mr. Muamba?"

It's a stacked court. The evidence is going to have to be overwhelming to win. "No, I am not."

As Banze returned to his seat, he smirked. "So you say."

It was early evening when Joseph left the court. There were huge crowds on the street, and heavily armed, nervous-looking soldiers manned the steps. As they separated to let him pass, the crowd saw him and started to chant, "Muamba, Muamba, Muamba," and the noise became deafening.

"Come on," Brett Kronk, said grabbing Joseph by the arm and pushing him into the back of the limo. "Those fuckers look like they could open fire at any time. Let's get out of here."

"We're safe, Brett." Leon laughed. "It'd take a nuclear bomb to penetrate this thing."

"What? What do you mean?" Joseph asked.

"This vehicle's as safe as Obama's," Leon replied. "Bullets from AK-47s will bounce off the glass, and the doors are impenetrable."

"But they're not heavy," Joseph said.

"The miracle of Kevlar, titanium, and metallurgy," Leon replied.

As the limo slowly maneuvered through the crowd, there were slaps on the panels and roof, and the chanting reached fever pitch.

"You're the most-liked person in the Congo," Kronk said, "and it makes you Bodho's number one target."

The drums beat through the night telling the story of a great savior who had returned to take his people to the Promised Land. Joseph didn't know it, but each day the crowds would grow larger, and the chanting would grow louder.

The next witness was a woman who had seen her twenty-two-year-old pregnant daughter gang-raped by at least half a dozen soldiers. When her daughter's husband had tried to save her, they had summarily executed him with a bullet to the back of his head. Her daughter had lost the baby and her mind. She now wandered around the village, singing, giggling, and crying. When villagers she had known all her life said hello, she didn't recognize them. Lidy was gentle with the girl's mother. Twice she broke down in tears as she recounted the terrible day. "Did you see any rebels?" Lidy asked.

"There were no rebels."

144

"Are you sure?"

"Yes."

"You are brave to be here testifying. Can you tell the court why you agreed to testify?"

"I wanted justice for my daughter and her husband."

"Are you scared?"

Banze leaped to his feet. "Objection. Why would she be? Counsel's question impugns the integrity of this court. It is an insult."

"Sustained," the senior judge said. "Counsel will confine his questions to what the witness saw."

Joseph looked over at the defendants. They were sniggering.

"After what you saw, are you scared of the soldiers?"

"No! They have killed and destroyed everything I loved. They can no longer hurt me."

"Your witness," Lidy said.

Banze was a skilled cross-examiner and spent the first few minutes sympathizing with the witness and putting her at ease. Then he moved on to the number of soldiers involved in what he called the "purported rape," asking, "Are you sure it was six soldiers?"

"I don't know. It could've been more."

"Could it have been less?"

The witness paused. "Perhaps."

"You have no idea how many soldiers were involved. Are you sure you saw your daughter raped? Aren't you just making it up because you hate the army?"

"No!" the woman sobbed.

"No, you didn't see her raped?"

"No, you're confusing me, and I'm telling the truth," the woman said, sniffling.

"Look at the defendants," Banze said, "and point out to the court those whom you can identify as raping your daughter."

The witness pointed out four soldiers, whom Banze asked to remain standing.

"Now point out the soldier who killed your daughter's husband."

The witness pointed to the second soldier standing.

"So it is not six as you claimed, but four."

"There were more. It happened quickly. I cannot identify them all."
The woman continued to sob.

"What would you say if I told you the defendant you've picked out
as a rapist and murderer never left the New Dawn gold mine? He was
never in the village."

"I-I don't know."

"You don't know! Could you have been mistaken?"

The witness paused and carefully looked at the defendant. "No,"
she said, "he was the first. When my daughter's husband intervened,
that soldier killed him."

"If what you say is true, surely your son-in-law charged at the
defendant?"

"Yes."

"Well, in that case, how could he have been shot in the back of the
head?"

"I-I – "

"You don't know," Banze sarcastically interrupted, as he sat down.
"No further questions for this witness, Your Honors."

The next witness was a mine worker. He told how soldiers forced him
and ten other miners into the back of a truck owned by the New Dawn
Gold Mining Company. The soldiers then drove the truck to a large ditch
on the outskirts of the mine. The workers were lined up on the edge of
the ditch and shot. The witness described his fear and how, as the shooting began, he fainted and fell into the ditch. When he came around, he
was suffocating and covered in blood from the bodies on top of him. He
couldn't recall the faces of any of the soldiers but distinctly remembered
Colonel Gizenga giving the order to load the workers into the truck.

"Was Colonel Gizenga one of the soldiers shooting?" Banze asked.

"No, but – "

"Just a yes or no will suffice. Did you hear Colonel Gizenga order
his soldiers to kill you and the others?"

"No, but he – "

"Thank you," Banze said. "I'm glad you survived, but are you
certain the other men in the truck weren't rebels?"

"They were miners."

"I'm sure you understand it's possible to be both a miner and a rebel. Are you 100 percent certain the other men in the back of the truck were not rebels?"

The witness cocked his elbow, closed his eyes, and rested his chin in his hand, before saying, "Yes, I am."

"For someone who's certain, you sure took your time answering. If, as you say, there were no rebels, who killed those two soldiers?"

I wish I could stand up and shout that I killed the thugs because they were going to rape a seven-year-old boy, Joseph thought. *Lidy's smart and doing his best, but he's getting no help from the judges.*

"I don't know."

"Don't worry." Banze sneered. "It's a familiar response."

A thin, frail-looking woman who said she was thirty-four but looked fifty was the next witness. She spoke in a whisper, and the senior judge asked her to speak up. She told how the soldiers shelled, fired on, and then pelted the village with hand grenades. She and her family had run to the safety of the jungle, but halfway there, her sixteen-year-old son became worried about his bike and had gone back to get it.

She never saw him again. When the gunfire stopped, she had ventured back to what remained of the village, hoping her son would be safe. The few remaining villagers told her they'd seen soldiers march him out of the village. Some of them were still there, selling the goods they had plundered back to the villagers. One of the soldiers had her son's bike and was trying to sell it. When she asked him where he had got it, he said he had bought it from her son. She told the court she knew he was lying.

Banze continued with the same line of cross-examination, saying the woman hadn't seen anything. She didn't even know whether her son was dead. He could be alive and living in another village. There was nothing to prove the soldier did not buy the bike. Lidy was like a bulldog making numerous objections, all of which were disallowed, in a vain attempt to save her from Banze's cruel savaging. By the time the cross-examination was over, she was shaking uncontrollably.

On the fifth day of the trial, Lidy called Yannick Kyenge, his last witness. If the looks on the faces of the soldiers in the gallery could have killed, he wouldn't have made it to the witness box. Joseph was sitting behind the prosecution table and winked at Yannick, who looked relieved to see someone he knew.

Yannick told how he had been in the forest when he heard gunfire and explosions. In fear of his life, he had hidden in the foliage and watched villagers running in blind panic across open space toward the safety of the trees as soldiers fired at them. Many didn't make it to the forest and were killed. He had crept to the edge of the village in the early hours of the morning and saw soldiers engaged in a drunken orgy. He choked up when telling how he'd watched the gang rape of women and young girls. A naked little boy, no older than six, had tried to escape the grasp of a soldier, who'd pulled out his pistol and shot him in the head. As the sun had edged over the horizon, the soldiers looted the huts and then set them ablaze.

Joseph knew that Yannick had crept back to the village, but other than the fires, he had not said anything about the atrocities he'd witnessed.

Paul Banze was as angry as the defendants, and the soldiers in the gallery. For the first time, he left the table and strode over to the witness box until he was no farther than two feet from Yannick. The judges said nothing. "You have some cheek, don't you?" he thundered.

"I don't know what you mean," Yannick replied.

"Oh, I think you do. Aren't you the leader of the rebels?"

"No. I work at the mine and live in the village."

"With the other rebels?"

"I am not a rebel, and nor are any of the mine workers or villagers. We went on strike for better wages and conditions. Nothing more. Then the soldiers came and executed the striking mine workers."

"How do you know? You weren't there. You've just testified you were sniveling in the forest."

Joseph clenched his fists. He wanted to leap over the prosecution table and smash them into Banze's face. He took a deep, calming breath and glanced around at the sullen soldiers sitting behind him. Colonel Donatien was staring at him, a mirthless smile on his face. *He hasn't been here before. Why is he here today? Oh, no,* Joseph thought.

"Once the soldiers had gone, I went back to the mine. I saw at least ten bullet-riddled bodies piled up on top of one another in a deep ditch. Only the soldiers had machine guns."

"You had weapons," Banze said. "Didn't you take the guards' rifles when you supposedly went on strike?"

"We didn't use them. We only took them to stop the guards using them on us."

"Really? Did you have a spear or spears?"

"Yes, only to protect myself."

"Do you own a knife?"

"Of course. All villagers do."

Banze paced up and down before the bench before abruptly turning. "Two soldiers were killed. Do you know how?"

"I heard one was killed by a spear, and the other had his throat cut."

"You *heard*." Banze sneered. "It was you who murdered them, wasn't it?"

"No, sir, I did not."

Joseph turned around to see a sea of angry faces all focused on Yannick. Fortunately, it was a few minutes to one, and the court was preparing to recess for lunch. Joseph leaned over and said to Lidy, "Take Yannick to one of the meeting rooms. I'll see you there soon. I have to talk to Leon."

Thirty minutes later, Joseph embraced Yannick. "You are courageous, my friend, but you are in great danger. As soon as you leave the court, they are going to arrest you. They'll hang you in prison or slit your wrists and make it look like you committed suicide. We have to get you to safety before they get hold of you."

Yannick frowned. "I knew they would arrest me if I testified. I am resigned to my fate. It's time I stood up."

"Rubbish," Joseph said. "We're going to get you to safety."

"Do you have a plan, Joseph?" Lidy asked.

"Yes. The toilets are at the back of the courthouse. A fire exit leads to an alley at the rear."

"Yes, yes, I know," Lidy said.

"Yannick," Joseph said, "just after four o'clock I want you to amble toward the toilets. Don't rush. Then go out the fire exit door and voila, you're free."

"They'll be expecting it," Lidy said, shaking his head. "It'll never work. If he runs, they'll shoot him in the alley."

"No, they won't," Joseph said. "As we speak, Leon is talking to the leaders of those huge crowds who have been at the front of the court."

"The crowds who have been chanting your name?" Lidy asked.

"Yes, they're going to pack into the alley at the rear of the court-house just after four o'clock."

"I shouldn't be listening to this." Lidy grinned. "But I'm glad I am."

"Now listen carefully, Yannick, and memorize what I tell you. When you go out the rear door, go low and stay hidden. The soldiers will follow you, but the crowd will press in on them and impede their progress. Work your way to the main street, and then turn right, but remain close to the ground because the soldiers on the steps will probably join in the chase. The crowd will stretch for at least four hundred yards. You should be in the clear by the time you reach the end of it. Stay on the main street until you reach Boulevard Kianze, where you will turn left.

"As you turn the corner, you'll see a man as big as a hippo with a cigarette dangling from his mouth, standing next to a black limousine. His name is Leon, and you can trust him with your life. On reflection, you will be. The rear door will be partly open. Get in and lay on the floor. Leon will take you to a safe house where some of his friends will get you out of Kinshasa," Joseph said, sliding $5,000 across the table.

"Thank you," Yannick said. "I shouldn't need it with the money you've been sending me, but it's all gone."

"It's emergency bribe money if you get caught," Joseph said, wondering how Yannick was managing to go through $1,000 a month.

Lidy smiled. "I think it'll work," he said. "The soldiers know there are those in the seething crowds who are armed, and probably carrying Molotov cocktails. They'll never run the risk of firing on them. The last thing they'll want when they're so hopelessly outnumbered is a bloody riot. It would be different if they were here in regiment force, though. You're an enterprising young man, Joseph."

Paul Banze asked Yannick his last question just before four o'clock, saying, "I think you led the rebels and murdered those two soldiers. What do you say to that?

"You're wrong, sir. I am not a rebel and did not commit murder."

Yuma Lidy called his last witness, a United Nations investigator.

Yannick made his way out of the courtroom, and a few seconds later Joseph followed him. As he walked down the aisle, two of the soldiers next to Donatien got out of their seats. Yannick was in the corridor about twenty yards in front of Joseph and could hear heavy footsteps directly behind him. As Yannick turned the corner leading to the toilets and fire exit, Joseph swung around and said to the soldiers, "I'm sorry. Can you tell me where the toilets are?"

They paused for just an instant before one said, "Get out of our way," and started to run.

Joseph strode to the corner to see the two soldiers racing down the corridor and the fire exit door closing. As they opened the door, he saw a crowded alley and then heard sustained booing. Yannick had escaped.

An hour later, when Joseph left the courtroom with Lidy, Colonel Donatien was waiting. "I know what you did," he snarled. "I should throw you in jail."

"What?" Joseph said. "I don't understand."

"You think you're smart playing your stupid games. I could snap my fingers, and you'd be dead."

"But you won't," Joseph replied, "because if you do, foreign aid will be cut off, and the president won't like that."

"I'll have my day, and when I do, I'm going to enjoy it," Donatien said, storming off.

"Don't antagonize him," Lidy said. "He's a dangerous man."

"So am I," Joseph replied.

Chapter 31

Yannick rushed out into the alley, immediately crouched low, and started to push his way through hundreds of legs. He could hear the chasing soldiers and felt the crowd closing behind him. He reached the main street and heard shouts of "Get out of the way, get out of my way," coming from the steps of the court. Sweat poured from his forehead, and fear drove him on as he half crawled, half stumbled through the crowd.

One hand was thrust deep into his pocket protecting the $5,000 he knew was his ticket back to the village. He felt ashamed accepting it after all the money Joseph had already given him. But once he'd agreed to testify, he hadn't expected to ever see his village again, so he'd withdrawn all the money in his bank account except for fifty dollars, and shared it amongst the villagers.

The crowd started to thin, and he could no longer hear the soldiers. He stood up and paused for just a second to let the blood rush into his aching thighs. Joseph had told him not to run, but resisting that urge was impossible. He didn't know the city, and panic set in as he passed street after street without finding Boulevard Kianze. Had he missed it? Did Joseph say it was on the left, or was it right?

It seemed like he'd been running for an hour, but it was less than ten minutes when he finally saw the street sign and turned the corner. The man waiting by the black limo was gigantic. As Yannick scrambled onto the floor, he heard the door close behind him.

"You made good time, Yannick, but you shouldn't have run. You were lucky some overzealous policeman didn't stop you. You'll learn to become invisible in the next few weeks."

Yannick was still gasping, but Leon's booming voice, which echoed around the limo, was comforting. He had no idea what the big man was talking about.

"Stay down until I tell you otherwise. It'll take fifteen minutes to get to the safe house. The people there are risking their lives for you, so don't get nosy or ask prying questions. They're not gonna answer, and all you're gonna do is piss 'em off."

"I won't, but how am I going to get back to my village?"

"It's not going to be easy. The soldiers will be waiting for you at N'djili Airport."

"I'll go overland. It's only a thousand miles."

"If you do, you'll be the first." Leon laughed. "Kikwit is two hundred miles to the east. If you're not held up by storms, rebels, gangs, and fake police, you might just get there. After that, you'll face mudslides, roads with impassable craters, wild animals, more gangs, and at night, insect swarms you couldn't imagine. If you get caught in heavy rain, everything turns to mud. They haven't invented the four-wheel drive that will get you from Kinshasa to your village. When something goes wrong, which it will, no one will be able to get parts to you. If it was possible, which it's not, it would take at least seven weeks."

"I wasn't thinking of a vehicle," Yannick said. "I know the bush and can cover more than forty miles a day on foot. I'll be back in three weeks."

Leon sighed. "If you don't get killed or eaten or die of starvation. Have you thought about the rivers and streams? Many have no bridges. Have you thought about getting across them?"

"I will find a way," Yannick said stubbornly.

Leon made a quick call on his cellphone and then pulled over to the side of the road. "You can get up now," he said. "The safe house is approximately a mile away. Take the next street on the left, and then look for number thirty-five. It's a cream brick bungalow barely visible from the street. Go around to the back and knock on the door. They're expecting you."

Yannick glanced around. The area was dense with palms, ferns, and foliage. "Where are we?"

"We're on the outskirts of Kinshasa. That's all you need to know. Once you leave, forget the street name, the house number, and the location. Oh, and no matter what happens, you must never come back here," Leon said, extending his hand. "Good luck."

Yannick pushed his way through the bushes and trees growing along the side of the concealed house. He knocked lightly on the back door, and a severe-looking, thirtyish woman opened it and said, "Quick, come in. I am Belvie, and this is my husband, Rishi."

Yannick hadn't been hungry, but a delightful aroma was wafting through the house. He closed his eyes for a split second and took a deep breath.

"Hello," he said. "Thank you for helping me."

"I think our friend is hungry," Belvie said, leading the way to the kitchen.

Rishi pulled out a chair for Yannick, and his bicep danced. "You are about to eat the finest goat stew in all the Congo." He laughed. "Are you hungry?"

The aroma of goat, herbs, spices, capsicum, and onion filled the small kitchen and overwhelmed Yannick. "Starved," he said.

As they ate, Yannick could feel Belvie sizing him up. She was thin and not unattractive, but her most pronounced facial feature was an eagle-like nose, on which she balanced a pair of wire-framed spectacles. "You are lucky to have such a powerful friend," she said, her face softening a little.

Yannick was feeling better than he had all day. His stomach was full, and two glasses of red wine had relaxed him. "How come you're working for the Americans?" he asked.

"Who said we are?" Belvie snapped.

"I'm sorry," Yannick replied. "I forgot, I shouldn't have asked."

"No, you shouldn't have," Rishi agreed, "and you must never forget — or it could cost you your life. In the next few weeks, we are going to teach you skills that will help you stay alive."

"I don't understand. I thought you were going to help me get back to my village."

"No, we're not," Rishi replied. "We're going to get you out of Kinshasa to Kikwit. Then you're on your own."

"Have you ever used a computer, the Internet, or a smartphone?" Belvie asked.

Yannick smiled grimly. "There's not much call for those things when you're a thousand yards under the ground."

"Before you leave here, you'll be a smartphone expert. It's the most powerful tool we can give you. Even more essential than the deadly skills Rishi will teach you."

"Have you ever fired a rifle, a handgun, or used a knife?" Rishi asked.

"I've fired rifles and machine guns into the air. Does that count? And of course I've used a knife. I've been using one all my life."

"To kill someone?"

"I've never killed anyone in my life," Yannick said, as he watched his hosts exchange almost imperceptible glances.

"Next week I will teach you how to use a Glock with a silencer and a knife to kill a man with minimal risk," Rishi said.

"I still don't understand. Why am I learning these skills?"

"Right now, you have no chance of getting back to your village alive. By the time we finish with you, you'll have a 50 percent chance. Does that answer your question?" Belvie said.

"Yes. Thank you," Yannick said. "I appreciate what you are doing for me, but you haven't told me how I'm going to get to Kikwit."

"There are two Belgians in Kinshasa planning to drive to Lubumbashi in three weeks' time. They will never make it, but God willing, they should get to Kikwit. You will go with them. They are traveling east whereas you will be heading north-east. Whether you stay with them after Kikwit is up to you," Rishi said.

"Fools!" Belvie said. "They will die. They've just driven across Siberia, and this is their next challenge. They don't understand. Siberia is a kindergarten, compared to here."

Chapter 32

The United Nations investigator said he had found evidence of executions, gang rapes, plundering, theft, extortion, and illegal detention by the soldiers.

Banze mocked what he called the purported evidence, saying it was hearsay, and the investigator could not have known what occurred because he wasn't there.

Joseph thought Lidy had done an excellent job, and that the case against the defendants was compelling. He had no doubt the court would convict and imprison the soldiers. "The prosecution rests, Your Honors," the feisty little prosecutor said.

Joseph tapped him on the shoulder and said, "Great job."

Colonel Gizenga was the star witness for the defense, and Banze carefully took him through his rehearsed testimony. He had been in Katanga when he'd received radio communications that the rebels had taken over the New Dawn gold mine, and the staff were fleeing in fear of their lives. Being cautious and wanting to learn more, he had not reacted immediately. Instead, he'd waited for the first helicopters to land, then questioned management and staff. After confirming the rebels were in control, he had sought permission from the mine's manager to use the helicopters to ferry his men to the mine. Presenting a picture of professionalism and sincerity, Gizenga swore he had done everything by the book. Lidy continually objected to his adversary's questions, to no avail.

"Were the rebels armed?" Banze asked.

"Objection," Lidy shouted. "It hasn't been established that there were any rebels."

"Disallowed," the senior judge said scornfully. "Counsel, if you continue with your frivolous objections, this trial will never conclude. Please refrain."

A smattering of laughter went around the courtroom. The defendants, except Boucher and Botha, nudged each other and grinned. They might as well have been at a Saturday afternoon barbecue for all the concern they expressed. Convinced the court would find them guilty, Joseph couldn't understand their demeanor, but it worried him.

Gizenga then told the court that when they landed at the mine, the rebels were in control and armed with rifles and spears. He said the rebels obviously outnumbered his men, and his immediate concern was for them. To placate the rebels, he had taken a megaphone and asked them to surrender their weapons. For all allhis peaceful efforts, they had immediately opened fire. After this, a pitched battle ensued, which — thanks to the bravery of his men — had seen rebels turn tail and run to the village where they had regrouped.

"When the fighting started in the village, can you be sure it was only rebels who were hurt and killed?" Banze asked.

"Sadly, no," Gizenga said hanging his head. "I suspect some of those killed were villagers, but I want to stress they were probably aiding and abetting the rebels. I don't think any of them were innocent."

"What do you say to the prosecution witnesses who say there were no rebels?"

"That is a ridiculous proposition. The rebels killed two of my men, and many others were injured."

"Thank you, Colonel," Banze said. "Your witness, Counsel."

Lidy sprang to his feet and said, "Your men killed eighteen women and seven children aged less than ten years old. Would you like to reconsider your answer that no innocents were killed?"

"No! I saw women and children handing spears to the rebels. There were no innocents," Gizenga said, folding his meaty arms across his chest.

Lidy shook his head. "The United Nations, in its report read to the court, stated your soldiers shot many villagers in the back with machine guns. The UN's lead investigator was adamant these poor unfortunates were not rebels. I ask you again, would you like to reconsider your answer?"

Gizenga smirked. "I never said villagers didn't get killed. I said there were no innocents. The villagers who were killed lost their lives because they were hiding and helping rebels. They may not have been rebels themselves, but they helped them."

A murmur of assent went around the court.

"Were you or the army paid by the New Dawn Gold Mining Company to put down the strike at the mine?"

"I resent your question." Gizenga bristled. "Neither my men or I received any payments. I know of no strike. I do know a gang of armed rebels threatened the management and staff and took control of the mine."

"Why then did the company pay for the hire of helicopters to transport you and your soldiers? Does the army usually use private transport resources?"

Gizenga rolled his eyes and looked at the judges. "As I said, the helicopters had just arrived from the mine, where employees had used them to escape the rebels. We were waiting at the airport when they landed, and the company's management, anxious to expediently put down the rebellion, suggested we take them. Do you have a problem with that?"

"Yes, I do," Lidy replied, "and I'll return to it later. When the helicopters landed at the mine, what happened?"

"I tried to talk the rebels into surrendering their weapons, but they engaged us in a fierce firefight. After we had got on top, they panicked and ran."

"And you chased them?"

"Yes."

"You ran after them?"

"No," Gizenga said. "We were in vehicles."

"You had vehicles at the mine?" Lidy asked, scratching his head.

"No, we used the mine's trucks."

"Really? You used the mine's helicopters. You used the mine's trucks. Are you sure you weren't on the mine's payroll?"

"No, we weren't!" Gizenga shouted. "It is easy to ask your smart questions now. At the time it was a life-and-death emergency requiring instant action. It would've taken eight hours to get to the mine by road."

"Life and death?" Lidy said. "How many of the mine's managers and staff were killed?"

"None."

"I'm sorry. I didn't hear your answer, Colonel. Could you please speak up?"

"None," Gizenga hissed.

"I put it to you that it wasn't a life-and-death emergency. The management and staff were never under physical threat. There were no rebels. However, the mine's management asked you to shut down the strike, and you did, by murdering unarmed workers."

Banze was on his feet screaming, "Objection, objection, Your Honors."

"Sustained. Counsel, you are here to ask questions, not make statements," the lead judge admonished.

Lidy put his hand to his mouth to conceal a smile. "I'm sorry, Your Honors," and then said, "One last question, Colonel. You own a small office block in Lubumbashi. Who are the tenants?"

For the first time, Gizenga's face dropped, and he looked to Banze for help. "I have several tenants."

"Yes, but you have one major tenant. Who is it?"

"Objection," Banze said. "Counsel is fishing."

The senior judge paused for a long time. "I'll cut you some slack, this time, Counsel," he said to Lidy. "Don't abuse it."

"Well, Colonel, who?"

"Liberty Investments."

"And what does Liberty Investments do?"

"It's a company based in Mauritania."

"What business is it in?"

"I believe it's an investment company," Gizenga said, staring down at his feet.

"An investment company." Lidy smiled. "Do you know the New Dawn Gold Mining Company is a wholly owned subsidiary of Liberty Investments?"

"I'd heard rumors," Gizenga muttered.

"Colonel, why is the rent you receive from Liberty Investments 200 percent above the city's average?"

"I-I don't know."

"Does Liberty Investments transfer funds into an offshore bank account in your name or a company or trust controlled by you?" Lidy asked, now rapidly firing questions.

"No," Gizenga replied, but his arrogance had vanished.

"Are you on the payroll of the New Dawn Gold Mining Company or Liberty Investments? Is the rent inflated to pay for you to provide the services of the army when requested?"

"No, no."

"You do realize the penalty for perjury." Lidy smirked but, before Gizenga could reply, said, "Withdrawn."

For the next three days, Banze called the soldier defendants and painstakingly took them through their testimonies. On cross-examination, Lidy attacked furiously in a futile attempt to break them down.

First thing on Friday, the tenth and what was expected to be the last day of the trial, Banze told Marc Boucher he wouldn't be in the witness box for long and that, immediately after cross-examination, the court would hear closing arguments.

Boucher explained in great detail how the rebels had attacked the mine and disarmed the guards. Fortunately, there were two helicopters at the mine site and another two in Kilwa. Boucher said he feared for the lives of his staff and hastily made the decision to evacuate.

When he returned with the soldiers, the mine was in the hands of the rebels. Colonel Gizenga had tried megaphone diplomacy and sought their surrender. They had responded by opening fire on the soldiers, and a fierce battle had ensued.

He had not traveled with the soldiers after they had chased the rebels from the mine and had no idea what had occurred at the village.

Banze thanked Boucher for his testimony, which had taken less than thirty minutes.

Lidy was quickly on his feet, armed with the information Joseph had given him.

"Mr. Boucher, are you wanted in South Africa for the manslaughter of twenty-one miners?"

"Objection," Banze shouted. "Relevance?"

"It goes to the character of the witness, Your Honors."

"I'll allow it," the chief judge said.

"Well, Mr. Boucher?"

"Yes, but the charges were trumped up."

"Really? If they're trumped up, why have you strenuously resisted extradition proceedings? Why not go back and clear your name?"

"I intend to, just as soon as I get some time."

"Are you saying the South African police and courts have to wait until you can fit them in?" Lidy laughed. "Are you serious, Mr. Boucher? Would you insult this court in the same manner?"

Lidy's questions struck a nerve with the judges, and they craned their necks, waiting for a response.

"I am innocent of all charges," Boucher replied, "and the courts here agree. They have rejected both applications for extradition."

"Weren't those rejections made because of technicalities? The courts here have said nothing about your innocence or guilt. Isn't what you just said a lie?"

"Objection!" Banze screamed. "Badgering the witness."

"Sit down, Counsel," the lead judge said. "I want to hear this."

"I-I might ha-have got my wor-words wrong. I-I'm not a lawyer. I think that's what they told me."

"Is that so?" Lidy asked, his tone dripping with sarcasm. "Tell me how you managed your escape. You said the supposed rebels took over the mine."

"There was nothing supposed about them," Boucher said, with a touch of his earlier arrogance. "I got a call from the guards at the front gate and moved immediately."

"You ran as fast as you could?"

"You might smirk, but I had the safety of my employees to think of."

"Oh, I see. Just like your South African employees?"

"Objection. Objection!"

"Withdrawn." Lidy grinned.

For the next two hours, Lidy hammered Boucher with questions about whether the soldiers were on New Dawn's payroll and why he had provided them with the helicopters and trucks. Boucher responded by saying he had acted intuitively and, given the same situation in the future, he would act in an identical manner.

The lead judge, who was continually looking at his watch, said, "Are you nearly finished, Counsel?"

"Not even close, Your Honor," Lidy cheerfully responded.

The judge frowned. "Very well, continue."

"I put it to you there were no rebels. The soldiers did not get fired on, and you witnessed the slaughter of more than ten workers in a ditch no farther than four hundred yards from your office."

"No, no," Boucher shouted, his mustache bristling. "We were under attack. I saw no one slaughtered."

"Then how do you account for the bodies in the ditch?"

"I can't. When we returned, I was in my office with the door locked. Perhaps they were the bodies of rebels killed in the fighting, and the soldiers dragged them to a communal grave." Boucher smirked, at the cleverness of his answer.

Gizenga looked over at Boucher and gave him the thumbs up.

"Why does Liberty Investments pay a rental premium to lease offices from Colonel Gizenga?" Lidy abruptly asked, hoping to catch Boucher off guard.

"I'm glad you asked." Boucher smiled. "The colonel tries to help impoverished youth by taking them off the streets and meeting with them. He tries to point them in the right direction. Liberty Investments pays a little more rent to help out. Our owners like to contribute to the community."

Joseph grimaced. Boucher had known the question was coming and had come up with a pat answer.

"Did New Dawn or Liberty Investments transfer monies into an offshore account of Colonel Gizenga or any company or trust associated with him?"

"No," Boucher confidently responded.

It was nearly five o'clock when Lidy asked, "Mr. Boucher, who owns the shares in Liberty Investments?"

"I have no idea. It's an investment company. I don't know who owns them."

"All right, who is your boss?"

"I don't understand. I run the mine. I am solely in charge."

"Yes, but we all have bosses. You don't own the company. You're not a director. You have someone to whom you report. Who is it?"

Boucher visibly squirmed and looked over at Banze, who leaped to his feet. "Objection. Relevance," he shouted.

"Your Honors, I am trying to establish whether the witness was acting on the instructions of others."

Before the judge could respond, Boucher said, "All decisions were mine and mine alone."

"Really? Didn't you communicate with your boss and seek instructions from him? Didn't you receive an email instructing you to let the army solve the problem? I remind you, you're under oath," Lidy said, looking down at his legal pad.

Boucher's face collapsed. "I-I don't know wha-what you're talk-talking about."

"Please tell the court who your boss is," Lidy said as he picked up his legal pad and strode toward the witness box.

Boucher seemed to lose his balance and almost fell.

"The witness is exhausted, Your Honors," Banze said.

"Can you go on, Mr. Boucher? How do you feel?" the lead judge asked.

"I feel dizzy, Your Honor. I'm not well."

"Can we adjourn until Monday, Your Honor?" Banze asked.

"Yes," the lead judge responded. "I hope you recover over the weekend, Mr. Boucher."

As Joseph and Lidy walked down the steps, the crowd in front of them started chanting, "Muamba, Muamba, Muamba," as they had every day at the close of proceedings.

"You're well-liked enough to be president," Lidy said.

"I don't know why. Mr. Lidy, you shook Boucher up. He nearly had a coronary when you asked him who his boss was. He faked his collapse to get out of the witness box. He has no idea what you have on him. He's probably asking Banze right now what lies he can get away with telling. I can't wait until Monday."

"The judges gave me some latitude today. They don't like his arrogant manner, and he did say he made all decisions himself. I'd love to produce those emails."

"You can't. It'll tip whoever Thibault is off, and we may never find out who he is."

"We'll find out on Monday, Joseph, when Boucher tells us who his boss is. If he doesn't, I'll demand the court send him to prison for contempt."

Chapter 33

Just before ten o'clock on Monday morning, Joseph entered the courtroom, with Bennett and Kronk on either side of him, and searched in vain for Lidy. As they approached the prosecution table, counsel assisting Lidy rose and said, "I am sorry to inform the court that thieves broke into Mr. Lidy's house on the weekend. Unfortunately, when he disturbed them, they brutally assaulted him. I have just been informed that he has just come out of a coma but is still in a bad way. He has broken ribs, a punctured lung, and several facial fractures. He will be in the hospital for many weeks."

Gizenga was grinning at someone in the gallery. When Joseph turned around, he saw Donatien nodding his head. Boucher was in the witness box patting his mustache and didn't seem to have a care in the world.

"That is terrible," the senior judge said. "When you see Mr. Lidy, please convey our best wishes for a speedy recovery. Have the police caught the culprits?"

"Thank you, Your Honor. No, there have been no arrests made, but the police are confident there will be."

"Let's hope so, Counsel. Are you prepared to continue cross-examination?"

"Yes, Your Honor, I have no further questions for this witness."

"What?" Joseph said, quite loudly from behind the assistant prosecutor. "Of course you do. Ask him who his boss is."

Bennett tugged on Joseph's sleeve and said, "Shut up!"

The senior judge rapped his gavel on the bench. "Silence, silence in the court. Another outburst like that and I'll remove you from the court. Counsel, please confirm you have concluded your cross-examination."

"I have, Your Honor."

"Thank you, Counsel. The witness is excused," the judge said. "Are you ready to make your final submission, Counsel?"

"Yes, Your Honor."

A smiling Marc Boucher departed the witness box.

The assistant prosecutor's final argument was concise and well-put-together, but it lacked Lidy's passion and fire. Just before one o'clock, the court recessed, the senior judge saying that the court would hear the defense's final argument after lunch. Joseph tugged on the assistant's sleeve on the way out, saying, "Why didn't you continue cross-examining Boucher?"

"The information you were seeking had nothing to do with the trial. It was for your personal use. I had no further questions."

"Your boss would have. You let him down. You let me down. Why?"

As they reached the corridor, the assistant turned abruptly and stared at Joseph. "I have a wife and four young children. You should see what they did to poor Mr. Lidy. He's lucky to be alive," he said, pausing. "Or perhaps he's unlucky to be alive."

"It was Donatien?"

"You saw them laughing in court."

"I didn't realize. I'm sorry," Joseph said. "I will visit Mr. Lidy before I leave."

"I told my wife and kids about you. I had such high hopes. I said you would change things for the better. I was wrong. You are no match for them. They're having lunch now, laughing at you. All the defendants are going to be acquitted, and there's nothing you can do about it."

"Perhaps in this court, but not in The Hague or the International Criminal Court. If they're acquitted, we'll appeal."

Lidy's assistant shook his head and smiled mirthlessly. "Do you know what double jeopardy is?"

Joseph frowned, putting his hand to his chin, and then it dawned on him. "No, no, it can't be!"

"But it is. If they're acquitted, which they will be, they can't be tried for the same offenses in any other court. It was a setup right from the time the president allowed the trial to proceed. In America, criminals pay the most expensive lawyers in the hope of getting off. In the Congo, criminals pay judges, knowing they'll get off. O.J Simpson's famed lawyer, Johnnie Cochran, would have struggled to get a conviction in this court."

"So it's over?"

"I thought that it was over from the first day. However, you provided Mr. Lidy with a glimmer of hope, but that was all it was, a faint glimmer."

An hour later, the court reconvened, and Paul Banze delivered a scathing final argument saying that the prosecution had failed dismally and its star witness, Joseph Muamba, had proven to be an unmitigated liar. Just before four o'clock, Banze completed his submission. Joseph thought the court would adjourn and hand down judgment in the morning. Instead, the three judges put their heads together, and then the senior judge said they were ready to deliver judgment.

For the next hour, the senior judge summarized the case, saying the court had been able to attach little credibility to the testimony of witnesses Muamba and Kyenge. They had not been forthright, had been evasive with their answers, and in many instances had not been believable. He further said the court would make a recommendation to the Ministry of Justice to examine the evidence given by witness Muamba to ascertain whether he'd committed perjury. In direct contrast, the witnesses for the defense, particularly Colonel Gizenga and Mr. Boucher, had been transparent and open and had not sought to evade any questions. As a result, the prosecution's case was weak, and it was impossible for the court to find any of the defendants guilty.

Just after 5:00 p.m. the senior judge asked the defendants to stand one at a time while he found them not guilty. The New Dawn Gold Mining Company had not been a defendant, but the judge, in a remarkable verdict, found it, its management, and its employees not guilty.

Joseph scratched his head. Charges had not been laid against the New Dawn Gold Mining Company, but it had been acquitted. Lidy's assistant was right. It had been a setup from the start. Worse, now they'd been acquitted and couldn't be tried again.

Lidy's assistant turned around and said, "I'm sorry. It is the way of the Congo."

"I'm sick of hearing that," Joseph replied. "Are you sure they can't be retried in The Hague?"

"Positive. Face it. They are far too smart for you. Go back to America. For all your education, wealth, and fame, you have not been able to achieve anything."

"There must be something we can do."

"You could bring a civil action against the military and New Dawn, but the result would be the same. The court would follow the decision made today," the assistant said, and then smiled.

"You've thought of something," Joseph said.

"Yes. If you could find out where the real owners reside or where the management emanated, you might be able to bring an action in that jurisdiction, without the court relying on today's decision. It's a long shot, though."

Gizenga and Donatien were in the corridor surrounded by a group of laughing soldiers when Joseph left the courtroom. Gizenga smiled, but his eyes were cold, and he ran his index finger across his throat. Standing conspicuously at the entrance were Bennett and Kronk.

The crowd was still chanting as Joseph came down the steps, but the enthusiasm and rhythm of the previous evenings had evaporated. Leon was holding the door of the limo open, and as Joseph got in, he said, "Take me to the hospital, please. I want to see Mr. Lidy."

Bennett climbed in the backseat next to Kronk. "We need to fly out tonight."

"We can wait until the morning," Joseph replied. "There's no rush."

"No rush? You don't have the luxury of time. Didn't you hear what the judge said about perjury charges? The morning might be too late."

"If only Mr. Lidy had finished cross-examining Boucher on Friday. Then I'd know who owns the mine and who's pulling the strings," Joseph said.

Kronk looked over at Bennett and grinned before saying, "Boucher's hotel is on the way to the airport. If we stop by on the way, we can have your answer in ten minutes, can't we, Chuck?"

"More like five."

"No," Joseph said. "I'll be as bad as they are if I employ those tactics. What are you going to do? Threaten to pull his fingernails out with pliers?"

"Jesus!" Kronk exclaimed. "The last time you were here, you killed two soldiers and a general. Now you're getting all sanctimonious. Do you want to know who owns the mine?"

"Yes, but not that way."

Bennett's cellphone buzzed, and after he'd finished the call, he said, "That was our embassy. There's no time to go to the hospital. The Congolese are preparing a warrant now. They'll arrest you when they serve it. What do you have at the hotel?"

"Just clothes."

"You've got your passport, laptop, and cellphone with you now?"

"Yes."

"Head to the airport, Leon, and don't waste a minute."

"Did you tell anyone when we were leaving, Joseph?" Kronk asked.

"I told Lidy's assistant that it'd be first thing in the morning."

"You might've just saved yourself. They're probably waiting at the hotel and, with luck, won't have notified customs."

"I'm a U.S. citizen," Joseph said. "They wouldn't dare hold me."

"And you're an Olympic gold medalist too," Bennett said. "It means diddly squat here. I won't be happy until we're out of the DRC's airspace. Fortunately, that'll only take ten minutes. Come on, Leon, faster."

Chapter 34

Those who can afford the luxury of private jets do not stand in long lines waiting to have their passports stamped. A young, fawning customs official ushered Joseph and his two de facto bodyguards into a private room. The man asked Joseph for his autograph, saying he'd watched him on television and prayed he would be victorious before the start of the fifteen hundred. Joseph chatted amicably while Bennett nudged him in the back of his leg.

As they walked across the tarmac, Kronk said, "One phone call and we're screwed, and here you are carrying on like you'd just found a long-lost friend."

The flight attendant was at the top of the stairs and said, "We're cleared for takeoff as you instructed, Mr. Bennett. Please hurry or we'll lose our slot."

The plane was already moving as the door shut behind them. "Seatbelts, gentlemen," the flight attendant said. As they taxied onto the runway, they heard the thrust of the engines, but a few seconds later they were idling.

Bennett jumped out of his seat and ran to the cockpit. "What's wrong?" he demanded of the captain.

"They cleared us for takeoff, but they've just told us to hold."

Bennett couldn't see any planes on the runway in front of them, and when he scanned the sky, he couldn't see any circling or approaching to land. He looked at the terminal and saw two army vehicles and an officer wildly waving his hands. "Take off! Take off now!" he shouted, as the first of the vehicles sped toward them.

"I can't. I don't have clearance."

"Captain, I'm not asking. I'm telling. Now get this fucking thing in the air."

"I-I – "

"See that Jeep?" Bennett yelled. "If it blocks our runway, you won't get out of Kinshasa for a year. If you want to see your family again, move it now."

The co-pilot stared out the window at the speeding Jeep and said, "I think he's right."

"I'm going to lose my license over this," the captain said, as the engines roared back to life.

The Jeep drew level. Bennett looked down to see a furious Colonel Donatien waving his fist. Bennett grinned and gave him the finger as the jet accelerated to over a hundred miles an hour.

"Did you see Donatien and his gang?" Bennett said, sitting down next to Kronk and opposite Joseph. "We were lucky to get out. I told you not to waste time chatting and signing autographs."

"I didn't think … I didn't think they'd go that far," Joseph said. "I didn't do anything wrong."

"Other than calling the president a liar in court." Kronk grinned.

"I told the truth."

"Thank Christ it's over and we're in the clear," Bennett said, as the jet passed over the Congo River and out of the DRC's airspace. "I need a Jim Beam."

"It's not over," Joseph said, opening his laptop.

Back at the palace, the president was beside himself with rage. "He is on a plane on the way back to the U.S. laughing at me!" he screamed. "You said he wouldn't get out of the country, Colonel."

"He-he wasn't meant t-to go until th-the morning, Mr. President," Donatien replied.

"You babbling idiot. This should have been a wake-up call to the Americans that we won't put up with their sly ways. You should have arrested him straight after the trial, thrown him in prison, and then worried about the warrant."

Donatien wanted to say, *You were there when we discussed the plan to issue a warrant and arrest Muamba*, but dared not. "I'm sorry, Mr. President."

"We got to the airport in time," Gizenga said, "and the pilot took off without clearance."

President Bodho picked up a vase and hurled it at Gizenga. He ducked, and it smashed into the wall. "If you'd gotten there in time, he'd be in prison. And you want to take Zamenka's job? You're not a shadow of him. Neither of you are!"

"Do you want to commence extradition proceedings?" Donatien asked.

Bodho groaned. "The people love him. The crowds at the airport would be enormous. And you want to haul him down the steps of a plane shackled in handcuffs. We'd face massive riots. You are stupid. If you'd done what you were supposed to do, he'd be locked up, and we'd be planning his accidental death. Instead, I'll be listening to those infernal drums again tonight."

"Yes, Mr. President."

"Have you at least managed to find the rebel leader?"

"He's disappeared," Gizenga said. "There's no sign of him."

"He's never been in Kinshasa before. He's an ignorant villager. He knows no one. Yet, he outsmarted you two. Have you frozen his bank account in Kalemie, and do you have someone watching the bank?"

"Yes, Mr. President. I doubt he'll get to Kalemie, but if he does and tries to withdraw any money, we'll have him," Donatien said.

"That's what you said when he was in court, and yet he slipped through your fingers, you fool. Get out of my sight before I do something I regret."

As the two colonels walked down the corridor, Donatien said, "Lidy — the prosecutor — died."

"Thank God we got something right," Gizenga replied.

During the twenty-nine-hour flight to LA, Joseph skimmed thousands of Boucher's emails, looking for anything that would identify Thibault. One email from Thibault said, "You know better than to use my name. Delete the email, send it to your recycle bin and empty. Advise me when it is done." It confirmed what Joseph already knew: Thibault was paranoid about keeping his identity hidden.

When Lidy had cross-examined Boucher about whom he reported to, he had shaken the mine manager, and he had done everything not to answer. That same night, Lidy had been savagely assaulted — in the previous nine days of the trial, he had asked some penetrating questions, none of which had resulted in his being beaten up.

It was 10:00 a.m. when the plane touched down in Los Angeles. Frank and Michelle were waiting. Michelle hugged and kissed Joseph, then told him he was never going back to that terrible place.

"He can't," Frank said. "He's a wanted man."

"Word travels fast," Joseph said. "Where are Maya and Moise?"

"College and school," Michelle said. "They wanted to come, but they now have their routines, and I didn't want to interrupt them."

"What she means," Frank said, "is she wanted to chew your ear off in private and get you to agree never to set foot in the Congo again."

"There's nothing you can do," Michelle chipped in, "even if you could go back. Don't you understand there's nothing you can change? Do you think they're all going to become honest overnight because of you? If you hadn't had those State Department bodyguards with you, you'd be in Kinshasa sitting in a dirty jail."

"That's if he was lucky," Frank said. "It's more likely he'd be dead."

"What is this?" Joseph laughed. "Bad cop and worse cop? I know I can't go back. It's over."

"You forget, we know you, Joseph," Michelle said. "You think you're bulletproof. You're not."

"Mom, I promise you I won't go back so long as there is a warrant out for my arrest. Are you happy with that?"

"I'd rather you'd said never, but yes, I'm pleased. Jack Costigan's adamant that they'll never lift the warrant and might even apply to extradite you. He told us not to worry. No court in the U.S. would sanction your extradition," Michelle said.

"Let's go home," Joseph said. "How's Moise?"

"Energetic." Frank laughed. "He wants to throw the football every night. I can't keep up with him. Maya's got a good arm and has been helping out, but I'm glad you're back. Oh, I nearly forgot. George Faraday's been driving me up the wall. He told me he wants to see you the minute you're back in the office."

"Phooey," Michelle said. "George is so full of self-importance."

"He's a good friend," Frank said, "and don't forget, if it weren't for him, Joseph wouldn't be our son. He deserves our respect."

"Dad, I'll call him and set up a meeting. Are you going to attend?"

"No, he wants to see you by yourself."

Joseph caught up on a few hours' sleep and picked Moise up from school in the afternoon. The little boy sprinted out of the gate and leaped into Joseph's arms.

"You're not going away anymore, are you?" he asked.

"No, I'm back to stay."

"Good. Can we throw the football when we get home?"

Joseph laughed. "Is that the only reason you missed me?"

Moise looked down at his feet. "I thought those evil men might put you in jail. I worried you weren't going to come back."

"Moise, you mustn't ever worry about me. I can look after myself. Let's go home and see if your throwing has improved."

That night over dinner, there was a lot of laughing and rejoicing. The family was glad Joseph wasn't going back to the Congo, but Maya was pensive. It was just after 2:00 a.m. when she crept into his bedroom expecting him to be sound asleep. He wasn't. Instead, he was sitting behind his desk, reading emails and making notes on a legal pad. He didn't get up, and Maya rested her hands on his shoulders. "I knew you wouldn't give up," she said.

"I can't, the answers I'm looking for are somewhere in these emails. I was skimming them, but now I'm reading all of them. I'm making notes on the amounts transferred, the recipients, and the names of the tax haven banks. Fifty million was transferred to an account in the Bahamas just after the permit for New Dawn was granted."

"You told everyone you weren't going back. Your parents are going to be terribly disappointed."

"I'm not going back so long as that warrant's hanging over my head, but I'm certain Thibault doesn't reside in the Congo. I'm guessing he lives in France or Belgium. He gave instructions to Boucher to get out of the mine and call in the army. If I can find him, I might be able to have him charged with murder in his home country. If I can't, at least I'll be able to expose him for bribery, tax evasion, money laundering, and profiting from the proceeds of blood gold."

"But you are going back one day?"

"Yes, it is my calling."

Maya laughed. "Have you finally worked out what it is?"

"Yes."

"Tell me."

"Not yet," Joseph said, standing up and kissing her. "I missed you."

"And me, you," she whispered, pulling back the bed covers and climbing in. "Come here, and show me how much you missed me."

Chapter 35

Three weeks after he had arrived at the safe house, Yannick was ready to start his journey back to the village. Belvie and Rishi had filled a large backpack with rations, bottled water, a solar phone charger, a ten-inch razor-sharp knife, bandages, antiseptic, matches, ammunition, and two silencers. He was wearing a shoulder holster under his shirt and packing a Glock. In the front pocket of his jeans was what Belvie called his most important item — a smartphone. He hugged her tightly, thanking her for all she had done. Rishi was still giving him lessons. "Remember, the silencer will make you invisible. No one will see the flash, but as you know, it will not completely muffle the sound. Only use the gun as a last resort. It's safer to use the knife."

Belvie added, "And when something appears on the Internet that shouldn't, or when you are suspicious, go with your gut. There are some devious people on the Net."

"You have both been so kind. Thank you."

It was just after five o'clock when they heard the vehicle pull up. Belvie said, "That's your ride. We won't come out. Good luck."

Yannick gave her one last hug and shook Rishi's hand. "Goodbye, and thanks again."

He pushed through the foliage along the side of the house and saw an army brown four-wheel-drive Toyota waiting for him. He climbed into the back and was shocked to see a smiling young woman sitting in the front passenger's seat. She said something in a guttural language he had never heard before. Then her partner smiled and said something in the same harsh tone. Yannick smiled back and spoke a few words in French-Swahili. When there was no reaction, he tried Lingala without success, then finally the few words of French he knew. The woman responded, but Yannick had no idea what she was saying. He held his hands out, palms up, and shrugged as the two Belgians burst out laughing.

The paved road was better than what Yannick had expected. When he looked at the speedometer, they were doing fifty miles an hour. At that rate, they would be in Kikwit in four hours. He was checking the weather on the Internet when he felt the vehicle noticeably slow. When he looked up, half a dozen men were blocking the road at an intersection approximately three hundred yards away. As the driver eased off the accelerator, Yannick shouted, "Faster, faster," and gesticulated wildly with his hands.

The Toyota surged again, but when it was fifty yards from the men, the driver started braking. "Faster!" Yannick screamed, gripping his shoulder.

At the last minute the men jumped out of the way. When Yannick looked back, they were shaking their fists furiously. He looked at the woman, grinned, and formed a circle with his thumb and forefinger, but she looked scared. Her face said, *We have a lunatic in the back seat.*

The pavement soon ran out and was replaced by a sandy dirt road riddled with potholes and ruts. They could travel no faster than twenty miles an hour. There were virtually no other vehicles on the road, and Yannick became sleepy. He closed one eye, before dropping off to sleep for two hours. Again he was alerted by the Toyota slowing. He looked up to see a large beam supported by two flimsy trestles blocking the road. Yannick wanted to crash through but knew there was no point shouting at the Belgians.

As they came to a complete stop, he noticed three motorcycles and was glad he hadn't shouted. He opened the backpack and slowly slid the knife out, before wrapping his hand around the butt of the Glock under his shirt. Five men were manning the blockade. Their leader sauntered over, saying in Lingala that he was a government tax collector, and the toll was $100. In any language, there were three clear words: *one hundred dollars.*

The driver was looking for his wallet when Yannick rolled down his window and demanded to see some identification. Two other men joined their leader and stared menacingly at Yannick. He had never been confident, but the past three weeks had transformed him. He felt no fear.

The leader smiled and said he'd left his identification at home but he was most definitely a tax collector, and unless he got paid, the Toyota wouldn't be moving.

Again the driver went to pay, and again Yannick seized his arm, which seemed to infuriate the men.

Yannick beckoned the leader over, and the man put his head through the window. "We know you are not a tax collector. Please let us pass. We mean you no harm."

Infuriated, the man shouted, "You are not supposed to be on this road. Where is your permit?"

In one smooth movement, Yannick rested the barrel of the Glock on the man's forehead and said, "Here it is. Is it in order?"

The arrogance in the men's eyes turned to fear as Yannick waved the gun around. "Back away," he said, as he pushed the door open and herded them into a compact group. Taking his knife, he walked over to the motorcycles. Soon the sound of six slashed tires hissing in unison filled the air.

"You'll pay for this," the leader said with false bravado.

Yannick pointed the Glock directly at his head and shouted, "Move the beam."

As soon as they were moving again, the Belgians fixed their gaze on the road, and didn't utter a word for miles. It was apparent they were more terrified of their passenger than the gangs who were trying to rob them.

There were two more attempts to collect tax before they arrived on the outskirts of Kikwit. In each instance, Yannick was able to talk the supposed tax collectors out of their folly without having to produce Mr. Glock, for which he was grateful. The two-hundred-mile trip to the city with a population of nearly four hundred thousand had taken just over nine hours.

Yannick was happy to sleep in the vehicle, but the Belgians had their smartphones out, and he knew they were looking for a hotel. As he watched them, his phone rang, and a distinctly familiar voice said, "Where are you?"

"Hello, Leon. We're in Kikwit looking for somewhere to stay."

"Listen to me. Joseph has chartered a small plane to fly you to Kalemie. You're leaving at dawn, and you'll be in Kalemie by eight o'clock. With luck, you'll be back in your village by nightfall. The pilot's staying in the Kikwit Airport Hotel. I want you to go there. He's in room number 324 and has the key to the adjoining room. Are you close to the airport?"

"I could've made it back to my village on foot," Yannick defiantly said. "I'm less than two miles from the airport."

"How do you know?"

"I'm looking at Google Maps."

"Oh my God," Leon roared. "They said they were going to teach you how to use a smartphone. I don't believe it."

"What are you going to do about the Belgians?"

"Nothing, Yannick. They're not my responsibility. They're going to Lubumbashi. Can they hear you?"

"Yes, but I can't understand them, and they can't understand me. If you don't help them, they'll be dead within the week. I don't think they could get back to Kinshasa safely without me."

There was a long pause before Leon said, "Let me talk to them."

Yannick passed his phone to the woman and then watched as she shook her head, patently disagreeing with what Leon was saying. The man then shouted into the phone in support of his partner. When he had finished, he handed the phone back to Yannick, and Leon said, "They're more scared of you than any of the gangs. You were told only to use the gun as a last resort. What were you thinking? You terrified them. I told them what you said. They say you're overreacting. They're going to push on."

Yannick shook his head and sighed. "What should I do?"

"Leave them now. They'll be glad to see the back of you, and it's only a short walk to the hotel."

Chapter 36

Joseph called George Faraday to say he would be in the office the following morning. The entrepreneur testily said he would be waiting for him.

Faraday looked like he was going to explode. As he sat down opposite Joseph, he said, "What did you think you were doing?"

"Telling the truth," Joseph replied.

"What, by calling their president a liar? You jeopardized every one of those deals we did. How would you have felt if the Chinese had ended up with Prescott's uranium project? Prescott and the other companies forked out hundreds of millions of dollars. You put their plans at risk. I had to call in every favor owed to me in order to salvage them."

"None of them have started construction," Joseph said. "The monies they paid were bribes. They did nothing to help the Congolese."

"You're bloody naïve. Pure. So wet behind the ears. Don't you understand how much your firm made while we were in the Congo? Didn't your father tell you?"

"George, I didn't do anything wrong. All I did was tell the truth."

"You didn't have to go. The prosecution didn't subpoena you. You went of your own volition."

"I don't like murderers not paying for their crimes!"

"Jesus, as if you can talk about murderers."

"I killed in self-defense. There's a big difference."

"You don't understand anything. There have been millions killed in the Congo over the past twenty years. It's the way things are, and there's nothing you can do to stop it."

"I might surprise you one day," Joseph said and smiled. "Have you managed to recall who you sold the New Dawn gold mine to?"

Faraday rolled his eyes and slowly shook his head. "What is it with you? I told you I didn't remember. If you know what's good for you, you'll back off. Capel & Lambert have a lot of clients who tread on the edge of the law. You keep poking and prodding, you might unearth some skeletons your father and his partners would prefer not to know about."

"So you do remember! You're just not telling. That's okay. I'll find out who it was, and when I do, I'll also know why you're so anxious to keep it secret."

"We should have left you to rot in the jungle. You're gonna get yourself killed. If you're not worried about yourself, think about your parents. They've given you everything — love, a good home, and a great life. You've wanted for nothing," Faraday said, standing up abruptly. "Oh, and think about Maya's brother and sister."

"Are you threatening me?"

"I'm telling you to grow up. The people you're antagonizing are some of the world's most powerful. You think your parents are wealthy and influential. They're not," Faraday said, as he paused at the door. "There's nothing you can change in the Congo, and if you try, all you'll do is hurt those you love."

Two days later, the devastating news of Yuma Lidy's death reached Joseph. He had been a courageous, good man, and courageous good men in the Congo were rare.

After the heated meeting with Faraday, life returned to normal for Joseph, even though he continued to use every spare hour to hunt through Boucher's emails. His relationship with Maya continued to grow, but they were both sick of creeping around at nights. When they discussed moving into an apartment, they always came up with the same problems. "How will we look after Moise?" Maya asked. "I'm at college, and you have your work."

"We'll do what other people do," Joseph replied. "We'll get him looked after."

"He'll miss your parents. There is nothing Michelle won't do for him, and Frank comes home early especially to throw the football with him. While you were away, he was in a sprint race at school, and Frank took the afternoon off to watch him."

"I know. He won." Joseph smiled.

"And he's got the swimming pool, and that big backyard to play in. He's not going to have those facilities in an apartment."

"We could lease a house."

"Yes, but we can't lease your mom and dad. I think it'll break their hearts if we go. Let's stay. They know what's going on with us. It's nothing to be ashamed of."

"I'll talk to Dad," Joseph said. "He'll think of something."

When Yannick's flight landed in Kalemie, he immediately emailed Leon and asked him to forward the email to Joseph. An hour later he received an email from Joseph saying, "I can't believe it, my friend. Welcome to the twenty-first century. You're in my address book. Be careful. Good luck."

Yannick was greeted as an all-conquering hero on his return to the village, but he knew he could not stay there. He was a wanted man — a rebel leader, according to the army — and if he stayed, he would put the villagers in danger. But he had rationalized on the plane that if he was going to die for being a rebel, he might as well perform the part. With $5,000 to buy food and guns, he and a small group of young, similar-minded villagers could live in the jungle and wreak havoc on the mines for years.

Within three months, his band of freedom fighters had grown to fifty, and he realized that after buying weapons and ammunition, $5,000 didn't go far. Fortunately, Joseph had continued making transfers. When Yannick checked on the Internet, the balance in his account was slightly more than $3,000. One small trader, who had been providing groceries, had refused to continue supplying without a $500 payment. When Yannick punched in his details and hit pay, nothing happened. After confirming the trader's banking details, Yannick tried again, without success. He smiled as he recalled Belvie's last message: "When you are suspicious, go with your gut."

The following morning before dawn broke, Yannick, nine of his best men, and a sixteen-year-old boy who had learned to become a whiz on the Internet in only a few days, set off in an old truck for the one-hundred-fifty-mile drive to the bank in Kalemie. They arrived on the outskirts of the city just after noon, parked in dense foliage, and again went over their plan. Two of the men remained with the truck, while the others broke into groups of three and headed for the bank. One had been a powder monkey at the mine and carried a small suitcase packed with explosives. Yannick hoped he wouldn't have to use them.

Five minutes before closing time, the young boy went to the ATM at the front of the bank and attempted to withdraw 100,000 Congolese francs, the equivalent of $100, from Yannick's account. Nothing happened, and when he tried again, four soldiers came out of the front door of the bank and seized him. Yannick raised his hand to caution the others, wanting to make sure there were no more soldiers. They started to march the boy into the bank, and as they reached the front doors, Yannick gave the signal. Such was the soldiers' excitement, they had been oblivious to anyone else, and were shocked to feel the cold steel of handguns thrust into their ribs. "Drop your weapons," Yannick said, "and you won't get hurt."

Another of Yannick's men locked the doors of the bank and pulled down the drapes. Three others waved their handguns around and shouted at the customers and staff to get on the floor. The boy collected their cellphones, turned them off, and piled them in the middle of the floor.

Yannick quickly took control. "Find two bags or satchels for the guns and phones," he shouted to one of his men. Then he demanded to see the manager. "I am not here to steal," he said. "All I want is what is in my account. It was transferred in U.S. dollars, and that is what I want."

"We-we don't hav-have any U.S. dollars," the trembling little man replied.

Yannick slowly removed the Glock from his shoulder holster and gently tapped the barrel into his palm, never taking his eyes off the manager. "Are you sure?" he asked.

The manager's eyes were watering, and without warning he vomited all over the floor.

Yannick gave him thirty seconds to recover, then said, "No more messing around. Get my money."

The manager went to one of the tellers' cages with Yannick close behind and counted out $3,050 in U.S. bills. "Thank you. Show me the vault."

The size of the enormous vault brought a smile to Yannick's face. His men herded the soldiers, customers, and staff into it. "There's not enough air in here for us to survive until morning," the manager whined.

"I don't believe you," Yannick said, as his men closed the heavy door.

One of the men said, "We should clean out the tellers' cages. We'll never get another opportunity like this."

"No," Yannick said, "we got what we came for. We'll leave in twos at one-minute intervals. Whatever you do, don't run. Act naturally. I'll go last. Make sure the truck is running and ready to go by the time I get back."

As Yannick nonchalantly walked down the main street, he emailed Joseph and asked him to stop transferring funds. When he reached the truck, he ordered his men to get rid of the bags and phones in the foliage. On the trip back to his jungle headquarters, he asked himself, not for the first time, whether he should have stolen from the bank. Running, feeding, and funding an ever growing army was not an easy task. He told himself he had done the right thing. He was not going to steal money from the banks or their customers.

Then out of the blue, a thought came to him, and he smiled. His money problems were over, and he'd never need to bother Joseph again. For the next two weeks, he meticulously planned an operation that would enable him to feed, clothe, and arm his freedom fighters.

Fifty miles south of the New Dawn gold mine in a heavily treed area, a sharp bend swung hard left on the gravel road leading to Lubumbashi. Just after five o'clock on Friday morning, Yannick and twenty-five of his heavily armed freedom fighters crammed into two old trucks and converged on the area. After hiding the vehicles, five men manning shovels started digging around the roots of a mukula tree approximately sixty feet tall. Two men carrying long, thick ropes scaled it. After they had wrapped the ropes securely around the upper trunk, they dropped them to the ground. An hour later, with some strenuous pulling on the ropes, the tree came crashing down across the road. Yannick checked the tree's base and was pleased to see the root system had concealed any sign of the digging. After carefully checking the area, he positioned his men, ensuring there was no possibility of them being hit by crossfire, and then called for complete silence. Having spent weeks planning the attack, he was nervous but confident. He silently prayed another vehicle would not be using the road and foil his plan.

He heard the small convoy when it was still a mile away and fought off another bout of nerves. A Jeep carrying an officer and three soldiers sped around the bend, coming to an abrupt halt at the sight of the tree. Immediately following was a compact black truck bearing the New Dawn Gold Mining Company signage. Bringing up the rear was another Jeep and four more soldiers. The officer leaped out onto the road and looked nervously around him before inspecting the base of the tree. "Uprooted," he shouted, "get the chainsaws."

The soldiers visibly relaxed. Some put their machine guns on the ground, another rolled a cigarette, and two others took chainsaws from the back of the truck. Finally, the two men in the truck got out, and as they did, Yannick stood up and shouted, "Drop your weapons and you'll come to no harm."

As the soldiers looked up, they saw more than twenty guns pointing directly at them. One soldier moved to pick up his machine gun, and Yannick screamed, "Don't do it, or you're dead."

"What do you want?" the officer demanded.

Yannick laughed. "I thought it would be obvious. Tell your men to take their clothes off. Everything! You do the same."

"No," the officer shouted.

Yannick nodded to the man next to him and a bullet smacked into the ground no further than six inches from the officer's feet. "No more talking. Now," he said.

"You will die for this," the officer snarled, removing his shirt.

"Tie them up," Yannick said, "hands behind their backs and ankles. Let's see what we've got."

One of the men took the keys out of the truck ignition and opened the rear doors to reveal a heavy safe with two keyholes in the door. "Where are the keys?" Yannick asked the officer.

"You can't open it," he responded. "I have one key, and the other is at the airport. The have to be simultaneously inserted. You'll never get it open without the second key."

Yannick called his powder monkey over and showed him the safe. Another of his men moved the rear Jeep out of the way, and the powder monkey and one of his helpers reversed the truck a hundred yards. Five minutes later an almighty explosion tore the truck apart. Yannick ran down the gravel road to see parts of the safe everywhere, and seven large ingots.

"Sorry," the powder monkey said, "I might have used a little too much explosive."

"You did great." Yannick grinned. "Bring the Jeep up and load these in the back. We have to get out of here."

He walked back to his men and told them to bundle up the soldiers' clothes and their weapons.

Yannick gave his smartphone to his sixteen-year-old assistant. "Get some photos of them before we leave," he said.

"You can't leave us tied up without clothes or guns," the officer whined.

"If you reversed our roles, you would've killed us," Yannick said, cutting the bindings from the officer's hands. "We're going to leave you a Jeep, a chainsaw, and a pistol. You'll be all right."

"You'll pay for this."

"Shut up and watch," Yannick said, as he hurled the pistol deep into the bush, followed by the keys to the Jeep. "That should keep you busy. If you want to find me, I'll be in the jungle, but if you come after me, you'll die."

Two days later, *The Congo Daily Times* reported the biggest robbery in the country's history. Rebels had stolen gold ingots valued at more than $5 million from the New Dawn Gold Mining Company while the precious metal was being transported to the airport. Soldiers guarding the gold arrived in Lubumbashi, naked, weaponless, and humiliated. Photographs of the soldiers, naked and bound, appeared next to the article. Yannick Kyenge was declared public enemy number one. The government offered a reward of 100 million Congolese francs ($100,000) for information leading to his apprehension, dead or alive.

Yannick knew the army would send in a huge contingent of soldiers to recover the gold, and kill him and his freedom fighters. On his return to the village, he immediately evacuated the villagers deep into the jungle, a place the soldiers lived in mortal fear of, and would never venture. For a week they searched the outskirts of the jungle and then, in frustration, set the village on fire. Yannick watched from afar, knowing he could replace the huts and that for once, the soldiers would go back to Kinshasa without having raped or murdered any villagers.

Chapter 37

Joseph couldn't catch a break and was becoming increasingly frustrated. He had read every email in Boucher's inbox, plus the sent and deleted items folders, over an eight-year period, but he still didn't know who Thibault was. The emails showed that the New Dawn Gold Mining Company was incredibly profitable, paid hardly any income tax, and made sizeable transfers to tax haven bank accounts of senior military personnel and politicians. By far the largest transfers were made to a numbered account in the Virgin Islands. Joseph knew it had to be Thibault's account.

As the first anniversary of his escape from Kinshasa approached, Joseph despaired of ever finding out who the real owners of the New Dawn Gold Mining Company were. He was sure the mysterious calling he had experienced was inextricably linked to the mine, and each night he prayed the day would come when the answers he was desperately seeking revealed themselves.

He was skimming the financial news on his iPad one morning before leaving for the office and pondered whether that day had finally come. An article in *The Wall Street Journal* had a photo of Marc Boucher, baton under his arm, surrounded by delegates at a Mining in Africa Conference in London. Boucher was the keynote speaker, and the journalist spoke glowingly of his thirty-year mining career in the "Dark Continent." Joseph had an overwhelming urge to jump on a plane.

The following morning another article — far more exciting — appeared in *The Wall Street Journal*. The South Africans had discovered Boucher was in London and had applied to have him extradited. In an astonishing turn of events, he had fled to the Embassy of the Democratic Republic of the Congo in London and sought asylum.

Joseph was intrigued by what was occurring in London and, knowing

Jack Costigan would know precisely what was going on, called him. The State Department man was gruff. "You've got some nerve calling me after what you got up to in the Congo. If the Chinese had shafted us on that uranium deal, I would've lost my job. Where do you get off calling their president a liar?"

"Jesus, Jack, that's old news. We didn't lose any deals. Besides, without me, you never would've gotten them in the first place."

"So you say. What do you want? I'm a busy man."

"Have you been following the Marc Boucher saga in London?"

"Ah, you want to know what's going on. Are you going to storm the embassy because he weaseled his way out of answering the prosecutor's questions? That horse has bolted. It's over. There's nothing you can do. Forget about it, and get on with your life."

"I'm just curious," Joseph said. "Will he have to remain permanently in the embassy? Virtually under house arrest?"

Costigan laughed. "You don't know anything about diplomacy, do you? The Brits invented it. Put yourself in their shoes. The South Africans need their capital, and they export huge volumes of everything to the U.K. Whereas the Brits, like the rest of the world, are desperate for a piece of the action in the Congo. What do you think they're going to do?"

"But the extradition application is to the British courts. There's nothing the diplomats can do."

"You have a lot to learn. Here's what's going to happen. The courts will say they don't have jurisdiction and dismiss the application. The diplomats will go back to the South Africans, who they've just screwed, and tell them how hard they tried, and the court's decision stinks. Then they'll tell the Congolese it was their backroom maneuverings that resulted in the court throwing the application out."

"That's terrible. I can't believe it."

"Diplomacy: the art of simultaneously deceiving your wife and your girlfriend with the utmost sincerity." Costigan raucously laughed.

"So you're saying Boucher will be free?"

"Within seventy-two hours. Thanks for the laugh, Joseph, but I have pressing matters that need my attention. Goodbye."

Yes, and I can be in London in twelve hours. "Thanks, Jack."

As Joseph put the phone down and pondered what he should do, his father came into his office and sat down. "You look perplexed, Son. Is there anything I can do to help?"

Joseph quickly related what had occurred with Boucher.

"You said he wouldn't answer questions in court. What makes you think he's going to talk to you in London?"

"I-I don't know. I just have this gut feeling I should go."

"You've been on this quest for over a year, and I don't want to criticize you, but you've neglected Maya and Moise. You've even drifted away from your mother and me. Some of my partners say your work's falling behind. It's making it difficult for me. I'm supposed to retire when I turn seventy, but I'm resisting because I'm worried about you. Don't you think it's time you gave up? Even if you find out who's behind New Dawn, what can you do?"

Should I tell him I'm regularly exchanging lengthy emails with Yannick? "I won't know that until I find out. It's a chicken-and-egg situation. However, I sense it's big and will alter the lives of tens of thousands in the Congo."

"Your calling?"

"Yes."

"You've been over thousands of emails, and you've spent more than two weeks in court. Ron's pored over the corporate structure and has come up with nothing. I've seen some incredibly smart people try to conceal things, but they always make at least one mistake that brings them down. Think of Nixon, Clinton, and even Bernie Madoff. I'm sorry, but my gut feeling says despite all your hard work, you've missed something. You've probably seen something you didn't think was important and passed over it.

"I suspect you're not going to get anywhere in London, and you'd be better off reviewing what you've already done. I'm betting there's a clue you've overlooked, but if you can't find it within a month, it's time to move on — calling or no calling."

"That sounds like an ultimatum."

Frank reached out and put his hand on Joseph's forearm. "I love you, Son. I would never threaten you with an ultimatum. I'm worried you've become obsessed. You haven't trained or competed since Beijing. You have a beautiful young woman who loves you and a little boy who adores you, yet you're cutting them out of your life. And the partners are more than unhappy — they're pissed off."

"I'm sorry, Dad. I am going to go to London. I'm not going to give up, but when I return, I'll ease up. I didn't realize I was neglecting the people I love."

Each of the seven 25-pound ingots stolen from New Dawn was worth $750,000. However, Yannick soon found their bulk and their stamping were major drawbacks. Seeking payment in cash, in U.S. dollars, didn't help, and the black market dealers didn't have the funds or currency to consummate a deal. Eventually, an Indian dealer in Kalemie offered to buy two of the ingots for a total of $600,000. Yannick had no choice but to accept.

Realizing he would need a permanent base, Yannick took his ever growing army deep into the jungle. Fortunately, weapons were not as difficult to buy as large ingots were to sell. He quickly added Russian-made, hand-held rocket launchers to his arsenal.

More importantly, he purchased a set of one ounce to one pound graphite molds, propane torches, and gold smelting pots.

Chapter 38

Like most consumed people, Joseph hadn't realized how over-whelming his obsession had become until the conversation with his father. What Frank said had been fair, and Joseph resolved to continue his investigation only after Moise and Maya were asleep.

Frank and Michelle, horrified by the thought that the three of them may leave, had modified a wing of the house for them. It had two bedrooms, a bathroom, kitchen, living area, and a study. Moise was a typical American kid, and they crowded into his room to play Left 4 Dead before his bedtime. He was well-liked, an above-average student, and by far the fastest sprinter in his age group. Copying Joseph, he also loved the 49ers.

"Joseph, are you going to take me to a game this season?" Moise asked.

"We'll all go. We'll introduce Maya to football," he said, putting his arm around her.

"I like it when you play with us. Have you finished all your work?"

"I like it too. I've been cooped up for too long. After you finish your homework, we can play every night."

"Good," the little boy said, climbing onto Joseph's lap.

"Okay, it's time to turn the computer off and for you to get to bed," Maya said.

"Oh no. We're having fun. Can I stay up late tonight?"

Joseph was going to say yes when Maya said, "No, Moise. You won't get out of bed for school tomorrow morning. You can stay up late on Friday night. Now clean your teeth, and we'll say a prayer, then you're off to bed."

"Are you going to say a prayer with us, Joseph?"

"If you like," Joseph said, pulling back the covers on Moise's bed.

After they had tucked him in, he asked, "Are you going to marry Joseph, Maya?"

Maya giggled. "He hasn't asked me."

"Why don't you ask her, Joseph?"

"Come on, Maya. This little devil needs to get to sleep," Joseph said, getting up from Moise's bed. "Do you want to watch some television?"

"Why the big change?" she laughed. "We haven't seen you for months, and now you're Mr. Family Man."

"Dad had a talk with me. I didn't realize I'd become reclusive. Some of his partners are unhappy with my work performance, and they've been pressuring him. He wants to retire but is protecting me. He also told me I've been neglecting you and Moise. He's right."

"Ah, now I understand. But how can you drop your investigation into New Dawn? Aren't you going to follow your destiny?"

"Sometimes I feel like dropping the investigation, but there's always the chance the next email or website I open might have the answers. I'll just have to squeeze it in while everyone else is asleep. As for my destiny, I'm not sure I have one."

"Of course you do. What you're doing is of vital importance for the future of our nation. Your father's right about Moise. He's missed you. You can't neglect him, but you don't have to worry about me. I have my studies. Let's forget the television and go to bed."

Thirty minutes later, Maya was lying nestled into Joseph's shoulder when she started to giggle. "Did you enjoy the sex, Boss?"

"What's that supposed to mean?"

"You're staring at the ceiling, saying nothing, and willing me to go to sleep so you can go to your study." Maya laughed.

"Is it that obvious?"

"Poor, serious Joseph. If only you'd smile more. I told you not to worry about me. Now go," she said, putting both of her feet on his thigh, and pushing him out the bed.

As he reached the door, carrying his clothes, he turned and said, "Ten out of ten."

"What?"

"The sex." He smiled.

"Ha-ha," she said, throwing a pillow at him. "I can't believe you made a joke, feeble as it was."

It was nearly midnight when Joseph sat down, turned his computer on, and started rereading emails. The frustration was wearing him down, and he was losing enthusiasm. What had his father said? "I think you've missed something. You've probably seen something that you didn't think was important and passed over it." Two hours later he snuggled up to Maya. "Did you find anything?" she murmured.

"Nothing. Go back to sleep."

"All right. I'll help you tomorrow. Maybe a fresh set of eyes will see something."

"I doubt it."

The following night, Maya positioned herself next to Joseph behind his desk. After an hour of reading emails, she said, "Do you have any current photos of Boucher?"

"Sure, there's not many, though. He likes to fly under the radar," Joseph said, Googling "*The Wall Street Journal* + Marc Boucher." "That's him. He's the keynote speaker at a mining conference in London."

"Oh my God, I've seen him before," Maya exclaimed. "He's aged, and that wasn't his name. I'll never forget seeing that ridiculous Hitler mustache. How old is he?"

"You're right. He changed his name from Jacques Le Roux to Marc Boucher after he fled South Africa. He's in his mid-fifties. Where did you see him?"

"I was in South Africa when he was charged and skipped bail. It was front-page news. Who are those people with him?" Maya asked, slowly moving her slender fingers under their faces.

"Just delegates to the conference. Most probably miners."

"And this man," Maya said, holding her finger under the face of a heavy-jowled, older man.

"I don't know," Joseph said. "It's not important. Why don't you go to bed and I'll keep reading emails."

"Ah, I'm not helping, and you'd rather be by yourself. You are so transparent. I've seen that man or his photo before. I just can't remember when."

"You mean where."

"No, I was in South Africa, but I can't remember when I saw his picture. It must have had something to do with Le Roux."

"Are you sure?"

"No, it's more a feeling." Maya grinned. "Trust me, Boss."

"Let's see if I can help," Joseph said, as he Googled "Jacques Le Roux + mining + photos + South Africa."

Unsurprisingly, only a dozen images of a much younger Jacques Le Roux appeared.

"Blow that one up," Maya said, tapping a photo on the screen with the end of her pen.

The photo of Le Roux standing on the steps of the court in Johannesburg took the whole screen. Joseph had seen it many times before and had assumed the men standing around him were his lawyers.

"There." Maya pointed at the image of a man partially hidden behind the lawyers. "That's him," she exclaimed. "He's the man in the photo taken in London at the mining conference. Who is he?"

"I have no idea," Joseph said, "but it may be significant. What a remarkable memory you have."

"Thank you. I also remember this serious big boy who used to call me Sis. Now he's my lover." She giggled. "I'm tired. I'm going to bed. Are you coming?"

"You're such a temptress, but no, I'm going to keep going over emails for another hour."

After Maya had left, Joseph studied the two photos and wondered whether they might be the breakthrough. He saved them, circled the man's face, and emailed Ron Patterson with the message: "Ron, please find out who this man is ASAP. Thanks, Joseph."

Chapter 39

When Joseph got to his office the following morning, Ron was waiting for him.

"Sir Richard Corson-Devlin," he said. "He's a British billionaire, famous for his philanthropy."

"Good morning to you too, Ron. Then what was he doing in Johannesburg for Boucher's bail application?"

"Sorry, Joseph. Good morning. It could've been a coincidence. He has business interests all over the world. He guards his privacy fiercely, but he reputedly gave more than £100 million to charity last year. He sits on the boards of the Spastic Society, Cambridge Orphanage, and Help Underprivileged African Kids, and helps countless other charities. He provides his service gratis."

"Does he have any mining interests?"

"Of course, but he also has investments in manufacturing, banking, media, health services, and retail. He's chairman of the second-largest mining company listed on the London Stock Exchange, Euro Minerals PLC. He was one of the speakers at the mining conference in London. That accounts for why he was there. He's a pillar of British society and beyond reproach."

"Thanks, Ron. I thought he might have been the mysterious Thibault. It was always a long shot. I'll keep looking through the emails."

Yannick Kyenge's army had grown to more than five hundred men and women, and they wreaked havoc on Katanga's mining companies. Described as the Congo's worst terrorist and the leader of rebels terrorizing foreign-owned mines in Katanga, his fame rapidly spread across the nation. Six months after the New Dawn robbery, Yannick and his freedom fighters held up another mine and stole the week's gold production. After that, pairs of identical helicopters carrying heavily armed soldiers picked up gold from the mines on a random basis, rather than the scheduled pickups they used to make.

Yannick thought of using rockets to blow them out of the sky, but he only killed when he had to. Besides, he knew only one of the choppers carried the gold, while the other was a decoy. The thought of blowing them both out of the air sickened him. He had more than enough cash and bullion to maintain and equip his fighters for years but was acutely aware he needed to keep them busy. Capturing soldiers and sending them back to their units naked — his trademark form of humiliation — only occupied his army infrequently. When they kidnapped a senior mine manager from Kalemie's Lakeside Motel and held him for ransom, the mining companies and the media went crazy. Helicopters flew over the jungle searching for him and his army without success.

Food was always a problem, and a more regular operation was stealing from convoys delivering supplies to the mines. Initially, villagers suspected of helping him were beaten, tortured, and — in some cases — killed. In every instance, Yannick extracted revenge tenfold. The soldiers became wary of mistreating the villagers. They hated Yannick and lived in fear of retribution.

Deep down, Joseph had given little credence to the possibility of the photographs leading to a breakthrough. Over dinner, he explained to Maya what Ron had told him. Undeterred, she said they had to keep looking, and she would continue to help. It was nearly midnight, and she sat in the study at Joseph's desk Googling New Dawn + Boucher + gold mines in Katanga when she asked, "What was the Englishman's name?"

I wish you'd go to bed, so I could get some work done. "Sir Richard Corson-Devlin," he sighed.

"Hmmm," she murmured, Googling his name. "Wow. He's aristocracy all right. Sir Richard Theobald Harcourt Winston Corson-Devlin. What a mouthful."

"What? What? Say that again!"

"Sir Richard Theobald Harcourt Winston Corson-Devlin. Why are you so excited?"

"'Theobald' is the English version of 'Thibault.' I've been looking for a Belgian or Frenchman. Maybe I've been looking in the wrong place."

"But you said he's a pillar of society and donates generously to charities."

"Before Bernie Madoff was found to be a crook, everyone thought he was a pillar of society."

"So I might have found something."

"Yes," Joseph said, lifting her from the chair and brushing his lips across hers. "Now go to bed. I've got work to do. Lots of work."

"Is that all the thanks I get?" Maya pouted.

"You've been fantastic, but this is one of those times when one set of hands and one mind is faster than two. I'll tell you what I find in the morning. Goodnight. Love you."

"Hmmm, you never tell me that. It must be good. All right, but I want to help you tomorrow night. Love you too."

For the next three hours, Joseph pored over articles about Sir Richard Corson-Devlin on the Net. It was evident he deplored publicity. There were many instances of articles where journalists said, "We invited Sir Richard to comment, but he declined." To use Ron's words, he seemed to be beyond reproach. He appeared to be happily married, there were no sordid stories about affairs, and he hadn't been associated with any failed companies. As far as Joseph could glean, he had not had so much as a parking ticket. He tried to play down his charitable activities but was widely thought to be Britain's most generous philanthropist. No lesser figure than the queen had asked him to head The Royal Foundation for Impoverished Children.

Photographs were scarce, and those on the Net were mainly group shots with either the boards he served on or members of the royal family. Joseph guessed he'd had no choice but to smile and bear it out of respect for those people. One article in particular caught Joseph's attention: It talked about Sir Richard residing in his country estate while architects arranged for renovations to his recently acquired penthouse in St. James near Buckingham Palace. *Who pays £45 million for a penthouse and then has it refurbished?* he thought.

Joseph hadn't known Sir Richard was chairman of Euro Minerals, but he knew the company. It was a large, diversified mining company with operations all over the world. He clicked on its website and saw it was holding its annual general meeting in London in ten days' time. All of the world's large miners had been involved in improprieties, usually environmental. Joseph Googled "Euro Minerals + scandals + current." Sure enough, there had been problems on a small Indonesian island. The operation under attack from locals on Urlu Island was an open-cut cyanide leach mine, the same as New Dawn's open-cut mine. Mine wastes containing more than three dozen dangerous chemicals — including arsenic, lead, mercury, and cyanide –had contaminated the sea where local villagers fished. The color of the water had turned a nasty red, marine life was wiped out, and villagers no longer cooked with or swam in the water. Strangely there were only half a dozen articles and no mention of the United Nations or Greenpeace. Joseph found the lack of interest strange and pondered whether Euro Minerals had paid someone off in exchange for the villagers' silence.

It was 2:00 a.m. when Joseph clicked on Euro Minerals' current annual report. The company had earned a record profit, was wallowing in cash, and had provided for a significantly higher dividend than in the previous year. The report ran to more than three hundred pages. Joseph skimmed the directors' report, looking for any mention of the Indonesian mine. There was none. Then he perused the accounts, and buried in the back of the notes was: "After twenty years, the Urlu Island mine in Indonesia reached the end of its working life. During the year, the company paid £25 million to the Indonesian government in full obligation of its reinstatement commitments under the conditions of the mining permit."

The mine had produced half a million ounces of gold the prior year with a value close to $1 billion. Twenty-five million pounds was a drop in the bucket for a company that had produced close to $10 billion worth of gold over the mine's lifetime. The villagers would never get their trees, foliage, water, and fishing habitats back. It was apparent the reinstatement monies were no more than a bribe paid to senior Indonesian politicians to ensure the problem disappeared.

Joseph doubted Sir Richard even knew about it, as £25 million was not a significant sum in a behemoth company. If he did, it would severely tarnish his pristine image.

The following morning, Joseph buzzed Ron and said, "Please buy me one thousand shares in Euro Minerals at market."

"In your name?"

"Yes, and Ron, I'm going to London next week for their annual general meeting. With luck, Marc Boucher will still be there."

"Is there anything else I can do?"

Joseph paused for a few seconds. "Yes, yes there is. Euro Minerals had a mine on Urlu Island. They quit it nine months ago. It's part of the Indonesian archipelago. Find out if any reclamation or reinstatement works have commenced. If you can get some photographs, it'll be a big help."

Chapter 40

UA923 landed at Heathrow just after midday on Tuesday. It was unusually warm, and Joseph folded his suit coat over his arm. Ninety minutes later, he checked into The Dorchester. After unpacking his small suitcase, he changed into jeans, a T-shirt, and Nikes before taking a casual stroll through Hyde Park. The park was busy with joggers, teenagers playing badminton on the manicured lawns, and mothers enjoying coffee or tea while they watched their children play. Joseph stopped at the memorial fountain to Princess Diana and reflected on how much she had cared for the poor and needy. He thought of her as an inspiration and, in some ways, a soul mate.

He checked his cellphone. It was only two miles to St. James, and he was curious to see what a £45 million penthouse looked like, even if it was just from the outside. Thirty minutes later, he approached an extended two-level rendered cream building set back from a curved tiled driveway. Three grand entrances faced the driveway. Chauffeurs stood chatting next to Rolls-Royces and Bentleys while they waited for their bosses to appear. Joseph could almost smell the money as he started to walk back to The Dorchester.

Early the following morning, he caught a cab to the Waldorf Hilton in the West End of London. He climbed the steps to the lobby and asked the concierge where he could find the mining conference.

"It's in the Adelphi Suite," he replied, pointing. "Are you a delegate, sir?"

"No," Joseph replied. "I only just found out about it, but I'm particularly anxious to attend."

"It's sold out. The organizers said that the demand was so strong, they could've filled two rooms. I'm sorry, but there are no seats." The concierge smiled.

"I'm prepared to pay anything. I'm keen to hear Mr. Boucher's speech."

"That won't help, sir. Mr. Boucher made the keynote address on the first day, and he isn't scheduled to speak again."

"Is he staying here?"

"He was, but I believe he's returned to Africa. Is there anything else I can help you with?"

"No — yes, I mean yes. What day is Sir Richard Devlin-Corson speaking?"

"You're having a bad run, sir. Sir Richard presented on the first day, too, and attended the following day, but hasn't been in attendance since."

"Thank you," Joseph said, sliding a twenty pound note under his hand across the counter.

As he stepped back on the sidewalk, he silently cursed. The day was going to waste. He punched the address of the Euro Minerals building on Fenchurch Street into his cellphone. It was less than two miles away, and he was disappointed it wasn't further. Thirty minutes later, he stared up at a glass skyscraper discreetly signed "Euro Minerals." He entered the lobby and checked the directory. The executive offices were on the top level and the meeting room immediately below it. Other than that, there was little to see in the bustling lobby, so he headed back to The Dorchester.

It was a six-mile walk, but he had plenty of time and was enjoying London's warm July weather. He walked slowly, pondering what the meeting might reveal. Back in his room, he brought up Euro Minerals' annual report on his laptop and read it again, adding to his list of questions.

The following morning, Joseph arrived at the Euro Minerals building early. He took the lift to the twenty-ninth level and, along with other shareholders, was greeted by an attractive young woman in the foyer. She directed them to a desk adjacent to the meeting room door, where they signed the attendance register. There was a semi-elevated stage at the front of the large room, and the company's ten directors were behind a long table. The portly Sir Richard Corson-Devlin was sitting in the middle of the table talking to the company's CEO. Joseph glanced around the room, guessing there were approximately four to five hundred shareholders in attendance.

A large electronic sign hung on the wall behind the directors showing a chart of the company's share price, and a little cheer erupted as it broke through twenty pounds. The mood was jubilant, and small groups congregated in the aisles chatting animatedly. One larger cluster at the rear of the room caught Joseph's eye, and he saw the unmistakable mustache and baton of Marc Boucher.

Joseph checked his watch, quickly left the meeting, and found a quiet area in the foyer away from the entrance. He punched Euro Minerals' number into his cell phone and when the receptionist answered, whispered, "This is Mr. Boucher. I have to speak to Sir Richard urgently. It's critical."

"He's unavailable, Mr. Boucher. I'll put you through to his PA."

"No, no! I don't have time. Get the message to him. It's a matter of life and death. Do you understand?"

"Ye-yes. Does he ha-have your number?"

"Of course. You don't have a second to waste," Joseph hissed, hitting the end button.

After returning to the meeting room, he didn't have long to wait. A harried-looking middle-aged woman entered the room, went on the stage and handed Sir Richard a piece of paper. He shook his head, and then the woman turned her palms up in apparent response to a question before being dismissed. Still shaking his head, he took out his cellphone. Joseph turned to watch Boucher, who a few seconds later answered, then started waving his free arm around. Joseph smiled. He wasn't positive but felt he might have just found out who Thibault was.

Five minutes later, Sir Richard rose and called the meeting to order. The vest of his three-piece navy blue pinstriped suit strained under the pressure of his well-rounded stomach. "Welcome, my friends," he said, "If there are any members of the media in attendance, I'd ask them to leave now. I would also ask shareholders to turn off their smartphones, recorders, and not to take any photographs."

Joseph's cellphone was on silent and recording. He didn't turn it off.

Sir Richard moved quickly through the formalities before spending fifteen minutes delivering the chairman's address. "We achieved record sales and record profits, increased our resources, and paid a special dividend. Better still, we are on track to exceed all those records this year. Our CEO will provide more details." He concluded by saying, "There are scones, jam and cream, and beverages in the adjoining room. I hope you don't have too many questions."

Laughter went around the room, and shareholders broke out into spontaneous applause.

The CEO delivered his presentation, repeating much of what Sir Richard had covered, and finished by saying the company was on track to increase net profit after tax by 30 percent. He received a round of rapturous clapping.

Sir Richard rose again, his ruddy jowls jiggling as he spoke. "If you have any questions, I would ask you to raise your hand, wait to be acknowledged, stand, identify yourself, and an usher will pass you a microphone. I would remind you the scones are getting cold."

Several shareholders complimented Sir Richard and the CEO on the great results they had achieved.

"Are there any more comments or questions?" Sir Richard beamed.

Joseph raised his hand and when acknowledged said, "Joseph Rafter, Mr. Chairman. Note 66 to the accounts states, 'After twenty years, the Urlu Island mine in Indonesia reached the end of its working life. During the year, the company paid £25 million to the Indonesian government in full obligation of its reinstatement commitments under the conditions of the mining permit.' Can you enlighten me regarding the progress made to date?"

Sir Richard smiled. "You're too modest, Mr. Rafter, or, should I say, Mr. Muamba. To those who don't know, Mr. Muamba is the reigning Olympic decathlon champion. It's an honor to have you on our share register."

Warm applause went around the room.

"With respect, Mr. Muamba, your question would be better addressed to the Indonesian government. Any liability the company had ceased on payment to the Indonesians."

"Were you aware of the assignment, Mr. Chairman?"

"What a strange question. Of course, I was."

"The company vacated the mine over nine months ago. Would it surprise you to know the reinstatement work has not commenced? The water the villagers rely on to live is still poisoned, and the foliage has not regrown. Further, the damage is extensive, and it will be impossible to restore the land and water to its pre-mine condition for £25 million."

Sir Richard's smile froze. "How do you know, and how do you know how much it will cost to reinstate the area?"

"I have photos that were taken last week," Joseph replied, holding them up. "Would you like to see them? I've had mining experts look at them, and they say more than double the amount you paid wouldn't get the job done. Meanwhile, villagers and their families are starving because of the damage the company rendered."

The mood of the meeting changed, there was some hissing and booing, before one man in the audience said, "Why don't you go back to America? If you don't like the way our company does business, sell your shares."

"Hear, hear," other shareholders said.

"Is it the company's policy to abrogate its environmental and humanitarian responsibilities by making payments to third parties? I don't believe the liability can be legally assigned. Morally, I'm certain it can't be assigned."

"Bloody socialist do-gooder," another shareholder said, followed by more catcalling and hissing.

"Mr. Muamba, I'm surprised by your comments. The Indonesian government has far more money than the company and has accepted the liability for reinstatement under the assignment. If the landowners and villagers are unhappy, their recourse is against the government. Surely you're not impugning the integrity of the Indonesian government, are you?" Sir Richard smirked.

Oh, you're good, you slimy bastard. "No, I'm not. However, I thought the company, after paying £25 million, would like to see some action for its money."

"Quite right. While we have no legal liability, I will personally ensure the reinstatement responsibilities are taken up with the

Indonesian government. Are there any other matters you'd like to raise?"

Short of calling the Indonesians crooks, what can I say? "No, thank you. Could you please be so kind as to let me know the outcome of your inquiries?"

"Of course."

A shareholder quickly moved to close the meeting with a vote of thanks to the chairman. Numerous seconders raised their hands, and the meeting was over.

"Please join my fellow board members and me for beverages. Let's hope the scones are still warm." Sir Richard beamed.

Joseph turned and looked back to where Marc Boucher had been sitting. His chair was empty.

Most of those who had attended the meeting stayed for refreshments and to personally congratulate Sir Richard and his co-directors. Joseph stood in a corner by himself, sipping mineral water and fending off dirty looks from otherwise happy shareholders. The portly Sir Richard left a group of backslappers and made his way over to Joseph.

"You made quite an impression, Mr. Muamba," he said extending his hand.

Joseph gently grasped Sir Richard's damp and pudgy hand. "Judging by the reaction of your shareholders, not a good one."

"They're not like you and I. They couldn't care less about the environment. All they're worried about is the size of their next dividend."

"You and I, alike? Surely you are joking. I care about the cyanide and heavy metals destroying the villagers' land and water. You know as well as I do the Indonesians pocketed the monies you paid them. They're not going to clean up the environment you destroyed."

"You didn't say anything derogatory about them in the meeting."

"You know I couldn't insult a sovereign government."

"Yes, and I know why. Your father's firm has many clients with investments in Indonesia. That's why you didn't say anything. As I said, we're the same." Sir Richard smiled, putting a Cuban in his mouth. "Don't worry. I'm not going to light it. I like the feel and taste."

"No, we're not the same. You're like your shareholders. All you care about is the gold. Water is far more important to the villagers — they can't eat gold."

"You're wrong. If it were true, I wouldn't have paid the Indonesians £25 million. And you forget, the mine provided jobs for over twenty years. Without it, the villagers wouldn't have survived."

"That's not true," Joseph said, unable to keep the anger from his voice. "They survived for thousands of years before you built your mine. They fished, hunted, and lived off the land. When you destroyed their land and water, you consigned them to a life of misery."

"They can always relocate. Urlu is a big island."

"I don't understand. You are famous for your philanthropy. Have you no conscience?"

"Ah, my philanthropy." Sir Richard smirked. "Sometimes all is not as it seems. For instance, why are you here? You don't care about those villagers on Urlu Island. You've never even been there. You bought a thousand shares in the company last week for less than £20,000. Then you jumped on a plane in LA to attend an annual general meeting in London. Who does that when their investment is so small? I'll ask you again: Why are you really here?"

"You're wrong. I do care about those villagers and thousands of others like them around the world. I think you know why I'm here."

"Perhaps. It's been nice chatting with you, Mr. Muamba, but I have other shareholders to look after. How much longer are you in London?"

"Three days."

"We must have a drink before you go back. I'll call you."

As Joseph reached into his suit coat pocket for a business card, Sir Richard grasped his arm and said, "I have your number. I'll be in touch."

Chapter 41

During the flight from Lubumbashi to Kinshasa, Colonel Donatien had unsuccessfully racked his brain for excuses. General Gizenga had been terse, saying, "The president wants to see you at nine o'clock tomorrow morning. After you have landed, you are to go to the palace immediately. We will be waiting for you."

Donatien arrived a few minutes early. He expected to be seen in the president's reception chamber but instead found himself shown to a small, windowless room with just a desk and three chairs. He paced around the room, unable to sit down for fear of what he was facing. The sweat under his arms was clammy. When he had asked the general why he'd been summoned, he had replied, "It's not good."

Over thirty minutes had elapsed before the door crashed open, and the president stormed in, with Gizenga close behind. Dressed in full white military attire and the medals on his tunic clanking, the president flopped himself in the chair behind the desk.

"Good morning, Mr. Pres–"

"Sit," Bodho snapped, nodding at the chair directly in front of him before turning to Gizenga and saying, "Newspaper."

Gizenga sat down next to Donatien and spread the front page of yesterday's *Congo Daily Times* across the desk. There was a photograph of twenty naked soldiers in the back of an open truck captioned: "Soldiers lose their clothes — again!"

"What do you see?" Bodho shouted, crashing his fist onto the newspaper. "What do you see?"

"Mr. Pres–"

"Shut up. I hadn't finished. I see the army being held up to ridicule. The people in the streets are laughing, all because you can't capture one scrawny rebel in Katanga. Why, why, why?"

Donatien paused, waiting for the president to continue.

"Are you mute? Answer me!" Bodho screamed.

"He has an army of more than a thousand men and women. They are well-armed and have even blown up our trucks with rocket launchers. Once in the jungle they are impossible to fin–"

"They're well-equipped because they stole your men's weapons and vehicles. Then they hoisted the gold from under your nose to buy rocket launchers and machine guns. If you'd stopped them before they got entrenched, we wouldn't be in this position."

"Bu-but that wasn't me. General Gizenga was still in Katanga when the gold was stolen."

Gizenga sat bolt upright and glared at Donatien. "You're mistaken, Colonel. If you remember, after General Zamenka's untimely death, I assumed his position."

"Yes, but – "

"Enough!" Bodho shouted. "Enough! I don't want to listen to your bickering. I want this rebel and his gang killed or captured. The mining companies' executives are angry. Some are even saying they're going to stop our payments. They can't operate without provisions, and we don't have enough helicopters to service them. What are you going to do, Colonel?"

"I-I don't know. Once they're in the jungle, they vanish into thin air. That's where they've captured my men."

"And they're returned to you without their weapons or uniforms," Bodho taunted. "What do you say, General?"

Gizenga stroked his chin before saying, "We'll surround the jungle and send in five units of a thousand men all coming from different directions. We'll use our superior numbers."

"Five thousand men?" Bodho said. "What do you think, Colonel?"

Still smarting from Gizenga's lie, Donatien said, "It won't work. The jungle is enormous. You could put twenty thousand soldiers in there, and they still wouldn't be successful. Yannick Kyenge and his gang know every blade of grass in there."

Gizenga started to protest, but Bodho held up his hand and silenced him.

"I need to do your thinking for you. Like leading a bee to honey, we will draw this criminal out, and when he surfaces, we will have him. The honey will be New Dawn's gold. Now listen to me."

Ten minutes later the two officers were congratulating and fawning over the president. "It is a great plan, Mr. President," Donatien said.

"Yes, it is," Bodho said, "and something you two should have devised. I never thought I'd miss General Zamenka so much. When I think of Muamba murdering him, my blood boils."

"Speaking of Muamba," Gizenga said, "Boucher called to say he's in London. We could launch extradition proceedings. As they proved when they rejected the South Africans' extradition application, the English are anxious to stay in our good graces."

Bodho rolled his eyes to the ceiling. "You've learned nothing," he hissed. "If our English partner's worried, he can take care of Muamba. Let him get his hands dirty for once. Besides, the English diplomats wouldn't do anything to jeopardize their relationship with the U.S. More importantly, as I've repeatedly told you, I'll be pleased if Muamba never sets foot in Kinshasa again. The faster the people forget him, the better. Only a fool would seek to extradite him, and unlike you, General, I am not a fool."

Donatien put his hand up to his mouth to conceal a smile but wasn't fast enough.

"Don't smile, Colonel," Bodho growled. "If you fail to capture or kill the rebel leader, it'll be your head on the block. Now get out of here and put my plan into action. I'm sick of the pair of you."

Joseph was almost certain Thibault and Sir Richard were one and the same. His only doubt came as a result of the knight's generous charitable donations. He hadn't been able to find one web page that consolidated Sir Richard's donations, but when he listed those made over the previous year, they aggregated more than £125 million. *Why would someone so generous be so ruthless and uncaring with his workers? Why would someone chairing large public companies invest in small, private, African companies?* What had he meant when he said, "Sometimes all is not as it seems?" As he stared out at Hyde Park, he felt the buzz of his cellphone.

A refined voice said, "Mr. Muamba, my name is Aaron Price. I'm Sir Richard Corson-Devlin's private secretary. Sir Richard has requested the pleasure of your company for drinks at his St. James residence tonight. I'll text the address. Is eight o'clock convenient?"

"Yes, I'll be there."

Chapter 42

Joseph dressed in a smart blue sports jacket, a white business shirt, casual fawn slacks, and sneakers for drinks with Sir Richard. The weather was balmy when he left The Dorchester. He walked slowly, enjoying the sights and sounds of Mayfair.

Thirty-five minutes later, he entered the private entrance to Sir Richard's penthouse and was greeted by the knight's concierge, who wore a black morning suit. Joseph wondered whether he should have worn a suit.

"Good evening, Mr. Muamba," he said. "Please take the lift to the first floor. Sir Richard is waiting for you."

Joseph sunk in the lift's carpets. Seconds later the doors opened to reveal a white marble tiled reception area and a valet dressed identically to the concierge. Large vases housed freshly picked roses, which gave off a delightful fragrance. The valet bowed to Joseph, and said, "Welcome, Mr. Muamba. Sir Richard is in the library. Please follow me."

On the short walk to the library, they passed two more reception areas and a large carpeted living room. The valet opened the lofty walnut double doors and took a step back to let Joseph enter. He gasped. The room was at least six times the size of his hotel room. Matching fully laden walnut bookshelves almost concealed the four walls, extending from the lush royal purple carpet to the ceiling. Sir Richard was sitting behind a hand-carved desk, in a black leather chair resembling a throne. On either side of the desk were full height windows, the only break from books in the room. Three matching recliners sat in front of the desk.

Sir Richard stood up and extended his hand. He was wearing a dark brown smoking jacket and loafers. "I'm glad you could come. Would you like something to drink?"

"Mineral water, thank you."

Sir Richard pressed a button on his desk and said, "James, mineral water for my guest and Macallan neat for me."

There was a pause, and Sir Richard said, "Of course 1972. Need you ask? Bring the bottle."

In less than a minute, James appeared in a morning suit carrying a silver tray bearing the drinks.

"Mr. Muamba, what we are going to discuss is highly confidential," Sir Richard said. "James is ex-MI5 and also handles my personal security. I don't want to offend you, but do you mind if he pats you down, and takes your cellphone? I'm afraid if you say no, we'll just have to discuss cricket and soccer, games you're probably not familiar with."

With those few words, Joseph knew he had found the beneficial owner of the New Dawn Gold Mining Company. "I don't have any objection," he replied, turning his cellphone off before handing it to James. He then stood and raised his hands above his head while the ex-MI5 man thoroughly patted him down. "I'll take your watch, and the gold ingot and chain too," he said.

When he had finished, he said, "He's clean, Sir Richard."

"Good. That will be all for now, James."

"You're a cautious man," Joseph said.

"I am. Now, why don't you tell me why you came to London?"

"I wanted to talk to the beneficial owner of the New Dawn Gold Mining Company."

"One of the beneficial owners. George Faraday told me you were snooping. How did you find me?"

"So you did buy the mine off Faraday?"

"Yes. Now answer my question."

"There was a photo of you standing on the steps of the Supreme Court building in Johannesburg with Jacques Le Roux — or should I say, Marc Boucher — at his bail hearing."

Sir Richard looked puzzled. "If memory serves me, it was a group photo. How did you connect me to New Dawn?"

"I didn't. I had no idea who you were. A friend and I were looking at a photo of Marc Boucher at the African Mining Conference, and you were in the background. My friend remembered seeing the

Johannesburg photo. We thought the probability of coincidence was remote."

"One tiny slip-up." Sir Richard grimaced. "Your girlfriend's astute."

Now it was Joseph's turn to be taken aback. Before he could respond, Sir Richard said, "You'd be amazed by what we know about you. Your girlfriend was in South Africa at the time of Boucher's bail application. Of course, it was her who put two and two together. Then you pulled your little phone trick today, and it confirmed my relationship with Boucher. You think you're so smart."

"No, I don't, but I am surprised by your transparency."

"Why? I haven't done anything wrong. Well, nothing you can prove. I'm not in the least worried about you. What I can't understand is why you came to London."

"There are men, women, and children dying in the New Dawn gold mine every day. They have no protective clothing. Some even work in their bare feet. They're grossly underpaid, and recently more than seventy workers and villagers were killed by the army at the direction of Marc Boucher."

"You have proof?" Sir Richard asked, sipping his whiskey.

"New Dawn provided the helicopters and trucks that carried the murderers. Is that enough proof for you?"

"Calm down, Mr. Muamba. Shouting and losing your temper doesn't make what you say right. Didn't the court in Kinshasa exonerate the company and its management?"

"A military court more interested in protecting its own than delivering justice."

"That's a scurrilous, unfounded allegation. You can't prove bias. While we're talking off the record, let me ask you some questions. Didn't you kill those two soldiers in the jungle? And didn't you throw General Zamenka into the Congo River?"

Joseph paused, and a mirthless smile crossed his face. By his insistence that they were speaking off the record, Sir Richard had just revealed that he was in fact recording their conversation. "You were misinformed. I have no idea who killed those soldiers, and I tried to save General Zamenka."

The permanent smile on Sir Richard's momentarily disappeared as he topped up his glass. "I was also told you're clever, or are you just blessed with rat cunning?"

"That is for others to judge. It is evident you know what is going on and don't care. I don't understand. Your generosity to the underprivileged and handicapped is legendary. Why can't you see and empathize with the plight of those in the mines? Marc Boucher is a cruel, ruthless manager. Why do you employ him?"

"Marc Boucher is the best mine manager in the whole of Africa. Over the years, he has rewarded my partners and me generously. It cost a lot of money to get him out of South Africa after those workers were killed, but it was worth every cent."

"You own the South African mine?"

"And many more," Sir Richard said, nipping the end off a Cuban and lighting it. "Tell me, do you think your father's rich?"

"It's of no interest to me. Why do you ask?"

"Let me help you. He's worth perhaps $50 million. Do you think he's rich?"

"I told you, I'm not interested. What game are you playing?"

Sir Richard blew a smoke ring, smirked, and threw his legs up on the desk. "I give away five times that amount every year. He's not even close to being rich."

"What's your point?"

"My point? Simple. You are a nosy young man who thinks he can pry into other people's business without repercussions. My friends and I could break your father, and at this late stage of his life, he'd never recover. You'd be wise to give that serious consideration."

Joseph wanted to leap across the table, take Sir Richard's paunchy neck in his hands, and wring it.

As if reading his mind, Sir Richard said, "You'd like to kill me, just like you killed General Zamenka, wouldn't you?"

"I've never killed anyone, but leave my father out of it. You haven't answered my question. Why do you give so much money away, but treat your mine workers so poorly?"

"Ah, the philanthropy I'm famous for." Sir Richard smirked. "I give away three-quarters of my yearly income. Dividends from public companies, directors' fees and consulting fees. More than £130 million last year. I get a huge tax deduction, but more importantly, I get the plaudits of the people. I wonder if their feelings would be so warm if they knew I was earning over £600 million a year from my offshore mining investments and not paying a single penny in taxes. A cynic might say the government is paying those donations that I'm supposedly making. Ironic, isn't it? The people who are feting me are the people who are making the donations."

"Why are you telling me? What's to stop me from going to the Serious Organized Crime Agency or the media and exposing you? You'll end up in jail for the rest of your life."

"For someone who's supposed to be clever, you are naïve. You have no proof, and I would deny your claims as the ramblings of a madman. Further, no one in SOCA is going to investigate me. I not only make charitable donations, but monetarily help government ministers and their opposition too. Did Rupert and James Murdoch go to jail over phone hacking? Of course not. They were too influential. The fear of what they might do in the future had our politicians protecting their collective asses. I'm far more powerful, and you are no more than a nosy little pissant. The media owners know I'll sue them if they put a foot out of place. There is nothing you can do to me."

"Why did you summon me then?"

"My partners thought I should talk to you. We can drive an enormous amount of business through your father's firm. Enough to make him genuinely wealthy. All you have to do is stop this silliness and put an end to your friend's sabotage in the Congo. I have a partner in the U.S. who is one of the wealthiest men in the world. He could make your father's firm the next Goldman Sachs. Think it over."

"Who is he?"

Sir Richard laughed. "You found me. You won't find any of my partners. What do you think?"

"Tell your partners I intend to have them and you charged with the murder of seventy-four men, women, and children."

"You're a fool. Fortunately, you won't even get close to causing us any serious problems. If you do, the forces I unleash against you and those who you love will make you regret the day you were born," Sir Richard said, pressing the button on his desk.

The ex-MI5 man appeared almost instantly. "James, Mr. Muamba is leaving. Please show him out."

Joseph reached the door and turned around. "I'll see you in court," he said.

"For your sake, I hope not," Sir Richard replied.

Chapter 43

Yannick Kyenge led a small army of a thousand freedom fighters, but he wasn't a natural leader. If Joseph was still in the Congo, he would lead from the front, being first in any attack, and his men would follow him through hell. Yannick was a planner, a skilled tactician who always carefully weighed the risks before launching a campaign. Some of the young hotheads called him an old woman behind his back and threatened to form a breakaway rebel group.

When word reached Yannick that due to the unavailability of helicopters, New Dawn would transport its ingots to Lubumbashi by road the following week, he was immediately suspicious. The hotheads were not. They were elated by the news and demanded to be part of the unit that they thought should attack the convoy. Yannick had reservations about launching an attack.

Equipping and feeding his freedom fighters' families was an expensive exercise. Yannick had enough gold to fund his ever growing army for another six months, but the idea of an easy heist was tempting. Despite this, he was not going to make a decision until he had fully considered the risks. The emboldened young hotheads called him a coward to his face and demanded he stand down as their leader. Wiser heads prevailed, but Yannick remained under pressure to make a decision. If he decided to attack, he would need to start moving men and equipment within forty-eight hours. Equally importantly, he knew those who opposed him were using his decision as a test of his leadership.

Many of Yannick's fighters had relatives who worked for New Dawn, and this was how he had found out the gold was going to be transported by road. It concerned him that the sensitive information had leaked far too easily. *Surely it should have been more closely guarded*, he thought. Fifty soldiers were being transported to the mine on Thursday to guard the gold shipment to Lubumbashi the following day. Yannick knew they would be heavily armed, but so were his men. If need be, he could have two hundred hidden in the jungle along the road. There would be loss of life on both sides, but there was no way fifty could win against two hundred.

He couldn't put his finger on it, but something wasn't right. Luckily, it was a clear day, and there were no problems with the satellites when he turned on his smartphone. He Googled helicopter hire companies at Lubumbashi International Airport and jotted down the phone numbers of two companies. He called the first and inquired about hiring a helicopter for the latter half of next week. Availability wasn't a problem. The receptionist at the second company gave him the same answer. She even offered a discount if he'd make the booking and give her a credit card number. Yannick put the smartphone back in his pocket and smiled. He knew what the army was up to and was almost positive they wouldn't run the risk of shipping the gold. They would most likely fill the safe with rocks.

When he informed the hotheads they wouldn't be attacking the convoy, they were furious. He implored them not do anything and assured them if they still opposed his leadership after Friday, he would stand aside.

Fifty soldiers in four trucks and two Jeeps noisily entered New Dawn's mine site on Thursday. The next morning, they roared out just after five o'clock for the eight-hour trip to Lubumbashi. Two soldiers guarding the entrance stood at attention and saluted. More than three thousand soldiers lay hidden at strategic locations along the road. Four helicopters carrying heavily armed soldiers were hovering at strategically positioned intervals high in the sky, waiting to respond when notified of the attack. Colonel Donatien was in the front Jeep. His informants had told him the rebels had been moving men and equipment to the south. He knew they were going to attack, and that fool Kyenge, who called himself a leader, would soon be dead. He was going to make President Bodho proud, and with luck, the president might even offer him Gizenga's position.

At 5:00 a.m., Yannick and twenty of his best men — all toting machine guns and wearing army uniforms — marched at double pace through the jungle to where they had hidden the stolen vehicles. Yannick wore a major's uniform at least two sizes too big for him. One of his men, a former powder monkey at the mine, was carrying six sticks of dynamite. Yannick got into the passenger seat of a Jeep, and three of his men joined him. The others climbed into a truck, and the little convoy set off for the New Dawn mine.

The soldiers at the entrance paid little attention to the approaching army vehicles until Yannick leaped out of the Jeep, and ordered them to stand to attention. They were confused and did not recognize the uppity major. When they saw the machine guns leveled at them, the penny dropped. Yannick ordered two of his men to stand guard at the entrance, while the two soldiers were stripped, bound, gagged, and thrown in the back of the truck.

The convoy continued for half a mile into the mine site until Yannick could see the smelter. The only heavily secured building on the site was fifty yards from the smelter. It was where the ingots were stored before dispatch. Two bored-looking soldiers snapped to attention when Yannick got out of the Jeep. With a minimum of fuss, they soon joined their comrades in the back of the truck.

Yannick rapped sharply on the fortified door. A small panel slid away to reveal a snarling Afrikaner, who said, "*Wat is dit?*"

"I am Major Patel. The rebels know the gold is still here. There are more than five hundred marching toward the mine. They're less than fifteen minutes away and heavily armed. I've been ordered by Colonel Donatien to get you and the ingots to safety. There's no time to waste."

Another Afrikaner put his face up to the panel. "*Ek weet nie dit nie jou!*" he said.

"I don't understand Afrikaans. I was sent from Lubumbashi to provide extra security for the mine, but we can't hold out against five hundred," Yannick said, stepping back from the door so the Afrikaners could see two rows of perfectly lined-up soldiers. "I'm not risking their lives for you. Are you coming with us or not?"

There was a short, fierce exchange of Afrikaans on the other side of the door. One of the Afrikaners then said in English, "I'm not going to die here, Major. We're coming with you," and Yannick heard bolts and padlocks opening.

There were three Afrikaners in what was a sparsely furnished room. One was opening a large safe, another was packing documents in a box, and the third, a brute of a man, eyed Yannick suspiciously. "Show me some identification," he said.

"We don't have time. We have to get out."

"Identification. Now!" the man demanded.

Jesus! The safe's still not open, and I don't want to have to blow it. "All right," he said, slowly reaching into his tunic pocket, as he heard the safe door click open.

"Hurry up."

"Sorry, wrong pocket," Yannick said, dropping his hand to his waist and placing the barrel of his pistol in the middle of the man's forehead. "Is Mr. Glock enough identification for you?"

"Shut the safe door!" the man shouted, but it was too late.

"Bind them, and get the gold loaded," Yannick ordered.

"Do we strip them?"

"No, we only do that to the soldiers. How many ingots are there?"

"Eight."

Six million. That's more than I dared hope for. "Let's get out of here."

The convoy stopped at the entrance to pick his two men up. "What will we do with the prisoners?" the driver of the truck asked.

"Remove the soldiers' bindings on their legs, and have them stand in front of the New Dawn sign," Yannick said, putting his smartphone in camera mode. "Turn them around. I want them facing me. Oh, they're great photos. Bind them again, and throw them in the back. We'll dump them twenty miles down the road."

As they sped away from the mine site, Yannick emailed the photos to *The Congo Daily Times.*

Colonel Donatien's trip was disappointingly uneventful, and he arrived in Lubumbashi just after midday. The rebels hadn't taken the bait, and he wondered how the president would react. It wasn't his fault. He had done everything the president asked. He poured himself a cold drink before calling General Gizenga and telling him the mission had failed. Gizenga sounded sympathetic, but there was an underlying cheeriness in his voice. Donatien put the phone down and cursed. He could just imagine Gizenga's disdainful comments while he relayed the news to the president.

Just before 3:00 p.m., Donatien's adjutant poked his head in the door, and said, "Mr. Boucher from the New Dawn mine is holding for you, sir. He sounds angry."

"Put him through," Donatien said. He might have to take shit from Bodho and Gizenga, but he wasn't going to cop it from some civilian.

Before Boucher could speak, Donatien said, "We did everything by the book. It wasn't our fault the rebels didn't take the bait. I've had a long, tiring day, and I don't want to hear you ranting."

"What are you talking about? The rebels stole the gold from our depot. They were dressed up like soldiers and driving army vehicles. How did they get those uniforms and vehicles? I have a call into the president. I don't know what we're paying him and you for."

Donatien fought back the bile in his throat. "Bu-but how di-did they know?"

"Someone leaked," Boucher screeched, "probably one of your men."

"My-my men did-didn't know. They thought we were car-carting ingots. It-it mus-must have been someone from th-the mine."

"Bullshit. I knew, my assistant knew, and the three Afrikaners who work in dispatch knew. None of us talk to or socialize with fucking kaffirs. The leak was from your end. Damn you."

Donatien was going to respond, but all he heard was the dial tone. He held his head in his hands. There was going to be hell to pay, and he knew who was going to take the blame.

When Yannick Kyenge marched into his camp, he was mobbed. His leadership would never again be questioned or challenged.

That night the drums of the Congo went into a frenzy, telling the story of the imminent return of the great leader and the heroics of his loyal friend.

Chapter 44

Joseph's father's words rang in his ears on the flight back to LAX: "Never show your cards unless someone pays." Not knowing that Joseph had a copy of Marc Boucher's hard drive, Sir Richard had contemptuously shown his hand. With what the knight had told him and the emails, Joseph had more than enough information to file a complaint with the Serious Organized Crime Agency but was wary of Sir Richard's influence. Even if SOCA investigated, he didn't know whether it had the power to access tax haven bank accounts. Without accessing those bank accounts, there was nothing to prove Thibault and Sir Richard were one and the same. Pondering this, he thought of applying pressure by approaching the media, but knew the British courts were plaintiff-friendly in defamation actions. It was unlikely any media organization would blow the whistle on Sir Richard.

Joseph's flight landed midafternoon at LAX, and that night, after they'd eaten, he asked his father and Maya whether he could have a word with them in private. "I didn't want to worry Mom," he said, before telling them what had occurred in London. "Do you know Sir Richard, Dad?"

"I know of him. Old money. He's British aristocracy. Other than satisfying your curiosity, I'm not sure you have anything. You have no proof he sent those emails resulting in the deaths of those workers and villagers."

"I have bank details and account numbers of every transfer to a tax haven. The IRS and SEC can access the details of those accounts. When they do, they'll find Sir Richard and the names of his partners."

Frank shook his head. "I admire your passion, Son, but our authorities don't have the power to investigate a British citizen. I know everything you say is true, but Sir Richard hasn't broken any U.S. laws. Besides, those bank accounts were probably set up by lawyers and accountants. There may be no connection to him."

"What about his U.S. partner?" Maya asked.

"We don't even know his name," Frank said. "Joseph, you can hardly file a complaint with the IRS and SEC about an American billionaire whose name you don't know, who you claim is guilty of tax evasion, money laundering, and possibly an accessory to murder. They'll laugh you out of their offices."

"What if I approach the media? It's just the type of story *Sixty Minutes* runs."

"What a great idea," Maya said. "You can expose the president, the army officers, and the politicians. The people are sick of getting ripped off by their leaders. It might bring the whole nasty regime down."

"*Sixty Minutes* won't touch it," Frank said. "You've got no hard proof, and while our defamation laws are nowhere as stringent as the Brits', no media organization is going to aid your crusade. Besides, defamation law is complicated. I don't think there's anything to stop Sir Richard commencing an action in Britain, despite the defamation taking place in the U.S. Our networks won't touch it."

"He won't sue in Britain or here," Joseph said. "No way."

"Yes, but the media doesn't know that. There's no way they'll run your allegations. I'm sorry, Son. It's over."

"No," Maya said, "exposing Sir Richard will bring the government down and improve the lives of millions in the Congo. You can't drop it."

"I agree," Joseph said. "Dad, Sir Richard said he'd hurt those who I loved if I caused any trouble, and he'd break you. If you're worried, I won't pursue him."

Frank paused before saying, "I've always told you to do what you think is right. I'm not going to change now. Don't worry about me."

"Thanks, Dad," Joseph said, reaching out and grasping his father's forearm.

"I still don't know what you're going to do."

"Nor do I," Joseph said. "Nor do I."

Before Joseph had left for London, he'd been teaching Moise how to play poker. The boy was a quick learner and loved playing three-handed poker. "Was it cold in England?" he asked, as Joseph dealt the cards.

"No, it was warm, but not as warm as the Congo."

"Two cards, please," Maya said.

"None for me." Moise grinned, making the maximum bet of eight matchsticks.

"Oh, you're lucky, Moise. I'm out," Maya said, throwing in her cards.

"Your eight, and I'll raise you eight," Joseph said.

Moise's face dropped. "How did you know I was bluffing?" he demanded.

"You were too arrogant. Too full of yourself. You tried to bully the table, and the fastest way to fix a bully is to up the stakes."

"Just because he's not smiling doesn't mean he's not joking." Maya smiled. "Lighten up, honey."

"Yes, yes," Joseph said. "Now I know what I have to do. I have to increase the stakes. Thank you, Moise."

Moise frowned and scratched his head.

"What are you talking about?" Maya asked.

"I have the solution," Joseph said.

President Bodho and Gizenga were already in the small interrogation room when Donatien arrived at the palace. *The Congo Daily Times* was on the desk with a photo of the four naked soldiers captioned "our naked army," with appropriate blackouts, on the front page.

"You messed up my plan," Bodho said in a scarily calm voice.

"They-they knew. Someone mus-must have leaked," Donatien replied.

"I've thought about it," Bodho replied. "They could have found out about the three thousand men hidden in the jungle, but how did they know the gold was still at the mine? Who did you tell, Colonel?"

"No one. It must hav-have been one of Bouch-Boucher's men."

"The plan was perfect," Bodho said, "but somehow you two ruined it."

"I was in Kinshasa," Gizenga protested. "It had nothing to do with me."

"You forget, General. You lead an army of one hundred and fifty thousand soldiers. This rebel Kyenge has thrived under your leadership. The army is a laughing-stock. I had a call from a prominent investor in London, to say I had promised I would protect his mines in Katanga. He's most unhappy."

"Do you want me to take over in Katanga?" Gizenga asked.

"If memory serves me, you were there when Kyenge created his ragtag gang. I don't see you doing any better job than the colonel."

"Mr. President –"

"Shut up, Colonel. I haven't finished. I'm giving the pair of you ninety days to crush the rebels. If you can't, I'll replace you both with officers who can," Bodho said, as he stood up and opened the door.

After the president had left, Donatien said, "I like him better when he rants and raves. At least I know what he's thinking. That was nerve-racking."

Their rivalry now replaced by a joint fear, Gizenga agreed, "You're right. He's at his most dangerous when he's cold. If we can't bring him Kyenge's body, he'll make us privates. Are you sure you didn't tell anyone about the gold?"

"Positive. The leak came from the mine. I'm certain. Do you have any idea how we're going to find Kyenge?"

"Yes. The villagers must be tipping him off to our every move. How else could he always be a step in front of us? We'll take ten thousand men into Katanga and systemically burn their villages. We'll teach them a lesson they'll never forget. If he's the hero they think he is, it'll smoke him out. When it does, we'll slaughter him and his followers."

"I like it." Donatien grinned.

Chapter 45

Floyd Coffey's career had blossomed since his interviews with Joseph in 2008, and his profile in sports journalism rivaled that of Morley Safer in world affairs. His Sunday night prime-time show on Fox, *Sporting Heroes*, was a ratings juggernaut.

Floyd didn't think there was anything unusual when Joseph called to suggest they meet up for coffee. They kept in regular contact and never went longer than a month without catching up. As they sat in their favorite coffee shop sipping lattes, Joseph said, "Great interview with Mayweather. How did you get him?"

"You mightn't believe this, but his people approached my producer. They wanted to show his softer side. We told them if he came on, it wouldn't be scripted. I'd be asking the questions, and they'd cover his relationships and convictions. They agreed."

Joseph laughed. "I thought he was going to knock you out when you asked him why the Australians wouldn't let him into their country. I didn't know. Why did he even want to go there? There are no challengers Down Under."

"They were going to pay him a shitload to fight a few exhibitions, and sign some autographs."

"Jesus, it's not like he needs the money."

"Yeah, I thought the same. I called you last week. You were in London. What was it, business or pleasure?"

"Business. I need to tell you about it."

After Joseph had finished, Floyd asked, "How come I've never heard of this Sir Richard dude?"

"Probably because he has nothing to do with sport, plus he likes to keep a low profile. If I was doing what he's doing, I'd want to fly under the radar too."

"But you've got no proof."

"He told me what he was doing."

"Yeah, and he also said he'd make your life hell if you pursued him, and he's got the resources to do it. Let's cut to the chase. What do you want me to do?"

"The London Olympics are just around the corner. I'd like you to interview me. You could ask me whether I'm going to defend my title, then follow up with a question about the reception I received in the Congo."

"Jesus! Do you know what you're asking me to do?"

"I've bounced it off a few current affairs journalists. They'd love to run with it, but their bosses think it's poison. They're scared shitless."

"No wonder. I don't know that you're right when you say our courts are tougher on plaintiffs. You admitted you've got no hard evidence linking the English dude to the emails. You've got nothing! Of course he'll sue."

"No. I can guarantee he won't. He'll threaten, and his lawyers will write fearsome letters, but the last place he wants his dirty laundry aired is in a court."

"I need another cup of coffee," Floyd said, signaling a waiter. "Short black, two shots, Miss. Anything for you, Joseph?"

"I'll sit on this." Joseph frowned, sipping his latte.

"I'd like to help, but as you know my program is on every second Sunday night, and I've got guests booked for six months. I don't see how I can get you on."

"Floyd, you ran special programs after Drew Brees won the Super Bowl, and when Chris Henry got killed in that truck accident. You can squeeze me in."

"Yeah, and they were special programs because there were exceptional circumstances. You don't fit the bill."

"You don't think the defending Olympic champion switching from the Congo to Team U.S.A. is exceptional? Name another athlete who has switched countries and won consecutive golds. It's a huge story."

"You told me you're not going to compete in London."

"I haven't told anyone else. I might compete."

"Bullshit! How long has it been since you trained?" Floyd grinned.

"In all the time I've known you, have I ever asked a favor? Do this for me, Floyd. Please."

"I'll probably get fired, but okay, I'll do it. Not this Sunday night, the one after."

"You won't get fired. It'll make you bigger than what you already are. After it airs, *Sixty Minutes* will probably offer you a gig."

That night Maya snuggled up in bed to Joseph and said, "When do you think you'll be going back?"

"I don't know. If I go back now, I'll get thrown into prison. That won't help anyone."

"When you go, I'm coming with you. I'll finish my degree this year. I'll do my residency in Kinshasa Mercy Hospital."

"I sometimes wonder if I'll ever get back," Joseph sighed. "If fate had taken a different twist, I'd still be there fighting with Yannick. Who would have thought he'd ever lead a rebel army?"

"You'll get back," Maya said, gently stroking his face. "It is your destiny. No, it's our destiny. Yours, Yannick's, and mine. We can change the Congo."

"I hope you're right."

"I am. Your interview with Floyd will be the first step in getting rid of corruption."

"Turn the light off," Joseph said, kissing her passionately.

Truckloads of heavily armed soldiers poured into Katanga and almost immediately attacked two villages to the north of Kilwa. They tortured and then killed villagers who refused to reveal anything about Yannick and his freedom fighters. Women and children were gang-raped. When the soldiers finished, they looted the villages and then set them ablaze.

Word traveled fast and soon reached Yannick. Villages to the south of Kalemie, and to the east of Kamina were also under attack. Yannick knew it was a trap and that the army wanted to draw him out into the open. Other than to avenge villagers, he had gone out of his way not to kill soldiers, preferring to humiliate them, but now they had forced his hand. His fighters would be outnumbered three to one, but they would have the advantages of surprise, rocket launchers, and the jungle.

A third village to the north of Kilwa — not far from the towns already destroyed — was an obvious next target for the army. Yannick moved swiftly to herd the villagers to the safety of the surrounding jungle. He and fifty of his best fighters, including those with rocket launchers, took up positions in the village. Two hundred hid on either side of the route to the village, and four hundred were a mile to the south. If all went to plan, the rearguard would capture the retreating soldiers as they fled in panic.

There was nothing discreet about the soldiers, and Yannick could hear the rumble of their trucks in the distance. Mortars landed in and around the village, and the ack-ack-ack of randomly fired machine guns created an explosive cacophony. Yannick put his field glasses to his eyes. The trucks were moving slowly, almost leisurely, and a large contingent of soldiers marched behind them. Those with mortars and small cannons had positioned themselves around a half mile away and were raining shells on the village. Yannick had a dozen men lying at the entrance with rocket launchers. When the first truck was in sight, he said, "Fire one," and a rocket whooshed past the truck and exploded in the jungle.

"Fire two," he yelled, and watched in amazement as the truck disintegrated in a puff of fire.

Two trucks with turret-mounted machine guns sprayed the village with bullets. Yannick gave the order to fire three, then four. One of the trucks exploded, its machine gun being catapulted twenty yards into the sky. The fifth missile hit a large, old tree and blew it to smithereens. Some of the soldiers started to retreat, and machine guns on either side of them opened up. As Yannick had anticipated, some of the soldiers broke into a run, and then it was a stampede.

Ten minutes later, the deafening sound of gunfire came from the jungle, and hundreds of soldiers were gunned down. Others stopped, dropped their weapons, and held their hands in the air. By the time Yannick arrived in his Jeep, the rout was complete, and his freedom fighters had rounded up more than a hundred soldiers in a huddle. A young man said, "I'm sorry, sir. Many escaped. Do you want us to go after them?"

"Don't worry about them, son, and don't call me sir. Yannick will do."

"Yes, Yannick. What do want us to do with them?"

Bodies littered the ground, and Yannick fought back a wave of nausea. "Order them to strip, but let them keep their boots. Give them shovels, and tell them to bury their comrades," he said, taking out his smartphone, and swiping the camera icon. "After they've finished, let them go. Gather up their uniforms and weapons and the weapons of the dead. Take them back to the camp."

Yannick had never expected such a resounding success but knew unless he moved quickly, he would lose the advantage of surprise. It wouldn't take long before word of the Kilwa defeat reached the officers in Kalemie, but Yannick surmised they wouldn't tell their soldiers for fear of demoralizing them. The last thing the regiment would be expecting was an attack mounted from three hundred miles to the south.

It was dusk when Yannick arrived back at the camp to be greeted by rapturous cheering. He jumped out of the Jeep and held his hands up for silence. "We are going to attack the regiment in Kalemie but only have transport for five hundred. I need volunteers!" he shouted. "We leave in two hours."

Another rousing cheer erupted, and a sea of hands rose into the air.

Chapter 46

The television studio held four hundred, and there wasn't a vacant seat to be found. Joseph sat in a leather recliner facing Floyd over a coffee table with a carafe of water and half a dozen glasses sitting on it. The heat from the overhead lights was uncomfortable. Joseph wiped a bead of sweat from his forehead. "We're on in one minute," Floyd's producer said and then, "Five, four, three, two, one. We're on."

"I'm with a man who many describe as the greatest athlete on the planet. Joseph Muamba, how does that description sit with you?"

"I'm naturally flattered, but I'm sure fans of Usain Bolt and LeBron James would disagree. It's subjective."

"Did you have a hero when you were growing up?"

"I think we all did. I dreamed of being Steve Young, but there were better quarterbacks than me. In my opinion, Muhammad Ali is the greatest athlete of all time. I would have loved to see him fight at his peak. He is also a great man, a trailblazer for humanity."

"You were something of a boxer yourself."

"No, I learned a little self-defense. That's all."

"I heard different," Floyd said, peering over the top of his spectacles. "I was told you could have been a Golden Gloves champion."

"You were misinformed."

"I doubt it. Anyhow, let's not belabor the point. You haven't competed for over a year. Are you retired? Are you training? Are you going to defend your title in Britain?"

"The danger of overtraining is peaking too early. Thanks to Greg Foreman, I peaked on those two days in Beijing. I've been training lightly," Joseph lied.

"Does that mean you're going to defend your gold medal by competing for the Democratic Republic of the Congo again?"

"No. I will try out for Team U.S.A."

There was a smattering of applause from the audience.

"It would be a unique achievement winning gold for different countries at consecutive Olympics. Is that what appeals to you?"

"No. Unfortunately, the government of the Democratic Republic of the Congo is corrupt. The president, the generals, and the politicians have been receiving bribes from Western and Chinese mining companies. There's not even two thousand miles of sealed roads across the whole country, it's in terrible condition, and poverty reigns. This in a resource rich country a quarter of the size of the U.S. Those in privileged positions have been the recipients of huge sums of money transferred to bank accounts in tax haven countries. Now that I know the extent of the corruption, I couldn't possibly compete for the DRC."

There was a loud gasp from the audience.

"Those are serious allegations. Do you have any proof?"

"I have copies of emails authorizing the transfers."

"May I ask how you obtained these emails?"

"No, you may not, but be assured the proof I have is irrefutable."

The audience was in shock. Sports interviews didn't focus on bribery, corruption, and geopolitics.

"You recently appeared at a murder trial in Kinshasa. Why were you there?"

"Seventy-four striking miners and villagers were massacred by the Congolese army at the instruction of a British-owned mining company. I was a witness for the prosecution."

"Hold on," Floyd said, "I happen to know all those on trial were acquitted, and the court found those killed were rebels."

"Seven children less than the age of ten were murdered. Would you call them rebels?"

"There's collateral damage in all wars. The court found the soldiers not guilty. Surely that brings the legal action to an end."

"The court was also corrupt. The government laid the charges so the perpetrators could be found not guilty, and thus not have to face a properly convened court. The trial was a travesty of justice."

Floyd's producer was waving his arms and shaking his head.

"I don't understand."

"Double jeopardy. Once acquitted, these murderers need never fear facing charges again. They are free."

"I understand your concern, but it appears there is nothing you can do."

"The order to commit murder emanated from London. The man who issued it has yet to face court. If the murdered mine workers and villagers are to attain any justice, he must be charged and convicted."

"Can you name him?"

"Yes. Sir Richard Corson-Devlin. He and his partners own the New Dawn Gold Mining Company in Katanga, even though you'd never know it. If you searched the company, you'd find Liberty Investments incorporated in Mauritania owns all the shares. If you searched the ownership of Liberty Investments, you would find countless other companies and trusts, but if it were possible to lift the corporate veil, you'd find Sir Richard and his cronies."

Someone sitting close to the stage exhaled loudly, and someone else said, "My God."

"Do you know the names of Sir Richard's partners?"

"No, but one of them is an American billionaire. If they knew of the order to murder the strikers, then they're as culpable as Sir Richard."

Floyd's producer was out of his booth and on the edge of the stage. "Go to a station break," he hissed.

"How do you know about the American?"

"Sir Richard told me."

"Sorry, but I'm missing something. Why would he tell you?"

"Because he didn't think I had any evidence. If I said anything, it would be his word against my word. He's going to find out it's a lot more than that."

"After Sir Richard made his admissions, why didn't you take your allegations to the Serious Organized Crime Agency?"

"Sir Richard told me he controlled the politicians who control SOCA. I realized there was no point in making any claims in the U.K."

"What do you think will come of your revelations tonight?"

"I hope the authorities investigate the matters I have raised and bring the guilty parties to account."

"We'll take a station break and be back soon," Floyd said.

Floyd's producer was immediately on stage. "What are you doing?

The phones are ringing off the hook. Don Rankin called, and he's screaming bloody murder. He told me to close you down if you keep going on with that shit. What's it going to be, Floyd?"

"I didn't realize I'd overstepped," the gangly interviewer said. "Joseph's story was compelling. I know the audience was enthralled. Sorry, we'll focus on Joseph's defense of his title for the remainder of the interview."

"Who's Don Rankin?" Joseph asked as they walked back on stage.

"The station's legal counsel."

Forty-five minutes later the interview was over, and Joseph said, "Thanks, Floyd. I know you stuck your neck out for me. I owe you."

Waiting just off the stage was a silver-haired man whose red face looked like it would burst. "Oh shit," Floyd said. "It's Don Rankin. I'm in for it."

"Jesus, Floyd, what are you doing?" Rankin said, glaring at Joseph. "You're meant to interview sports stars about sports. You let him defame a president, politicians, a foreign army, a court, a knight of the realm, and say our closest ally's major crime-buster is corrupt. We're going to get our ass sued off. What were you thinking? You'll be lucky if you still have a job in the morn—"

"No one's going to sue," Joseph interrupted. "They might jump up and down and get their lawyers to send threatening letters, but they'll do nothing. Why? Because everything I said was true, and they have no idea what evidence I have. It wasn't Floyd's fault. I just got on a roll."

"Don't bullshit me. Floyd knew exactly what was going on. Even if you're right, which you're probably not, you've created an international incident. Not only that, our companies that have investments in the Congo are going to be falling over themselves apologizing for you in the morning. After they've said sorry, they're going to come after us for letting a lunatic like you have air time."

"I'm sorry you feel that way, Mr. Rankin. I didn't think Fox or you would condone oppression and murder in third-world countries. I thought you'd have a sense of justice. I'm sure I'm going to be interviewed by other media outlets. Would you like me to pass on your views?"

"Don't twist my words, young man, because I will sue you. Floyd, be in my office at nine o'clock in the morning. We need to discuss your future."

As the lawyer stormed out the studio, Joseph said, "I'm sorry, Floyd."

"Don't be, bro, I'm on your side."

Chapter 47

It was midnight when Joseph got home, but Maya was still awake. "You were wonderful," she said, kissing him. "Moise wanted to watch but fell asleep on my lap. Your mom and dad didn't say much, but I think they're worried about you. The phone rang off the hook with journalists after the interview was over. Did you get any calls?"

"I don't know. I turned my phone off before we started and didn't want to turn it back on. It can stay off. I've had enough media today. I think Floyd might be in trouble with Fox."

"They won't do anything. It's the highest-rated Sunday night show they've had this year. They'll most likely replay it tomorrow night. Facebook and Twitter are blowing up. There's enormous support for you, and there's a Facebook page called 'Charge Sir Richard Corson-Devlin with murder.'"

"I better listen to my messages," Joseph said, pulling out his cell-phone. "There's thirty." A few minutes later, he grimaced and turned it off.

"What's wrong? Was there a nasty message?"

"They were mainly journalists, but there were calls from George Faraday, and Jack Costigan. They're furious, particularly Faraday. He wants to know why I'm trying to ruin him."

"They're going to be livid when you leak those emails."

"If SOCA, the IRS, and SEC do their jobs, I mightn't have to use WikiLeaks."

"You will. I think you're going to find Sir Richard and his partners are as powerful as he boasted. I don't think the authorities are going to act with any enthusiasm. However, once you leak the emails, the pressure from the public will leave them no choice. And, when they read them in the Congo, they'll bring the government down. Stick to your plan, and do it just before the attacks."

Joseph grinned. "You're an assertive woman."

"Ah, a rare smile," Maya said, massaging his shoulders.

"That feels good."

"I can feel the pent-up tension. Let's go to bed. I'll help you relax."

Television crews, journalists, and photographers blocked the entrance when Joseph tried to reverse out of the driveway in the morning. He got out of his car and faced a barrage of questions.

"What evidence do you have to support your claims?" a hirsute, aggressive man asked, shoving a microphone in Joseph's face.

"Sir Richard Corson-Devlin called you deluded and said he's going to sue you, Fox, and Floyd Coffey. Are you worried?" a plump blonde butted in.

"The State Department's been critical of you and said if you had concerns, you should have gone through the proper channels. Why didn't you?" a balding, bespectacled man shouted from three deep in the rabble of journalists.

Flashing cameras blinded Joseph, and he pushed the thrusting microphones away from his face. He raised his arms and said, "I have nothing to add to what I said last night."

"Do you see yourself as a whistleblower?" someone shouted.

"You're not likely to be welcome in Britain for the Olympics. Why would you attack Sir Richard? He's one of the most generous men in the world," someone else asked.

Joseph shook his head, and started to climb back into his car when a petite brunette pushed her way through the crowd and said, "Do you accept responsibility for the riots and shootings in Kinshasa?"

"What?" Joseph said, turning around.

"You didn't know?" she said. "A crowd of forty thousand blocked the entrance to the president's palace. The army tried to disband them, and the crowd rioted. There have been sporadic exchanges of gunfire, and twenty civilians have been killed or injured. The president's declared a state of martial law in Kinshasa, not that it's had any effect. Some soldiers have deserted and joined the rebels."

Joseph rolled down his window and said, "Please get out of my way," as he reversed slowly past the crowd.

"The ambassador for the Democratic Republic of the Congo in Washington has called you a liar and a traitor," one journalist shouted as Joseph drove off. "Is that what you are?"

When Joseph arrived at the office, there was another throng of media waiting at the entrance to the underground parking garage. He kept on driving, parked a block away, and walked briskly back to the office, entering the building by a side door to the foyer. Two of the firm's partners were waiting by the elevators. One rolled his eyes, and the other looked at the floor and bit his lip. Neither acknowledged him.

An hour later, Joseph's father came into his office and sat down at the coffee table, motioning his son to join him. "I couldn't get out of the driveway until half an hour after you left. I wish you had talked to me before going on that show."

"I couldn't, Dad. I knew you'd try to talk me out of it. I had to do it."

"The firm's copping flak from all directions. We have a lot of wealthy clients who don't like the idea of the founder's son turning whistleblower. George Faraday called me at home to tell me he could no longer put deals the firm's way." Frank sighed. "I know you don't like George, but we've made significant profits because of our relationship. We're going to miss those funds. Needless to say, the partners aren't happy with you."

"Do you remember me telling you Faraday couldn't remember who bought the New Dawn gold mine from him? You'd know from last night that he lied. He and Sir Richard Corson-Devlin are as thick as thieves," Joseph said. "What am I saying? They are thieves."

"Yes, perhaps I just looked the other way because I thought of George as a friend."

"Sir Richard called you a pauper and threatened to break you and the firm."

"Compared to him I am." Frank frowned. "I can see you're worried about me. Don't be. I have more than $50 million in stocks, bonds, and property. For all his money, he can't hurt me."

"What about the firm?"

"Yes, he can hurt us. He may have already. George might have gone because of Sir Richard. He may be able to get to other clients, and if he mounts a campaign against you as a whistleblower, we'll lose others."

"No wonder the partners are pissed off at me."

"No one can understand why you had to go public. You could've told Jack Costigan at the State Department. He would've advised you what to do and who to tell."

"Dad, Jack knows what happened to those miners and villagers. He was in Kinshasa when they were murdered. It was his men who arranged to get me out of the jungle. One thing drives Jack, and that's keeping the Chinese out of the Congo."

"You're not finished yet, are you?"

"Last night was just the start. When the time is right, those emails are going on WikiLeaks."

"There's no other way?"

"No, Dad, this is the only way I can get justice for those murdered in Katanga."

"I admire what you're doing, Son, but I fear neither of us will have a job for much longer." Frank laughed. "I'm not worried for myself. I should be retired, but I am concerned about you."

"Don't be. I have big plans."

Late in the afternoon, Joseph received a six-page hand-delivered letter from Beaubien & Latham, the most influential law firm in Los Angeles, threatening him with every form of legal hell if he continued to defame Sir Richard Corson-Devlin. The final paragraph demanded that he immediately publish an unconditional apology to Sir Richard in the attached list of U.S., U.K., and African newspapers within forty-eight hours. Failing compliance, the lawyers threatened to mount defamation action for unspecified damages without further notice.

Joseph smiled and wondered whether Beaubien & Latham and Sir Richard would be so eager to commence litigation once the emails were on WikiLeaks.

Chapter 48

Mass rioting broke out on the streets of Kinshasa. More than forty thousand furious Congolese surrounded the entrance to the presidential palace chanting for Bodho's resignation. The president vowed to crush the uprising and instructed the Republican Guard to kill anyone who attempted to enter the grounds. He had established the ten-thousand-man Republican Guard specifically to guard his life, and they were the finest soldiers in the Congo. Much to the chagrin of Gizenga and Donatien, they reported directly to the president.

When Bodho took a call from an upset Sir Richard Corson-Devlin, the knight complained about paying for protection but not getting any. Bodho explained he was introducing policies to protect mining companies from prosecution for human rights violations. Sir Richard was grateful but expressed concern about the rebel attacks on convoys carrying provisions to the mines in Katanga. The president assured him the army had ten thousand men in Katanga to destroy the rebels. He didn't mention one of the regiments had been wiped out, or that his troops were bogged down in Kalemie fighting skirmishes with an invisible enemy.

Anticipating what *The Congo Daily Times* would print, the president sent the army in to take control of the presses. He also warned the television stations that if they showed or commented on Joseph's interview, they would lose their licenses.

Most in the seething crowds had already watched the interview on their cellphones and computers, and when they found the army had taken over the offices of *The Congo Daily Times*, it only served to fuel their anger.

"General Gizenga, when the riots die down, I want you to find the leaders and make sure they disappear," the president instructed. "Without the troublemakers leading them, they are a headless rabble."

"Yes, Mr. President."

"Our English friend suggested we throw some dirt back at Muamba.

Did you know he bribed an immigration official to forge documents enabling him to kidnap that young boy?"

"I didn't." Gizenga smirked. "But now that I do, I think we should seek his return."

Yannick Kyenge's hopelessly outnumbered fighters in Kalemie fought bravely and managed to prevent a regiment of over two thousand men from plundering villages, by attacking and running. The attacks were sporadic, usually occurring at night or in the early hours of the morning. The soldiers lived in fear of the sound of whooshing rockets. When the freedom fighters fled, they stayed just far enough in front of the soldiers to entice them into the jungle. Once they entered, they rarely got out alive. As Yannick had anticipated, the officers hadn't told the soldiers of the terrible rout in Kilwa. When they finally found out, a sense of doom pervaded the regiment in Kalemie.

After four days, Yannick and twenty of his men left Kalemie to return to his camp. The destruction of the villages by the army had led to another three hundred recruits and the surrender of seven soldiers.

"They say they deserted the army to join us. I don't trust them," one of Yannick's commanders said, shoving a young, well-muscled soldier with his wrists bound, in front of him. "This thug's name is Alain Bukasa. He's been doing all the talking."

"Why do you want to join us?" Yannick asked.

"I did not join the army to kill old men, helpless women, and children," Bukasa said, spitting on the ground. "General Gizenga is a pig. The men have no respect for him."

"How widespread is the disrespect?"

"It is common, but no one speaks of it. The officers have their spies amongst the men. No one dares speak ill of the president or the general."

"I like your attitude, but how can I trust you? What can you do for us?"

"You caught us off guard, and we weren't expecting rocket launchers. Some of my former comrades ran. They were terrified. Then the rest of the regiment panicked. Your fighters are very brave, but they have no idea how to use their weapons. Without the rocket launchers, we would have slaughtered them. We can teach your fighters how to use rifles, machine guns, grenades, and small cannons. We can turn them into an army," Bukasa said, his eyes blazing.

Yannick sensed the young man was telling the truth but wasn't prepared to trust his instincts. He took out his knife and sliced through Bukasa's bindings. "You shall be free in the camp, but you will not have any weapons. You will teach my men by telling them or showing them what to do using unloaded weapons. Until I am sure I can trust you, you will not be armed. Remember, if you do anything stupid, you'll never leave the jungle alive. Go and tell your men."

After the soldier had gone, Yannick said, "Have them watched twenty-four hours a day. If they look like they're causing trouble, kill them. The next time we go into battle, make sure they're on the front-line. Then we'll find out whether they can be trusted. If they're genuine, they'll be invaluable."

Three days after the Fox interview, Joseph had a visit from two IRS investigators, to whom he handed over a copy of the emails and a detailed list of bank transfers. They expressed little enthusiasm, explaining that as there were no American citizens or companies involved, there was little they could do, and they seemed skeptical about the unnamed American billionaire. When they asked Joseph whether there was any mention of the American in the emails and his response was in the negative, they shook their heads in resignation. It was the reaction Joseph had anticipated; he'd had little expectation of anything different from the SEC.

On the same day, he received another letter from Beaubien & Latham, this time four pages, telling him he had not complied with their earlier letter and threatening that unless he did so before Friday, they would commence legal action without further notice. *What a waste of paper,* he thought. *They're not going to do anything other than threaten.*

On Friday Joseph received the call he had been hoping for. A lady with a distinctly English voice said, "Mr. Muamba, my name is Susan Crennan. I'm with the Serious Organized Crime Agency. They were grave allegations you made about Sir Richard Corson-Devlin and this office. You've put a lot of noses out of joint."

"I'm glad to hear it."

"You said you had emails evidencing the purportedly illegal transactions."

"Ms. Crennan, there is nothing purportedly illegal. The transactions are without a doubt illegal. The emails and bank transfers prove bribery, tax evasion, money laundering, and murder. Is that enough for you? As far as your office goes, Sir Richard was adamant that there would be no investigation because he had the ears of prominent people."

"Well, he's wrong. When can you come to London to give us your evidence and make a statement?"

"Not so fast. Can you access bank accounts in the Virgin Islands?"

"Yes. We can be just as persuasive as the SEC and your Justice Department."

"Good. Before I provide you with any information, I want a guarantee that you'll provide me with the name of the others, particularly the American. There'll be payments to him or entities controlled by him from the Virgin Islands bank."

There was a long pause. "I can't do that, but we work closely with your authorities. I can undertake to provide copies of what we find to the CIA and Justice Department insofar as it relates to American citizens and corporations. Will that suffice?"

"Not good enough," Joseph replied. "I want all the names and confirmation of Sir Richard's. I can't bring criminal action, but I can take civil action on behalf of the families shafted by the military court in Kinshasa."

Joseph held the phone hard to his ear. He could hear raised voices arguing animatedly before a man said, "Give him the bloody names. The PM's turning up the heat. He's desperate to know. If it's true, he'll cut Corson-Devlin loose, but if it's not, he doesn't want to lose one of the party's major donors."

He could hear Susan Crennan sigh before responding, "Mr. Muamba, if your allegations are valid, we'll be able to provide the names. Now, when can you come to London?"

"Sorry. If you want the information, you'll have to come to LA. I want to make sure you're serious."

There was another long pause before she said, "We'll see you at 9:00 a.m. on Monday."

In London, the entrance to Sir Richard Corson-Devlin's penthouse was besieged by journalists and television crews. He denied all allegations, called Joseph a lunatic, and said he had instructed his lawyers to commence defamation action against Joseph, Floyd, and Fox. Sir Richard hated publicity and was fuming, but he was also wary, not knowing whether Joseph had any hard evidence to support his allegations. After watching the Fox interview, he had called Marc Boucher and vigorously interrogated him. Boucher told him not to worry. Joseph was bluffing. There was no way he could have gotten his hands on any of their emails.

Sir Richard's partners were not so nonchalant and told him that under no circumstances were their names to be disclosed. He was dismissive of their concerns, but his calm façade concealed an annoying uneasiness.

Chapter 49

Joseph was surprised by the coldness of Susan Crennan's long, bony fingers. She was tall and approximately forty-five, with a face made more severe by her tight, graying bun. The man with her, whom she introduced as Jeremy Spencer, was perhaps ten years younger, taller than his boss, and had a face no less severe. He placed a Dictaphone on Joseph's desk and said, "We'll be recording everything."

"As you wish. Would you like something to drink before we start?"

Crennan looked over the top of her black, thick-rimmed spectacles and said, "Thank you. No. We have no time to waste. We're on an eight o'clock flight tonight. Now, why don't you tell us all you know?"

For the next three hours, Joseph related everything that had occurred in the Congo and at the New Dawn mine while Crennan and Spencer peppered him with questions. When he finished, Crennan asked, "Where did you get these emails?"

"I can't say," Joseph replied, "but you should have no difficulty in determining their veracity. I'm sure when you pressure the Virgin Islands banks, they will confirm the transfers in the emails and on the spreadsheet I've given you."

"But you said that there's nothing in the emails that confirms the identity of Thibault," Spencer said, "and Sir Richard didn't admit anything."

"I didn't mention Thibault. I didn't want to tip him off to what I had. However, he didn't try to hide his control of New Dawn. He was quite open. It's why I know he has partners who he splits the booty with."

"Suspecting and knowing are vastly different," Spencer said.

"Humor me for a moment. If everything I told you stacks up, what charges will you lay?"

"Tax evasion, bribery, and money laundering, for starters," Crennan replied.

"What? Is that all?" Joseph said, rummaging through the papers on his desk. "Look at this. It warrants a murder charge."

Crennan read aloud the email Joseph gave her.

Marc,

Evacuate mine immediately. I have spoken to Z, and he will send soldiers to take care of the strikers. I have told him you will make helicopters available and, if need be, vehicles from the mine. Send key personnel to Lubumbashi, and advise others to make their way to Kilwa.

Thibault

"It hardly warrants a murder charge," she said.

"Forty-nine mine workers and twenty-five villagers were killed as a result of that email. The soldiers flew in on helicopters paid for by New Dawn and chased miners and villagers in vehicles provided by New Dawn. Of course it warrants a murder charge."

"Mr. Muamba, I'm a lawyer, so I can say with certainty that 'take care of' does not translate into murder, even if mine workers and villagers were murdered," Crennan said. "If we prove Thibault is Sir Richard, his lawyers will say 'take care of' was never meant to mean murder. We can't hold Sir Richard responsible because the soldiers overreacted. No, on what you've told us, we won't be pursuing murder charges. What was the reaction of the military court when the prosecutor tabled the email?"

"He didn't."

"Why not?"

"We didn't know who Thibault was then and didn't want to let Marc Boucher know we had his emails."

"It might have helped convict the soldiers. No, on reflection, it wouldn't have. From what you've told me, they were going to be acquitted, no matter how damning the evidence. You were wise not to table the email."

"So the most serious charges you'll lay will be related to white-collar crime." Joseph frowned. "That's disappointing."

"And we'll only lay them if we're 99 percent certain of getting a conviction," Crennan said. "Mr. Spencer is a forensic accountant. He and his team will be doing most of the grunt work. After he's finished, I'll make the recommendation of whether we prosecute. You shouldn't be too disappointed. If what you say is true, Sir Richard will be looking at ten years' hard time."

"I was holding out for a murder conviction. Then the families of the victims could've sued in the United Kingdom for damages."

"Sorry, it's not going to happen," Crennan said, glancing at her watch.

"Are your recommendations to prosecute usually accepted, Ms. Crennan?"

"Yes, but the director general will make the final decision. If it eases your mind, I've never had a recommendation rejected."

"It doesn't," Joseph said. "Sir Richard said he has your most powerful politicians in his pocket. Don't your funds come from the Home Office?"

"Your fears are unfounded," Crennan said, getting up from her chair. "If we can make a case, we'll prosecute. Thank you, Mr. Muamba. We have a plane to catch."

When Yannick called, he was elated. "Joseph, my friend, the soldiers have pulled out of Katanga. They left Kalemie with their tails between their legs. More than four hundred soldiers have joined my fighters."

"Fantastic. You have proved yourself to be a brave and skilled leader. What about the two regiments in Kamina?"

"The soldiers razed five villages. Then the villagers, knowing they would die if they didn't fight back, rose up. It is unbelievable. They randomly attacked the soldiers, always at night, with poison arrows and spears. It reached the stage where the soldiers refused to do sentry duty for fear of having their throats cut, or dying an excruciatingly painful death from poisons for which there is no antidote. Rebel groups have risen up across Katanga."

"We don't want that, my friend. You must go to Kamina and unify everyone under your control. If you can unite them, there's no reason why you can't take Lubumbashi. What's happened to the mines?"

"They are deserted. Once the soldiers pulled out, the management and staff couldn't leave fast enough. Northern Katanga is in our hands. I can't believe it."

"Keep your feet on the ground. You're going to have to feed an army of thousands. Employ those who know how to mine at New Dawn. They'll be able to produce twenty-five thousand ounces a month and allow you to fund an even larger army. How many of your men are in Kinshasa?"

"Two hundred."

"You need more. The day you take Lubumbashi, we'll also need to capture and hold N'djili Airport."

"Yes, yes, I know, and we must ensure the president's helicopter doesn't leave the palace. If he gets across the river to Brazzaville, he'll be free."

"You have to send more men to Kinshasa. Get them on planes while you still can."

"If you release those emails, the people will revolt. They were furious after they watched your interview. I've had my men on the streets egging them on. It won't take much more for them to attack the palace."

"No, I can't. Not yet. I don't want to show our hand to Sir Richard while he's still under investigation. He doesn't know what cards we're holding, but once he does, I'm sure he'll prove adept at covering his tracks."

Chapter 50

The late afternoon call from Jack Costigan was unexpected. "Joseph, if I had known what you were going to do, I would've made sure you never set foot in the Congo," he said. "I've been mopping up for you ever since that interview. Bodho's first reaction was to throw all U.S. companies out of the country. I've been groveling for the past month to save them. Did you give any thought to the impact your claims would have?"

"Jack, the feeling's mutual. I wish I'd never represented those companies. They get their permits through bribes and then rape the country. They don't pay taxes, and they work the Congolese to death for a pittance. I'm not sorry I spilled the beans."

"You might be. Their Department of Justice is claiming you bribed immigration officials before you kidnapped Moise. They want him back."

"You were there. You know there's not an ounce of truth in that. I have papers."

"Didn't you hear me? They're claiming those documents were forged by the officials you bribed."

"That's bullshit! I didn't kidnap him."

"I told you once before, you didn't know what you were doing. Welcome to the big leagues. Did you think you could tip a bucket of shit all over them, and they'd smile and walk away? They're a sovereign nation. They've imprisoned the immigration officials, and they want Moise back and you charged."

"What's going to happen?"

"I don't know. The Justice Department's handling it. I only got wind of it today. It doesn't look good."

"It's bullshit."

"I heard you the first time. Does Maya want to go back to the Congo to practice medicine?"

"You know she does. She's a citizen."

"So what?" Costigan laughed. "It's not the U.S. or the U.K. If they don't want to let her in, they won't, and she won't be able to do anything."

"What's that have to do with Moise?"

"Nothing, but they're not going to let her back into the country. They're going to do you over every which way. You attacked some dangerous people. Didn't you think they'd hit back?"

"Moise's my son. No one's taking him from me."

"That's no longer in your hands. If the government says he has to go back, there's nothing you'll be able to do to keep him here."

"He'll go back over my dead body," Joseph growled.

"I hope not," Costigan replied.

As Joseph was about to respond, his secretary came in and whispered, "Sir Richard Corson-Devlin's holding for you. He's an arrogant pig. He demanded I cut Mr. Costigan off."

"Jack, I have to go. Keep me informed."

"This is a surprise," Joseph said. "I never expected to hear from you. What do you want?"

"That's hardly the way to greet an old friend." Sir Richard laughed. "I don't want anything. I just called to see how you're holding up."

"Don't play games. Get to the point."

"You're very testy. Calm down. I called to find out how you're feeling now that SOCA's dropped the investigation into your ludicrous claims."

"What? What are you talking about?"

"Oh, hasn't that silly Crennan woman told you? Did you believe her when she said her recommendation would be rubber-stamped by the director general? Like you, she's an insignificant pissant."

"I-I don't under-understand."

"Of course you don't. Surely you never thought the British government would assist a kidnapper. Once the DRC filed charges against you, there was no possibility of SOCA continuing to investigate your unfounded claims. Don't worry, though. My lawyers say it is unlikely they'll extradite you. In some ways, it's a shame because the little boy you kidnapped will be going back to the Congo alone."

"It was you, you bastard! You told Bodho to rig that kidnapping charge and the extradition charges."

"I don't know what you're talking about." Sir Richard laughed. "Truth be told, you should be facing murder charges. If I were you, I'd think myself lucky."

"No one's taking Moise away from me."

"Enjoy your last few days with him. You're going to find the Congo's minerals are far more important to the U.S. than a kidnapped little boy. I warned you not to mess with me. You didn't listen. Now you're going to pay."

"You won't get away with it."

"I already have," Sir Richard said. "I don't expect we'll talk again. Goodbye, Mr. Muamba. Have a nice life."

Joseph sat behind his desk, stunned. He stared out the window to see the last of the setting sun and the offices in the buildings around him lighting up. He knew what he had to do, but moving early would be risky. He would let Maya and his father know what he had to do after dinner.

Joseph couldn't conceal his disquiet, and conversation around the dinner table was stilted. After dinner they adjourned to his father's study, where Joseph related what had occurred during the day.

"Corson-Devlin's a nasty piece of work," Frank said. "The firm's lost some major clients, no doubt as a result of his and his partner's influence. You were right about George Faraday, Son. Money is more important to him than loyalty or friendship."

"Why didn't you tell me, Dad?"

"You had enough on your plate, and there's no direct link to you and the loss of those clients."

"I'm sure your partners aren't as understanding. You've been fighting to save my job, haven't you?"

"It's irrelevant. Saving Moise from being returned and you from extradition is all that counts."

"According to Jack Costigan, the application to extradite me will fail, but Moise's another matter."

"He's our son," Maya sniffled. "If he's sent back to the Congo without us, his life will be destroyed. So will ours."

"I'll brief the best lawyers money can buy," Frank said. "We're not going to let them take Moise."

"It won't work, Dad. Sir Richard said the minerals are more important than Moise. Lawyers might stall Moise's return, but that's all. I have to go back to the Congo."

"I knew this day would come, even though I prayed it wouldn't," Frank said. "You think your calling's the presidency?"

"Yes, but after I take power, I'll hold elections within nine months and let the people choose who they want to lead them."

"My God. You should listen to yourself. You don't have the means to overthrow the government. If you go back, they'll throw you in prison. We'll never see you again."

"Dad, there's more than five thousand in Yannick's army, and he controls northern Katanga and all the mines. He is preparing to take Lubumbashi."

"So it's your friend! The rebels taking over the mines is not going to help the nation or the people. Foreign companies aren't going to invest in a war-torn country where the government can't guarantee it will protect their investments. Without foreign capital, the Congo will grind to a standstill."

"Dad, they're not rebels, they're freedom fighters. I'm sorry, but you're starting to sound like George Faraday and Jack Costigan. It's rubbish. The New Dawn Gold Mining Company paid $375,000 in taxes when it should be paying $150 million a year. Without penalties, New Dawn owes more than a billion in taxes. That's vastly more than the size of Sir Richard's and his partners' investment. Multiply that by every foreign company, and the Congo doesn't need foreign investment — it needs to collect the taxes it's entitled to."

"What you say may be true, but your friend doesn't have the firepower to topple the government. Even if he can get his freedom fighters to Kinshasa, they'll be hopelessly outnumbered. The president has an army of one hundred fifty thousand. Yannick might take Lubumbashi, but he'll never take Kinshasa."

"Soldiers are already deserting to join him, and the people are angry. After watching my interview with Floyd, they blockaded the streets for a week. All they need is a catalyst, and they'll revolt. I'm going to give them one."

"What? What can you do from here?" Frank asked.

"He can leak the emails to WikiLeaks," Maya said, "and name those in them. The people are already disgruntled. After they see the size of the payments to Bodho, Zamenka, Gizenga, and the others, they'll be furious."

"If all goes to plan, the people will rise up, and the soldiers will desert en masse and join Yannick," Joseph said.

"He's going to stage a coup," Frank said in disbelief. "Thank God you won't be there."

"But I will be. I'm flying into Kilimanjaro in Tanzania. Then I'll cross the border into the Congo by boat and join him."

"You're going to enter illegally. If they catch you, you're dead. It's suicidal."

"I'll be all right, Dad, and Yannick's counting on me. The drums have been beating about my return for months. The people will expect me to be there. I can't let them down."

"Your mother's going to be distraught. How are you going to break the news to her?"

"Dad, it's something I have to do. I know she's going to be upset. You can help me by not bringing up what you see as the dangers in front of her."

"What I see as the dangers?" Frank laughed cynically. "When are you going?"

"Next Friday. That'll give Yannick enough time to get another three hundred men to Kinshasa."

"Jesus! Why so soon?"

"It has to be. If Moise's returned, they'll use him as a pawn. They'll threaten to kill him."

"They'll use him to stop the coup."

"Yes, but it won't work. Freeing the country from the president and his cronies is more important than any one person, even if he is my son. Once the revolt starts, there'll be no stopping."

"So the proceedings for the return of Moise forced your hand?"

"Yes. I have no choice. I have to move now."

"It seems so rushed. Aren't you worried, Maya?"

"I'm going to go with Joseph," she said, making little fists with her hands.

"I wish you'd reconsider, Maya," Joseph said. "There's no need for you to come."

"I'm going, and that's final." Maya pouted.

"Who's going to look after Moise if something happens to you?" Frank asked.

"Dad, if we're unsuccessful, Moise will be returned to the Congo. I know you'll try to save him, but Jack Costigan left me in little doubt of what the outcome of the proceedings will be."

"I'll book a plane."

"No," Joseph replied. "We're traveling by commercial flight. We don't want to draw any undue attention to ourselves."

Chapter 51

Moise was in bed, and Joseph and Maya were on the sofa watching the late night news. She nestled into his shoulder and said, "I wish there was another way. I'll never be able to practice medicine. When we have kids, they'll need guarding around the clock. When Moise joins us, he'll have to be driven to and picked up from school every day. It's a horrible life."

"How can you be so confident? Dad thinks they'll throw us in prison if the coup fails, but you know what will really happen. We'll be found guilty of treason and publicly hanged as a warning to others. I wish you'd think again. You don't have to come with me."

"You of little faith," she said, punching him in the chest. "Ever since we got back together in Kinshasa, all you've talked about is your calling. Why do you now think it's false? I have belief. Why don't you?"

"I do. I'd just feel better if you stayed here."

"Well, I'm not. I'm going to have to get used to living in a fishbowl, and this might be one of the few remaining instances where I have a choice."

"My calling is to free the country from thugs and rid it of corruption. I don't need to be president to do that, and like you, I want to lead a normal life."

"What? Have you lost your senses? Of course, you'll be president. Yannick says the people are still chanting your name. You're the great savior the drums beat for."

"Yes, but only until there are elections. If the coup is successful, I'll call them within nine months. I don't intend to be a career president. I'll miss the London Olympics, but I'm going to compete in Rio. No one has ever skipped an Olympics and come back to win gold in the decathlon. I'll be the first."

"Don't be silly. Who else is going to be president? Don't say Yannick. He is brave and has a good heart, but he's uneducated. There is no one else."

"There is someone. You don't know him."

"Who?" Maya grinned disbelievingly.

"I'll let you know when the time is right."

It was a cloudless, humid day when General Gizenga's motorcade drove into the grounds of the palace. The president was waiting in the reception chamber, a bottle of malt whiskey and full glass on the table next to him. He pointed to a chair but did not offer the general a drink. "How could a small group of rebels defeat ten thousand of the army's finest?" he shouted. "How?"

"They attack and run. It's not like fighting another army. Once they're in the jungle, they're impossible to find. Most of the soldiers killed died in the jungle. We tried to – "

"Enough," Bodho interrupted. "You sound like you're defending that incompetent Colonel Donatien. Are you?"

"No, definitely not."

"When you left Katanga, he was your choice to replace you. It reflects poorly on you. The man is a coward and an idiot. He still had seven thousand men when he returned to Lubumbashi. What was he thinking?"

"Well – "

"I haven't finished," Bodho growled, downing his whiskey in one gulp. "Who are you going to get to replace him? We need someone who'll take no prisoners."

"Do you want me to return?"

"No. There is too much unrest on the streets here, and those infernal drums never stop. How many troublemakers did you catch after the riots?"

"Twenty-three. They're in prison."

"Get rid of them. It will send a message to those plotting against us. It'll also make the soldiers think twice about deserting."

"All of them?" Gizenga asked, unable to hide his shock.

"I'm surprised you need to ask, General. You saw what happened in Katanga with Colonel Donatien. No one respects or fears weakness. I hope you aren't getting squeamish."

"Of course not. We can't have twenty-three accidental hangings, though."

Bodho sighed and rolled his eyes. "I never had to think for General Zamenka. You'll put them in the back of a truck and drive out into the bush. It'll give your men some machine gun practice."

"Yes, Mr. President. What do you want me to do with Colonel Donatien?"

"Do what you want with him. Bring him back here, if he can help you. If not, send him to an outpost where he won't have to lead men into battle. The rebels only ever got a foothold because of him. If he hadn't let Kyenge escape, we wouldn't be in this position."

Yannick was shocked when he received Joseph's call to say he wanted the coup moved forward. Yannick liked to plan the minutest details, and rushing distressed him. Not only did he have to take Lubumbashi, but Joseph wanted leaflets printed and dropped by helicopter for those who couldn't access the Internet. He also wanted more men in Kinshasa.

"Yannick, strike Lubumbashi in the early hours of the morning," he said. "You'll have the advantage of surprise. If all goes well, it will be a bloodless coup. It's going to be far tougher for me in Kinshasa."

Chapter 52

It was midday, and LAX was buzzing. Joseph begged Michelle to stay in the car, but she wouldn't hear of it. "I'll never see either of you again," she sobbed.

Frank held her hand and said, "Calm down, darling. They'll be all right."

Moise had his arms wrapped around Maya's legs. "Don't go. Please don't go," he whimpered.

"Mom, you're upsetting Moise," Joseph said, putting his arm around her. "We know what we're doing. Nothing's going to happen to us. We have to go."

Frank shook Joseph's hand before embracing him. "Make sure what you told your mom is true," he said, fighting back the tears.

"Don't worry, Dad, we know what we're doing," he said, picking up Moise. "I'm leaving you here to look after Grandma and Granddad. Can you do that?"

"Ye-yes," the little boy said. "I-I don't want you to go."

Maya wiped Moise's eyes and said, "We'll see you in three weeks, I promise. You know I never tell fibs."

"Come on," Joseph said, taking Maya's hand.

As they joined the line to present their passports, Maya said, "Poor Moise."

"Yes, I'm glad that's over and hope we didn't lie to him."

"We didn't. Remember, it's your destiny," Maya said, squeezing his hand.

KM0602 took off for Kilimanjaro via Amsterdam on time at 1:45 p.m. Joseph pushed his business class seat back. "I'm going to have a snooze. You should do the same. After we land at Kilimanjaro tomorrow, it will be the end of sleep for God knows how long. We'll cross the lake and be home before midnight."

"Home?" Maya laughed. "So deep down you're not really an American boy."

"Go to sleep."

It was 7:45 p.m., and hot and sticky when they landed at Kilimanjaro Airport. They cleared customs, and a small, old, toothless man wearing a faded New York Yankees cap approached them. "Mr. and Mrs. Afua?" he asked.

"Yes," Joseph replied. "Are you our pilot?

"I am. Please follow me," he said, picking up their suitcases. "I'm cleared for takeoff."

The plane was an old Cessna with patched-up wings and a corroded fuselage. Joseph nudged Maya and said, "Hardly a Gulfstream. I hope it gets us there."

The seats were torn and the interior smelled of aviation fuel. "Strap yourself in," the pilot shouted, over the engine noise.

"How long is it going to take to get to Tabora?" Joseph shouted back.

"Not long. It's only four hundred miles. We should be there in ninety minutes."

"I can't wait to see Grace and Roland," Maya said.

Surprisingly, the flight was uneventful, and the pilot made a perfect landing at the small, ill-lit Tabora Airport. "My nephew is ready with your helicopter," he said, carrying the suitcases down the stairs.

Joseph handed him $100, but he shook his head. "I was paid plenty for this job. I knew it was someone important but never would've guessed it was you, Mr. Muamba."

Joseph's face dropped, and the pilot continued. "Don't worry, I won't breathe a word. Nor will my nephew. You may not realize it, but yours is the most famous face in all of Africa. We cheered for you in Beijing as much as the Congolese did. You're not going to be able to fool anyone in this continent with a false name."

"Thank you." Maya laughed. "He doesn't know how famous he is."

"Good luck," the pilot said. "The drums of Africa have been foretelling your return for months. Come on, I'll introduce you to my nephew, Paul. He's a good boy, and like me, he won't breathe a word."

The helicopter was a four-seater Robinson that looked like it had been patched up by the same repairer who had worked on the Cessna.

"It's an honor to meet you, Mr. Muamba. One day I'll tell my kids the president of the Congo flew in my helicopter," Paul said.

"Call me Joseph."

"I'll take those suitcases, Uncle," Paul said. "Did he look after you? Did you have a good flight, Mr. Muamba?"

Joseph sighed and shook his head. "How long before we're at Lake Tanganyika?"

"Not long. You just relax, Mr. President. Mr. Kyenge has arranged everything. We'll be there soon enough."

As the helicopter took off, Maya nudged Joseph and giggled. "I told you it was your destiny, Mr. President."

Two hours later, the helicopter flew over the vast lake. "There's a speedboat waiting in that small cove," Paul said, as a light beam flashed three times. "We're in the clear. You don't have to worry about government officials. Another forty miles and you'll be back in the Congo."

Another set of light beams lit up a clearing fifty yards from the edge, and Paul made a perfect landing. The angry roar of engines shattered the night silence, and the young man waiting for them on the jetty said, "Mr. Muamba, I am Alain. Yannick sent me to pick you up. Sorry about the din. They're Mercury 250s. There's not a faster boat in all of Africa. No one's going to catch us."

Two other men carrying machine guns bowed to Joseph and Maya as they climbed onboard. Alain took the wheel, and the speedboat idled out of the cove. "We're nearly home, Maya."

"Yes," she replied. "See how those men are intimidated by you? You must be careful when you are with Yannick not to undermine him. He has built his army without your help. You must not assume leadership."

"Why would they be intimidated?"

"You killed two men with your bare hands, and then you slew the most feared man in the Congo. The return of the great savior is played out on the drums every night. Of course they're in awe of you. You need to ensure you don't sound as though you're talking down to or ordering Yannick around."

"What would I do without you?" Joseph said. "I would never

intentionally put Yannick down, but yes, I'll be careful about how I address him."

"You look sad. What's wrong?"

"I'm thinking of Anatole and the others trying to get across this vast expanse of water on a flimsy raft. They never stood a chance. I'm glad I killed Zamenka, but it won't bring them back."

Maya put her arm around his shoulders. "And here I am talking about how much I'm looking forward to seeing Grace and Roland when you have lost all of your family. I'm sorry."

An hour later, a blaze of lights lit up the jungle on the other side of the lake. "What's that, Alain?" Joseph asked.

"It's Yannick waiting to welcome you."

"What's he doing, telling the world we've returned?" Joseph muttered.

Maya elbowed him sharply. "Remember, Boss, you must not disrespect him in front of his men. Without him, we wouldn't be here."

There were three Jeeps and a truck on shore, all with their lights on high. As the boat pulled into the shallows, four men waded into the water and dragged it to the shore.

"Yannick, Yannick," Maya said, leaping out of the boat and throwing her arms around him. "You've changed. You look terrific."

"It's wonderful to see you, Maya. We eat better in the jungle than we ever did in the village. We live off mine provisions, and if they run short, we have plenty of gold to buy more. We feed more than six thousand, twice a day. No one goes hungry."

Joseph shook Yannick's hand, and said, "You've lost ten years, and added twenty pounds. Leading an army of freedom fighters agrees with you."

"Thank you," Yannick said. "Listen to the drums. They're beating out the message of your return. The Congo will be in a frenzy tonight."

"Where are we?" Maya asked.

"Fifty miles south of Kalemie. Tanzania's border security rarely patrols where you crossed."

"Yannick," Joseph said, "I don't want to criticize, but why are your vehicles' high beams on? It will only draw attention to us."

Yannick slapped his thigh and roared with laughter. "We control all of northern Katanga, the roads, the mines, and the villages. We no longer need to sneak through the bushes and trees. The light show is to greet you."

Joseph was amazed. Not by what Yannick had done, but by his friend's assertiveness and confidence. The skinny, nervous man who had escaped in the alley at the rear of the court had transformed himself into a vibrant leader.

"You have conquered Katanga, my friend. What an incredible achievement."

"Not until I've taken Lubumbashi," Yannick replied, "and God willing, you will take Kinshasa on the same day. Come on. It's a five-hour drive to our camp. You'll be surprised by where I have relocated it."

Chapter 53

The sun was rising as they drove into the camp, and Joseph was taken aback not by the location, but by its enormity. There were tents and temporary huts for as far as the eye could see. An area had been set aside for equipment and vehicles. There were more than a hundred army Jeeps and trucks, but taking the place of honor was a Sikorsky. "How did you capture a helicopter?" Maya gasped.

"We didn't. The pilots deserted and joined us. You haven't said anything about the location, Joseph."

"I guessed. Where's your tent pitched? Next to the old baobab tree?"

"You know me too well." Yannick laughed. "We are close to the village. The equipment is readily accessible, and if need be, we can retreat into the jungle."

Screams of joy interrupted their conversation as Maya caught sight of Grace and Roland coming toward them. Joseph watched as they hugged and kissed, and was overcome by sadness. "We still have some planning to do," Maya said. "I will catch up with you after. You look wonderful, Grace. Oh, and so do you, Roland."

"How many fighters are here, Yannick?" Joseph asked, trying to forget how despondent he felt.

"I don't know exactly. More than five thousand, and there are another thousand on the outskirts of Lubumbashi. I'm still adding to the four hundred now in Kinshasa, and I have men at all the regional airports in Katanga."

"Excellent. Tell me your plans."

"I need to look at my notes," Yannick said, heading toward the jungle with Joseph and Maya close behind.

"God," Maya said, "you've pitched your tent in the same position where we used to meet. Seventeen years ago, who would've thought three scruffy kids from Katanga would overthrow the government?"

Yannick picked up his notes and knelt down in front of his tent and, with a small branch, made a mark in the dirt. "We are here. To get four thousand men to Lubumbashi, we'll need to use every vehicle and make two trips," he said, drawing a line. "If the army gets wind of what we're doing, they'll fly in more troops. We need to move quickly. I'll be ready to attack on Wednesday. That's seven days."

"I thought you said there were more than five thousand fighters here," Maya said.

"There are. You will stay with those we leave behind. If we fail, you'll take them back into the jungle and keep the fight going."

"No!" Maya said. "I'm going to Kinshasa with Joseph."

"No, you're not," Joseph said. "One of us has to stay here."

"And Joseph will be undertaking the most dangerous part of the operation," Yannick said. "We'll be lucky to have five hundred fighters in Kinshasa by Wednesday, so he'll need to turn the crowd and then the army. If he can't, he's dead."

"It's unfair," Maya said, shaking her head. "Joseph, you would not even be here if it were not for me. I have never had any doubts. It is you who needed convincing about your calling. I want to be with you. If they kill you, I'll have nothing to live for."

"No one is going to kill me, but if something happens it is important that the cause goes on. That responsibility will fall on your shoulders, Maya. And if they're successful in bringing Moise back, your first task will be to free him." Joseph said.

"Maya, I know you want to be with Joseph on the frontline but one of us has to remain here. I'm leaving Grace and Roland behind to support you, not that you'll need any support," Yannick said. "Joseph, what's your plan for leaking the emails?"

"I'd like to make it look like Marc Boucher leaked them, but I don't have the computer expertise."

"Don't worry," Yannick said. "There's a woman in the safe house in Kinshasa. Her name is Belvie. She taught me how to use a computer and smartphone. There is nothing she does not know. She'll leak the emails through anonymous servers and make it look like it was Boucher. I'll call her. When do you want them leaked?"

"Saturday. That'll leave four days to circulate them. All of the

Congo will know their president, the army, and their politicians cheated them out of billions by Sunday. The people will be furious."

"Let's hope they are angry enough to revolt in Kinshasa. You're going to need all the help you can get."

"Get your men to stir the people up, but make sure they don't take to the streets until Wednesday. That's when I'll need them. Are you going to do the same in Lubumbashi?"

"I won't need any help," Yannick replied.

"Why are you so confident?"

"We'll move at four o'clock in the morning. I'll have five thousand fighters with me, and we'll have the advantage of surprise. Lubumbashi will be in our hands by six. I wish I could be in Kinshasa with you. Can you think of anything else I can do to help?"

"Can you get someone to teach me how to use a machine gun?"

"I'll do it myself."

"Thank you, Yannick, and do you trust those two helicopter pilots?"

"Implicitly. Why?"

"When I fly out of Kilwa for Kikwit, I want one with me."

"I don't understand. I've already arranged for a helicopter for you at Kikwit. You don't need a helicopter pilot."

"I will when I get to Kinshasa," Joseph said. "Someone who I can trust and who will follow my orders without question."

"Consider it done, my friend."

The president's motorcade — with Jeeps carrying soldiers in the front and rear — was surrounded by motorcycles on Saturday morning as it traveled slowly through the streets of Kinshasa. There was no cheering or waving, and when President Bodho looked out the window, all he saw were surly, unhappy faces. General Gizenga glanced nervously out the other window. "The people are restless," Bodho said. "I wonder if it's those damn drums. They've been feverish the past three days."

"They're angry," Gizenga replied. "They know we killed the prisoners."

"Angry? They're not angry. They're scared. None of them can hold my gaze. They look away or down at their feet. They know if they stir up trouble, they'll die."

"We need to be careful, Mr. President. If we push them to the point where they have nothing to lose, they'll revolt, and next time, they mightn't stop."

"Rubbish! When will you ever learn? They respond to power and brutality. The Romans knew fear was the greatest motivator, and nothing has changed. When Germany occupied France, Hitler killed ten civilians for every German soldier murdered by the French resistance. He knew the power of fear."

Gizenga wanted to say, *The Romans were overthrown, and despite the civilian deaths in France, the French freedom fighters continued to kill German soldiers for the duration of the war,* but he bit his tongue. "You know best, Mr. President."

"Yes, I do. What have you decided to do with Colonel Donatien?"

"He's flying into Kinshasa tonight. I can use him to handle time-consuming administrative duties. It'll free me up to undertake more important tasks."

"Good, good, as long as he is not leading men into battle. Who are you replacing him with?"

"There is a young captain who oversaw the execution of the prisoners. He personally finished those who he thought weren't dead or were faking with a bullet to the back of their heads. He is one of my most capable officers. He was hit by friendly fire in an attack on the rebels six months ago and has been recuperating ever since. He's fully recovered and dying to get back to Katanga. He says he'll rout the rebels within a week."

"He sounds like my type of man. Is he flying out tonight?"

"He has some loose ends to tidy up. He'll take up his new position next weekend."

"You're leaving Lubumbashi without a commander for six days. Is that wise?"

"There's nothing to worry about," Gizenga replied. "Colonel Donatien was often away for longer than a week. It's not as if anything is going to happen."

"Yes, you're right. Offer the captain $100,000 if he can retake Katanga in a week."

"That's unusual. It'll create a precedent. Are you sure you want to do it?"

"The British, Canadians, and Americans are screaming about the rebels closing their mines. That pain in the ass, Sir Richard Corson-Devlin, calls me every day. They've stopped making payments. They say without the income from the mines, they don't have the funds to pay us. Liars! They're all billionaires. We'll make them pay for their deceit once Katanga is back in our hands."

As the motorcade approached the palace, protesters carrying placards demanding an end to government-sanctioned murder paraded in front of the gates. They didn't look scared. They looked angry. "Get your men to clear them out, General. If they don't go, throw them in prison. Better still, give them to your captain for revolver practice."

"I'll get rid of them, Mr. President."

"Oh, and what is happening with the boy? Every time the Englishman calls, he wants to know if we have the boy. I think he hates Muamba even more than we do."

"The Americans are stalling. They're throwing up legal roadblocks. We'll get him back. It's just a matter of time. He's not a refugee. He's one of our citizens. I've sworn an affidavit saying the adoption papers were falsified. They have no choice but to return him, and they know it."

"Call that State Department official. I can't remember his name. The one with the big mouth. Tell him we're looking at the status of the Prescott uranium project and are considering reopening permit negotiations so the Chinese can bid. He'll get the message. The boy will be back here within the week." Bodho grinned. "They take us for fools, but we know who the fools are. Right, General?"

"Yes, Mr. President."

Chapter 54

On Sunday morning the cities, towns, and villages of the Congo bristled. Those who had computers or cellphones showed the emails to their friends, and the drums broadcast them to the wider populace. The people had known their leaders were corrupt but were staggered by the size of the bribes they had accepted. Miners who were paid three dollars for a twelve-hour shift fumed when they saw the millions transferred to the president, generals, and the politicians. Yannick's freedom fighters worked the crowds and bars telling the people to maintain their rage, but not to do anything until Wednesday.

Despite the freedom fighters' advice, hundreds of placard-carrying citizens marched in front of the palace gates. President Bodho and General Gizenga were beside themselves with rage. They wasted no time dispatching soldiers to Marc Boucher's hotel, instructing them to return with him, whether he liked it or not. When they dragged him into the small interrogation room, he was still protesting. "It wasn't me!" he insisted. "It wasn't me!"

"Why did you say you lied in court and that you heard me order my soldiers to murder those miners and villagers?" Gizenga shouted, holding up a printed copy of that particular email in front of Boucher's eyes.

"It wasn't me. I didn't send that email. Look at the sender's email address. It's not mine."

"Why did you say Thibault was Sir Richard? He's fuming."

"I know. He woke me in the early hours of the morning. I told him what I'm telling you."

"And why did you name us?" Gizenga snarled.

"I told you it wasn't me!"

"So the emails aren't genuine?" Bodho asked.

"I haven't looked at all of them. There are thousands."

"What about the ones you have looked at?" Bodho asked, his top lip turned up in an ugly sneer.

Boucher looked down at the floor. "They appear to be genuine."

"'They appear to be genuine,'" Gizenga mimicked. "I know they're genuine. I've checked the dates and the amounts transferred. The question is, how did they get out into the public?"

"Sir Richard asked me that. I don't know. My computer must have been hacked," Boucher whimpered.

"I don't believe you," Bodho said. "Who paid you? Why did you do it?"

"I didn't. If I had, do you think I would've stayed in the Congo? It wasn't me. I promise."

"Throw him in a cell," Bodho said to the soldiers. "It'll give him some thinking time to come up with the truth."

"No, no!" Boucher yelled, as the soldiers dragged him from the room.

"The baobab tree hasn't changed in seventeen years," Maya said, kneeling in the shadow in front of it. "Do you remember we used to say it will be dead next year? It might outlast us."

"I don't think so," Yannick said. "We'll know our fate within forty-eight hours. Is there anything else I can do before you leave for Kilwa, Boss?"

"No, nothing," Joseph said. "Just remember, no announcements before six o'clock on Wednesday morning."

Maya held her hand out, palm down. Yannick put his on top of it, Joseph put his on Yannick's, and they repeated the process until six hands were stacked. "We'll never be separated," she said.

"Never," echoed Joseph and Yannick.

It was dusk when Joseph and his helicopter pilot, Beni, boarded a twin-engine Cessna in Kilwa for the five-hour flight to Kitwit. "How long were you in the army, Beni?" Joseph asked.

The middle-aged man ran his fingers through his short, graying beard. "Too long. I saw too much death and cruelty. More than twenty years."

"Do you have a family?"

"A wife and three kids."

Joseph frowned as he related what he wanted the helicopter pilot to do. "If we fail, you'll die. I wish I had known you had a family."

"Don't worry, Mr. Muamba. I knew the risks I was taking when I deserted," Beni said, a twinkle in his eye. "I can do things with a helicopter that no other pilot in Africa can. I don't intend to die, and I'm going to make sure I protect my new president, too."

"Get some sleep, Beni, and forget the 'Mr. Muamba.' Call me Joseph."

Except for the airport, Kitwit was asleep. The pilot made a perfect landing and taxied over to a waiting helicopter. "Good luck, Mr. Muamba," he said.

As Joseph boarded the helicopter, he said, "It seems everyone knows my plans, Beni."

"No, they don't, Joseph. They all know something's going to happen, though. Listen to those drums. They're feverish."

It was 1:00 a.m. when the helicopter landed in a clearing on the outskirts of Kinshasa. As Joseph came down the stairs, a familiar voice said, "Welcome home, Mr. President."

"Leon, what a surprise. What's the CIA doing here?" Joseph asked, gripping the humongous man's hand.

"Ex-CIA. I'm your chauffeur and bodyguard. One day I want to tell my grandkids I helped free the Congo."

"You're optimistic."

"There is dissent in the army. The people are seething. Once you move, they will follow. Get in. I'll take you to the safe house."

Ten minutes later, Leon pulled into the driveway of a barely visible cream brick bungalow. Leon hid the limo in the dense, surrounding foliage, and led the way through bushes to the rear of the house. The back door was open, and the veranda light was on. "Hello, Belvie, hello, Rishi," Leon said. "Let me introduce you to Joseph and Beni."

"Welcome, Mr. Muamba," Belvie said. "It is an honor to meet you."

"Please call me Joseph. I would not be here if it were not for you two. The time you spent training Yannick turned him into the finest general in the Congo."

"Yes, we have watched him from afar," Rishi said. "Who would think he'd never held a revolver two years ago?"

"Or used a smartphone," Belvie said. "He has become a superb strategist and tactician. We have much to go over before Wednesday morning. Do you want to do it now, or do you want to get some rest?"

"Let's do it now. Tell me how you've deployed our forces."

"One hundred at the airport. Fifty at the radio and television station, and three hundred on the streets to stir up the crowds."

"Make it one hundred and fifty at the airport. I want to make sure that once we've taken it, word doesn't leak out. That means moving fast and shutting down all form of communication, particularly cellphones. Can you make sure that instruction filters down?"

"Yes," Belvie said, "but it will leave us short on the streets."

"It has to be done," Joseph said. "Let's go over the rest of the plan."

Chapter 55

At four o'clock on Wednesday morning, Yannick's youngest commander and one hundred of his men took control of a quiet Lubumbashi International Airport. A few weary commuters sleeping overnight in the terminal were shocked to have their cellphones taken from them. Other than some angry words, though, the seizure was achieved without incident.

At the same time, Lubumbashi's national radio and television office was seized and closed down by fifty freedom fighters. There were less than twenty personnel, who, after having their cellphones taken from them, were locked up in a large office.

The army barracks were in Lubumbashi's least desirable area — made so by the drunken antics, rapes, and bashings committed by the soldiers. Yannick carefully positioned more than three thousand of his freedom fighters in the streets around the barracks. Another two thousand formed an outer ring to prevent soldiers from escaping. At 5:15 a.m., with only fifty minutes to sunrise, Yannick gave the signal, and his men moved with blinding speed to disarm the still sleepy sentries.

By 5:55 a.m., just as Yannick had hoped, he controlled Lubumbashi without firing a shot or losing a life. Thirty minutes later, he appeared on national television to say he had taken Lubumbashi in a bloodless coup on behalf of the Congo's new president, Joseph Muamba.

At 1:30 a.m., on the outskirts of Kinshasa, Joseph, Beni, and Leon left the safe house and headed for N'djili. "What a shame the airport and army barracks are both in N'djili," Joseph said. "We must take the airport without gunfire and ensure no one uses their cellphone to sound the alarm."

"Our fighters know what to do. You don't have to go with Beni. There are those who are far more competent than you with a machine gun. It's a silly risk. What if they shoot you down? That will end the revolution."

"Yes, I do, and what you say is not right. If something happens to me, you will take over, Leon. You have the skills to lead."

"Even if what you say is true, the people aren't going to rise up for me. They love you. You're their hero."

"He's right," Beni said. "Without you, there is no revolution."

"My mind is made up," Joseph said. "Now tell me about the airport."

"The one hundred and fifty you want at the airport is too many," Leon said. "It doesn't open until six o'clock in the morning. There will only be a skeleton staff maintaining it. We will take it without any problems."

"Perhaps you are right — but one call on a cellphone, and our plans are up in flames. And don't forget, we have to hold it. Where are our fighters? I want to talk to the leaders."

"Within walking distance of the airport."

A cacophony of pounding drums permeated every inch of the Congo. Cities, towns, and villages remained awake in anticipation of what the night might hold. At five o'clock in the morning, an ever increasing crowd started to congregate before the entrance to the palace. The Republican Guards manning the gates were alert and on edge. Just before six o'clock, an army helicopter hovered over the entrance, and some in the crowd pulled back, not knowing whether it was going to attack them.

"Beni, there must be fifty thousand down there," Joseph said.

"And look at the streets," Beni replied. "Thousands more are joining them."

"Let's get it done. Take me around to the back of the palace, and remember, bring it down slowly as if you're going to land."

"I know what to do," Beni replied. "You only need to take out one rotor."

"I'll take them both out," Joseph said, cradling an AK-47. "I want to make sure the president has no means of escape."

As Beni lowered the helicopter, rifle-toting guards put their hands over their eyes and looked up. Thirty feet from the ground, Joseph opened fire and, in less than twenty seconds, sprayed the presidential helicopter with two hundred rounds. "Climb, climb," he shouted, as bullets bounced off the fuselage.

Instead, Beni skillfully maneuvered the helicopter, putting the palace between it and the guards. "Don't forget the leaflets," he said, as they flew over the crowd.

"Did I get the rotors?" Joseph asked as he shoved leaflets out the door.

"It doesn't make any difference." Beni laughed. "You decapitated it. No one's going to fly that bird."

The leaflet had a picture of Joseph with a statement below it, saying he had taken over the presidency and vowed to rid the country of corruption. The bottom line in pronounced bold type called on the people to help him. One of Yannick's men in the crowd started to chant, "Muamba, Muamba, Muamba," and soon it drowned out everything.

"I've never seen so many people," Beni said. "The streets are packed."

President Bodho had had a late night and consumed too much alcohol, but the machine gun and rifle fire had awoken him. As he looked at the remains of his helicopter, he asked one of the guards whether they'd been attacked. "No, Mr. President, they just destroyed the helicopter and fled."

"What is that chanting?"

"There is an enormous crowd at the entrance chanting Joseph Muamba's name."

Bodho hurried back into the palace and called General Gizenga but got the busy signal. "Here," he said, hurling the phone at one of his assistants. "Keep trying until you get the general."

As Joseph and Beni approached the airport, they could see flashes of gunfire. Beni landed behind one of the hangars, and they made their way to the terminal where the fighting was taking place. "What's happening, Leon?" Joseph shouted.

"The army mounted a counterattack thirty minutes ago. We're hopelessly outnumbered. We've already lost more than twenty men. I've called our people in Kinshasa for help."

"There are only two hundred and fifty," Joseph replied. "What help are they going to be? It looks like our bluff has failed. I hate the idea of our people dying for a lost cause. I'm afraid we misjudged, my friend."

"Cease fire!" a loud voice over a megaphone shouted, and the soldiers stopped shooting. "Joseph Muamba, my name is Captain Sunga. Look out the window at the southern end of the terminal. I have ten of your men. I will execute them unless you surrender. Come out with your hands above your head by yourself, and I will let them live."

"It's a trap," Beni said, "don't go."

"He's right," Leon agreed.

"Look at them," Joseph said, "kneeling on the tarmac with their hands tied behind them. I can't let them die."

"He's going to kill them no matter what you do. Our reinforcements will be here soon."

"Two hundred and fifty." Joseph frowned. "Look at the truckloads of soldiers pouring in. We're outnumbered twenty to one. I thought the soldiers would turn. I was wrong."

"You have one minute, Muamba. If you're not out here by then, I'll kill the first of your rebels."

Joseph heard the captain ask someone a question. Then he shouted, "Her name is Junelle, and she's only nineteen. Do you want her blood on your hands?"

"I'm coming!" Joseph shouted back. "Beni, Leon, there is no need for you to stay. You can get away by helicopter. Take as many of our fighters as you can."

Leon folded his massive arms across his chest and said, "I'm not going anywhere."

"Nor me," Beni added.

"Thirty seconds," the captain screamed.

"I'm coming!" Joseph yelled again.

The sun was coming up as he left the terminal. When he reached the soldiers, they immediately seized him and manhandled him over to their captain. "The famous Joseph Muamba." He sneered. "Your fame's not going to help you now. Get on your knees."

"You said you'd let them go."

"I lied," the captain said, punching a number into his cellphone. "They'll die with you. Damn, General Gizenga's phone's busy. You have a few minutes extra to live."

Joseph lifted his head and caught the eye of a nervous-looking young corporal. He glanced around and saw hundreds of soldiers surrounding the terminal before he felt a rifle butt slam into the back of his head. His face crashed into the tarmac. "Keep your head down," a soldier grunted.

"How many men do you have in the terminal?" the captain snarled.

Joseph felt blood trickling down his neck but sat upright and defiantly said, "I don't know."

The captain's boot slammed into his ribs. "It makes no difference. They are all going to die. I'm only letting them live so they can see you beg for mercy before I kill you."

"It's never going to happen," Joseph said, spitting just in front of the captain's boots.

Another boot crashed into his ribs, but he didn't grunt or show any pain.

The captain pulled out his cellphone and said, "You have less than a minute to live."

Chapter 56

Joseph heard the captain say, "Yes, General, I will put it on speaker mode."

Then he heard Gizenga's voice. "You fool, Muamba, you thought you'd come back with your ragtag rebels and overthrow the president. You've come back to die."

"You're not at the palace are you, General? When I flew over it an hour ago, the crowd was trying to break down the gates, and the Republican Guards were running. Are you sure the president is still in power?"

Gizenga laughed mockingly. "I've just spoken to him. You're a liar. Yes, there is a mob at the gates, but the guards have not run, and the president remains in control. Once you are dead, this foolishness will be over."

"It won't make any difference if I die. The people know you stole from them. They know you are guilty of murder. They want retribution. If it's not me, it will be someone else."

"They're a rabble without leadership. Once you are dead, they'll come to their senses. If they don't, a few public hangings will soon bring them into line. Enough talking. Kill him, Captain. Goodbye, Muamba, and good riddance."

As the captain withdrew his pistol the doors of the terminal burst open, and Leon came out with his hands above his head. "Stop!" he shouted. "Listen. Listen."

The soldiers trained their guns on Leon, and the captain said, "What are you talking about, you fool? Do you want to die with him?"

"Listen," Leon said. "Listen!"

The chant was angry, and it was still a way off. Joseph heard it. They had shouted his name in front of the palace in exultation. Now it was in anger.

One of the soldiers said, "I can hear it."

Leon didn't need a megaphone. His booming voice carried across the tarmac. "There's an angry crowd of more than fifty thousand on their way to the airport. If you kill their president, they will tear you apart from limb from limb. None of you will leave the airport alive. Why do you want to be loyal to a president who has stolen billions from you? Lay down your weapons."

Some of the soldiers dropped their eyes while others looked in the direction of the ever increasing crescendo.

"Shut up! Once he is dead, they'll lose their enthusiasm," the captain said.

"Look at the windows of the terminal!" Leon said. "See those cell-phones? They're videoing every move you and your men make, and uploading it direct to Facebook. They have close-ups of your faces. Are you married, Captain? You might like to call your wife and kids and say goodbye."

The first of the open trucks appeared on the road with men shouting and randomly firing rifles into the air while the angry chant increased in intensity.

The captain rested the barrel of his pistol on the back of Joseph's head and said, "They're too late."

"No! No!" Leon shouted, charging at the captain.

"Stop!" the corporal yelled, leveling his AK-47 at Leon.

"Kill him," the captain ordered, preparing to pull the trigger.

Then Leon watched in amazement as the corporal pointed the machine gun at the captain. "No, he is right. Joseph Muamba is our country's hero. He is honest. He will rid the country of corruption and poverty. Drop your pistol, Captain."

"Kill him," the captain screamed at the other soldiers. "He is a deserter, and you know what happens to deserters."

The trucks swung onto the tarmac, and there was a fierce exchange of gunfire. The soldiers looked at each other, not knowing what to do, before one of them said, "I am with Corporal Bilenga."

"So am I," another said, and the others followed.

As the captain swung his pistol back on Joseph, the corporal fired one short burst that ripped through the captain's chest. "Untie them," he said.

Leon seized the megaphone, and his booming voice carried across the tarmac. "It is over. Your captain is dead. You are outnumbered fifty to one. Cease firing. Celebrate our new president. He will bring honesty and prosperity to our country."

There were a few random shots and then joyous chanting: "Muamba, Muamba, Muamba."

"You saved my life," Joseph said, grasping Leon's hand.

"He saved both our lives," Leon said, grinning at the corporal. "You're a brave young man."

"Is there anything I can do to help, Mr. President?" the corporal asked.

"Yes," Joseph said. "Come with us to the palace."

Joseph and Leon sat in the back of a Jeep crawling along the teeming road to Kinshasa. Thousands followed in cars and trucks, firing guns into the air. The joyous crowd sang, drank, and chanted. Kinshasa's streets were bursting at the seams, and a crowd of more than two hundred thousand pressed up against the tottering palace gates. Heavily armed Republican Guards behind the gates, knowing they would eventually collapse, couldn't conceal their fear. Finally, the Jeep made it to the entrance, and Leon leaped out and shouted, "Open the gates for President Joseph Muamba."

The crowd broke out into raucous cheering, and the chanting intensified.

"Nothing will happen to you," Leon yelled. "We know you think you are protecting the president, but Mr. Bodho's been deposed. We have a new president."

As Leon was talking, the gates gave way. Joseph climbed on the bonnet of the Jeep and held his arms up. "Stop," he shouted. "We want no more bloodshed. No more lives lost." He then turned to the guards. "I am your president. I am coming in with fifty of my men. Please, for your sake, do not attempt to stop us."

"You heard the president!" Leon shouted. "Lower your weapons."

Joseph put his hand on Corporal Bilenga's shoulder and said,

"Secure the gates after we have entered. The crowd knows you are with me, so it shouldn't be a problem. Try to avoid violence."

"Yes, Mr. President."

Guards at the entrance to the palace lowered their rifles as the convoy bearing Joseph and his freedom fighters came to an abrupt halt. Likewise, the guards at the doors to the presidential chamber stood aside when Joseph and Leon marched through the door with half a dozen of their men. Bodho was sitting by himself. He looked dazed. "I should have never signed those adoption papers seventeen years ago."

"But you did," Joseph replied. "Where are General Gizenga and Colonel Donatien?"

"The fools who let you escape from court? I don't know. I don't care. You were so lucky to get out of the country."

"They won't get far."

"So lucky. So lucky," Bodho muttered.

"It was destiny."

"Are you going to kill me?"

"My first official act as president will be to abolish capital punishment. You're not going to hang, but you might spend the rest of your life in a cell. That will be up to the courts to decide."

"What?" Leon said. "They're murderers. They killed thousands. You can't abolish the death penalty."

Joseph held his hands up. "I understand your anger, Leon, but I have my reasons. Trust me."

"Yes, Mr. President."

"Mr. President," Bodho scoffed. "He is not the president. He is the leader of a rabble. No one has elected him."

"You're right. That is why I will hold elections within nine months. The people will choose their president, but in the meantime, I will fill the role of caretaker president."

"The governments of countries who have investments here will be furious. You'll have another fight on your hands before you know it."

"Without those emails going public, you might have been right. However, the world knows you and the others stole from the poor who you were meant to be helping. They want to see you brought to justice. No one is coming to your rescue, and you're going to return all those monies you misappropriated."

Bodho smiled. "If you let me go and leave me with $100 million, I'll return the rest."

"Forget it," Joseph replied. "If you return all the stolen funds, I'll ask the Justice Department to go easy on you in court. You might get your sentence reduced from life to fifteen years."

"Fifteen years?" Bodho gasped. "I'll be dead before then. I can't go to prison. I'll get the money transferred back here. I promise."

"You're a liar. You have numerous overseas bank accounts, and it would take a magician to find them. But we have all the time in the world. While you are rotting in prison, I'll have investigators going through banks' and companies' records. When we find them, we'll inform the tax haven banks that the funds in the accounts are the property of the Democratic Republic of the Congo. They will return them, or we will confiscate any assets they have here. You would be wise to accept my offer and come clean."

One of Joseph's men touched him on the arm and said, "Mr. President, the man who was the boss of the New Dawn mines is in the cells."

"Marc Boucher!" Joseph exclaimed, a huge smile on his face. "What a bonus. Throw this one in with him."

"No, no," Bodho shouted, "I'll tell you where the money is. We can do a deal."

"Take him away," Joseph said.

"What would you like me to do, Mr. President?" Leon asked.

"Round up Gizenga, Donatien, and the others, and throw them in the cells. Then come and see me."

"Yes, Mr. President. I thought you'd be pleased to know that Yannick will be here this afternoon, and Maya is flying in from Kilwa. She will be here this evening."

"Good, we'll have a celebratory dinner."

Chapter 57

Joseph called Frank, Michelle, and Moise to tell them he was safe and well and was now caretaker president of the Democratic Republic of the Congo. They were happy and relieved, but it didn't stop Frank from calling him a danged fool. "I love you, Son," he said.

"We all do," Michelle said. "Don't ever do anything so dangerous or stupid again."

"There was no danger, Mom."

"I miss you, Joseph," Moise said. "When am I going to see you?"

"Soon, little man, soon."

Midafternoon, Joseph was being taken on a tour of the palace. He had never realized the enormity of it and resolved to move the Justice Department from its pokey offices into the palace. Then he heard cheering and clapping and turned to see Yannick. As they embraced, Yannick said, "It's good to see you're still in one piece, Mr. President. I heard it was a close call."

"Oh, no! Not you with the 'Mr. President' too. You will soon be leading the army. Would you like me to call you General?"

"No." Yannick laughed.

"Seriously, though, without you, this would never have happened. You were magnificent, my friend."

"So were you, Joseph. So were you."

Just after five o'clock, Joseph and Yannick sat in the back of a four-wheel-drive surrounded by freedom fighters riding police motorcycles. The streets were festive, and when the crowds saw Joseph, the chanting started anew. "They love you," Yannick said.

"Life can be unfair. It is your name that they should be chanting."

"I'm not in the least concerned. You're going to be living in a fishbowl for years to come. I could never cope."

"No, I won't," Joseph replied.

"What?"

"I'll explain over dinner. What time did you say Maya's flight is landing?"

"Six o'clock."

Joseph tapped the driver on the arm. "I know it's difficult with the crowds, but we have to be at the airport by – "

"I heard, Mr. President. I'll get you there on time," the driver replied, stomping on the accelerator.

The motorcade drove onto the tarmac, and Joseph and Yannick got out. A few minutes later a small jet landed two hundred yards away, and Maya made her way down the stairs. Joseph loped across the tarmac to greet her, and as they kissed, she started laughing. "What's wrong?" he asked.

"That was funny," she said. "You had at least a dozen men running behind you. I thought they were going to attack me."

Joseph turned around to see a group of smiling faces staring at him. "I'm never going to get used to this."

"Oh, I nearly forgot," Maya said curtsying. "Hello, Mr. President. Is there anything I can do for you?"

"If we weren't in public, I'd put you over my knee. On reflection, I can do anything. I'm the president."

Maya laughed. "You wouldn't."

"No, I wouldn't," Joseph said, as Yannick joined them and embraced Maya. "Let's get going. Leon is joining us for dinner tonight."

"I thought it would be just us three." Yannick frowned.

"I'm sorry," Joseph said, "but I don't think you'll be disappointed."

Dinner was served in a small room three doors from the kitchen. "This is the only room in the palace with a round table," Joseph said, "and I didn't want to eat in the great hall. Leon, did you find Gizenga and Donatien?"

"Yes. We threw them in the same cell as Bodho and Boucher. They're squabbling like two-year-olds. I think that for the first time, they're not scared of Bodho, and they're giving him hell."

"Good. We have much to get through tonight."

"Before we start, a toast," Leon replied, "to a new Congo."

"To a new and honest Congo," Joseph said, clinking glasses. "I have told the kitchen not to serve our meals for an hour. After we get the politics out of the way, we can enjoy dinner. Leon, I want you to relocate the Justice Department to the palace as quickly as you can. And do you remember the deputy prosecutor?"

"The one who was too scared to ask questions after Yuma Lidy was beaten up?"

"Yes. He will head the Justice Department."

"What? Why? He's a coward."

"He's honest, and he's not a coward. He has a wife and family, and they were under threat. Anyhow, being scared does not make you a coward. I was petrified when the barrel of that gun was resting on the back of my head today. Are you telling me you weren't scared at the airport, Leon?"

"A little," the big man said.

"Rubbish! You were as scared as I was. The most courageous warrior in the land admits to being scared. Tell him, Yannick."

Yannick glowed with pleasure at the compliment his friend had just paid him. "I'm always scared," he said, "but I force myself to fight through the fear."

"And therein lies the definition of courage," Joseph said. "Make the appointment tomorrow, Leon. Oh, and abolish capital punishment. I want it promulgated this week."

"Hold on," Leon said. "I have no authority. I am nothing."

"No authority?" Joseph scoffed. "You're my vice president."

Yannick looked shocked but not as shocked as Leon. Maya smiled like the cat who'd swallowed the canary. "What are you talking about?" Leon asked.

"You're ex-CIA, and you are honest, love the Congo, love the people, speak six languages, have two degrees, and, best of all, have a foghorn voice that terrifies everyone. You're perfect."

"It's something I've never considered. I don't know what to say."

"You don't have to say anything," Joseph said. "In nine months' time I'd like you to run for the office of president."

"Wha-what di-did you just say?"

"You heard me."

"But what are you going to do? The people love you. They don't know me. They'll never vote for me."

"They mightn't now, but they will in nine months, and if I vote for you, so will they."

"My God. I don't know what to say. I will not let you down, Joseph. There is so much to do, so much to change," Leon said. "I promise I will make the Congo a better place for everyone, but why don't you want the presidency?"

"Yes, why?" asked a stunned Yannick. "The people love you, Joseph."

"We want to lead everyday lives," Maya said. "We don't want to be surrounded by bodyguards, twenty-four hours a day. We want to add to our family, and I want to practice medicine at Kinshasa Mercy Hospital."

"A white picket fence," Leon said.

"Yes," Maya agreed.

"What about me? I thought I'd be your right-hand man, Joseph, just like old times," Yannick said.

"You will head up the army, and yes, you will be the president's right hand, but I will not be the president forever. You are a great hero, Yannick, and the people know it."

"If that is what you wish," Yannick said, resting his hand on Joseph's forearm.

Joseph glanced at Maya before saying, "Yannick, I have a favor to ask. There was an incredibly brave young soldier at the airport today. Leon and I would not be here if it were not for him. His name is Corporal Bilenga. Could you take him under your wing? He reminds me of a younger you."

Maya smiled her approval. "I'm hungry," she said. "Have we nearly finished with politics?"

"Nearly," Joseph said, "bear with me a little longer. Because of the military court verdict, we are unable to charge Marc Boucher with anything."

"You want to let him go?" Leon asked. "I don't believe it."

"Mr. Vice President, you need to be more circumspect with your responses," Joseph laughed. "I want you to instruct the new head of the Justice Department to contact the South Africans and ask them to refile their application for his extradition."

Maya grinned. "It's so good to hear you laugh, Mr. President."

"Caretaker president, and only for nine months," Joseph said.

"You're going to leave a big hole," Leon said.

"With your permission, I'd like to stay on in an unofficial role for a further two years."

"Doing what?" Yannick asked.

"I'd like to oversee the Justice and Taxation Departments.'"

Leon understood immediately. "You're going to go after all the foreign banks and companies that haven't been paying taxes and have been underpaying their workers."

"That, and recovering the bribes and kickbacks paid to the army officers and our politicians."

"What if the banks won't cooperate?" Maya asked.

"I'll cancel their banking licenses and the licenses of any bank that acted as an intermediary. There's a pecking order with the banks. If I close down operations of a large bank that was used as a conduit by a smaller, tax haven bank, the larger bank will soon bring the smaller one to account."

"Are you going to charge Gert Botha and the Afrikaner supervisors?" Yannick asked.

"Yes. The maltreatment at New Dawn must have occurred at the other mines too. We will bring all those responsible before the courts."

"We have much to do," Yannick said.

"Yes, and Maya is going to oversee our health system. She will remove the barriers to our young people studying medicine. She also told me that once I've recovered the stolen funds, she's going to build new hospitals in the regional cities," Joseph said. "Without Maya, none of us would be here today."

"A toast to Maya," Leon said, topping up the glasses.

"Yes, a toast to Maya," Joseph said, "and then I think we can eat."

Epilogue

Seven days had elapsed since the coup, and Joseph was warming to his new role. He knew Sir Richard would call, and when he did, he was angry. "I should have gotten rid of you when you were in London, Muamba. Those emails have caused me no end of trouble."

"Mr. President," Joseph said coldly.

"All right, Mr. President. My partners and I would like to know what's happened to our mine."

"Who are your partners?"

"You'll never find the answer to that question."

"You might be surprised. Why did you say 'mine,' Sir Richard, when you have five mines that we know of here? How many more do you have that we don't know about?"

There was a long pause before Sir Richard said, "You haven't answered my question."

"Your mines are being assessed for taxation, which I believe might run to billions."

"That's ridiculous," Sir Richard spluttered. "We won't pay."

"That's fine. If you don't, we will seize the mines in lieu of the debt and sell them."

"You're going to nationalize mining?"

"No, I'm going to collect the tax rightfully due."

Joseph could hear angry breathing before Sir Richard said, "You bastard. Still, for all your games, it's had no impact on my lifestyle. Sure, some politicians are causing me grief, but when the next election comes around, they'll be begging me for donations."

"No, they won't. You'll be here facing murder charges."

"You have a strange sense of humor." Sir Richard laughed cynically. "How do you propose to get me there?"

"I'll have you extradited," Joseph said.

"You idiot! No English court will extradite me," Sir Richard yelled, before slamming down the phone.

It took a few minutes for Sir Richard to regain his composure. He had lost billions, and there were many powerful politicians — and those in the legal profession — who had once been friends but who now would like nothing better than to see him extradited.

He smiled. He wasn't concerned. No English court would ever consider an extradition application from a country that still had the death penalty on its books.

Reviews:
Good, bad or indifferent are important for readers and authors alike. The Amazon links are:

U.S. http://a.co/bO3FqKb
U.K. http://amzn.eu/7n88WNS
Canada http://a.co/d8EvLmU
India http://amzn.in/j8XL1AI

Other Books By Peter Ralph

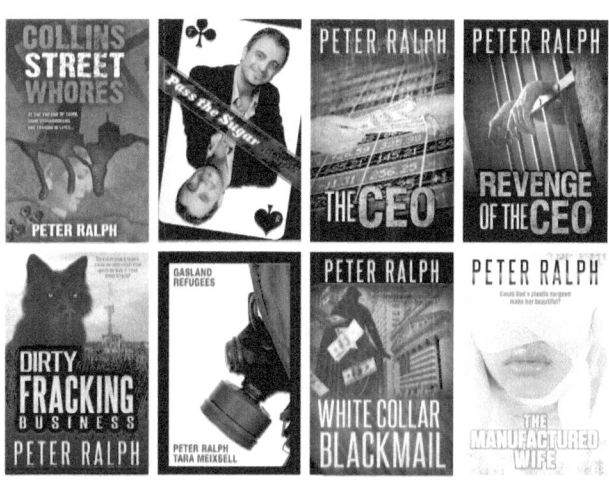

More white collar crime suspense thrillers by Peter Ralph are on the drawing board.

For updates about new releases, as well as exclusive promotions, visit the author's website and sign up for the VIP mailing list at http://www.peterralphbooks.com/

Visit here to get started:
Amazon USA: http://goo.gl/Ya6GB7
Amazon UK: http://goo.gl/Uxc4ly

FREE DOWNLOAD

FOG CITY FRAUD

Why is an irate investor holding his advisor's receptionist hostage on the 16th level of a high rise building?
Sign up for Peter Ralph's reader's group and get your free copy of the novella Fog City Fraud: a financial suspense thriller.

Visit here to get started:
http://www.peterralphbooks.com/